Mario Vargas Llosa was born in Arequipa, Peru. He attended the University of San Marcos in Lima, and later obtained his doctorate from the University of Madrid. His novels include *Conversation in the Cathedral, The Green House, Aunt Julia and the Scriptwriter*, *In Praise of the Stepmother*, *The Notebooks of Don Rigoberto*, and more recently, *The Feast of the Goat* and *The Way to Paradise*. He lives in London.

the GREEN HOUSE

Also by Mario Vargas Llosa

The Time of the Hero

Conversation in the Cathedral

Captain Pantoja and the Special Service

The Cubs and Other Stories

Aunt Julia and the Scriptwriter

The War of the End of the World

In Praise of the Stepmother

The Notebooks of Don Rigoberto

The Feast of the Goat

The Way of Paradise

a novel

the GREEN HOUSE

Mario Vargas Llosa

Translated by Gregory Rabassa

NEW YORK • LONDON • TORONTO • SYDNEY

HARPER PERENNIAL

HarperCollins books may be purchased for educational, business, or sales promotional use. For information please write: Special Markets Department, HarperCollins Publishers, 10 East 53rd Street, New York, NY 10022.

Published by Harper & Row in 1968.

FIRST RAYO EDITION PUBLISHED 2005, REISSUED IN HARPER PERENNIAL 2008.

Library of Congress Cataloging-in-Publication Data

Vargas Llosa, Mario
[Casa verde. English]
The green house : a novel / Mario Vargas Llosa : translated by Gregory Rabassa.—1st Rayo ed.
p. cm.
ISBN 978-0-06-073279-0
I. Rabassa, Gregory. II. Title.

PQ8498.32.A65C413 2005
863'.64—dc22

2004063259

10 11 12 QK/RRD 10 9 8 7 6 5 4

For Patricia

THE SERGEANT TAKES A LOOK at Sister Patrocinio and the botfly is still there. The launch is pitching on the muddy waters, between two walls of trees that give off a burning, sticky mist. Huddled under the canopy, stripped to the waist, the soldiers are asleep, with the greenish, yellowish noonday sun above: Shorty's head is lying on Fats's stomach, Blondy is breathing in short bursts, Blacky has his mouth open and is grunting. A thin shadow of gnats is escorting the launch, and butterflies, wasps, horseflies take shape among the bodies. The motor is snoring evenly, it chokes, it snores, and Nieves the pilot is holding the rudder in his left hand as he uses his right to smoke with, and his face, deeply tanned, is unchanging under his straw hat. These savages weren't normal, why didn't they sweat like other people? Sitting stiffly in the stern, Sister Angélica has her eyes closed, there are at least a thousand wrinkles on her face, sometimes she sticks out the tip of her tongue, licks the sweat from her upper lip, and spits. Poor old woman, she wasn't up to these chores. The botfly moves its blue little wings, softly pushes off from Sister Patrocinio's flushed forehead, is lost as it circles off into the white light, and the pilot goes to turn off the motor, they were getting there, Sergeant, Chicais was beyond that gorge. But he was telling the good Sergeant that there wouldn't be anybody there. The sound of the engine stops, the nuns and the soldiers open their eyes, raise their heads, look around. Standing up, Nieves the pilot moves the rudder pole from left to right, the launch silently approaches the shore, the soldiers get up, put on their shirts, their caps, fasten their leggings. The vegetable palisade on the right bank suddenly opens up beyond the bend in the river and there is a rise, a brief parenthesis of reddish earth that descends to a tiny inlet of mud, pebbles, reeds, and ferns. There is no canoe on the bank, no human figure on the top of the rise. The boat runs aground. Nieves and the soldiers jump out, slosh in the lead-colored mud. A cemetery, a person's feelings could always tell, the Mangaches were right. The Sergeant leans over the prow, the pilot and the soldiers drag the launch up onto dry land. They should help the sisters, make a hand chair for them so they wouldn't get wet. Sister Angélica is very serious as she sits on the arms of Blacky and Fats, Sister Patrocinio hesitates as Shorty and Blondy put their hands together to receive her, and as she lets herself down, she turns red as a shrimp. The soldiers stagger across the shore and put the nuns down where the mud ends. The Sergeant jumps out, reaches the foot of the hill, and Sister Angélica is already climbing resolutely up the slope, followed by Sister Patrocinio, both are using their hands, they disappear among clouds of red dust. The soil on the hill is soft, it gives way with every step, the Sergeant and the soldiers go forward, sinking to their knees, hunched over, smothered in the dust, Fats is sneezing and spitting and holds his handkerchief over his mouth. At the top, they all brush off their uniforms and the Sergeant looks around: a circular clearing, a handful of huts with conical roofs, small plots of cassava and bananas, and thick undergrowth all around. Among the huts, small trees with oval-shaped pockets hanging from the branches: paucar nests. He had told her, Sister Angélica, here was the proof, not a soul, now they could see for themselves. But Sister Angélica is walking around, she goes into a hut, comes out and sticks her head into the next one, shoos away the flies by clapping her hands, does not stop for a second, and in that way, seen from a distance, hazy in the dust, she is not an old woman but a walking habit, erect, an energetic shadow. Sister Patrocinio, on the other hand, does not move, her hands are hidden in her habit, and her eyes run back and forth over the empty village. A few branches shake and shrieks are heard, a squadron of green wings, black beaks, and blue breasts flies noisily over the deserted huts of Chicais, the soldiers and the nuns follow them with their eyes until the jungle swallows them up, the shrieking lasts for a moment. There were parrots around, good to know if they needed food. But they gave you diarrhea, Sister, that is they loosened up a person's stomach. A straw hat appears at the top of the hill, the tanned face of Nieves the pilot: that was why the Aguarunas were afraid, Sisters. They were so stubborn, you couldn't tell them not to pay any attention to him. Sister Angélica approaches, looks here and there with her little wrinkled eyes, and she shakes her gnarled, stiff hands with dark brown spots in the Sergeant's face: they were nearby, they hadn't taken away their things, they had to wait for them to come back. The soldiers look at each other, the Sergeant lights a cigarette, two paucars are coming and going through the air, their black and gold feathers giving off damp flashes. Birds too, there was everything in Chicais. Everything except Aguarunas, and Fats laughs. Why wouldn't they attack unexpectedly?, Sister Angélica is panting, maybe you didn't know them, Sister, the cluster of white hairs on her chin trembles slightly, they were afraid of people and they hid, they wouldn't think of coming back, while they were there they wouldn't even see their dust. Small, pudgy, Sister Patrocinio is there too, between Blondy and Blacky. But they hadn't hidden last year, they had come out to meet them and they had even given them a fresh gamitana, didn't the Sergeant remember? But they hadn't known then, Sister Patrocinio, now they did. The soldiers and Nieves the pilot sit down on the ground, take off their shoes, Blacky opens his canteen, drinks and sighs. Sister Angélica raises her head: they should put up the tents, Sergeant, a withered face, he should have them put up the mosquito nettings, a liquid look, they would wait for them to come back, a cracked voice, and you shouldn't make that face, she had experience. The Sergeant throws away his cigarette, grinds it out, what difference did it make, you guys, you should move it. And just then there is a cackling and the bushes spit out a hen, Blondy and Shorty shout with glee, a black one, they chase it, with white spots, catch it, and Sister Angélica's eyes flash, bandits, what were they doing, she waves her fist in the air, did it belong to them?, they should let it go, and the Sergeant should tell them to let it go, but, Sisters, they were going to need food, they didn't feel like going hungry. Sister Angélica would not stand for any abuses, what confidence would they have if we stole their animals? And Sister Patrocinio agrees, Sergeant, stealing it would be an offense against God, with her round and healthy face, didn't he know the commandments? The hen touches the ground, clucks, picks a flea from under her wing, waddles off, and the Sergeant shrugs his shoulders: why were they fooling themselves, since they knew them as well or even better than he did. The soldiers go off toward the slope, the parrots and paucars are screeching in the trees again, there is a buzzing of insects, a light breeze shakes the yarina leaves that form the roofs of Chicais. The Sergeant loosens his leggings, mutters between his teeth, twists his mouth, and Nieves the pilot slaps him on the back, Sergeant: you shouldn't get upset, you should take things easy. And the Sergeant furtively points at the nuns, Don Adrián, little jobs like this were too much. Sister Angélica was very thirsty and probably a little feverish, her spirit was still eager, but her body was already getting weak, Sister Patrocinio, and she no, no, you shouldn't say that, Sister Angélica, as soon as the soldiers came back she would take a lemonade and she would feel better, you'd see. Were they whispering about him?, the Sergeant looks about with distant eyes, did they think he was a man or not?, he was fanning himself with his cap, that pair of buzzards!, and suddenly he turns toward Nieves the pilot: keeping secrets together was bad manners and anyone who saw them, Sergeant, the soldiers come back on the run. A canoe?, and Blacky yes, with Aguarunas?, and Blondy, yes Sergeant, and Shorty yes, and Fats and the nuns yes, yes, they come and ask questions and go off in all directions, and the Sergeant has Blondy go back to the top of the hill and tell him if they are coming up, the others should hide, and Nieves the pilot picks the leggings up off the ground and the rifles. The soldiers and the Sergeant go into a hut, the nuns are still in the open, Sisters, you should hide, Sister Patrocinio, quick, Sister Angélica. They look at each other, they whisper, they go into the hut opposite and, from the bushes where he is hiding, Blondy points at the river, they were getting out now, Sergeant, and he didn't know what he should do, you should come and hide, Blondy, you shouldn't fall asleep. Stretched out on their bellies, Fats and Shorty are spying out from behind the crosshatching of the wall made out of tucuma strips; Blacky and Nieves are standing back in the hut and Blondy comes running, squats down beside the Sergeant. There they were, Sister Angélica, there they were now, and Sister Angélica may have been old but she had good eyes, Sister Patrocinio, she could see them, there were six of them. The old woman, with long hair, is wearing a whitish loincloth and two tubes of soft dark flesh hang down to her waist. Behind her two men of indeterminate age, short, big-bellied, with skeletal legs, their sexes covered with pieces of ochre-colored cloth tied with thongs, their buttocks naked, their hair cut in bangs around their heads. They are carrying bunches of bananas. After them come two girls with straw headbands, one has a ring in her nose, the other leather hoops on her ankles. They are naked, just as is the little boy who follows them, he looks younger and is thinner. They look at the deserted clearing, the woman opens her mouth, the men shake their heads. Were they going to talk to them, Sister Angélica? and the Sergeant yes, there went the sisters, you should be on your toes, boys. The six heads turn at the same time, remain fixed. The nuns advance toward the group with a steady pace, smiling, and, at the same time, almost imperceptibly, the Aguarunas draw together, soon form one earthen and compact group. The six pairs of eyes do not leave the two figures in dark folds that float toward them, and if they resisted we would have to come out running, boys, no shooting, no scaring them. They were letting them approach, Sergeant, Blondy thought they would run away when they saw them. And the girls were nice and tender, young ones, right, Sergeant?, there was no holding that Fats. The nuns stop and, at the same time, the girls draw back, they stretch out their hands, they clutch the legs of the old woman, who begins to pat them on the shoulders, each pat makes her long breasts shake, makes them swing back and forth: might the Lord be with them. And Sister Angélica grunts, spits, pours out a flow of scratchy, rough, and sibilant sounds, interrupts herself to spit, and ostentatiously, martially, goes on grunting, her hands move about, they trace figures solemnly in the air before the motionless, pale, impassive Aguaruna faces. She was talking to them in pagan, boys, and the little old sister was spitting just like the redskins. They must have liked that, Sergeant, having a white woman talking their language, but not so much noise, boys, if they heard you they'd get scared. Sister Angélica's grunts reach the hut very clear, robust, out of tune, and now Blacky and the pilot too are spying on the clearing with their faces against the wall. She had them in her pocket, boys, the little old sister was smart, and the nuns and the two Aguarunas smile at each other, exchange bows. And she had a good education, did the Sergeant know that at the Mission they made them study all the time? They were most likely praying, Shorty, for the sins of the world. Sister Patrocinio smiles at the old woman, the woman turns her eyes away and is still serious, her hands on the girls' shoulders. I was wondering what they were saying, Sergeant, what they were talking about. Sister Angélica and the two men make faces, gesture, spit, interrupt each other, and suddenly the three children leave the old woman, run about, laugh loud. The kid was looking at them, boys, he wasn't taking his eyes off them. Look how skinny he was, did the Sergeant notice?, a great big round head and a skinny little body, he looked like a spider. From under his mat of hair, the boy's large eyes are staring at the hut. He is as dark as an ant, his legs are curved and sickly. He suddenly raises his hand, shouts, the little bastard, Sergeant, and there is a violent agitation behind the wall, oaths, bumping into each other, and guttural shouts break out in the clearing as the soldiers invade it running and tripping. You should lower those rifles, you dunces, Sister Angélica shows the soldiers her angry hands, oh, the Lieutenant would hear about this. The two girls bury their heads on the old woman's chest, they flatten out her soft breasts, and the little boy is out of orbit, halfway between the soldiers and the nuns. One of the Aguarunas drops his bunch of bananas, the hen is cackling off somewhere. Nieves the pilot is standing in the doorway of the hut, his straw hat thrown back, a cigarette between his teeth. What did the Sergeant think he was doing, and Sister Angélica takes a little leap, why did you interfere if you weren't called? But if they lowered the rifles you wouldn't see them for their dust, Sister, she shows him her freckled fist, and he you should put down your Mausers, boys. Gently she continues, Sister Angélica talks to the Aguarunas, her stiff hands sketch slow figures, persuasively, little by little the men lose their stiffness, now they answer with monosyllables and she, smiling, inexorable, keeps on grunting. The boy goes over to the soldiers, smells the rifles, touches them, Fats gives him a pat on the forehead, he crouches down and shrieks, he didn't trust him, the bastard, and a laugh shakes Fats's flabby waist, his jowls, his jawbones. Sister Patrocinio blushes, embarrassed, what was he saying, why was he disrespectful like that, the boor, and Fats a thousand pardons, he shakes his confused oxhead, it came out without his realizing it, Sister, he is tongue-tied. The girls and the little boy circulate among the soldiers, they examine them, touch them with their fingertips. Sister Angélica and the two men are grunting in a friendly way and the sun is still shining in the distance, but a cloak has come over the place, another forest of white and heady clouds is piling up over the forest: it was probably going to rain. Sister Angélica had insulted them before, Sister, and what had they said. Sister Patrocinio smiles, dunce wasn't an insult, just a kind of pointed hat just right for their heads, and Sister Angélica turns toward the Sergeant: they were going to eat with them, they should bring up the gifts and the lemonade. He agrees, gives instructions to Shorty and Blondy, pointing at the hill, green bananas and raw fish, a banquet fit for a mother whore. The children sit in a circle around Fats, Blacky, and Nieves the pilot, and Sister Angélica, the men, and the old woman put banana leaves on the ground, go into the huts, bring out clay pots, cassavas, light a small fire, wrap catfish and bocachicas in leaves that they tie together with reeds and put near the flames. Were they going to wait for the rest of them, Sergeant? It would never end and Nieves the pilot throws his cigarette away, the others weren't coming back, if they had gone away it meant that they didn't want any visitors, and these would leave too at the first chance they got. Yes, the Sergeant was aware, but it was no use fighting with the sisters. Shorty and Blondy come back with the bags and the thermos bottles. The nuns, the Aguarunas, and the soldiers are sitting in a circle facing the banana leaves, and the old woman is shooing away the insects by clapping her hands. Sister Angélica distributes the gifts and the Aguarunas take them without showing any signs of enthusiasm, but then, when the nuns and the soldiers begin to eat small pieces of fish that they pick off with their fingers, the two men, without looking at each other, open the bags, fondle mirrors and necklaces, divide up the colored beads, and greedy lights suddenly come on in the eyes of the old woman. The girls fight over a bottle, the little boy is chewing furiously, and the Sergeant was going to get sick to his stomach, God damn it, he was going to get diarrhea, he was going to swell up like a fat-bellied hualo toad, lumps would grow on his body, they would break and give off pus. He has the piece of fish next to his lips, his small eyes blink, and Blacky, Shorty, and Blondy are screwing up their faces too, Sister Patrocinio closes her eyes, swallows, makes a face, and only Nieves the pilot and Sister Angélica keep reaching toward the banana leaves and with a kind of hasty delight break up the white meat, clean out the bones, put it in their mouths. All jungle people had a little redskin in them, even the nuns, the way they ate. The Sergeant belches, everybody looks at him, and he coughs. The Aguarunas have put on the necklaces, they show them to each other. The glass beads are garnet-colored and contrast with the tattoo on the chest of the one who has six beaded bracelets on one arm, three on the other. What time were they going to leave, Sister Angélica? The soldiers watch the Sergeant, the Aguarunas stop chewing. The children stretch out their hands, they timidly touch the shiny necklaces, the bracelets. They had to wait for the rest of them, Sergeant. The Aguaruna with the tattoo grunts, and Sister Angélica yes, Sergeant, did you see?, you should eat, they were offended with all the faces you were making. He was not hungry, but he wanted to say something, Sister, they couldn't stay in Chicais any longer. Sister Angélica's mouth is full, the Sergeant had come to help, her small and stony hand drains the lemonade from a thermos, not to give orders. Shorty had heard the Lieutenant, what had he said?, and he too that they should come back before a week was out, Sister. Five days had already gone by and how many would it take to get back, Don Adrián?, three days as long as it didn't rain, did you see?, they were orders, Sister, so she shouldn't be angry with him. Along with the sound of the conversation between the Sergeant and Sister Angélica there is another sound, a harsher one: the Aguarunas are conversing animatedly, they hit their arms and compare their bracelets. Sister Patrocinio swallows and opens her eyes, and if the others didn't come back?, and if they took a month in coming back? of course it was only an opinion, and she closes her eyes, maybe she was wrong, and swallows. Sister Angélica wrinkles her brow, new wrinkles appear on her face, her hand strokes the tuft of white hairs on her chin. The Sergeant takes a drink from his canteen: worse than a laxative, everything got hot in this region, it wasn't the kind of heat they had where he came from, the heat here rotted everything. Fats and Blondy are lying on their backs with their caps over their faces, and Shorty wanted to know if anyone was sure of that, Don Adrián, and Blacky really, Don Adrián should continue and tell some more. They were half fish and half women, they lived at the bottom of lagoons waiting for people who had drowned, and as soon as a canoe tipped over they would come and grab the people and take them down to their palaces. They would put them in hammocks that were not made out of jute but made out of snakes and they would have fun with them there, and Sister Patrocinio were they talking about superstitions now?, and they no, no, and did they call themselves Christians?, nothing like that, Sister, they were talking about whether it was going to rain. Sister Angélica leans toward the Aguarunas, grunting softly, smiling insistently, she has her hands clasped, and the men, without moving from the spot, sit up little by little, stretch out their necks like cranes sunning themselves on a riverbank when a steamboat comes along, and something frightens them, dilates their pupils, and the chest of one puffs up, the tattoo grows clear, is erased, grows clear, and they gradually approach Sister Angélica, very attent, serious, silent, and the long-haired old woman opens her arms and clasps the girls. The little boy is still eating, boys, the rough part was coming, you should stay awake. The pilot, Shorty, and Blacky are quiet. Blondy gets up with red eyes and shakes Fats, an Aguaruna looks at the Sergeant out of the corner of his eye, then at the sky, and now the old woman is hugging the girls, pressing them against her long and drooping breasts, and the eyes of the little boy go back and forth between Sister Angélica and the men, from them to the old woman, from her to the soldiers and to Sister Angélica. The Aguaruna with the tattoo begins to speak, the other man follows him, the old woman, a storm of voices drowns out the voice of Sister Angélica, who says no now with her head and with her hands and suddenly, without stopping their snorting and spitting, slowly, ceremoniously, the two men take off their necklaces, their bracelets, and there is a rain of glass beads on the banana leaves. The Aguarunas reach out toward the remains of the fish, across which a narrow river of brown ants is flowing. They were already getting a little wild, boys, but they were ready, Sergeant, whenever he gave the word. The Aguarunas clean off the remains of the blue and white flesh, catch the ants in their fingernails, squash them, and very carefully wrap the food in the veiny leaves. Shorty and Blondy were to take care of the kids, the Sergeant orders, and Fats the lucky guys. Sister Patrocinio is very pale, she moves her lips, her fingers close tightly over the black beads of her rosary, and you should remember, Sergeant, they were little girls, he knew, he knew, and Fats and Blacky would keep the naked savages quiet and the Sister should not worry, and Sister Patrocinio, oh, if they committed any brutalities, and the pilot would take care of carrying the things, boys, no brutalities: Holy Mary, Mother of God. All of them look at the bloodless lips of Sister Patrocinio, and she, Pray for us, is shedding the little black balls in her fingers, and Sister Angélica you should be calm, Sister, and the Sergeant now, now was the time. They get up slowly. Fats and Blacky dust off their pants, they squat down, pick up their rifles, and now there is running, screams and at the hour, trampling, the little boy covers his face, of our death, and the two Aguarunas stay rigid, amen, their teeth chatter and their eyes look perplexedly at the rifles that are pointed at them. But the old woman is on her feet struggling with Shorty, and the girls are slippery as eels in Blondy's arms. Sister Angélica covers her mouth with a handkerchief, the dust cloud grows and thickens, Fats sneezes, and the Sergeant ready, they should make it to the top of the hill, boys, Sister Angélica. And someone should help Blondy, Sergeant, couldn't you see that they were getting away from him? Shorty and the old woman are rolling around together on the ground, Blacky should go help him, the Sergeant would take his place, he'd keep his eyes on the naked savages. The nuns walk toward the hill holding each other by the arm, Blondy drags along two intermingled and gesticulating figures, and Blacky pulls the old woman furiously by the hair until she lets go of Shorty and he gets up. But the old woman jumps on them, catches them, scratches them, and the Sergeant ready, Fats, they would slip away. Still keeping aim on the two men, they retreat, heel their way back, and the Aguarunas get up at the same time and advance, as if attracted by the rifles. The old woman is dancing like a monkey, she falls and clutches two pairs of legs, Shorty and Blacky stumble, Mother of God, they fall down too, and Sister Patrocinio should not shout like that. A sudden breeze comes up from the river, it scales the slope and brings up active, enveloping, orange-colored, and thick grains of earth that fly like botflies. The two Aguarunas docilely face the rifles and the slope is very close. If they attacked him, would Fats shoot? and Sister Angélica stupid man, he was capable of killing them. Blondy takes one girl by the arm at the top of the hill, why didn't they go down, Sergeant?, he has the other one by the neck, they were getting away from him, they were getting away from him and they are not shouting but they are pulling, and their heads, shoulders, feet, and legs struggle and kick and vibrate, and Nieves the pilot goes by loaded down with thermos bottles: you should hurry up, Don Adrián, have you left anything behind? No, nothing, whenever the Sergeant wanted to. Shorty and Blacky are holding the old woman by the shoulders and the hair and she sits down shrieking, sometimes she swats them weakly on the legs and blessed was the fruit, Mother, Mother, of her womb, and they were getting away from Blondy, Jesus. The man with the tattoo looks at Fats's rifle, the old woman gives a hoot and cries, two wet threads open narrow channels on the crust of dust on her face, and Fats should not act crazy. But if they attacked him, Sergeant, he would open up somebody's skull, only with his rifle butt, Sergeant, and the joke would be over. Sister Angélica takes the handkerchief away from her mouth: stupid, why were you saying such evil things?, why did the Sergeant allow it?, and Blondy would he start going down?, those wild girls were skinning him alive. The girls' hands cannot reach Blondy's face, only his neck, already full of purple scratches, and they have torn his shirt and pulled off the buttons. Sometimes they seem to lose their spirit, their bodies go limp and they moan and they attack again, their naked feet kick at Blondy's leggings, he curses and shakes them, they follow along mutely, and the Sister should go down, what was she waiting for, and Blondy too and Sister Angélica why was he holding them like that if they were only children? of her womb Jesus, Mother, Mother. If Shorty and Blacky let the old woman go, she would pounce on them, Sergeant, what were they going to do?, and Blondy she would grab them, you should see, Sister, couldn't she see how they were scratching him? The Sergeant shakes his rifle, the Aguarunas balk, take a step backward, and Shorty and Blacky let go of the old woman, they keep their hands ready to defend themselves, but she does not move, she only rubs her eyes, and there is the little boy looking as if he were isolated by the whirlwinds: she squats down and buries her face between her flowing breasts. Shorty and Blacky are going downhill, a rose-colored wall of dust soon swallows them up, and how in hell was Blondy going to carry them down all by himself, what was the matter with them, Sergeant, why were those guys leaving, and Sister Angélica approaches him swinging her arms resolutely: she would help him. She stretches out her hands toward the girl on the slope but she does not touch her and she doubles over, and the small fist hits out again and sinks into the habit and Sister Angélica gives a little cry and withdraws: what did he tell her, Blondy shakes the girl like a rag, Sister, wasn't she an animal? Pale and wrinkled, Sister Angélica tries again, she catches the arm with her two hands, Holy Mary, and now they howl, Mother of God, kick, Holy Mary, they scratch, they are all coughing, Mother of God, and instead of so much praying they should have been going down, Sister Patrocinio, why in the world was she so frightened and how long, and how long, they should go down because the Sergeant was already getting hot, damn it. Sister Patrocinio turns, jumps down the slope, and disappears, Fats advances his rifle and the one with the tattoo draws back. The hate there was in his look, Sergeant, he looked angry, son of a whore, and proud: that was what the eyes of the chulla-chaqui devil must have been like, Sergeant. The heavy clouds that enveloped those descending are farther away, the old woman is crying, twisting around, and the two Aguarunas are watching the barrels, the butts, the round muzzles of the two rifles: Fats shouldn't get so excited. He wasn't getting excited, Sergeant, but what way was that to look at a person, damn it, what right did he have? Blondy, Sister Angélica, and the girls also disappear into the waves of dust and the old woman has crawled to the edge of the hill, she looks down toward the river, her nipples touch the ground, and the little boy is making strange shouts, he howls like a mournful bird, and Fats did not like to have them so close to the savages, Sergeant, how would they get down now that they were all alone. And then the motor on the launch snorts: the old woman grows silent and looks up, looks at the sky, the little boy follows her, the two Aguarunas do the same, and the bastards were looking for a plane. Fats, they weren't watching, now was the time. They draw back their rifles and suddenly thrust them forward, the two men jump back and make signs, and now the Sergeant and Fats go down backward, still aiming, sinking up to their knees, and the sound of the hoarse motor is growing stronger and stronger, it pollutes the air with hiccups, gargling, vibrations, and shaking, and it is different on the slope from up on the clearing, there is no breeze, only a hot vapor and reddish and biting dust that makes one sneeze. Dimly, there on top of the hill, hairy heads are exploring the sky, they move softly back and forth, searching among the clouds, and the motor was going and the kids were crying, Fats, what about him?, Sergeant, he couldn't make it. They cross the mud on the run, and when they reach the launch they are panting and their tongues are hanging out. It was time now, why had they taken so long? How did they think Fats was going to get on board, they had all got so comfortable, the devils, they should make room for him. But he had to lose some weight, they should just look at him, Fats was getting on board and the boat was sinking down and it was no time for jokes, they should get under way at once, Sergeant. They were leaving right away, Sister Angélica, Sister Angélica, of our death, amen.

1

A door slammed, the Mother Superior raised her face from her desk, Sister Angélica burst into the office like a meteor, her livid hands fell onto the back of a chair.

"What's wrong, Sister Angélica? Why do you look that way?"

"They've run away, Mother!" Sister Angélica stammered. "There isn't a single one of them left, God save us."

"What are you saying, Sister Angélica?" The Mother Superior had jumped up and was heading toward the door. "The pupils?"

"Oh Lord, oh Lord!" Sister Angélica nodded yes with short, identical, very quick movements of her head, like a hen pecking at grain.

Santa María de Nieva rises up at the junction of the Nieva with the upper Marañón, two rivers that embrace the town and form its boundaries. Across the way, emerging from the Marañón are two islands that the inhabitants use to measure the rising and falling of the waters. From the town, when there is no mist, hills covered with vegetation can be seen in the rear, and in front, downstream on the broad river, the mass of the Andes split into the Manseriche canyon by the Marañón: six violent miles of whirlpools, rocks, and torrents, which begin at one military outpost, that of Lieutenant Pinglo, and end at another, the one at Borja.

"This way, Mother," Sister Patrocinio said. "Look, the gate's open, they went through here."

The Mother Superior raised the lamp and leaned over: the underbrush was a uniform shadow flooded with insects. She rested her hand on the half-open gate and turned toward the nuns. Their habits had blended into the night, but the white veils were shining like the plumage of a crane.

"Go find Bonifacia, Sister Angélica," the Mother Superior whispered. "Bring her to my office."

"Yes, Mother, right away." For a second, the lamp lighted up Sister Angélica's trembling chin, her small blinking eyes.

"Go tell Don Fabio, Sister Griselda," the Mother Superior said. "And you the Lieutenant, Sister Patrocinio. They should go out and search for them at once. Hurry, Sisters."

Two white halos separated from the group in the direction of the Mission courtyard. The Mother Superior, followed by the other nuns, walked toward the Residence, hugging the garden wall, where at capricious intervals a cackling drowned out the flapping of the bats and the chirping of the crickets. Winks and sparks rose up among the fruit trees, fireflies, the eyes of owls? The Mother Superior stopped in front of the chapel.

"Go in, Sisters," she said softly. "Pray to the Blessed Virgin that nothing will happen to them. I'll be along shortly."

Santa María de Nieva is like an irregular pyramid whose base is formed by the rivers. The dock is on the Nieva, and around the floating wharf the Aguaruna canoes and the boats and launches of the Christians are rocking. Farther up is the ochre-colored earthen main square with two bald and corpulent capirona poles in the center. The soldiers use one of them for a flagpole on national holidays. And around the square are the commissary, the Governor's house, several Christian homes, and the bar owned by Paredes, who is also a merchant and a carpenter and knows how to prepare love potions. And still farther up, on two hills that are like the vertexes of the town, are the Mission buildings: corrugated metal roofs, props of adobe and pona wood, whitewashed walls, metal grating on the windows, wooden doors.

"Let's not waste any time, Bonifacia," the Mother Superior said. "Tell me everything."

"She was in the chapel," Sister Angélica said. "The sisters found her there."

"I asked you a question, Bonifacia," the Mother Superior said. "What are you waiting for?"

She was wearing a blue tunic, a sheath that hid her body from her shoulders to her ankles, and her bare feet, the same copper color as the planks of the floor, were lying side by side: two flat, polycephalic animals.

"Did you hear?" Sister Angélica said. "Speak up."

The dark veil that framed her face and the half light of the office accentuated the ambiguity of her expression, somewhere between shy and indolent, and her large eyes were staring at the desk; sometimes the flame of the wick, agitated by the breeze coming in from the garden, would reveal the green of her eyes, their soft twinkling.

"Did they steal your keys?" the Mother Superior asked.

"You'll never change, you careless creature!" Sister Angélica's hand was flying about Bonifacia's head. "Do you see what your negligence has done?"

"Let me handle this, Sister," the Mother Superior said. "Let's not waste any more time, Bonifacia."

Her arms were hanging by her side and she held her head low, the tunic barely revealed the movement of her breasts. Her thick straight lips were soldered into a harsh grimace, and her nose was dilated and opening and closing slightly with a very regular rhythm.

"I'm getting angry, Bonifacia. I'm talking to you with consideration, and it's as if you were listening to the rain falling," the Mother Superior said. "What time was it when you left them alone? Didn't you lock up the dormitory?"

"Speak up, you devil!" Sister Angélica tugged at Bonifacia's tunic. "God will punish you for your pride."

"You have all day to go to the chapel, but your duty at night is to take care of the pupils," the Mother Superior said. "Why did you leave your room without permission?"

Two short knocks sounded on the office door, the nuns turned around. Bonifacia raised her eyelids a little and, for a second, her eyes were larger, green and intense.

From the hills of the town, a hundred yards away on the right bank of the Nieva River, the hut of Adrián Nieves can be seen, his small garden, and then nothing but a mass of vines, underbrush, trees with tentacular branches and very high crowns. Not far from the square is the Indian quarter, an agglomeration of huts built on tree stumps. The mud devours the wild grass there and the place is surrounded by ditches of stagnant water that boils with worms and tadpoles. Here and there, small and regular, are cassava patches, plantings of corn, pygmy gardens. From the Mission, a rough path goes down to the square. And behind the Mission an earthen wall resists the push of the forest, the furious onslaught of the vegetation. There is a bolted gate in that wall.

"It's the Governor, Mother," Sister Patrocinio said. "May he come in?"

"Yes, have him come in, Sister Patrocinio," the Mother Superior said.

Sister Angélica turned up the wick and drew two shadowy figures out of the darkness. Wrapped in a cape, a lantern in his hand, Don Fabio entered with a bow.

"I was in bed and I came as fast as I could, Mother; please excuse my appearance." He shook hands with the Mother Superior, with Sister Angélica. "How could something like this happen? I tell you I couldn't believe it. And I can imagine how you all must feel, Mother."

His bald head looked damp, his thin face was smiling at the nuns.

"Sit down, Don Fabio," the Mother Superior said. "Thank you for coming. Get the Governor a chair, Sister Angélica."

Don Fabio sat down and the lantern that was hanging from his left hand made a light: a golden circle on the chambira rug.

"They're already out looking for them, Mother," the Governor said. "The Lieutenant too. Don't worry, I'm sure we'll find them before morning."

"Those poor children out there all by themselves, just imagine, Don Fabio." The Mother Superior sighed. "Luckily it's not raining. You don't know what a fright this has given us."

"But how did it all happen, Mother?" Don Fabio asked. "It still doesn't seem possible to me."

"Carelessness on the part of this one," Sister Angélica said, pointing at Bonifacia. "She left them alone and went to the chapel. She probably forgot to lock the door."

The Governor looked at Bonifacia and his face took on a severe and pained look. But a second later he smiled and bowed to the Mother Superior.

"The girls have no idea, Don Fabio," the Mother Superior said. "They have no notion of the dangers. That's what worries us most. An accident, a wild animal."

"Oh, such girls," the Governor said. "Now you see, Bonifacia, you have to be more careful."

"Pray to God that nothing happens to them," the Mother Superior said. "Otherwise you'll have remorse for the rest of your life, Bonifacia."

"Didn't you hear them leave, Mother?" Don Fabio asked. "They didn't go through town. They must have gone into the woods."

"They went out through the gate in the orchard; that's why we didn't hear them," Sister Angélica said. "They stole the key from this fool."

"Don't call me a fool, Missy," Bonifacia said, her eyes wide open. "They didn't steal anything from me."

"Fool, big fool," Sister Angélica said. "Have you still got the nerve . . . ? And don't call me 'Missy.' "

"I opened the gate for them." Bonifacia barely opened her lips. "I had them run away, so you can see I'm not a fool."

Don Fabio and the Mother Superior leaned their heads toward Bonifacia, Sister Angélica closed and opened her mouth, snorted before she could speak.

"What did you say?" She snorted again. "You had them run away?"

"Yes, Missy," Bonifacia said. "I had them do it."

❦

"You're getting sad again, Fushía," Aquilino said. "Don't be like that. Come on, let's have a little talk and you'll get over your sadness. Tell me for the last time how you escaped."

"Where are we?" Fushía asked. "How much longer before we get to the Marañón?"

"We reached it a while back," Aquilino said. "You didn't even notice, you were sleeping like a child."

"You reached it during the night?" Fushía asked. "How come I didn't feel the rapids, Aquilino?"

"It was so light you would have thought it was dawn, Fushía," Aquilino said. "The sky was all stars and the weather was the best you could ask for, there wasn't even a fly moving. During the day there are fishermen, sometimes a launch from the garrison, it's safer at night. And why should you feel the rapids? I know them by heart. But get rid of that sad face, Fushía. You can get up if you want, it must be hot there underneath the blankets. There's no one around, the river's all ours."

"I'll just stay here where I am," Fushía said. "I can feel a chill and my whole body's shaking."

"All right, then, anything that makes you feel better," Aquilino said. "Come on, tell me once and for all how you escaped. What did they have you in for? How old were you?"

He had gone to school and that was why the Turk had given him a job in his warehouse. He kept accounts, Aquilino, in some big books called Debits and Credits. And even though he was honest in those days, he was already dreaming about getting rich. How he used to save, old man, he ate only one meal a day, no cigarettes, no drinking. He wanted a little capital to set up a business. And that's the way things go: the Turk got it into his head that he was robbing him, a complete lie, and he had him arrested. No one would believe that he was honest, and they put him in a cell with two crooks. It was damned unfair, wasn't it, old man?

"But you already told me about that when we left the island, Fushía," Aquilino said. "I want to hear how you escaped."

"With this picklock," Chango said. "Iricuo made it from a wire on his cot. We tried it out and it can open the door without any noise. You want to see, Jappy?" he said to Fushía.

Chango was the older one, he was in for drugs or something, and he was good to Fushía. Iricuo, on the other hand, was always making fun of him. A slippery guy who had swindled a lot of people with a story about an inheritance. He was the one who made the plans.

"And it happened just like that, Fushía?" Aquilino asked.

"Just like that," Iricuo said. "Haven't you noticed that on New Year's Eve they all get leave? There's only one of them left in the building. We've got to get his keys before he gets time to toss them through the bars. It all depends on that."

"Come on, open it up, Chango," Fushía said. "I can't take much more of it, Chango, open it up."

"You really ought to stay behind, Jappy," Chango said. "A year goes by fast. We've got nothing to lose, but if it doesn't work you've had it, they'll give you a couple of years more."

But he insisted and they got out and the building was empty. They found the jailer asleep beside the bars with a bottle in his hand.

"I hit him with the leg of the cot and he fell onto the floor," Fushía said. "I think I killed him, Chango."

"Let's get the hell out of here, I've got the keys," Iricuo said. "We've got to make it across the yard running. Did you get his gun?"

"Let me go first," Chango said. "The ones on the ground floor are probably drunk like this guy too."

"But they were awake, old man," Fushía said. "There were two of them and they were shooting craps. You should have seen the looks on their faces when we busted in."

Iricuo pointed the pistol at them: they were going to open the gate or he'd spray them with bullets, the bastards. And the first sound out of them and he'd start, and they'd better hurry up or he'd do it, the bastards, he'd spray them.

"Tie them up, Jappy," Chango said. "Use their belts. And stuff their neckties in their mouths. Hurry up, Jappy, hurry up."

"They won't work, Chango," Iricuo said. "None of these is for the main gate. We've got our asses in a sling, you guys."

"It's got to be one of those, keep on trying," Chango said. "What are you doing, kid, what are you kicking them for?"

"And what did you kick them for, Fushía?" Aquilino asked. "I don't understand, at a time like this the only thing a person thinks about is getting away and nothing else."

"I hated all those sons of bitches," Fushía said. "The way they treated me, old man. Do you know that I sent them to the hospital? The newspapers talked about Japanese cruelty, Aquilino, Oriental vengeance. It made me laugh. I'd never been out of Campo Grande and I was more Brazilian than anybody."

"Now you're a Peruvian, Fushía," Aquilino said. "When I first met you in Moyobamba, you still might have been a Brazilian, there was something funny about the way you talked. But now you talk just like the people around here."

"I'm not a Brazilian and I'm not a Peruvian," Fushía said. "A poor piece of shit, old man. Garbage, that's what I am now."

"What makes you so dumb?" Iricuo said. "What did you beat them up for? Now if they catch us they'll club us all to death."

"I'm getting it, no time for arguing," Chango said. "You and I'll hide, Iricuo, and you hurry up, Jappy, get the car and hurry back."

"In the cemetery?" Aquilino said. "Christians don't do things like that."

"They weren't Christians, they were crooks," Fushía said. "In the papers they said that they went to the cemetery to dig up graves. That's what people are like, old man."

"And you stole the Turk's car?" Aquilino asked. "How come they caught them and not you?"

"They spent the whole night in the cemetery waiting for me," Fushía said. "The police jumped them in the morning. I was already far away from Campo Grande."

"You mean you double-crossed them, Fushía?" Aquilino asked.

"Haven't I double-crossed everybody?" Fushía answered. "What did I do to Pantacha and the Huambisas? What do you call what I did to Jum, old man?"

"But you weren't bad back then," Aquilino said. "You told me yourself that you were honest."

"Before I went to jail," Fushía said. "That's when I stopped."

"And how did you get to Peru?" Aquilino asked. "Campo Grande must be a long way off."

"It's in Mato Grosso, old man," Fushía said. "The papers said that the Japanese was heading for Bolivia. But I wasn't that stupid. I was everywhere, I took my time in getting away, Aquilino. Finally I reached Manaus. From there it was easy getting to Iquitos."

"And that was where you met Señor Julio Reátegui, Fushía?" Aquilino asked.

"I didn't meet him that time," Fushía said, "but I heard about him."

"What a life you've had, Fushía," Aquilino said. "The things you've seen, the traveling you've done. I like to listen to you, you don't know how much I enjoy it. Don't you enjoy telling me all of this? Don't you feel that the trip goes quicker this way?"

"No, old man," Fushía said. "I don't feel anything except cold."

As it crosses the dune region, the wind that comes down off the Andes heats up and stiffens: reinforced with sand, it follows the course of the river, and when it gets to the city it can be seen floating between the earth and the sky like a dazzling layer of armor. It empties out its insides there: every day of the year, at dusk, a dry rain, fine as sawdust, ceasing only at dawn, falls on the squares, the roofs, the towers, the belfries, the balconies, and the trees, and it paves the streets of Piura with whiteness. Outsiders are mistaken when they say, *"The houses in this town are ready to collapse."* That nocturnal creaking does not come from the buildings, which are ancient but strong; it comes from the invisible, uncountable minute projectiles of sand as they hit the doors and windows. They are mistaken too when they think, *Piura is a bashful city, a sad one.* At nightfall people take refuge in their homes to escape the suffocating wind and the sand attack that stings their skin like pin pricks and turns it red and wounds it, but in Castilla, in the wattled shacks of Mangachería, in the chili places and chicha bars of Gallinacera, in the fine homes the important people have on the Malecón and the Plaza de Armas, they have a good time like people anywhere else, drinking, listening to music, chatting. The abandoned and melancholy look of the town disappears at the thresholds of its houses, even the humblest, those fragile houses laid out in a row along the riverbank on the other side of El Camal, the slaughterhouse.

The night is full of stories in Piura. The peasants talk about ghosts; in their corner, as they cook, the women gossip and discuss misfortunes. The men drink little gourds of light-colored chicha, heavy glasses of cane liquor. It comes from the mountains and is very strong: outsiders will get tears in their eyes when they try it for the first time. The children roll around on the ground, fight, plug up wormholes, make iguana traps, or, motionless, their eyes opened wide, they listen to the stories of their elders: bandits who hide in the canyons of Canchaque, Huancabamba, and Ayabaca and rob travelers and sometimes cut their throats; big houses where ghosts are weeping; the miraculous cures of witch doctors; hidden stores of gold and silver that announce themselves with moans and the sound of chains; rebel factions that split the landowners of the region into two bands and cover the desert in all directions looking for each other, attacking each other in the midst of great dust storms, and that occupy villages and districts, confiscating animals, enlisting men by force, and paying for everything with pieces of paper which they call national bonds, rebels whom the adolescents remember seeing come into Piura like a hurricane of riders, setting up their tents in the Plaza de Armas and spreading red and blue uniforms all throughout the city; stories of duels, adultery, and catastrophe, of women who saw the Virgin in the cathedral weep, raise her hand to Christ, smile furtively at the Infant Jesus.

There are usually parties on Saturdays. Happiness flows like an electric current through Mangachería, Castilla, Gallinacera, the shacks along the riverbank. In all Piura one can hear songs and dancing, slow waltzes, the huaynos that the mountain people dance as they beat their bare feet on the ground, agile marineras, the sad fugue of a tondero. As drunkenness becomes general and there is a stop to the singing, the plucking of guitars, the booming of the box drums, and the wailing of the harps, out of the shantytowns that ring Piura like an embracing wall sudden shadows appear that defy the wind and sand: illicit young couples slip away into the sparse carob grove that darkens sandy patches, hidden little beaches on the river, grottoes that open out toward Catacaos, the more daring to the edge of the desert. There they make love.

In the center of town, in the blocks around the Plaza de Armas, in the big houses with whitewashed walls and shuttered balconies, live the landowners, the merchants, the lawyers, the authorities. At night they gather in their gardens under the palm trees, and they talk about the diseases that threaten their cotton and cane fields this year, whether the river will be on time and rise, about the fire that devoured some of Chápiro Seminario's crop, about the Sunday cock-fight, about the barbecue being organized to welcome home the flamboyant local doctor: Pedro Zevallos. While they play their rocambor, dominoes, or ombre in parlors full of rugs and shadows, among oval oil paintings, large mirrors, and furniture lined with damask, the ladies say their rosary, arrange future betrothals, program receptions, and benefits, assign duties for the Procession and the decoration of the altars, organize bazaars, and comment on the social gossip in the local newspaper, a colorful sheet called *Ecos y Noticias*.

Outsiders are not familiar with the inner life of the city. What do they dislike about Piura? Its isolation, the vast stretches of sand that separate it from the rest of the country, the lack of roads, the long trips on horseback with a roasting sun and bandit attacks. They arrive at the Estrella del Norte, the hotel on the Plaza de Armas, a large, colorless building, as tall as the bandstand where retreat is played on Sundays and in whose shade beggars and bootblacks settle, and they have to stay in there after five in the afternoon and watch the sand take over the solitary city. *"This isn't like Lima,"* they say. *"There's no fun; the people in Piura are a bad lot; did you ever see such stiff-necks, such stay-at-homes?"* They would like to have some spots that stay open all night so they could burn up their money. That is why, when they leave, they are apt to speak badly of the city, to the point of calumny. And are there, perhaps, any more hospitable and cordial people than those in Piura? They give outsiders a triumphant welcome, they fight over them when the hotel is full. Those cattle dealers, cotton buyers, every official who arrives, all are shown a good time by the important people as best they know how: they organize deer hunts in their honor in the Chulucanas mountains, they invite them to their ranches, they give them barbecues. The doors of Castilla and Mangachería are wide open to Indians who come down from the mountains and reach town hungry and frightened, to witch doctors expelled from their villages by priests, to notion vendors who come to try their luck in Piura. Chicha makers, water carriers, irrigators, they make them one of the family, they share their room and board with them. When they leave, the outsiders always take gifts with them. But nothing seems to satisfy them, they thirst for women and cannot stand the Piura nights, where the only thing awake is the sand that falls down out of the sky.

Those ingrates wanted women and nighttime fun so much that finally heaven (*"the devil, you mean, that cursed trickster,"* Father García says) ended up giving them exactly what they wanted. And that was how it came to be, noisy, frivolous, and nocturnal: the Green House.

Corporal Roberto Delgado fidgets a good while outside the office of Captain Artemio Quiroga and has a hard time deciding. In between the ashen sky and the Borja garrison, blackish clouds are slowly passing by, and on the nearby parade ground the sergeants are drilling the recruits: attention God damn it, at ease God damn it. The air is heavy with moisture. After all, a fine was the most he could get, and the Corporal pushes open the door and salutes the Captain, who is in his office, fanning himself with one hand: what was it, what did he want, and the Corporal a pass to go to Bagua could it be arranged? What was the matter with the Corporal, the Captain is now fanning himself furiously with both hands, what bug had bitten him. But bugs didn't bite Corporal Roberto Delgado, because he was a jungle boy, sir, from Bagua: he wanted a pass to see his family. And there it came again, that blasted rain. The Captain gets up, closes the window, goes back to his chair, his hands and face wet. So bugs didn't bite him, wasn't it most likely because his blood was no good?, maybe they didn't want to get poisoned, that was why they wouldn't bite him, and the Corporal agrees: it could be, sir. The officer smiles like a robot and the rain is filling the room with sound: the large drops are falling like stones on the calamine roof, the wind whistles in the chinks of the wall. When had the Corporal had his last pass?, last year? Oh, well, that was a different story and the Captain's face twitches. Then he was due for a three-week furlough and his hand goes up, was he going to Bagua?, he could buy some things for him, and he slaps himself on the cheek and it reddens. The Corporal has a very serious expression. Why wasn't he laughing?, wasn't it funny that the Captain slapped his own face?, and the Corporal no, of course not, sir, he didn't understand. A jolly spark crosses the eyes of the officer, makes his acid mouth sweet, country boy: he'd better give a nice loud laugh or there'd be no furlough. Corporal Roberto Delgado is puzzled, looks at the door, at the window. He opens his mouth and laughs, first with a reluctant and artificial laugh, then naturally and, finally, joyously. The mosquito that had bitten the Captain was a girl one, and the Corporal is shaking with laughter, only the females bit, did he know that?, the males were vegetarians, and the Captain what the hell did he mean, the Corporal is silent: he should be careful or the animals would eat him for a clown on the road to Bagua. But it wasn't a joke, it was a scientific fact, only the females sucked blood: Lieutenant de la Flor had explained it to him, sir, and what the hell did the Captain care whether they were males or females if it itched just the same and who had asked him anyway, was he turning into a professor? But the Corporal wasn't making fun, sir, and you should know that there was a cure that never failed, an ointment that the Urakusas put on themselves, he would bring him a jar, sir, and the Captain wanted him to talk like a white man, who were the Urakusas. Except how was the Corporal going to talk like a white man if that was what the Aguarunas called themselves, the ones who lived in Urakusa, and had the Captain maybe ever seen a redskin bitten by bugs? They had their secrets, they made their ointment from resins on trees and they daubed themselves with it, any mosquito that got close died, and he would bring some back, sir, a big jar, he would bring some back, on his word. The Corporal was in a good mood this morning, I'd like to see what kind of face he'd put on if the heathens shrank his noggin, and the Corporal that was very funny, very funny, sir: he could already see his head this size. And why was the Corporal going to Urakusa? Just to bring back that ointment? and the Corporal of course, of course, and besides because it was a short cut, sir. If he didn't, he'd spend his whole furlough traveling and he wouldn't be able to have any time with his family and friends. Was everybody in Bagua like the Corporal?, and he worse, as crafty?, much worse, sir, he'd never imagine, and the Captain laughs heartily and the Corporal imitates him, observes him, measures him with his half-closed eyes, and suddenly could he take along a pilot, sir?, a porter?, could he? and Captain Artemio Quiroga what was that? The Corporal thought he was pretty wise, didn't he?, he was softening him up with his clownishness, the Captain would laugh and he'd try to get something out of him, wasn't that it? But if the Corporal was all alone it would be terrible, sir, were there any roads?, how could he get to Bagua and back in such little time without a pilot, and all the officers would give him errands, he needed someone who could help him with the packages, he should let him take a pilot and a porter, he gave his word that he would bring back that bug-killing ointment, sir. Now he was working on his pity: the Corporal knew all the tricks, and the Corporal you're a wonderful person, sir. There was a pilot among the recruits who had come last week, he should let him take that one and a porter who was from the region. All right, three weeks, not one day more, and the Corporal not one day more, sir, he swore. He clicks his heels, salutes, and at the door he stops with he should be excused, sir, what was the name of the pilot? and the Captain Adrián Nieves, and the Corporal he was going now he was behind in his work. Corporal Roberto Delgado opens the door, goes out, a damp and burning wind invades the room, ruffles the Captain's hair slightly.

There was a knock on the door, Josefino Rojas went over to open it and there was nobody outside. It was getting dark, the lights on the Jirón Tacna had not been turned on yet, a breeze was slowly blowing through the city. Josefino went a little way toward the Avenida Sánchez Cerro and saw the Leóns on a bench in the square next to the statue of the painter Merino. José had a cigarette between his lips, Monk was cleaning his nails with a matchstick.

"Who died?" Josefino asked. "Why those funeral faces?"

"Hang on or you'll fall over backward, champ," Monk said. "Lituma just got into town."

Josefino opened his mouth but he did not say anything; he blinked for a few seconds with a perplexed and apathetic smile that made his whole face twisted. He began to rub his hands together softly.

"A couple of hours ago, on the Roggero bus," José said.

The windows of the San Miguel School were lighted, and at the main door a monitor was hurrying the boarding students along by clapping his hands. Boys in uniform were coming down the Calle

Libertad talking to each other under the whispering carob trees. Josefino had put his hands in his pockets.

"You better come along," Monk said. "He's waiting for us."

Josefino went back across the avenue, locked the door of his house, returned to the square, and the three of them started walking in silence. A few feet past the Jirón Arequipa, they met Father García, who was coming along wrapped in his gray scarf, all doubled over and dragging his feet and panting. He shook his fist at them and shouted, "Heathens!" "Firebug!" Monk answered, and José "Firebug! Firebug!" They were going along the sidewalk on the right, with Josefino in the middle.

"But the Ruggero buses get in early in the morning or at night, never at this time," Josefino said.

"They got stuck in Cuesta de Olmos," Monk said. "They had a flat. They changed it and then they got two more. Some luck."

"We froze when we saw him," José said.

"He wanted to start celebrating right away," Monk said. "We left him cleaning up while we came to get you."

"He caught me off guard, damn it," Josefino said.

"What are we going to do now?" José asked.

"Whatever you say, cousin," Monk said.

"Bring the old buddy along, then," Lituma said. "We'll have a few drinks with him. Go get him, tell him that champ Number Four has arrived. See what kind of face he puts on."

"Are you serious, cousin?" José asked.

"Absolutely," Lituma said. "I've got a few bottles of Sol de Ica with me. We'll empty one with him. I'd kind of like to see him, I mean it. Go ahead while I change my clothes."

"Every time he mentions you, he calls you buddy, the champ," Monk said. "He thinks as much of you as he does of us."

"I suppose he loaded you with questions," Josefino said. "What stories did you make up?"

"You're wrong, we didn't talk about that at all," Monk said. "He didn't even mention her. Maybe he's forgotten all about her."

"As soon as we get there, he's going to pepper us with questions," Josefino said. "We've got to get this settled today, before they get to him with the story."

"You take care of it," Monk said. "I don't dare. What are you going to tell him?"

"I don't know," Josefino said. "It all depends on how things look. If we'd only known he was coming, at least. But blowing in like this all of a sudden. God damn it, I wasn't ready for it."

"And quit rubbing your hands so much," José said. "I'm starting to catch your nervousness, Josefino."

"He's changed a lot," Monk said. "He's showing his age a little, Josefino. And he isn't as fat as he used to be."

The lights on the Avenida Sánchez Cerro had just gone on and the houses were still broad and sumptuous, with light walls, carved wooden balconies, and bronze door knockers, but at the end of the street, in the blue death rattle of the dusk, the twisted and hazy outline of Mangachería was beginning to appear. A caravan of trucks was heading along the street toward the New Bridge, and on the sidewalks there were couples huddled against the doorways, gangs of boys, slow old men with canes.

"The whites have become very brave," Lituma said. "Now they walk through Mangachería as if they owned it."

"It's because of the avenue," Monk said. "It was a real low blow against the Mangaches. While they were building it, the harp player said they were screwing us, everybody was going to stick his nose into the neighborhood. And that's just what happened, cousin."

"You can't find a single white man now who doesn't finish off his parties in the chicha bars," José said. "Have you noticed how big Piura has got, cousin? New buildings all over the place. But that wouldn't impress you, coming from Lima."

"I'll tell you one thing," Lituma said. "I'm through with traveling. I've been thinking about it all this time and I found out I had bad luck because I hadn't stayed home like you. I've learned one thing at least, this is where I want to die."

"He might change his mind when he finds out what's been going on," Josefino said. "He'll be ashamed to have people pointing at him on the street. Then he'll leave again."

Josefino stopped and took out a cigarette. The Leóns made a screen with their hands so that the breeze would not put the match out. They continued walking, slowly.

"What if he doesn't go away?" Monk said. "Piura's going to be too small for the both of you, Josefino."

"It'll be hard for Lituma to leave, because he's turned into a Piuran right down to his bones," José said. "It isn't like it was when he came back from the jungle, when he thought everything here stank. He got a feeling for his home town in Lima."

"No Chinese places," Lituma said. "I want some Piura food. A good seco de chabelo, a piqueo, and oceans of light chicha."

"Let's go to Angélica Mercedes' place, then, cousin," Monk said. "She's still the best cook in town. You haven't forgotten about her, have you?"

"How about Catacaos, cousin?" José said. "The Carro Hundido, they've got the best light chicha I know of there."

"The pair of you sure are happy to have Lituma back," Josefino said. "You're both acting as if it was a holiday."

"He is our cousin, after all, champ," Monk said. "It's always nice to see someone in the family again."

"We've got to take him somewhere," Josefino said. "We've got to tune him up a little before we talk to him."

"Wait a minute, Josefino," Monk said. "We haven't finished telling you."

"Let's go to Doña Angélica's tomorrow," Lituma said. "Or to Catacaos if you'd rather. Right now I know already where I want to celebrate my coming home; you have to let me have my way."

"Where the fuck does he want to go?" Josefino asked. "To the Reina, to the Tres Estrellas?"

"To Chunga Chunguita's," Lituma said.

"How about that," Monk said. "The Green House, no less. Wake up, champ."

2

"You're a regular devil," Sister Angélica said as she leaned over Bonifacia stretched out on the floor like a dark, compact animal. "A wicked woman, an ingrate."

"The ingratitude is the hardest to take, Bonifacia," the Mother Superior said slowly. "Even animals are thankful. Haven't you ever seen the frailecillo monkeys when people throw them bananas?"

The faces, hands, and veils of the sisters appeared phosphorescent in the half light of the pantry; Bonifacia remained very still.

"Someday you'll realize what you've done and you'll be sorry," Sister Angélica said. "And if you don't repent, you'll go straight to hell, you devilish rascal."

The pupils sleep in a long, narrow room that looks like a deep well; on the bare walls are three windows that open out over the Nieva; the single door leads to the wide courtyard of the Mission. On the floor, leaning against the wall, are the army cots: the pupils fold them up when they get up, unfold and stretch them out at night. Bonifacia sleeps on a wooden cot on the other side of the door in a little room that is like a wedge between the dormitory and the courtyard. Over her bed there is a crucifix, and next to it a trunk. The sisters' cells are across the courtyard, in the Residence: a white structure with a pointed roof, several symmetrical windows, and a solid wood railing. Next to the Residence is the Refectory, and then the Workroom, where the pupils learn to speak like Christians, spell, do sums, sew, and embroider. The classes in religion and morals are given in the chapel. In a corner of the courtyard is a place that looks like a hangar, next to the Mission garden; its tall reddish chimney stands out against the invading branches of the woods: it is the kitchen.

"You were this size, but it was already easy to see what you would turn out to be." The Mother Superior was holding her hand a foot and a half off the floor. "You know what I'm talking about, don't you?"

Bonifacia nodded, raised her head; her eyes examined the Mother Superior's hand. The chattering of the parrots in the garden reached even into this corner of the pantry. The foliage of the trees could be seen through the window, dark now, inextricable. Bonifacia leaned her elbows on the floor: she didn't know, Mother.

"And you don't know what we've done for you, eh?" Sister Angélica exploded as she walked back and forth clenching her fists. "And you don't know what you were when we took you in, eh?"

"How could I know," Bonifacia whispered. "I was very little, Missy, I don't remember."

"Listen to the little voice she's putting on, Mother, how gentle she seems," Sister Angélica shouted. "Do you think you're fooling me? Do you think I don't know you? And who told you you could keep on calling me 'Missy'?"

After evening prayers, the sisters go into the Refectory, and the pupils, led by Bonifacia, go to the dormitory. They set up their cots, and when they are in bed Bonifacia puts out the resin lamps, locks the door, kneels down beneath the crucifix, prays, and goes to bed.

"You used to run through the garden; you'd dig in the ground, and as soon as you found a worm or a caterpillar you'd put it in your mouth," the Mother Superior said. "You were always sick, and who cured you, who took care of you? Don't you remember that, either?"

"And you were naked," Sister Angélica shouted. "It used to be a great pleasure for me to make dresses for you and you would take them off and run out exposing yourself to everybody, and you must have been over ten years old. You had bad instincts, you devil, you only liked dirty things."

The rainy season was over and night came on rapidly: behind

the curls of the branches and leaves at the window, the sky was a constellation of sparks and dark shapes. The Mother Superior was sitting on a bag, very erect, and Sister Angélica was walking back and forth, shaking her fist; sometimes her sleeve would rise up and her arm would appear, a thin little white snake.

"I never would have imagined that you could be capable of such things," the Mother Superior said. "What was it, Bonifacia? Why did you do it?"

"Didn't it occur to you that they might starve to death or drown in the river?" Sister Angélica asked. "That they might catch a fever? Didn't you think about anything, you wretch?"

Bonifacia sobbed. The pantry had become impregnated with an odor of acid earth and damp vegetables that was rising and growing stronger in the shadows. A thick, sharp smell, nocturnal, it seemed to come in through the window mixed in with the chirping of the crickets and the locusts, quite clear now.

"You were like a little animal and we gave you a home here, a family, a name," the Mother Superior said. "We also gave you a God. Doesn't that mean anything to you?"

"You didn't have anything to eat or to wear," Sister Angélica said, with a grunt, "and we brought you up, we dressed you, we taught you. Why have you done this to the girls, you wicked woman?"

From time to time a shudder would run through Bonifacia's body, from her waist to her shoulders. Her veil had become loose and her straight hair was covering part of her forehead.

"Stop your crying, Bonifacia," the Mother Superior said. "Come, now, speak up."

This Mission wakes up at dawn, when the sound of the insects follows up the song of the birds. Bonifacia goes into the dormitory ringing a small bell: the pupils jump out of their cots, recite their Hail Marys, put on their smocks. Then they break up into groups according to their chores in the Mission: the smallest ones sweep up the courtyard, the Residence, the Refectory; the older ones do the chapel and the Workroom. Five pupils drag the garbage bags out to the courtyard and wait for Bonifacia. Guided by her, they go down the path, cross the Plaza de Santa María de Nieva, go through the planted fields, and a little before where the pilot Nieves has his cabin, they turn in to a narrow path that winds among capanahuas, tucumas, and chambiras and comes out into a small clearing which is the town dump. Once a week, Mayor Manuel Águila's workers make a large fire with the trash. The Aguarunas in the neighborhood come to eat in the place every afternoon, and some of them dig into the garbage looking for something to eat or items that can be used at home, while others shout and wave sticks to chase away the meat-eating birds that float greedily over the clearing.

"Doesn't it make any difference to you whether or not the girls go back to live in innocence and sin?" the Mother Superior asked. "Whether or not they lose everything they've learned here?"

"You still have the soul of a heathen, even though you speak like a Christian and don't go around naked," Sister Angélica said. "It isn't just that it doesn't bother her, Mother, but she helped them to escape because she wanted them to go back to being savages."

"They wanted to leave," Bonifacia said. "They went out into the courtyard and came over to the gate, and I could see in their faces that they wanted to go along with the two girls who arrived yesterday."

"And you let them have their way!" Sister Angélica shouted. "Because you were angry with them! Because they meant work for you and you hate to work, you loafer! You devil!"

"Calm yourself, Sister Angélica." The Mother Superior stood up.

Sister Angélica put a hand to her breast, touched her forehead: these lies were driving her crazy, Mother, she was very sorry.

"It was because of the two you brought in yesterday, Missy," Bonifacia said. "I didn't want the others to leave, just those two, because I felt sorry for them. You shouldn't shout like that, Missy, you'll get sick. You always get sick when you get mad."

When Bonifacia and the garbage pupils return to the Mission, Sister Griselda and her helpers prepare the morning meal: fruit, coffee, and a roll baked in the Mission oven. After they eat, the pupils go to chapel, have their catechism and church history, and learn their prayers. At noon they go back to the kitchen, and under the direction of Sister Griselda—red-faced, always moving about, and talkative—they get the noon meal ready: vegetable soup, fish, cassava, two rolls, fruit, and distilled water. Then the pupils are allowed to play for an hour in the courtyard and in the garden, or they can sit in the shade of the fruit trees. Then they go up to the Workroom. Sister Angélica teaches the new ones Spanish, the alphabet, and numbers. The Mother Superior has the classes in history and geography, Sister Ángela drawing and home care, and Sister Patrocinio arithmetic. At dusk, the sisters and the pupils say their rosary in the chapel and the girls once more break up into work groups: kitchen, garden, pantry, Refectory. The night meal is lighter than the morning one.

"They told me about their village to convince me, Sister," Bonifacia said. "They offered me everything and I felt sorry for them."

"You don't even know how to lie, Bonifacia." The Mother Superior unfolded her hands and their whiteness waved about in the blue shadows and came together again in a round shape. "The girls Sister Angélica brought from Chicais didn't know how to speak like white people, you see. It's no use for you to keep on sinning."

"I can speak the Indian language, Mother, except that you didn't know that." Bonifacia lifted her head, two green little sparks flashed beneath the mat of hair. "I learned by listening so much to the little Indians and I never told you."

"That's a lie, you devil," Sister Angélica shouted, and the round shape broke in two and fluttered softly. "Look what she's making up now, Mother. You bandit!"

But she was interrupted by some grunts that broke out as if some animal had hidden in the pantry and, suddenly infuriated, was revealing itself with howling, snorting, and rumbling, spitting out high and squeaky sounds from the darkness in a sort of savage challenge.

"You see, Missy?" Bonifacia said. "Could you understand what I was saying in Indian language?"

There is a mass every day before the morning meal. It is celebrated by the Jesuits from a neighboring Mission, usually by Father Venancio. The chapel opens its side doors on Sundays, so that the people of Santa María de Nieva may attend the services. The authorities are never absent, and sometimes farmers come, rubber workers from the area, and many Aguarunas who stay in the doorway, half naked, huddled together and timid. In the afternoon, Sister Angélica and Bonifacia take the pupils to the riverbank, where they let them splash around, fish, and climb trees. On Sundays, the morning meal is bigger and there is usually meat. There are some twenty pupils, from six to fifteen years of age, all Aguarunas. Sometimes there is a Huambisa girl among them, and even a Shapra. But that is not too frequent.

"I don't like feeling useless, Aquilino," Fushía said. "I wish it was the way it was before. We used to take turns, remember?"

"I remember," Aquilino said. "It was you who made me what I am now."

"That's right. You'd still be selling water from door to door if I hadn't come to Moyobamba," Fushía said. "You were sure afraid of the river, old man."

"Only the Mayo, because I almost drowned there when I was a boy," Aquilino said. "But I always used to go swimming in the Rumiyacu."

"The Rumiyacu?" Fushía asked. "Does it go through Moyobamba?"

"It's that easy-flowing river, Fushía," Aquilino said. "The one that goes through the ruins, near where the Lamistas live. Where there's a bunch of orange orchards. You don't remember the sweetest oranges in the world, either?"

"I'm ashamed to see you sweating all day and me here like a dead man," Fushía said.

"There's no need to row or do anything, man," Aquilino said, "just steer. Now that we're going through the canyon, the Marañón does the work all by itself. What I don't like is for you to be so quiet and be looking at the sky as if you'd seen the chulla-chaqui."

"I've never seen it," Fushía said. "Here in the jungle, everybody's seen it once except me. I even have bad luck in that."

"Good luck, you mean," Aquilino said. "Did you know that once it appeared to Señor Julio Reátegui? In a canyon on the Nieva, they say. But he saw that it was limping a lot, and all of a sudden he discovered its little leg and he filled it with bullets. By the way, Fushía, why did you have a fight with Señor Reátegui? You must have given him one for sure."

He had given him many, and the first one before he even knew him; he had just got into Iquitos, old man. He told him about it much later, and Reátegui had laughed, so you were the one who put the squeeze on Don Fabio, and Aquilino Don Fabio, the Governor of Santa María de Nieva?

"At your service, sir," Don Fabio said. "What can I do for you? Are you going to stay in Iquitos for long?"

He would stay for a fair time, maybe for good. Some business about lumber, did he know?, he was going to set up a sawmill near Nauta and he was waiting for some engineers. He was behind in his work and he would pay him more, but he wanted a large room, comfortable, and Don Fabio of course, sir, he was there to take care of the customers, old man: he swallowed the whole thing.

"He gave me the best one in the hotel," Fushía said. "With windows on a garden with jipijapas. He invited me to have lunch with him, and he talked on and on about his boss. I could barely understand him; my Spanish was very bad in those days."

"Wasn't Señor Reátegui in Iquitos?" Aquilino asked. "Wasn't he rich yet then?"

"No, he really got rich later on, through smuggling," Fushía said. "But he already had that little hotel and he was beginning to trade with the Indians; that's why he went to Santa María de Nieva. He was buying rubber and skins and he sold it in Iquitos. That was when I got the idea, Aquilino. But it's always the same thing, you need a little capital and I didn't have a cent."

"And did you get away with much money, Fushía?" Aquilino asked.

"Five thousand *soles*, Don Julio," Don Fabio said. "And my passport and some silverware. I'm terribly upset, Señor Reátegui. I know what you must think of me. But I'll make it up to you, I swear, with the sweat of my brow, Don Julio, down to the last cent."

"Haven't you ever felt sorry, Fushía?" Aquilino said. "I've been asking you that question for quite a few years now."

"For robbing that bastard Reátegui?" Fushía asked. "That guy is rich because he stole more than I did, old man. But he had something to begin with and I didn't have anything. That was always my bad luck, I always had to start from scratch."

"And what's your head for, then?" Julio Reátegui asked. "How come it didn't ever occur to you to ask to see his papers, Don Fabio?"

But he had asked to see them and his passport looked brand new; how could he have known that it was forged, Don Julio? And besides he was dressed so well when he arrived and he spoke in such a convincing way. He even said that as soon as Señor Reátegui got back from Santa María de Nieva, I would introduce him and they would do a lot of business together. A person can get careless, Don Julio.

"And what were you carrying in that suitcase, then, Fushía?" Aquilino asked.

"Maps of the Amazon region, Señor Reátegui," Don Fabio said. "Great big ones like they have in the barracks. He put them up on the wall in his room and he said it was so he could know where we would get the wood from. He had drawn some arrows and notes in Brazilian, it was very strange."

"There's nothing strange about it at all, Don Fabio," Fushía said. "Besides wood, I'm interested in trading too. And sometimes it's useful to have contacts with the Indians. That's why I wrote down the names of the tribes."

"Even the ones on the Marañón and the ones from Ucayali, Don Julio," Don Fabio said, "and I thought what an enterprising man; he'd make a good partner for Señor Reátegui."

"Do you remember how we burned your maps?" Aquilino asked. "Nothing but junk. People who make maps don't know that the Amazon is like a hot woman, she's never the same. Everything is on the move here, the rivers, the animals, the trees. What a crazy land we've got for ourselves, Fushía."

"He knows the jungle very well too," Don Fabio said. "When he gets back from the upper Marañón, I'll introduce you and you'll get to be good friends."

"Here in Iquitos everybody tells me such wonderful things about him," Fushía said. "I'm very anxious to meet him. Don't you know when he'll be back from Santa María de Nieva?"

"He has business there and, besides, official duties take a lot of his time, but he always has his little escapades," Don Fabio said. "A will of iron, sir. He got it from his father, another great man. He was a big man in rubber, when things were good in Iquitos. He shot himself after the crash. He lost his shirt. But Don Julio came back, all by himself. A will of iron, I tell you."

"They gave him a lunch in Santa María once and I heard him give a speech," Aquilino said. "He was very proud of his father, Fushía."

"His father was one of his favorite topics," Fushía said. "He was always talking to me about him too, when we worked together. Oh, that bastard Reátegui, shit lucky. I was always jealous of him, old man."

"So white, so loving," Don Fabio said. "And to think that I played with him, licked his boots. He would come into the hotel and Jesucristo would stop twitching his tail, he was so happy. What a terrible man, Don Julio."

"In Campo Grande kicking the jailers, and in Iquitos killing a cat," Aquilino said. "Your goodbyes are something, Fushía."

"That really doesn't bother me so much, Don Fabio," Julio Reátegui said. "What I'm sorry about is that he got away with my money."

But he was very sorry, Don Julio, hung from the mosquito netting by a sheet, and when he went into the room and saw it all at once, dancing in the air, stiff, its eyes bulging! Evil just for the sake of evil was something he didn't understand, Señor Reátegui.

"A man does what he has to in order to live, and I can understand your stealing," Aquilino said. "But why do that to the cat? Was it because you were mad at not having the money you needed to get started with?"

"That's right," Fushía said. "And besides the animal stank and he'd wet my bed God knows how many times."

And something about Orientals too, Don Julio, they do the dirtiest things, who could imagine, and he'd seen it and for example the Chinese in Iquitos raised cats in cages, they fattened them up on milk and then they put them in the pot and ate them, Señor Reátegui. But he wanted to talk about the purchases now, Don Fabio, that's why he'd come from Santa María de Nieva, they should forget about sad things, had he bought anything?

"Everything you ordered, Don Julio," Don Fabio said, "the small mirrors, the knives, the cloth, the beads, and at a good discount. When are you going back to the upper Marañón?"

"I couldn't go into the jungle alone to trade, I needed a partner," Fushía said. "And I had to try to find him far away from Iquitos after that episode."

"That's why you came to Moyobamba," Aquilino said. "And you made friends with me so I could go to the Indians with you. So you began imitating Reátegui even before you'd ever seen him, before you went to work for him. The way you used to talk about money, Fushía: come with me, Aquilino, within a year I'll make you rich. You used to drive me crazy with that little song."

"And look at us now; take a good look," Fushía said. "I've sacrificed myself more than anyone ever could, no one has taken the chances I have. Is it fair for it to end up like this, Aquilino?"

"That's for God to decide, Fushía," Aquilino said. "It's not up to us to judge things like that."

One hot December dawn, a man arrived in Piura. On a mule that was slowly dragging itself along, he rose up suddenly out of the dunes to the south: a silhouette beneath a broad-brimmed hat, wrapped in a light poncho. In the reddish light of dawn, as the sun tongues snaked their way out across the desert, the stranger must have been happy to see the first cactus plants, the singed carob trees, the white houses of Castilla that huddle together and multiply as they approach the river. He advanced on toward the city through the heavy atmosphere, and now it could be seen on the other shore, like the flash of a mirror. He crossed the one street in Castilla, nobody on it yet, and when he reached the Old Bridge he dismounted. He took a few seconds to look at the buildings on the other side, the paved streets, the houses with their balconies, the air thick with small grains of sand that were softly falling down, the massive tower of the cathedral with its round, soot-colored belfry, and, toward the north, the greenish splotches of the farm plots that followed the course of the river as it headed toward Catacaos. He took the reins of his mule, he crossed the Old Bridge and, hitting his leg with the whip from time to time, he went along the main street, the one that leads, elegant and straight, from the river to the Plaza de Armas. There he stopped, tied the animal to a tamarind tree, sat down on the ground, and lowered the brim of his hat to protect himself from the sand that was mercilessly puncturing his eyes. He must have had a long trip: his movements were slow, fatigued. When the rain of sand was over and the first inhabitants came out upon the square that was all bright in the sunlight, the stranger was asleep. Beside him lay the mule, with greenish froth on its nose, showing the whites of his eyes. No one dared to wake him. The news spread through the neighborhood, and soon the Plaza de Armas was filled with the curious, who were elbowing each other and whispering about the stranger as they shoved up close to him. Some climbed up on the bandstand, while others watched him from up on the palm trees. He was an athletic young man, with broad shoulders; his face was bathed in a small curly beard, and his buttonless shirt showed a chest full of muscles and hair. He was sleeping with his mouth open, softly snoring; between his parched lips his teeth were peeping out like those of a mastiff: yellow, large, carnivorous. His pants, his boots, the faded poncho, all were tattered, filthy, the same as his hat. He did not have any weapons.

When he awoke, he jumped up and took a defensive stance: his eyes, under their swollen lids, uneasily took in the mass of faces. Smiles broke out on all sides, spontaneous hands, an old man shoved his way up to him and handed him a gourd of fresh water. The stranger smiled then. He drank slowly, savoring the water greedily. There was a growing murmur, everybody fought to say something to the newcomer: they asked him about his trip, they were sorry that his mule had died. He was laughing strongly now, shaking all the hands. Then he tugged the saddlebags off the animal and asked about a hotel. Surrounded by solicitous people, he went across the Plaza de Armas to the Estrella del Norte: there were no rooms. The people gave him assurances, many voices offered him their hospitality. He put up in the house of Melchor Espinoza, an old man who lived by himself on the Malecón, near the Old Bridge. He had a small plot some distance away on the banks of the Chira, where he went twice a month. That year, Melchor Espinoza had broken a record: he had put up five outsiders. Usually, they would stay in Piura just the time necessary to buy a cotton crop, sell some cattle, place some merchandise; a few days, that is, a few weeks at most.

This stranger, quite the opposite, stayed. The people could not find out much about him, almost all of it what he was not: he was not a cattle dealer, or a tax assessor, or a traveling salesman. His name was Anselmo and he said that he was a Peruvian, but no one could identify his accent: he did not have that dubitative and effeminate speech of Lima people, or the singsong intonation of a Chiclayan; he did not pronounce his words with the luxuriant perfection of people from Trujillo, nor could he have been from the mountains, because he did not crack his tongue on the *r*'s and the *s*'s. His accent was different, quite musical and a little languid; the expressions and idioms that he used were strange, and when he argued, the violence of his voice brought to mind an outlaw chief. The saddlebags, which were all of his luggage, must have been full of money: how could he have crossed the desert without being attacked by bandits? The people were unable to find out where he came from, or why he had chosen Piura as his destination.

The day after he had arrived, he appeared in the Plaza de Armas, clean shaven, and the youth of his face surprised everybody. In the store owned by the Spaniard Eusebio Romero, he bought a new pair of pants and boots; he paid cash. Two days later he had Saturnina, the best hat weaver in Catacaos, make him a white straw hat, the kind a person can put into his pocket and pull out later without a wrinkle in it. Every morning, Anselmo would go to the Plaza de Armas and settle down on the terrace of the Estrella del Norte, and from there he would invite passers-by to have a drink. That was how he made friends. He was good at conversation and he had lots of jokes, and he won the people over by praising the charms of their city: the delightful people, the beauty of the women, their splendid sunsets. He soon learned the ways of local speech and its warm and lazy melody: after a few weeks he was saying "Guá" to show surprise, he was calling children "churres" and donkeys "piajenos," he was making superlatives out of superlatives; he knew how to distinguish light chicha from thick chicha, and all the varieties of hot seasonings; he knew people's names by heart, the streets too, and he could dance the tondero like any Mangache.

His curiosity had no limits. He had a consuming interest in the customs and manners of the city, he kept himself informed with a luxury of details about lives and deaths. He wanted to know everything: who the richest people were, and why, and since when; whether the Prefect, the Mayor, and the Bishop were honest and well-liked, and what the people did for fun; what adulteries, what scandals there were among church-ridden women and the priests; how the people followed their religion and morals; what forms love took in the city.

Every Sunday he would go to the Coliseo and cheer at the cockfights like an old man, at night he was the last one to leave the bar in the Estrella del Norte, he would play cards with elegance, betting heavily, and he knew how to win or lose and keep his composure. In that way, he won the friendship of the merchants and landowners and he became quite popular. Important people invited him to go hunting in Chulucanas and he amazed them all with his marksmanship. When they passed him on the street, the peasants would call him by his name and he would give them rough and cordial pats on the back. People like his jovial spirit, the ease of his manners, his generosity. But they were all intrigued by where his money came from and by his past. Small myths grew up about him: when they reached his ears, Anselmo would celebrate them with a great laugh and would neither confirm nor deny them. Sometimes he would hit all the Mangache chicha bars with friends, and he would always end up at Angélica Mercedes', because there was a harp there, and he was an accomplished harpist, inimitable. While the others would be stomping and toasting, he would sit hour after hour in the corner, caressing the docile white strings and making them whisper, laugh, sob.

The only thing that people deplored was that Anselmo was rude and would look at the women boldly when he was drunk. Barefoot servants crossing the Plaza de Armas on their way to the market, vendor women with clay jars or pitchers on their heads as they came and went offering mango and canistel juice and fresh cheeses from the mountains, ladies with gloves, veils, and rosaries parading toward the church, to all he would make propositions under his breath along with improvised off-color verses. *"Watch out, Anselmo,"* his friends would say to him. *"Piurans are very jealous. An offended husband, a father with no sense of humor, someday he'll challenge you to a duel when you least expect it. You should show respect toward women."* But Anselmo would answer with a laugh, raise his glass, and toast Piura.

During his first month in the city, nothing happened

❂

It isn't so bad and besides everything worked out in this world, the sun is sparkling in Julio Reátegui's eyes, and the bottles are sitting in a tub of water. He does the pouring himself: the white foam bubbles up, swells, and breaks down into small craters: they shouldn't worry and, before anything more, another glass of beer. Manuel Aguila, Pedro Escabino, and Arévalo Benzas drink, wipe their lips with their hands. Through the screen one can see the square of Santa María de Nieva, a group of Aguarunas are grinding cassava into some fat-bellied receptacles, several children are running around the capirona trunks. Up above, on the hillside, the nuns' Residence is a fiery rectangle and, in the first place, it was a long-term project and projects didn't do too well here, Julio Reátegui thought that they were worrying over nothing. But Manuel Águila no, nothing like that, Governor, he stands up, they had proof, Don Julio, a small man, short and bald, with bulging eyes, those two guys had subverted them. And Arévalo Benzas too, Don Julio, stands up, there was proof, he had said that there was something else behind those flags and those books and he had been against the teachers' coming, Don Julio, and Pedro Escabino bangs his glass on the table, Don Julio: the cooperative was a fact, the Aguarunas were going to sell for themselves in Iquitos, the chiefs had got together in Chicais to talk about that, and that was the way things were and a person had to be blind. Except that Julio Reátegui didn't know a single Aguaruna who knew what Iquitos or a cooperative was, where did you get such a story from, Pedro Escabino?, and he begged them please to speak one at a time, gentlemen. The glass sounds dry and hollow again against the table, Don Julio, he spent a lot of time in Iquitos, he had a lot of business there, and he didn't know how the region had been all stirred up since that pair had come. Julio Reátegui's voice is still smooth, Don Pedro, the Governorship had made him lose time and money, but his eyes have hardened, and he didn't want to accept it, and Pedro Escabino was one of those who insisted most, he would please watch his words. Pedro Escabino knew how much they owed to him and he didn't want to offend him: only he had just got back from Urakusa and for the first time in ten years, Don Julio, dry and hollow twice against the table, the Aguarunas refused to sell him even one little ball of rubber, to hell with progress, and Arévalo Benzas: they even showed him the cooperative. Don Julio, he should not laugh, they had built a special hut and they had it filled with rubber and skins and they refused to sell to Escabino and they told him they were going to Iquitos to sell. And Manuel Águila, short and bald behind his popeyes: did the Governor see? Those guys should never have been allowed among the Indians, Arévalo was right, they only wanted to stir them up. But no more of them were coming, gentlemen, and Julio Reátegui fills up the glasses. He didn't go to Iquitos just on his own business but on theirs too, and the Ministry had canceled the plan for the jungle cultural extension and the teacher brigades were over. But Pedro Escabino dry and hollow for the third time: they'd already come and the damage was done, Don Julio. So they couldn't even get together with the redskins? He would soon see that they got along very well and they had brought the interpreter that that pair had taken to Urakusa, and he himself would tell him, Don Julio, and he would see. The copper-colored barefoot man who is squatting beside the door gets up, advances confusedly toward the Governor of Santa María de Nieva, and Bonino Pérez how much did they pay for a pound of rubber, he should ask him that. The interpreter begins to grunt, he moves his hands, he spits, and Jum listens in silence, his arms crossed on his naked chest. Two thin reddish "X"s decorate his greenish cheeks and three horizontal lines are tattooed on his square nose, thin, like small worms, his expression is serious, his posture solemn: the Urakusas crowded into the clearing do not move and the sun spears down on the trees, down on the huts of Urakusa. The interpreter is silent and Jum and a small old man gesticulate and chew with grunts, and the interpreter for good quality one, for regular a half a sol a pound, boss, saying, and Teófilo Cañas blinks, costing, a dog barks in the distance. Bonino Pérez knew it, brother, God damn them, what bastards, and to the interpreter: bad Peruvians, they sold it for ten a pound, bosses screwing them, they should not let them, man, they should take the rubber and skins to Iquitos, no more business with these bosses: translate that for him. And the interpreter telling them?, and Bonino yes, bosses robbing them telling them?, and Teófilo yes, bad Peruvians telling them?, yes, yes, boss screwing them telling? and they yes, yes, God damn it, yes: devils, thieves, Peruvians bad, that they shouldn't let them, yes God damn it, don't be afraid, translating that. The interpreter grunts, roars, spits, and Jum grunts, roars, spits, and the old man strikes himself on the chest, his skin has rough little folds, and the interpreter Iquitos never coming boss Escabino coming, bringing knife, machete, cloth, and Teófilo Cañas how about that, brother, they think Iquitos is a man, they didn't understand a thing, Bonino, and the interpreter saying, exchanging for rubber. But Bonino Pérez goes over to Jum, points at the knife that he has at his waist, come, how many pounds of rubber did that cost you: ask him that. Jum takes out his knife, lifts it up, the sun makes the white blade flame, dissolves its edges, and Jum smiles arrogantly and behind him the Urakusas smile and several of them take out their knives, lift them up, and the sun lights them up and makes them disappear, and the interpreter: twenty balls for Jum's, saying, the others ten, fifteen balls, costing, and Teófilo Cañas wanted to go back to Lima, brother. He had a fever, Bonino, and all this injustice and these people who didn't understand, better to forget about it, and Bonino Pérez counts on his fingers, Teófilo, he was never any good at figures, Jum's knife came out to be forty soles, didn't it?, and the interpreter telling?, translating? and Teófilo no, and Bonino tell him this: boss devil, this knife not cost even one ball, picked out of garbage, Iquitos not boss, city, downriver, down Marañón, they should take their rubber there, they would sell it a hundred times better, they would buy all the knives they wanted, or whatever they wanted, and the interpreter yes?, he did not understand, repeating slowly, and Bonino was right: you have to explain everything to them, brother, right from the beginning, don't get me down, Teófilo and maybe they were right but Julio Reátegui insisted: there was no reason to lose their heads.

Hadn't those two guys left? They'd never come back and it was only the Aguarunas who were stirred up, he'd had dealings with the Shapras the same as ever, and besides everything had a way out. Just that he had thought he would end his term as Governor in peace, gentlemen, and that they should see, and Arévalo Benzas: that wasn't all, Don Julio. Hadn't he heard what had happened in Urakusa to a corporal, a pilot, and a porter from the Borja garrison? Just last week, Don Julio, and he what, what had happened.

"You all ought to be happy now, we're in Mangachería," José said.

"The sand scratches, it tickles me. I'm going to take my shoes off," Monk said.

When the Avenida Sánchez Cerro ended, so did the asphalt, the white façades, the solid outside doors, and the electric lights; and wattled walls, straw, tin, and cardboard roofs, dust, flies, and twisted lanes began. Tallow candles and Mangache lamps glowed in the square little curtainless windows of the shacks, whole families were taking the night air in the middle of the street. At every step the Leóns would raise their hands to greet acquaintances.

"What are they so proud of? Why are they always praising it?" Josefino asked. "It smells bad and the people live like animals. At least fifteen of them in every shack."

"Twenty, if you count the dogs and Sánchez Cerro's picture," Monk said. "That's another good thing about Mangachería, there's no distinction made. Men, dogs, goats, all equals, all Mangaches."

"And we're proud because we were born here," José said. "We like to praise it because it's our home town. Deep down inside of you you're jealous, Josefino."

"The rest of Piura's dead this time of night," Monk said. "But over here, listen, life is just getting started."

"We're all friends or relatives here, and we're worth what we're worth," José said. "In Piura they only look at you for what you've got, and if you're not white you lick the whites' boots."

"Shit on Mangachería," Josefino said. "When they tear it down like Gallinacera, I'm going to celebrate by getting drunk."

"You're up on your high horse and you don't know who to get

mad at," Monk said. "But if you want to make cracks about Mangachería, you better whisper, or the Mangaches'll cut your heart out."

"We're acting like a bunch of kids," Josefino said. "This is no time for arguments."

The people sitting on the sand were quiet, and all the noise—songs, toasts, guitar music, clapping—was coming from the chicha bars, huts larger than the others, better lighted, and red and white flags flying in front at the top of a pole. The atmosphere was boiling with warm and contrasting smells, and as the streets disappeared, out came dogs, chickens, pigs that darkly, gruntingly, were rolling on the ground, staked-out goats with enormous eyes, and even thicker and noisier was the aerial fauna that hung over their heads. The champs were slowly advancing through the twisted trails of the Mangache jungle, stepping around the old people who had taken their mats out into the open, detouring around the untimely huts that burst up in the middle of the road like porpoises out of the sea. The sky was burning with stars, some large and shining proudly, others like the small flame of a match.

"The Marimachas are out now," Monk said; he was pointing at three very high, sparkling parallel points, the three Marys. "Look at them blink. Domitila Yara used to say that when you see the Marimachas that clear, you can ask them for a favor. Go ahead, Josefino."

"Domitila Yara!" José said. "Poor old woman. I used to be a little scared of her, but since she died I've had warm feelings about her. I wonder if she's forgiven us for that mess at her wake."

Josefino was walking along in silence, his hands in his pockets, his chin sunk down on his chest. The Leóns kept mumbling in chorus all along the way, "Good evening, Don," "Hello, Doña," and from the ground invisible and sleepy voices would return the greeting and call them by name. They stopped in front of a shack and Monk opened the door: Lituma, his back turned, was dressed in a reddish-yellow suit, the jacket bulging at the hips, and his hair was damp and shiny. Over his head a newspaper clipping was dancing, hung by a pin.

"Here's champ Number Three, cousin," Monk said.

Lituma spun around like a top, he crossed the room smiling and quickly, his arms open, and Josefino went to meet him. They embraced strongly, and they spent a good time patting each other on the back: a long time, brother, a long time, Lituma, and it's good to have you back again, rubbing each other like two hounds.

"That's some outfit you've got on, cousin," Monk said.

Lituma stepped back so that the champs could take their time in looking over his bright and motley clothes: a white shirt with a stiff collar, a pink tie with gray spots, green socks, and pointed shoes that shined like two mirrors.

"You like it? I'm wearing it for the first time, in honor of my home town. I bought it three days ago in Lima. The tie and the shoes too."

"You look like a king," José said. "The bestest, cousin."

"The outfit, just the outfit," Lituma said, pinching the lapels of his jacket. "The cloth is getting moth-eaten. But I can still get the girls. Now that I'm a little old bachelor, it's my turn."

"I almost didn't recognize you," Josefino interrupted. "I haven't seen you in civilian clothes for so long, buddy."

"You mean you just haven't seen me for so long," said Lituma and his face became serious; he smiled again.

"We'd forgotten what you looked like as a civilian too, cousin," José said.

"You're better like that than all trimmed up," Monk said. "Now you're a real champ again."

"What are we waiting for," José said. "Let's sing our song."

"You're all my brothers," Lituma laughed. "Who taught you how to dive off the Old Bridge?"

"And to take a swig and chase after whores too," José said. "You corrupted us, cousin."

Lituma embraced the Leóns, shook them affectionately. Josefino was rubbing his hands, and although his mouth was smiling, in his steady eyes something furtive and frightened was gleaming, and the position of his body, his shoulders thrown back, his chest stuck out, his legs slightly bent, was forced, restless, and watchful all at the same time.

"We have to sample that Sol de Ica," Monk said. "You promised and a promise is a debt."

They sat down on two mats, under a kerosene lamp hanging from the ceiling that, as it swayed, rescued from the adobe wall hidden in the half light, fleeting chinks, inscriptions, and a shabby niche where at the feet of a plaster Virgin and Child there was an empty candleholder. José put a candle in and lit it, and in its light the newspaper clipping showed the yellowed outline of a general, a sword, many decorations. Lituma had brought a suitcase over to the mats. He opened it, took out a bottle, uncorked it with his teeth, and Monk helped him fill four small glasses to the brim.

"I still can't believe I'm back here with all of you, Josefino," Lituma said. "I missed you a lot, the three of you. And my town too. Here's to our being together again."

The glasses touched and they drank them empty at the same time.

"Wow! firewater!" Monk roared, his eyes full of tears. "Are you sure this isn't rubbing alcohol, cousin?"

"Why, it's smooth," Lituma said. "Pisco is for Lima people, women, and children, it isn't like cane liquor. Have you forgotten how we used to drink cane liquor like soda pop?"

"Monk never was any good at drinking," Josefino said. "Two drinks and he's tight already."

"I may get drunk fast, but I can last longer than anyone else," Monk said. "I can go on like that for days on end."

"You were always the first one to pass out, brother," José said. "Remember, Lituma, how we used to drag him to the river and bring him to by tossing him in?"

"And sometimes just by slapping me on the cheeks," Monk said. "That must be why I haven't got any beard, from all the slapping you gave me to sober me up."

"I'm going to make a toast," Lituma said.

"Let me fill up the glasses first, cousin."

Monk took the bottle of pisco, began to pour, and Lituma's face was growing sad, two wrinkles made his eyes slant, his look seemed far away.

"Let's have that toast, champ," Josefino said.

"To Bonifacia," Lituma said. And he slowly raised his glass.

3

"Stop acting like a child," the Mother Superior said. "You've had all night to whimper as much as you liked."

Bonifacia grasped the skirt of the Mother Superior's habit and kissed it.

"Tell me that Sister Angélica won't come. Tell me, Mother, you're so kind."

"Sister Angélica was right when she scolded you," the Mother Superior said. "You've offended God and you've betrayed the trust we had in you."

"Just so she doesn't get mad, Mother," Bonifacia said. "You know that whenever she gets mad she gets sick. I don't mind if she scolds me."

Bonifacia claps her hands and the pupils' whispering diminishes but does not stop, stronger clap and they become quiet: now only the shuffling of sandals on the stones of the courtyard. She opens the dormitory, and as soon as the last pupil has gone through the door she locks it and puts her ear to it: it is not the usual noise, along with the everyday bustle there can be heard a soft whispering, secret and frightened, the same kind that was heard when they saw them arrive at noon between Sister Angélica and Sister Patrocinio, the same kind that bothered the Mother Superior during rosary. Bonifacia listens for a moment more and returns to the kitchen. She lights a lamp, takes a tin plate of fried plantains, opens the lock on the pantry door, goes in, and in the back, in the darkness, there is a sound like the running of mice. She raises the lamp and explores the room. They are behind the bags of corn: a thin ankle with a leather loop around it, two bare feet that rub against each other and curl up, trying to hide each other? The space between the bags and the wall is very narrow, they must have squeezed together, there is no sound of weeping.

"Maybe the devil tempted me, Mother," Bonifacia said. "But I didn't know it. I just felt sorry for them, believe me."

"What did you feel sorry about?" the Mother Superior asked. "And what does that have to do with what you did, Bonifacia, don't be foolish."

"For the little heathen girls from Chicais, Mother," Bonifacia said. "I'm telling you the truth. Didn't you see them crying? Didn't you see how they were hugging each other? And they wouldn't eat anything, either, when Sister Griselda brought them their meal; didn't you see that?"

"It wasn't their fault that they acted that way," the Mother Superior said. "They didn't know that it was for their own good that they were here, they thought we were going to hurt them. Isn't that the way it always is until they get used to it? They didn't know, but you knew that it was for their own good, Bonifacia."

"But I felt sorry for them just the same," Bonifacia said. "What did you expect me to do, Mother?"

Bonifacia kneels down, holds the lamp over the bags, and there they are: curled together like a pair of eels. One has her head sunk into the breast of the other, and that one, with her back against the wall, cannot hide her head as the light invades her hiding place, she can only close her eyes and moan. Neither Sister Griselda's scissors nor the burning, reddish disinfectant has been there yet. Heavy, dark, covered with dust, pieces of straw, and probably fleas, their hair rains down over their shoulders and thighs; they look like a little trash heap. Emerging from the mixed and dirty strands, their feeble arms and legs can be seen in the light of the lamp, patches of dark skin, their shoulders.

"It just happened, Mother, I didn't mean to," Bonifacia said. "I didn't mean to, I hadn't even thought about it, really."

"You hadn't thought about it and you didn't mean to, but you did let them get away," the Mother Superior said. "And not just those two, but the others as well. You'd been planning it all out with them for a long time, isn't that right?"

"No, Mother, I swear I didn't," Bonifacia said. "It was night before last, when I brought their meal to them here in the pantry. I can remember and I'm scared, I turned into someone else and I thought it was because I felt sorry, but most likely the devil was tempting me, the way you said, Mother."

"That's no excuse," the Mother Superior said. "Stop hiding behind the devil so much. If he tempted you, it was because you let yourself be tempted. What do you mean when you say that you turned into someone else?"

Beneath the underbrush of hair, the small and intertwined bodies have begun to tremble, their shaking is contagious, and the chattering of their teeth is like that of timid maquisapa monkeys when they are put into a cage. Bonifacia looks toward the door of the pantry, leans over, and very slowly, discordantly, persuasively begins to grunt. There is a change in the air, as if a fresh breeze had suddenly cooled the darkness of the pantry. The bodies stop trembling beneath their filth, two little heads start to move in a barely perceptible way, and Bonifacia keeps on croaking, clucking softly.

"The pupils got nervous as soon as they saw them," Bonifacia said. "They were whispering among themselves, and when I went over to them they started talking about something else. They were acting, Mother, but I knew that they'd been talking about the little Indians. Don't you remember how they were acting in chapel?"

"What were they so nervous about?" the Mother Superior asked. "It wasn't the first time that they'd seen two girls come to the Mission."

"I don't know, Mother," Bonifacia said. "I'm only telling you what happened, I don't know why they were acting that way. They must have remembered when they came themselves. Yes, that must have been what they were talking about."

"What happened in the pantry with those children?" the Mother Superior asked.

"Promise me first that you won't send me away, Mother," Bonifacia said. "I've been praying all night that you won't send me away.

What could I do all alone, Mother? I'll change if you promise me. And I'll tell you everything."

"Are you making conditions for your repentance?" the Mother Superior asked. "That's all we needed. And I don't know why you want to stay on at the Mission. Didn't you help the children escape because you were sorry for their being here? I should think you'd be happy to leave."

Bonifacia holds the tin plate out to them and they stop trembling, they are motionless and their breathing inflates their chests with an identically spaced rhythm. Bonifacia puts the plate down at the level of the girl who is sitting against the wall. She keeps on grunting, softly, familiarly, and suddenly the small head rises up, behind the cascade of hair there are two brief lights, two small and shiny fish that go from Bonifacia's eyes to the tin plate. An arm emerges and stretches out with infinite caution, a fearful hand is outlined in the light of the lamp, two dirty fingers seize a plantain, bury it under the growth.

"But I'm not like them, Mother," Bonifacia said. "Sister Angélica and you always tell me, 'You're out of the darkness now, you're civilized now.' Where can I go, Mother? I don't want to be a heathen again. The Virgin was good, wasn't she?, she pardoned everything, didn't she? Have pity, Mother, be good, you're like the Virgin for me."

"You can't buy me off with flattery, I'm not Sister Angélica," the Mother Superior said. "If you feel so civilized and Christian, why did you help the girls escape? Why didn't it bother you that they'd go back to being heathens?"

"But they'll find them, Mother," Bonifacia said. "You'll see how the soldiers will bring them back. Don't blame me for what they did. They went out into the yard and they wanted to leave. I didn't know what was going on, Mother, believe me, I'd turned into somebody else."

"You turned crazy," the Mother Superior said, "or into an idiot, not knowing that they were escaping right under your nose."

"Worse even than that, Mother, a heathen just like the ones from Chicais," Bonifacia said. "I think about it now and I'm scared, you have to pray for me, I want to repent, Mother."

The girl is chewing without taking her hand away from her mouth and she adds pieces of fried plantain as she swallows. She has pushed her hair aside and now it frames her face between two bands, and as she chews the ring in her nose swings slightly back and forth. Her eyes are fixed on Bonifacia and suddenly her other hand grasps the hair of the girl huddled against her chest. Her free hand goes to the tin plate, grabs a plantain, and the hidden head, forced by the hand that holds its hair, turns: this one does not have her nose pierced, her eyes are two small, irritated pockets. The hand descends, puts the plantain next to the closed lips, which tighten even more, mistrustful, obstinate.

"Why didn't you come and tell me?" the Mother Superior asked. "You hid in the chapel because you knew that you'd done something bad."

"I was afraid, not of you but of myself, Mother," Bonifacia said. "I thought it was a bad dream when I didn't see them any more, and that's why I went to the chapel. I kept telling myself it wasn't so, they haven't gone, nothing has happened, I've been dreaming. Tell me that you won't send me away, Mother."

"You've sent yourself away," the Mother Superior said. "We've done more for you than we have for anybody else, Bonifacia. You could have spent your whole life here at the Mission. But when the girls come back, they can't see you here. I'm sorry about it too, in spite of how you've misbehaved. And I know that it's going to be very hard on Sister Angélica. But you'll have to leave for the good of the Mission."

"Just keep me on as a servant, that's all, Mother," Bonifacia said. "I won't take care of the pupils any more. I'll just sweep up and carry trash and help Sister Griselda in the kitchen. I beg you, Mother."

The one lying down resists: tense, her eyes closed, she bites her lips, but the fingers of the other one dig implacably, persist against that stubborn mouth. The two are breathing heavily from the effort, clumps of hair are sticking to their shining skin. And suddenly it opens: the fingers swiftly put the almost dissolved remains of the plantain into the open mouth and the girl begins to chew. A few ends of hair have entered her mouth along with the plantain. Bonifacia indicates it to the one with the ring by a gesture, and she raises her hand again, her fingers grasp the trapped hairs and delicately pull them out. The girl who is lying down swallows now, a little ball goes up and down along her throat. Seconds later, she opens her mouth again and stays that way, her eyes closed, waiting. Bonifacia and the one with the ring look at each other in the oily light of the lamp. They smile at the same time.

"Don't you want any more?" Aquilino asked. "You have to eat something, man, you can't live on air."

"I keep thinking about that whore," Fushía said. "It's your fault, Aquilino, I've been seeing her and hearing her for two nights now. But she was such a young girl when I met her."

"How did you meet her, Fushía?" Aquilino asked. "Was it long after we split up?"

"It's been a year, more or less, Dr. Portillo," the woman said. "We were living in Belén then and with the flood the water was coming right up to the house."

"Yes, of course, Madam," Dr. Portillo said. "But tell me about the Japanese, do you mind?"

Where the river had overflowed, the Belén district looked like an ocean, and the Japanese would go by the house every Saturday, Dr. Portillo. And she I wonder who he is, and how strange he's so well-dressed and he comes to load the merchandise on board himself and doesn't have somebody do it for him. Those were the best times, old man. He was beginning to make money in Iquitos, working for that bastard Reátegui, and one day a girl couldn't cross the street because of the water, and he paid a stevedore to carry her across and her mother came out to thank him: a horrible old bawd, Aquilino.

"And he would always stop and talk to us, Dr. Portillo," the woman said. "Before he went to the docks, or afterward, and always so friendly."

"And did you know what business he was in?" Dr. Portillo asked.

"He seemed very decent and elegant in spite of his race," the woman said. "He used to bring us presents, Doctor. Clothes, shoes, and once he even brought a canary bird."

"For that barefoot daughter of yours, Ma'am," Fushía said. "So that it can wake her up with its singing."

They understood each other famously, even though they pretended that they didn't, old man; the bawd knew what he wanted and he knew that the old bitch wanted money, and Aquilino what about Lalita?, what did she have to say about it all?

"Her hair was already quite long," Fushía said. "And her face was clear then, not a single pimple. She was very pretty, Aquilino."

"He used to come with a parasol, wearing a white suit and his shoes were white too," the woman said. "He used to take us out walking, to the movies, once he took Lalita to that Brazilian circus that had come to town, do you remember?"

"Did he give you much money, Madam?" Dr. Portillo asked.

"Very little, practically none, Doctor," the woman said. "And not very often. He used to give us presents, nothing else."

And Lalita was already too old to go to school: he would give her a job in his office and her salary would be a great help to both of them, did Lalita like the idea? She had thought about the future of her daughter and about necessities, Dr. Portillo, about the hard times they were having: it all added up to Lalita's going to work for the Japanese.

"To live with him, Madam," Dr. Portillo said. "Don't be ashamed, a lawyer is like a confessor to his clients."

"I swear to you that Lalita always slept at home," the woman said. "Ask the neighbors, if you don't believe me, Doctor."

"And what kind of work did he have your daughter do, Madam?" Dr. Portillo asked.

Stupid work, old man, which would have made him rich for the rest of his life if it could have lasted a couple of years more. But somebody turned them in, and Reátegui got off scot-free as far as the blame went, and he had to load everything up and run away, and that was when the worst part of his life began. The most stupid kind of work, old man: receiving the rubber, storing it with plenty of talcum to take away the smell, packing it up to look like tobacco, and shipping it.

"Were you in love with Lalita during that time?" Aquilino asked.

"She was a virgin when I got her," Fushía said, "and she didn't know anything at all about life. She would start crying, and if I was in a bad mood I'd give her a slap, and if I was in a good mood I'd buy her some candy. It was like having a wife and a daughter at the same time, Aquilino."

"And why did you blame Lalita for that too?" Aquilino asked. "I'm sure she didn't tell on you. More than likely it was the mother."

But she only found out in the newspapers, Doctor, she swore by what was most holy. She may have been poor, but she was as honest as the day was long, and she was only at the warehouse once, and she what do you have in there, and the Japanese tobacco and in all innocence she believed him.

"Not tobacco, Madam," Dr. Portillo said. "The crates may have said that, but you know that there was rubber inside."

"The old bitch never found out anything," Fushía said. "It was one of those bastards who used to help me put on the talcum and pack it. In the papers they said that she was another one of my victims because I stole her daughter."

"It's too bad you didn't keep those newspapers and the ones from Campo Grande too," Aquilino said. "It would be fun to read them now and see how famous you were, Fushía."

"Have you learned how to read?" Fushía said. "When we worked together before, you didn't know how, old man."

"You would have to read them to me," Aquilino said. "But how come nothing happened to Señor Julio Reátegui? Why did you have to run away and they didn't bother him?"

"The injustices of life," Fushía said. "He risked his capital and I risked my skin. The rubber was in my name, even though I just got the crumbs. But I still would have got rich, Aquilino, the business was that big."

Lalita did not tell her anything, she showered her with questions, and the girl I don't know, I don't know, that was the truth, Dr. Portillo, why should she have suspected? The Japanese was always off on trips, but so many people went on trips, and besides how was she to know that shipping rubber was illegal and shipping tobacco wasn't.

"Tobacco is not a strategic material, Madam," Dr. Portillo said. "Rubber is. We must sell it only to our allies, who are at war with the Germans. Didn't you know that Peru is at war too?"

"You should have sold the rubber to the gringos, then, Fushia,"

Aquilino said. "You wouldn't have had any trouble and they would have paid you in dollars."

"Our allies buy rubber from us at wartime prices, Madam," Dr. Portillo said. "The Japanese would sell it secretly and they paid him four times the price. Didn't you know that, either?"

"This is the first I heard of it, Doctor," the woman said. "I'm a poor woman, I'm not interested in politics, I never would have allowed my daughter to go out with a smuggler. And are they sure he wasn't a spy too, Doctor?"

"Being so young, it must have been hard for her to leave her mother," Aquilino said. "How did you convince Lalita, Fushía?"

Lalita might have loved her mother very much, but she ate well with him and she wore shoes; in Belén she would have ended up as a washerwoman, a whore, or a servant, old man, and Aquilino just tales, Fushía: he must have been in love with her or he wouldn't have taken her along. It was much easier to get away alone than dragging a woman along, if he hadn't been in love he wouldn't have kidnapped her.

"In the jungle Lalita was worth her weight in gold," Fushía said. "Didn't I tell you she was pretty then? She could tempt anybody."

"Her weight in gold," Aquilino said. "As if you'd thought about using her for business."

"I did a good business with her," Fushía said. "Didn't that whore ever tell you? That bastard Reátegui will probably never forgive me for that. It was my revenge on him."

"And one night she didn't come home, or the next night either, and then I got a letter from her," the woman said. "Telling me she was leaving the country with the Japanese and that they were going to get married. I brought the letter with me, Doctor."

"I'll keep it, give it to me," Dr. Portillo said. "And why didn't you tell the police that your daughter had run away, Madam?"

"I thought it was love business, Doctor," the woman said. "That he might have been married and that was why he ran off with my daughter. It was only a few days later that it came out in the papers that the Japanese was a thief."

"How much money did Lalita send in her letter?" the lawyer asked.

"Much more than both bitches were worth together," Fushía said. "A thousand soles."

"Two hundred soles, see how cheap he was, Doctor," the woman said. "But I've already spent it all paying off debts."

He knew the old woman's heart: stingier than the Turk who had had him arrested, Aquilino, and Dr. Portillo wanted to know if what she had told the police was the same as what she had told him, Madam, down to the last detail?

"Except about the two hundred soles, Doctor," the woman said. "They would have taken it away from me, you know what they're like at headquarters."

"Let me study the matter carefully," Dr. Portillo said. "I'll send for you as soon as there's any news. If they call you to court or to the police, I'll go with you. Don't make any statement unless I'm present, Madam. Not to anybody, understand?"

"Anything you say, Doctor," the woman said. "But what about the damages? They all tell me I have the right. He deceived me and he stole my daughter, Doctor."

"When they catch him, we'll ask for reparations," Dr. Portillo said. "I'll take care of that, don't worry. But if you don't want any complications, you know, not a word unless your lawyer is present."

"So you saw Señor Julio Reátegui again," Aquilino said. "I thought that from Iquitos you went straight to the island."

And how was he going to get there: swimming?, crossing the whole jungle on foot, old man? He only had a few soles and he knew that bastard Reátegui would wash his hands of him, because his name didn't figure in it at all. It was lucky that he'd brought Lalita along, that people have their weaknesses, and Julio Reátegui was there, he'd heard everything, but was it true that the old woman didn't know anything? She had a look that wasn't to be trusted, friend. And besides he was worried because Fushía had taken a woman with him, people in love do foolish things.

"That's his worry if he does anything foolish," Dr. Portillo said. "He can't compromise you even if he wants to. I've studied the whole thing carefully."

"He never said a word to me about that Lalita," Julio Reátegui said. "Did you know that he was living with the girl?"

"Not a word," Dr. Portillo said. "He must be jealous, he probably had her under lock and key. The important thing is that the dear old lady doesn't know a thing. I can't see any danger, I imagine that the lovers are in Brazil by now. Do you want to have dinner together tonight?"

"I can't," Julio Reátegui said. "I got an urgent message from Uchamala. A worker came with it, I don't know what the devil is going on. I'll try to be back by Saturday. I imagine that Don Fabio must have got to Santa María de Nieva by now, we have to send him a message not to buy any more rubber for the moment. Until things cool off."

"And where did you go to hide with Lalita?" Aquilino asked.

"To Uchamala," Fushía said. "Some property on the Marañón that belongs to that bastard Reátegui. We're going to pass right by it, old man."

The cattle leave the ranches after noon and go into the desert as the first shadows fall. Wrapped in ponchos, with broad hats to resist the attack of the wind and the sand, the herdsmen drive the heavy animals all night long toward the river. At dawn, Piura can be seen: a gray mirage on the opposite bank, a motionless cluster. They do not go into the city over the Old Bridge, which is too weak. When the river is dry, they walk across it, raising a great cloud of dust. During floodtime, they wait on the riverbank. The animals nuzzle the earth with their broad snouts, they knock down the young carob trees with their horns, they low mournfully. The men chat calmly while they eat a cold breakfast and drink cane liquor, or they roll up in their ponchos and take a nap. They should not have long to wait, sometimes Carlos Rojas reaches the dock before the cattle. He has come along the river from the other side of town, where he has his place. The boatman counts the animals, calculates their weight, decides on the number of trips needed to ferry them across. On the other bank, the men from the slaughterhouse get the nooses, saws, and knives ready, and the barrel where they will boil that thick oxhead broth which only slaughterers can drink without fainting. When his work is over, Carlos Rojas ties his boat to one of the supports of the Old Bridge and goes to a bar in Gallinacera where the early risers gather. That morning, a good number of water carriers, sweepers, and market women are already there, all Gallinazos. They serve him a gourd of goat's milk, they ask him why he has that look on his face. Is his wife all right? And his kid? Yes, they're fine, and Josefino is walking already and he says papa, but he had something to tell them. And he continued on with his large mouth open and his eyes popping with fright, as if he had just seen the devil. For ten years he had been working with his boat and he had never found anybody on the streets except for the people from the slaughterhouse. The sun is not up yet, everything is black, it is when the sand comes down strongest, who would ever get the idea, then, to take a ride at that hour? And the Gallinazos, you're right, man, nobody would ever think of it. He was speaking forcefully, his words came out like shots, and he helped himself along with energetic gestures; during the pauses, his mouth still open and his eyes still popping. That was why he was frightened, damn it, because it was so strange. What's that? And he heard it again, very clear, the hoofs of a horse. He wasn't going crazy, he had looked all around, they should wait, they should let him tell: he had seen it going onto the Old Bridge, he recognized it right away. Don Melchor Espinoza's horse? The white one? Yes sir, that's exactly why, because it was white it was shining in the early dawn and it looked like a ghost. And the Gallinazos, disappointed, it probably got loose, that's nothing new, or did Don Melchor get the senile idea of taking a ride in the dark? That's what he thought, of course, the animal had run away, he has to be caught. He jumped out of the boat and climbed up the bank with long strides, it was just as well that the horse was not going very fast, he went up to it slowly so as not to frighten it, now he would stand in front of it and grab it by the mane, and with his mouth easy, so, boy, don't get wild, he would mount it bareback and bring it home to its owner. It was passing by, quite close now, and he could barely see it because there was so much sand, they were entering Castilla at the same time, and then he crossed himself and boom. Interested again, the Gallinazos, what happened, Carlos, what did you see? Yes sir, Don Anselmo who was looking down at him from the saddle, word of honor. He had a cloth over his face and, his first reaction, his hair stood on end: excuse me, Don Anselmo, I thought the animal was running away. And the Gallinazos, what was he doing there?, where was he going?, was he running away from Piura in secret like a thief? They should let him finish, damn it. Don Anselmo laughed as hard as he could, he was looking down at him and roaring with laughter, and the horse was rearing. Did they know what he said to him? Don't look so frightened, Rojas, I couldn't sleep so I came out for a little ride. Did they hear? That was just what he said. The wind was like fire, it was lashing hard, very hard, and he felt like asking him if he thought he was looking at a fool, did he expect him to believe that? And a Gallinazo, but you probably didn't say anything, Carlos, it isn't a question of lying to people and besides what did it matter to you. But that wasn't the end of the story. A while later he saw him again, in the distance, on the trail to Catacaos. And a Gallinazo woman in the desert?, the poor fellow, he must have had his face eaten away, and his eyes and his hands. The way it was blowing that day. That unless they let him speak he would shut up and leave. Yes, he was still on the horse and turning and turning, he was looking at the river, the Old Bridge, the city. And then he dismounted and played with his cape. He looked like a happy kid, he was playing and jumping like Josefino. And the Gallinazos, do you think Don Anselmo went crazy?, it would be too bad, such a nice person, do you think he was drunk? And Carlos Rojas no, he didn't seem to be either crazy or drunk, he had shaken hands when he left him, he asked him about his family and told him to give them his regards. But they could see that he had every right to be scared.

That morning, Don Anselmo appeared in the Plaza de Armas at his usual hour, smiling and talkative. He looked very happy, he toasted everyone who passed by the terrace. He was possessed by an irrepressible urge to joke; his mouth was pouring out, one after the other, stories with double meanings that Jacinto, the waiter at the Estrella del Norte, would applaud, doubling up with laughter. And Don Anselmo's laughter echoed across the square. The news of his nocturnal excursion had already spread all over town and the Piurans were besieging him with questions: he answered them with jokes and ambiguous expressions.

Carlos Rojas's story had the city intrigued and it was the subject of conversation for days. Some curious people even went to Don Melchor Espinoza looking for information. The old farmer did not know anything. And besides he was not going to ask his boarder any questions because he was neither nosy nor a gossip. He had found his horse unsaddled and cleaned. He did not want to know anything else, they should go away and leave him in peace.

When people stopped talking about that excursion, there was an even more surprising piece of news. Don Anselmo had bought a piece of land from the city. It was across the Old Bridge, beyond the last houses in Castilla, right in the desert, along where the boatman had seen him jumping about that morning. It was not odd for the stranger, if he had decided to settle down in Piura, to want to build a house. But in the desert! The sand would eat the house up in no time, it would swallow it up like the old rotten trees and the dead vultures. The desert is unstable, soft. The dunes change their location every night, the wind creates them, does away with them, and moves them at will, makes them larger and smaller. They appear menacing and multiple, they surround Piura like a wall, white at dawn, red at dusk, gray at night, and on the following day they have fled and they can be seen, scattered, distant, like a sparse eruption on the skin of the desert. During the night, Don Anselmo would be cut off and at the mercy of the sand. Effusive and in great numbers, the people tried to dissuade him from that madness; they abounded in arguments to discourage him. He should get a lot in town, he should not be stubborn. But Don Anselmo disdained all advice and he would answer with phrases that were like enigmas.

The boat with the soldiers comes about noon, it tries to land prow first and not alongside as reason dictates, the current catches it and pulls it away, hang on, boys: Adrián Nieves was going to help them. He jumps into the water, grabs the rudder pole, brings the boat to shore, and the soldiers, without saying thank you or why, throw a rope around him, leave him tied up, and run up to the village. Too late, boys, almost all the people have had time to escape into the woods, they only catch a half a dozen, and when they get back to the Borja garrison Captain Quiroga is angry, what possessed them to bring a cripple?, and to Vilano, beat it, gimpy, you're no good to the Army. Instruction begins the following morning: they get them up very early, they cut their hair short, they give them khaki shirts and pants and large shoes that pinch their feet. Afterward, Captain Quiroga talks to them about their country and divides them into groups. Nieves and eleven others are taken by a corporal and drilled: standing at attention, saluting, marching, running, stopping, attention God damn it, at ease God damn it. And every day like that and no way to escape, the vigilance is strict, kicks come from everywhere, and Captain Quiroga there isn't a deserter who doesn't get caught and then his time of service is doubled. And one morning Corporal Roberto Delgado comes, one step forward the recruit who is a pilot, and Adrián Nieves at his orders, Corporal, he was the one. Did he know the country upriver well? and he like the back of his hand, Corporal, upriver and downriver too, and then he should get ready because they were going to Bagua. And he now's the time Adrián Nieves, now or never. They leave the following morning, they, the small boat, and an Aguaruna porter from the garrison. The river is running high and they go along slowly, avoiding sand bars, guinea grass, trunks like amputated stumps that rise up before them. Corporal Roberto Delgado is happy as he goes along, he talks and talks, a lieutenant from the coast arrived who wanted to know the Pongo, they it's dangerous, sir, there's been a lot of rain, but he insisted, and he went and the boat capsized and they all drowned, and Corporal Delgado was saved because he had faked a fever so he wouldn't have to go along, he talks and talks. The porter did not open his mouth; Corporal, was Captain Quiroga an old jungle hand? Adrián Nieves was the one speaking to him. Far from it, two months ago they had gone on a mission on the Santiago and the mosquitoes had made the Captain's legs swell up. They were red, all full of bumps, he had them in the water and the Corporal frightened him: watch out for the yacu-mamas, watch out that they don't leave you stub-horned, sir, those boas will sneak up on you, stick out their snouts, and take off a leg with one bite. And the Captain: let them come and eat it. It burned so much he didn't feel like living, only the water cooled it, God damn his bad luck, shit. And the Corporal your legs are bleeding, sir, the blood will attract the piranhas and what if they take off a few slices? But Captain Quiroga got angry, you son of a bitch, that's enough of trying to scare me, and the Corporal was revolted by the sight of the legs: fat, full of scabs, with the brush of every branch they would open up and some white liquid would ooze out. And Adrián Nieves that's why the piranhas didn't come, Corporal, they could smell it, if they sucked on those legs they'd die of poison. The porter is silent, in the prow, measuring the depth with the rudder pole, and two days later they reach Urakusa: not a single Aguaruna, they have all gone into the woods. They had even taken their dogs with them, the sly buggers. Corporal Roberto Delgado is in the center of the clearing, his mouth wide open, Urakusas! Urakusas!, his teeth are like a horse's, strong, very white, aren't the Urakusas famous for being brave?, the evening sun is breaking the sky into blue spokes, come on out, you cowards, come on back! But not brave for the porter, Corporal, white men frightening, and the Corporal they should search the huts, they should make a bundle of anything that can be eaten, worn, or sold right now and hurry up. Adrián Nieves did not advise it, Corporal, they're probably watching, and if they robbed them they would jump them and there were only three of them. But the Corporal did not want advice from anyone, God damn it, had they asked him anything?, and let's just see them attack, he would take care of the Urakusas without even needing his pistol, with his bare fists, and he sits on the ground, crosses his legs, lights a cigarette. They go toward the huts, they come back, and Corporal Roberto Delgado is sleeping peacefully, the butt is burning up on the ground surrounded by curious ants. Adrián Nieves and the porter eat some cassava and catfish, they smoke, and when the Corporal wakes up he crawls over to them and has a drink from the canteen. Then he examines the bundle: a lizard skin, trash, a necklace of small beads and shells, was that all there was?, earthenware plates, bracelets, and the thing he had promised the Captain?, anklets, crowns, not even a little of that bug-killing resin?, a chambira basket and a gourd full of cassava beer, all trash. He poked the bundle with his foot and he wanted to know if they had seen anyone while he was asleep. No, Corporal, nobody. The porter thought that they were nearby and points at the woods, but the Corporal doesn't give a damn: they would sleep in Urakusa and they would continue on tomorrow early. He still grumbles, what was all this about hiding as if they had some disease?, he stands up, urinates, takes off his leggings, and goes toward a hut, they follow him. It is not hot, the night is damp and full of noises, a slow breeze brings the smell of rotting plants to the clearing, and the porter leaving, Corporal, much trouble here, saying, not staying, not liking, and Adrián Nieves shrugs his shoulders: who would like it, but he shouldn't tire himself out, the Corporal couldn't hear him, he was already asleep.

"How was it for you there?" Josefino asked. "Tell us about it, Lituma."

"How else would it be for me, buddy," Lituma said, his small eyes startled. "Very bad."

"Did they beat you, cousin?" José asked. "Did they put you on bread and water?"

"None of that, they treated me pretty well. Corporal Cárdenas had them give me more food than the rest. He'd served under me in the jungle, a half Negro, half Indian, a good person, we used to call him Blacky. But it was a pretty bad life, any way you look at it."

Monk had a cigarette in his hands, and suddenly he stuck out his tongue and winked. He was smiling, not paying any attention to the others, and he was practicing faces that would bring out dimples in his cheeks and wrinkles on his forehead. Sometimes he would applaud himself.

"They had a little respect for me," Lituma said. "They said, 'You've got the balls of a young goat, country boy.' "

"They were right, cousin, absolutely right, who'd ever doubt it."

"All Piura was talking about you, buddy," Josefino said. "Kids, grownups. A long time after you left they were still arguing about you."

"After I left?" Lituma said. "I didn't exactly go because I wanted to."

"We've got the newspapers," José said. "You'll see them, cousin. In *El Tiempo* they insulted you a lot, they called you a hoodlum, but in *Ecos y Noticias* and even in *La Industria* they admitted that you were a brave man."

"You were a he-man, buddy," Josefino said. "The Mangaches felt very proud."

"And what good has it all done me?" Lituma shrugged his shoulders, spat, and stepped on the saliva. "Besides, it was because I was drunk. If I'd been sober, I'd never have dared."

"We all belong to the Unión Revolucionaria here in Mangachería," Monk said, jumping up. "Faithful followers of General Sánchez Cerro, right down to the bottom of our hearts."

He went over to the clipping, made a military salute, and went back to the mat, laughing loudly.

"Monk is already lit," Lituma said. "Let's go to Chunga's before he falls asleep on us."

"We've got something to tell you, buddy," Josefino said.

"Last year an Aprista came here to live, Lituma," Monk said. "One of those who killed the General. It made me so damned mad!"

"I met a lot of Apristas in Lima," Lituma said. "They had them locked up too. They were cursing Sánchez Cerro all the time, they said he was a dictator. Something to tell me, buddy?"

"And you let them sound off in front of you about that great Mangache?" José said.

"A Piuran, but not a Mangache," Josefino said. "That's another one of your inventions. I'll bet that Sánchez Cerro never even set foot in this part of town."

"What have you got to tell me?" Lituma asked. "Come on, you've got my curiosity up."

"It wasn't just one person, it was a whole family, cousin," Monk said. "They built a house where Patrocinio Naya used to live and they hung an Aprista flag on the door. What do you think about that for crap?"

"About Bonifacia, Lituma," Josefino said. "I can tell by your face that you want to know. Why haven't you asked us anything, champ? Were you ashamed to? But we're all brothers, Lituma."

"We really put them in their place," Monk said. "We made life miserable for them. They had to run away wailing like a railroad engine."

"It's never too late to ask," Lituma said; he straightened up a little, rested his hands on the floor, and remained motionless. He was speaking very calmly. "She never wrote me a single letter. What's become of her?"

"They say Kid Alejandro was an Aprista when he was a boy," José said rapidly. "That once when Haya de la Torre came to town he was in the parade with a poster that read 'Master, Youth Acclaims You.' "

"All lies; the Kid is a great guy, one of the glories of Mangachería," Monk said, with a disjointed voice.

"Shut up, can't you see we're talking?" Lituma slapped the floor and a small cloud of dust rose up. Monk stopped smiling, José had lowered his head, and Josefino, very stiff, with his arms crossed, was blinking continuously.

"What happened, buddy?" Lituma asked, with an almost affectionate softness. "I hadn't asked anything, but you loosened up my tongue. Go ahead, now, don't be quiet."

"There are some things that can burn more than cane liquor, Lituma," Josefino said, in a low voice.

Lituma stopped him with a gesture.

"I'm going to open up another bottle, then." Neither his voice nor his expression revealed any distress, but his skin had begun to perspire and he was breathing heavily. "Alcohol helps when you get bad news, right?"

He bit the cork out of the bottle and filled the glasses. He drank his down in one swallow, his eyes became red and moist, and Monk, who was sipping his, his eyes closed, his whole face contracted into a grimace, suddenly choked. He began to cough and hit himself on the chest with his open hand.

"Good old Monk, always the ham," Lituma muttered. "Come on, buddy, I'm waiting."

"Pisco is the only drink that comes back into the world through your eyes," Monk sang, in a low voice. "The rest of them come out in your pee."

"She's become a whore, brother," Josefino said. "She's at the Green House."

Monk had another coughing spell, his glass rolled on the floor, and a small damp spot shrank and disappeared into the earth.

4

"Their teeth were chattering, Mother," Bonifacia said, "I talked Indian to them so they wouldn't be afraid. You should have seen how they looked."

"Why didn't you ever tell us that you could speak Aguaruna, Bonifacia?" the Mother Superior asked.

"Don't you see how all the sisters would have said, 'That's the savage coming out in you'?" Bonifacia said. "Don't you see how they would have said, 'You're eating with your hands, heathen'? I was ashamed, Mother."

She takes them out of the pantry by the hand, and on the threshold of her narrow room she indicates that they should wait. They stand together, huddled up against the wall. Bonifacia goes in, lights the lamp, opens the trunk, searches through it, takes out the old bundle of keys, and leaves. She comes back and takes the girls by the hand.

"Is it true that they tied the Indian to the capirona pole?" Bonifacia asked. "That they cut off his hair and left his head all white?"

"You must be crazy," Sister Angélica said. "All of a sudden you come out with the strangest things."

But she knew it, Missy: the soldiers brought him in a boat, they tied him to the flagpole, the pupils went up on the roof of the Residence to watch, and Sister Angélica spanked them. Were they still telling that story, the bandits? When did they tell Bonifacia?

"A little yellow bird that flew in told me," Bonifacia said. "Did they really cut off his hair? The way Sister Griselda did to the little Indians?"

"The soldiers cut it off, silly," Sister Angélica said. "There's no comparison. Sister Griselda cut the girls' hair so that they wouldn't be bitten. His was cut off as punishment."

"And what had the Indian done, Missy?" Bonifacia asked.

"Bad things, ugly things," Sister Angélica said. "He'd committed a sin."

Bonifacia and the girls go out on tiptoe. The courtyard is split in two: the moon lights up the angular façade of the chapel and the kitchen chimney; the other part of the Mission is a collection of damp shadows. The brick wall is cut off, imprecise, under the opaque arch of vines and branches. The sisters' Residence has disappeared into the night.

"You have a very unjust way of seeing things," the Mother Superior said. "The sisters worry about your soul, not the color of your skin or the language you speak. You're ungrateful, Bonifacia. Sister Angélica has done nothing but spoil you ever since you came to the Mission."

"I know, Mother; that's why I ask you to pray for me," Bonifacia said. "It's only that on that night I went back to being a savage, you'll see how horrible it was."

"Stop your crying at once," the Mother Superior said. "I already know that you went back to being a savage. I want to know what you did."

She lets them go, she indicates with a gesture that they should be quiet, and she starts to run, still on tiptoe. At first she is a little ahead of them, but halfway across the courtyard the two girls are running beside her. They reach the locked door together. Bonifacia leans over, tries the thick rusty keys from the bundle, one after the other. The lock squeaks, the wood is wet and it sounds hollow when they hit it with their palms, but the door will not open. The three of them are breathing heavily.

"Was I very small then?" Bonifacia asked. "How big, Missy? Show me with your hand."

"Like this, this high," Sister Angélica said. "But you were already a devil."

"And how long had I been at the Mission?" Bonifacia asked.

"A very short time," Sister Angélica said. "Only a few months."

That's it, the devil had already got into her body, Missy. What was that crazy girl talking about? Look at what she was coming out with now, and they had brought Bonifacia to Santa María de Nieva with that Indian. The pupils had told her; now Sister Angélica had to confess her lie. If she didn't, she'd go to hell, Missy.

"So why do you ask me, sly one?" Sister Angélica said. "It's a lack of respect and a sin besides."

"I was fooling, Missy," Bonifacia said. "I know that you're going to go to heaven."

The third key turns, the door gives way. But outside there is a tenacious concentration of stalks, thickets, and vines, nests, spider webs, mushrooms, and climbers that resist and tie up the door. Bonifacia puts her whole body against the door and pushes—there, very slight, several tearings and a breaking noise—until enough of an opening is formed. She holds the half-open door, she can feel the rubbing of soft threads against her face, she can hear the murmuring of the invisible foliage, and suddenly, behind her, a different kind of murmuring.

"I became just like them again, Mother," Bonifacia said. "The one with the ring in her nose ate, and I forced the other little Indian to eat. I put the plantain in her mouth with her fingers, Mother."

"And what does all that have to do with the devil?" the Mother Superior asked.

"One of them grabbed the other's hand and sucked her fingers," Bonifacia said. "Then the other one did the same thing. You can see how hungry they were, Mother."

Why shouldn't they be? The poor things hadn't tasted a mouthful since they'd left Chicais, Bonifacia, but the Mother Superior already knew that she was sorry for them. And Bonifacia could barely understand them, Mother, because they spoke in such a strange way. Here they would have something to eat every day and they we want to leave, here they would be happy and they we want to leave, and she began to tell them those stories about the Infant Jesus that the little Indians liked so much, Mother.

"That's what you're best at," the Mother Superior said. "Telling stories. What else, Bonifacia?"

And her eyes are like two fire beetles, get away, green and

frightened, go back to the dormitory, she takes a step toward the pupils, who gave you permission to leave?, and, pushed by the forest, the door closes noiselessly. The pupils watch her silently, two dozen fireflies and one single wide, deformed silhouette, the darkness hides faces and smocks. Bonifacia looks toward the Residence: not a single light is on. Again she orders them to go back to the dormitory but they will not move or answer her.

"Was that Indian my father, Missy?" Bonifacia asked.

"He wasn't your father," Sister Angélica said. "You were probably born in Urakusa, but you were somebody else's daughter, not that bad man's."

Wasn't she lying to her, Missy? But Sister Angélica never lied, silly, why would she lie to her. So that she wouldn't suddenly feel sorry for him, Missy? So that she wouldn't be ashamed? And didn't she think that her father was a bad man too?

"Why should he be?" Sister Angélica said. "He could have had a very good heart, there are many heathens like that. But why does that worry you? Don't you have a father now who is much greater and much better?"

They did not obey her this time either, go away, go back to the dormitory, and the two girls were at her feet, trembling, clutching at her habit. Suddenly Bonifacia turns halfway around, runs toward the door, pushes it, opens it, points into the darkness of the woods. The two girls are next to her but they do not dare cross the threshold; their heads go from Bonifacia to the dark opening, and now the fireflies come forward, their silhouettes are outlined opposite Bonifacia; they have begun to whisper, some to touch her.

"They were looking for them on each other, Mother," Bonifacia said, "and they would pick them off and kill them with their teeth. Not wicked, just playing, Mother, and before biting they would show them, saying look at what I got off you. Playing, and with love too, Mother."

"If they already trusted you, you could have told them," the Mother Superior said. "Told them not to do such dirty things."

But she was only thinking about the next day, Mother: that tomorrow would not come, that Sister Griselda would not cut off their hair, they shouldn't have it cut off and they shouldn't have disinfectant put on, and the Mother Superior what kind of nonsense is that?

"You don't see what they're like, I have to hold them down and I can see," Bonifacia said. "When they get bathed too, and the soap gets in their eyes."

Was she sorry that Sister Griselda was getting rid of those bugs that were eating up their heads? Those bugs that they swallowed and that made them sick and made their little bellies swell up? But the fact is that she still screamed at the thought of Sister Griselda's shears. It must have hurt her so much, Mother; that must have been why.

"You're not being very intelligent, Bonifacia," the Mother Superior said. "You should have been sorry to see those children turned into two little animals, doing what monkeys do."

"You're going to get even angrier, Mother," Bonifacia said. "You're going to hate me."

What did they want?, why didn't they pay any attention to her?, and a few seconds later, raising her voice, run away too?, go back to being heathens again?, and the pupils have swallowed up the two girls, all Bonifacia can see is a compact mass of smocks and greedy eyes. What did it matter to her, then, God would know, they would know, whether they went back to the dormitory or ran away or died, and she looks toward the Residence: still in darkness.

"They cut off his hair to get rid of the devil he had inside of him," Sister Angélica said. "And that's enough, don't think about that Indian any more."

She always remembered, Missy, about what it must have been like when they cut it off, and was the devil like lice? What was that crazy girl saying? In his case to get rid of the devil, in the case of the little Indian girls to get rid of lice. She meant that both of them got into the skin, Missy, and Sister Angélica how silly she was, Bonifacia, what a silly child.

They go out one after the other, in order, as on Sunday when they go to the river; as they pass by Bonifacia, some of them stretch out their hands and affectionately squeeze her habit, her bare arm, and she rapidly God would help them, would pray for them, He would care for them and she holds the door open with her back.

Every pupil stops on the threshold and turns her head toward the hidden Residence, she pushes, she makes them disappear into the vegetable opening, sink into the muddy earth, and get lost in the shadows.

"And all of a sudden she let go of the other one and came over to me," Bonifacia said. "The smaller one, Mother, and I thought she was going to hug me, but she began to look for lice on me with her little fingers, and that was why, Mother."

"Why didn't you take the children to the dormitory?" the Mother Superior asked.

"Grateful for what I'd given them to eat, don't you see?" Bonifacia said. "Her face was sad because she couldn't find any, and I hoped she would, I hoped she could find just one, the poor thing."

"And then you complain when the sisters call you a savage," the Mother Superior said. "Do you sound like a Christian now?"

And she was looking into their hair too, and it didn't disgust her, Mother, and every one she found she killed with her teeth. Disgusting?, yes, it probably was, and the Mother Superior you talk as if you were proud of that filthy behavior, and Bonifacia was, that was the terrible part of it, Mother, and the little heathen made believe she'd found one, and she showed her her hand and quickly put it into her mouth as if she were going to kill it. And the other one began too, Mother, and she worked on the other one too.

"Don't talk to me in that tone," the Mother Superior said. "And besides that's enough, I don't want to hear any more, Bonifacia."

And she that the sisters should come in and see her, Sister Angélica and you too, Mother, and she had even insulted them, how furious she was, how much she hated, Mother, and the two girls were no longer there: they must have left with the first ones, groping along quickly. Bonifacia crosses the courtyard; when she passes the chapel she stops. She goes in, sits down in a pew. The light of the moon is angling down onto the altar, dying beside the grating that separates the pupils from the faithful of Santa María de Nieva during Sunday mass.

"And you were a little wild animal besides," Sister Angélica said. "We had to chase you all over the Mission. You gave me a bite on the hand, you little bandit."

"I didn't know what I was doing," Bonifacia said. "Can't you see that I was a heathen? If I kiss you where I bit you, will you forgive me, Missy?"

"You tell me everything with a little touch of teasing and a devilish look that makes me want to spank you," Sister Angélica said. "Do you want me to tell you another story?"

"No, Sister," Bonifacia said. "I've been praying here for some time."

"Why aren't you in the dormitory?" Sister Ángela asked. "Who gave you permission to come to the chapel at this hour?"

"The pupils have run away," Sister Leonor said. "Sister Angélica is looking for you. Come on, hurry up, the Mother Superior wants to talk to you, Bonifacia."

"She must have been pretty when she was a girl," Aquilino said. "That long hair of hers caught my eye when I met her. It's too bad her face broke out so much."

"And that son of a bitch Reátegui with his go on, beat it, the police might come, you'll get me into trouble," Fushía said. "But that whore was under his nose all the time and he was falling for it."

"But you told her to do it, man," Aquilino said. "It wasn't a case of whoring, she was just obeying you. Why do you insult her like that?"

"Because you're beautiful," Julio Reátegui said: "I'm going to buy you a dress from the best store in Iquitos. How would you like that? But come away from that tree; come over here, come closer, don't be afraid of me."

Her hair is thin and loose, she is barefoot, her silhouette is outlined against the huge trunk, underneath a thick crown that vomits flame-like leaves. Her seat on the tree is the stump of a branch with a wrinkled, impenetrable, ash-colored bark, and inside it there is hard wood for the Christians, evil spirits for the heathens.

"Are you afraid of the lupuna tree too, boss?" Lalita asked. "I wouldn't have expected you to be."

She looks at him with mocking eyes and she laughs, throwing her head back: her long hair sweeps down across her tanned shoulders and her feet glow among the damp ferns, darker than her shoulders, with thick ankles.

"And shoes and stockings too, girl," Julio Reátegui said. "And a pocketbook. Anything you want."

"And what were you doing all that time?" Aquilino asked. "She was your mistress, after all, weren't you jealous?"

"My mind was only on the police," Fushía said. "She'd got him wild over her, his voice would tremble when he spoke to her."

"Señor Julio Reátegui drooling over a Christian girl," Aquilino said. "Over Lalita! I still can't believe it, Fushía. She never told me about that, and still I was her confessor and her crying-towel."

"Wise old women, those Boras," Julio Reátegui said. "No one knows how they make their dyes. See how strong the red is, the black. And they're twenty years old by now, maybe more. Go ahead, girl, put it on, let's see how you look in it."

"And why did he want Lalita to put the coat on?" Aquilino asked. "What an idea, Fushía. But what I can't understand is that you were so calm about it. Anybody else would have gone for his knife."

"The son of a bitch was in his hammock and she was at the window," Fushía said. "I was listening to their stories and breaking up laughing."

"So why aren't you doing the same thing now?" Aquilino said. "Why do you hate Lalita so much?"

"It's not the same thing," Fushía said. "This time it was without my permission, sneaky, for bad reasons."

"Don't even think about it, boss," Lalita said. "Even if you prayed for me and wept over me."

But he does, and the wooden fan, which works with the swaying of the hammock, gives off a broken sound, a kind of nervous stammer, and, wrapped up in the black and red cloak, Lalita is motionless. The metal window screen is a mass of constellations of little nebulae, green, white, yellow, and in the distance, between the house and the woods, one can see the young coffee plants, tender, good to smell.

"You look like a caterpillar in its cocoon," Julio Reátegui said. "One of those little butterflies that come by the window. What do you care, Lalita? Let me have some fun, take it off."

"That's crazy," Aquilino said. "First she puts it on and then she takes it off. That rich fellow has strange ideas."

"Haven't you ever had an urge, Aquilino?" Fushía asked.

"Anything you want," Julio Reátegui said. "Just ask me, Lalita, whatever it is, come on, come over here."

Her coat, on the ground now, is a round *Victoria regia* and she rises up out of it like an orchid on an aquatic plant, the girl's body, thin, handsome breasts with brown corollas and nipples like arrowheads. A flat stomach and firm thighs can be seen through her clothes.

"I pretended that I hadn't seen anything when I came in," Fushía said. "I was laughing so that the bastard wouldn't be embarrassed. He jumped out of his hammock and Lalita put on her coat."

"A thousand soles for a girl isn't something a good Christian would do," Aquilino said. "That's the price of a motor, Fushía."

"She's worth ten thousand," Fushía said. "It's just that I need money, I don't have to tell you, Don Julio, and I can't take any women along. I'd like to be able to get going today."

But they weren't going to get a thousand soles out of him just like that, more than what he had hidden. And besides Fushía could see that the rubber deal had gone to pot, and with the high water it was impossible to get any wood out this year, and Fushía those girls from Loreto, Don Julio, he already knew: like volcanoes, they make everything warm. It pained him to leave her behind, because she wasn't only pretty: she could cook and she had a good heart. Have you made your mind up, Don Julio?

"Did it really upset you to leave Lalita in Uchamala with Señor Reátegui?" Aquilino asked. "Or were you just saying so?"

"How could it upset me," Fushía said. "I was never in love with that whore."

"Stay in the water," Julio Reátegui said. "I'm coming in with you. You shouldn't be naked. What if there are canero fish? Put something on, Lalita, no, wait, not yet."

Lalita is squatting in the inlet and the water covers her, waves break around her, concentric circles. There is a rain of vines on the surface of the water, and Julio Reátegui could feel the caneros, Lalita, put something on: they were very small, they had little needles, they got in through small openings, girl, and once they were inside they scratched, they infected everything, and she would have to take some Bora medicine and have diarrhea for a week.

"They're not caneros, boss," Lalita said. "Can't you see they're little fish? And the plants on the bottom, that's what you feel. It's so nice and warm, delicious, don't you think?"

"Getting into the river with a woman, the pair of them naked," Aquilino said. "I never thought of it when I was young and now I'm sorry. It must be a lot of fun, Fushía."

"I'm going to Ecuador up the Santiago," Fushía said. "It's a rough trip, Don Julio, we won't ever see each other again. Have you decided yet? Because I'm leaving tonight. She's only fifteen and I was the first one to touch her."

"Sometimes I wonder why I never got married," Aquilino said. "But with the life I've led, it wasn't any use. Always on the go, I wasn't going to find any woman along the river. But you've got no cause to complain, Fushía. You've always had plenty of them."

"We're agreed, then," Fushía said. "Your boat and the provisions. It's a good deal for both of us, Don Julio."

"The Santiago is a long way off and you'll never get there without being seen," Julio Reátegui said. "And besides, upstream and at this time of year, it'll take you a month or so. Why don't you go to Brazil instead?"

"They're looking for me there," Fushía said. "At this end of the border and at the other one too, for something that happened in Campo Grande. I'm not that dumb, Don Julio."

"You'll never get to Ecuador," Julio Reátegui said.

"You never did, actually," Aquilino said. "You were in Peru all the time."

"It's always been like that, Aquilino," Fushía said. "My plans always come out backward."

"And what if she doesn't want to?" Julio Reátegui asked. "You'll have to convince her yourself before I give you the boat."

"She knows that my life will be jumping from one place to another," Fushía said, "that a thousand things could happen to me. No woman likes to follow a man who's always screwed up. She'll be glad to stay, Don Julio."

"Still, as you can see," Aquilino said, "she did follow you and she was a big help in everything. She lived the life of a wild boar like you and she didn't complain. In spite of everything, Lalita was a good woman, Fushía."

❧

This is how the Green House was born. The building of it took several weeks; the boards, the beams, and the adobe blocks had to be hauled from the other side of town, and the mules rented by Don Anselmo pulled painfully through the desert. Work would begin in the morning, when the dry rain was over, and would end when the wind grew strong. In the late afternoon and at night, the desert would swallow up the foundations and bury the walls, iguanas would chew the wood, vultures would build their nests in the incipient construction, and every morning it was necessary to redo what had been begun, correct the levels, put back the materials, in a slow struggle that had the city enthralled. "*When will the stranger quit*?" people asked each other. But the days went by, and without letting himself be downcast by bad luck or be caught up in the pessimism of friends and acquaintances, Don Anselmo continued to show a startling activity. He directed the work stripped to the waist, the underbrush on his chest was wet with perspiration, his mouth was full of euphoria. He passed out cane liquor and chicha to the workers, and he carried bricks himself, fastened beams, went back and forth through the city driving the mules. And one day the Piurans admitted that Don Anselmo would win, when on the other side of the river, across from the city, like an emissary on the edge of the desert, they could see an undefeated wooden skeleton. From then on, the work went rapidly. The people from Castilla and from the huts by the slaughterhouse came every morning to watch the work, give advice, and sometimes spontaneously lend the workmen a hand. Don Anselmo gave everybody drinks. During the last days, an air of public holiday reigned where the work was going on: women selling chicha, fruit, cheeses, candy, and soft drinks came to offer their wares to the workers and spectators. The ranchers would stop as they passed by, and from their saddles they would give words of encouragement to Don Anselmo. One day, Chápiro Seminario, the rich farmer, gave him an ox and a dozen jugs of chicha. The workers prepared a barbecue.

When the house was finished, Don Anselmo had it painted green all over. Even the children laughed hard on seeing those walls covered with an emerald skin where the sun sparkled and made fleeting reflections. Old and young, rich and poor, men and women made merry jokes about Don Anselmo's whim to daub his house like that. They immediately christened it "the Green House." They were amused not only by its color but also by its bizarre anatomy. It had two stories, but the lower one barely deserved the name: a spacious room cut by four beams, also green, that held up the roof, a half-covered courtyard paved with small stones that the river had polished, and a circular wall the height of a man. The second floor was made up of six tiny rooms lined up along a hallway with a wooden railing that hung over the first-floor room. In addition to the main entrance, the Green House had two rear doors, a stable, and a large storeroom.

At the store owned by Eusebio Romero the Spaniard, Don Anselmo bought matting, oil lamps, brightly colored curtains, and several chairs. And one morning two carpenters from Gallinacera announced that *"Don Anselmo ordered a desk from us, and a bar just like the one in the Estrella del Norte and a half a dozen beds!"* Then Don Eusebio Romero confessed, *"And six wash basins, six mirrors, and six chamber pots from me."* A kind of effervescence grew up all over the city, a noisy and agitated curiosity.

Suspicions grew. From house to house, from parlor to parlor, the church biddies were whispering, ladies looked at their husbands with mistrust, people would exchange mischievous smiles, and one Sunday during the twelve o'clock mass Father García declared from the pulpit, *"An attack upon morality is being prepared in this city."* The Piurans besieged Don Anselmo on the street, they demanded that he say something. But it was of no use: *"It's a secret,"* he would tell them, happy as a schoolboy. *"Have a little patience, you'll find out soon enough."* Indifferent to the uproar all over town, he kept on coming to the Estrella del Norte in the morning, drinking, making jokes, toasting and complimenting the women who passed by on the square. In the afternoon, he would shut himself up in the Green House, where he had moved after giving Don Melchor Espinoza a case of pisco and a tooled saddle.

A short time afterward, Don Anselmo went away. Riding a black horse that he had just bought, he left the city the same way he had arrived, one morning at dawn, unseen, in an unknown direction.

There has been so much talk in Piura about the original Green House, that first building, that no one knows for sure any more what it was really like or the authentic details of its history. The survivors from that period, very few, argued with and contradicted one another, and they have ended up confusing what they saw and heard with their own inventions. And the witnesses are so decrepit now, and their silence so obstinate, that it is no use questioning them. In any case, the original Green House no longer exists. Until a few years ago, on the spot where it had stood—the spread of desert bordered by Castilla and Catacaos—charred pieces of wood and domestic objects were found, but the desert and the road that was built and the small farms that sprang up in the area have erased all those remains, and no Piuran is able to locate that part of the desert where once it stood, with its lights, its music, its laughter, and that daytime glow of its walls, which from a distance and at night would be converted into a square and phosphorescent reptile. In Mangache tales they say that it was near the other side of the Old Bridge, that it was very large, larger than any other building at the time, and that there were so many colored lamps hanging in its windows that the light hurt one's eyes, staining the sand all around, and even lighting up the bridge. Its main virtue, however, was the music that punctually started up at the beginning of the evening, it would last all night and could be heard as far as the cathedral. Don Anselmo, they say, searched tirelessly in all the neighborhood chicha bars, and even those in nearby towns, looking for musicians, and from everywhere he brought guitar players, box-drum players, jawbone scratchers, flutists, bass-drum and cornet players. But never any harpists, because he played that instrument, and his harp unmistakably dominated the music in the Green House.

"It was as if the air had become polluted," the old women on the Malecón would say. *"The music penetrated everywhere, even though we would close our doors and windows, and we could hear it while we ate, while we said our prayers, and while we slept."*

"And the faces on the men when they heard it were something

to see," the church biddies wrapped up in their veils would say. *"And you should have seen how it took them away from their homes, and drew them into the street and toward the Old Bridge."*

"And there was no use praying," the mothers, wives, and sweethearts would say. *"Our weeping, our begging, the priests' sermons, the novenas, even the Holy, Holy, Holy, were of no use."*

"We have hell at our doorstep," Father García thundered. *"Anyone can see it, but you are blind. Piura has become Sodom and Gomorrah."*

"Maybe it's true that the Green House brought bad luck," the old men would say, licking their lips, *"but you certainly could have a good time there."*

A few weeks after Don Anselmo returned to Piura with his caravan of occupants, the Green House imposed its rule. At first, its visitors would sneak out of the city; they would wait in the darkness, discreetly cross the Old Bridge, and disappear into the desert. Then the incursions increased, and the young men, more and more imprudent, no longer worried about being recognized by the ladies hidden behind their blinds along the Malecón. In huts and in parlors, on the ranches, no one talked about anything else. The pulpits increased their warnings and exhortations, Father García stigmatized license with verses from the Bible. A Committee for Pious Works and Good Customs was organized, and the ladies who formed it went to see the Chief of Police and the Mayor. The authorities agreed, with their heads lowered: of course, they were right, the Green House was an affront to Piura, but what could they do? Don Anselmo was protected by laws made in that corrupt capital of Lima, the existence of the Green House was not against the Constitution or the Criminal Code. The ladies stopped saying hello to the authorities. Their houses were closed to them. In the meantime, adolescents, mature men, and even peaceful old codgers flocked to the noisy and glowing building.

The most serious, the most hard-working and upright Piurans all fell. In the city, which used to be so quiet, the nocturnal noise and movement became as regular as a nightmare. At dawn, when the harp and the guitars of the Green House fell silent, an undisciplined and collective rhythm would rise skyward from the city: the people coming back, alone or in groups, going through the streets, laughing loudly and singing. The lack of sleep showed on the men's faces, which were wounded by the bite of the sand, and at the Estrella del Norte they would tell wild tales that went from mouth to mouth and that the children would repeat.

"Now you can see, now you can see," Father García would say, in a trembling voice, *"all that remains is for hell's fire to rain down on Piura, all the evils of the world are descending upon us."*

Because it is true that this all coincided with bad luck. During the first year, the Piura River rose and continued to rise, it broke the dikes around the small farms, many fields in the valley were flooded, some animals were drowned, and the dampness spread over wide sections of the Sechura Desert: the men cursed, the children made castles in the affected sand. The second year, as if in reprisal against the curses thrown at it by the owners of the flooded lands, the river did not flow. The bed of the Piura became covered with grass and bushes which died soon after coming up, and there was only a long, scarred gully; the cane fields dried up, the cotton bloomed prematurely. In the third year, blights destroyed the harvests.

"These are the disasters of sin," Father García roared. *"There is still time. The enemy is in your blood, destroy him with your prayers."*

Witch doctors from neighboring settlements sprinkled the planted fields with the blood of young goats, they rolled about in the furrows, they made spells to attract the water and chase away the insects.

"My God, my God," Father García lamented. *"There is hunger and there is misery, and instead of learning from their experience, they sin all the more."*

For neither flood, nor drought, nor blight could stop the growing glory of the Green House.

The look of the city changed. Those tranquil provincial streets became crowded with outsiders who on weekends would come to Piura from Sullana, Paita, Huancabamba, and even Tumbes and Chiclayo, drawn by the legend of the Green House that had been spread all through the desert. They would spend the night there, and when they came to the city they were uncouth and boisterous, they would walk their drunkenness through the streets as if it were some act of prowess. The people hated them and sometimes there were fights, not at night and at the dueling place, which is the small flat spot below the bridge, but in broad daylight and on the Plaza de Armas, on the Avenida Grau, or anywhere. Brawls would break out. The streets were becoming dangerous.

When, in spite of the prohibition by the authorities, one of the occupants of the house would venture into the city, the ladies dragged their daughters inside their houses and drew the curtains. Father García would go out to meet the intruder, beside himself, the people would have to hold him back to prevent an attack.

During the first year, there were only four occupants, but the following year, when those left, Don Anselmo took a trip and came back with eight, and they say that at its height the Green House had twenty occupants. They would come directly to the structure on the outskirts. From the Old Bridge one could see them arriving, their shrieks and curses could be heard. Their colorful outfits, their scarves and jewelry would sparkle like crustaceans in the arid countryside.

Don Anselmo, on the other hand, did go into town. He would ride up and down the streets on his black horse, which he had taught to do cute tricks: to shake its tail merrily when a woman passed, to pick up its foot as a sign of greeting, to do dance steps when it heard music. Don Anselmo had put on weight, his clothes were too showy—a soft straw hat, a silk scarf, linen shirts, a hand-tooled belt, tight pants, boots with high heels and spurs. His hands seethed with rings. Sometimes he would stop for a few drinks at the Estrella del Norte, and many important people would not hesitate to sit at his table, chat with him, and then accompany him to the outskirts.

Don Anselmo's prosperity was translated into a horizontal and vertical expansion of the Green House. Like a living organism, it was growing, ripening. The first innovation was a stone wall. Crowned with thistles, pieces of broken bottles, barbed wire, and thorns to discourage thieves, it enclosed and hid the first floor. The space between the wall and the house was at first a stony courtyard, then a smooth-surfaced entranceway with potted cactus plants, then a circular parlor with a floor and a roof of matting, and finally wood replaced straw, the floor was paved, and the roof was tiled over. On top of the second story, a third one arose, small and cylindrical, like a watchtower. Every stone that was added, every tile or board, was automatically painted green. The color chosen by Don Anselmo gave the countryside a refreshing, a vegetable, an almost liquid note. From the distance, travelers would spy the building with green walls, half diluted in the bright yellow light of the sand, and they would get the feeling that they were coming to an oasis of palm trees and coconuts, hospitable, with crystalline water, and it was as if that distant presence promised all kinds of recompense for a fatigued body, goads without end for a spirit that had been depressed by the drowsiness of the desert.

Don Anselmo, they say, lived on the top floor, in that narrow dome, and no one, not even his best customers—Chápiro Seminario, the Chief of Police, Don Eusebio Romero, Dr. Pedro Zevallos—had access to that place. From there, without doubt, Don Anselmo would watch the parade of visitors through the desert, would see their silhouettes outlined by the whirlwinds of sand, those hungry beasts who browsed at the edge of town after the sun went down.

In addition to its occupants, during its good period the Green House sheltered Angélica Mercedes, a young Mangache girl who had inherited from her mother wisdom and the art of hot sauces. Don Anselmo would go to the market with her, to the stores, to order food and drink: merchants and vendors would bow like reeds in the wind when they passed. The kids, cavies, pigs, and lambs that Angélica Mercedes roasted with mysterious herbs and spices came to be one of the incentives for visiting the Green House, and there were old men who would swear, *"We only go there to enjoy that delicious food."*

The area around the Green House was always lively with the multitude of tramps, beggars, vendors of trinkets and fruits who laid siege to the customers who came and went. The children of the city would sneak out of their houses at night and, hiding behind the bushes, would spy on visitors and listen to the music, the laughter. Some scaled the wall, scratching their hands and legs, and looked covetously at the inside. One day (which was a holy day of obligation), Father García stationed himself in the desert a few yards from the Green House, and he harangued the visitors one by one and exhorted them to return to the city and repent. But they invented excuses: a business meeting, a punishment they had to undergo because otherwise they would poison their souls, a wager that was a matter of honor. Some made fun of Father García and invited him to come along with them, and there were some who were offended and drew their pistols.

New myths about Don Anselmo arose in Piura. According to some, he took secret trips to Lima, where he kept his money and was buying property. According to others, he was only the front man for a business group that had the Chief of Police, the Mayor, and several ranchers among its members. In popular fantasy, Don Anselmo's past became enriched, sublime or bloody deeds were daily added to his biography. Old Mangaches were sure that they saw in him an adolescent who years back had committed holdups in the district, and others asserted, *"He's an escaped prisoner, a former rebel, a politician in disgrace."* Only Father García dared say, *"His body smells of sulfur."*

And at dawn they get up to continue on their way, they go down the bank and the boat is not there. They start to look for it, Adrián Nieves on one side, on the other Corporal Roberto Delgado and the porter, and suddenly shouts, stones, naked people, and there is the Corporal surrounded by Aguarunas, they beat him with sticks, the porter too, and now they have seen him and the redskins run toward him, holy Christ, Adrián Nieves, your time has come, and he jumps into the water: cold, rapid, dark, don't stick out your head, deeper, let the current take you, arrows?, let it carry you downstream, bullets?, stones?, Christ, his lungs need air, his head is spinning like a top, watch out for cramps. He comes up and he can still see Urakusa and, on the bank, the Corporal's green uniform, the redskins are beating him, it was his fault, he had warned him, and the porter would he get away?, would they kill him? He lets himself float downstream, grabbing a log, and then, when he climbs up the right bank of the river, his body hurts. He goes to sleep right there on the beach, he still hasn't got his strength back, and a scorpion stings him freely. He has to light a fire and put his hand over it, that's it, let him sweat even though it burns so much, he sucks the wound, he spits, he rinses out his mouth, you never know about the sting of a mother-fucking scorpion. Then he goes on, through the woods, no redskins anywhere, but he'd better head for the Santiago, and what if a patrol catches him and takes him back to the garrison at Borja? He can't go back to the town either, the soldiers would find him there tomorrow or the next day and, for the present, he will have to build a raft. It takes him a long time, oh, if you only had a machete, Adrián Nieves, his hands are tired and do not have the strength to knock down thick trunks. He chooses three dead trees, white and worm-eaten, which fall with the first push, he ties them together with some vines, and he makes two poles, one to take along as a spare. And no thought now of going out onto the main river, he looks for channels and inlets to follow, and it is not difficult, the whole region is full of waterways. Except how will he find his way, these uplands are not his country, the water has risen a lot, will he reach the Santiago that way?, just one more short week, Adrián Nieves, you were a good pilot, he opens up his nostrils wide, the smell does not deceive him, it's the right direction, and balls, man, lots of balls. But where is he going now, the channel seems to spin around him and he is navigating in the dark, the woods are thick, the sun and the air can barely penetrate, it smells of rotting wood, mud, and so many bats besides, his arms hurt, his throat is tired from scaring them off, just one more week. Neither backward nor forward, neither going back up the Marañón nor reaching the Santiago, the current carries him wherever it wants, his body is tired no end, and to top it off it is raining, it rains day and night. But finally the channel ends and he comes out into a lagoon, a small inlet with chambiras that are just like stakes along the bank, the sky is growing dark. He sleeps on an island, when he wakes he chews some bitter grasses, he continues on his trip, and only two days later does he kill a skinny tapir with a stick, he eats the half-raw meat, his muscles can no longer move the pole, the mosquitoes have been biting him at their leisure, his skin burns and his legs are like Captain Quiroga's, which the Corporal was telling him about, what would become of him?, would the Urakusas let him go?, they were furious, would they kill him right there? Perhaps it would have been better to have gone straight back to the garrison at Borja, better to be a soldier than a corpse, a sad thing dying of hunger or fever in the jungle, Adrián Nieves. He is lying on his belly on the raft and a handful of days like that, and when the channel ends and he comes out into an enormous lagoon, look at that, so big it looks like the Lake, look at that, Lake Rimache?, he couldn't have come that far, impossible, and in the center there is the island and on top of the bank there is a wall of lupunas. He pushes the rudder pole without getting up and, finally, among the trees full of humps, naked forms, holy Christ, are they Aguarunas?, help me, are they friendly?, he waves at them with both hands and they move about, shout, help me, they jump, they point at him, and when he lands he sees the white man, the white woman, and his head gets dizzy, Mister, you don't know how glad I am to see a white person. He had saved his life, Mister, he had thought it was all over and he is laughing and they give him another drink, the bittersweet taste of the anisette and behind the boss there is a young white girl, her face is pretty, her long hair is pretty, and it was as if he were dreaming, Ma'am, you saved me too: he thanked them in the name of heaven. When he wakes up, they are still there, next to him, and the boss come on, that's enough, man, he had slept a whole day, he was finally opening his eyes, did he feel all right? And Adrián Nieves yes, very well, but were there any soldiers around here? No, there weren't, why did he want to know, what had he done, and Adrián Nieves nothing bad, boss, I didn't kill anybody, he had only deserted, he couldn't live cooped up in a barracks, there was nothing like the open air for him, his name was Nieves, and before the soldiers tied him up he was a pilot. A pilot? Then he must know the jungle well, he must know how to take a boat anywhere and at any time of the year, and he of course he could, boss, he'd been a pilot since the day he was born. He was lost now because he had got caught in the strong currents in the middle of high water, he didn't want the soldiers to see him, couldn't he stay, boss? And the boss yes, he could stay on the island, he would give him work. He would be safe here, neither soldiers nor police would ever come: this was his wife, Lalita, and he, Fushía.

"What's the matter, buddy?" Josefino asked. "Don't get all worked up."

"I'm going to Chunga's!" Lituma roared. "Are you coming with me? No? I don't need any of you, either. I'm going alone."

But the Leóns held his arms and Lituma stayed where he was, wheezing, sweating, his small eyes rolling anxiously around the room.

"What for, brother?" Josefino said. "We're fine here. Take it easy."

"Just to hear the harp player with the golden fingers," Lituma moaned. "That's the only reason, champs. We'll just have one drink and then go home, I swear."

"You were always a good man, buddy. Don't turn weak now."

"I'm a better man than anybody," Lituma babbled. "But I've got a heart this size."

"Try crying," Monk said tenderly. "That relieves you, cousin, you don't have to be ashamed."

Lituma had begun to look off into space and his canistel-colored suit was covered with stains of earth and saliva. They were silent for a fair time, each one drinking on his own, without toasting, and echoes of tonderos and waltzes reached them, and the air had become impregnated with the smell of chicha and frying food. The swinging of the lamp would enlarge and diminish the four forms projected on the mats with a precise rhythm, and the candle in the niche, very short now, was giving off a curled and dark wisp of smoke that wrapped the plaster Virgin in long hair. Lituma stood up with great effort, brushed off his clothes, let his eyes wander around, and suddenly he put a finger in his mouth. He was poking his finger down his throat under the attentive look of the others, who saw him grow pale and finally vomit, noisily, with spasms that shook his whole body. Then he sat down again, cleaned off his face with his handkerchief, and, exhausted, hollow-eyed, he lit a cigarette with trembling hands.

"I feel better now, buddy. Just keep on telling your story."

"We don't know very much, Lituma. That is, how the thing happened. When they locked you up, we took off. We'd been witnesses and they could have got us involved. You know that the Seminarios are rich people, with a lot of influence. I went to Sullana and your cousins went to Chulucanas. When we got back, she'd left the house in Castilla and no one knew where she was staying."

"So the poor thing was all alone," Lituma murmured. "Without a penny and pregnant too."

"Don't worry about that, brother," Josefino said. "She didn't give birth. After a while, we found out that she was hanging around the chicha bars, and one night we ran across her in the Río Bar with some guy and she wasn't pregnant any more."

"And what did she do when she saw you?"

"Nothing, buddy. She said something fresh to us. And later on we used to run into her here and there, and she always had someone with her. Until one day we saw her in the Green House."

Lituma wiped his face with his handkerchief, dragged hard on his cigarette, and blew out a great mouthful of thick smoke.

"Why didn't you write to me?" His voice was getting hoarser all the time.

"You already had enough trouble, locked up far away from home. Why should we make life worse for you, buddy? That's not the kind of news you give someone who's all screwed up."

"Enough, cousin, I think you just like to suffer," José said. "Let's change the subject."

From Lituma's lips a thread of shining saliva ran down to his neck. His head was moving, slowly, heavily, mechanically, following the precise oscillation of the shadows on the matting. Josefino filled the glasses. They continued drinking, not speaking, until the candle in the niche went out.

"We've been here for two hours," José said, pointing at the candleholder. "That's how long the wick lasts."

"I'm glad you're back, cousin," Monk said. "Don't look like that. Laugh. All the Mangaches are going to be happy to see you. Laugh, cousin."

He went over to Lituma, he hugged him, and he was looking at him with his large eyes, bright and burning, until Lituma patted him on the head and smiled.

"That's the way I like it, cousin," José said. "Long live Mangachería. Let's sing the theme song."

And suddenly the three of them—José, Monk, and Lituma—began to talk, they were three kids and they were jumping over the adobe walls of the public school to swim in the river, or riding somebody's donkey, they would go along sandy paths, through farm plots and cotton fields, toward the mounds of Narihualá, and there was the uproar of carnivals, the confetti, and the balloons raining down on furious passers-by, and they would also drench dandies who were afraid to haul them out of their hiding places on rooftops and in trees, and now, on hot mornings, they would play furious games of soccer with a ball that was made out of rags on the infinitely large playing field that was the desert. Josefino listened to them in silence, his eyes filled with envy, the Mangaches chiding Lituma, did you really enlist in the Civil Guard?, you renegade, you yellowbelly, and the Leóns and Lituma laughed. They opened another bottle. Still silent, Josefino blew smoke rings, José was whistling, Monk held the pisco in his mouth, pretended that he was chewing it, gargled, made faces, I don't feel any sickness or fire, just that unmistakable little heat.

"Take it easy, champ," Josefino said. "Where are you going? Grab him."

The Leóns caught him at the door, José held him by the shoulders and Monk around the waist, they shook him furiously, but his voice was bewildered and weepy.

"What for, cousin? Don't go, you'll just make your heart bleed. Listen to me, Lituma, cousin."

Lituma clumsily stroked Monk's face, rumpled his curly hair, pushed him away softly, and stumbled out. They followed him. Outside, next to their houses made of wild cane, the Mangaches were sleeping under the stars, they formed silent human clusters on the sand. The noise from the chicha bars had increased, Monk was repeating the songs between his teeth, and when he heard a harp, he would open up his arms: but there's no one like Don Anselmo! He and Lituma were in front, arm in arm, zigzagging; sometimes a protest would come up out of the darkness, "Watch where you're going!," and they, in unison, "Beg your pardon, sir," "Terribly sorry, lady."

"That story you told him was like a movie," José said.

"But he believed it," Josefino said. "I couldn't think of anything else. And you people didn't help me, you didn't open your mouths once."

"It's too bad we're not in Paita, cousin," Monk said. "I'd jump in the water clothes and all. That would be a lot of fun."

"In Yacila there are waves, that's real ocean," Lituma said. "At Paita it's just a little lake, the Marañón is rougher than the ocean there. We'll go to Yacila on Sunday, cousin."

"Let's go to Felipe's," Josefino said. "I've got some money. We can't let him go, José."

The Avenida Sánchez Cerro was deserted, insects were buzzing in the shadows of the oily lights from every lamppost. Monk had sat down on the ground to tie up his shoes. Josefino went over to Lituma:

"Look, buddy, Felipe's is open. All the good times we had in that bar. Come on, let me buy you a drink."

Lituma shrugged off Josefino's grip. He spoke without looking at him:

"Afterward, brother, on the way back. The Green House now. We had a lot of good times there too, more than anywhere else. Isn't that right, champs?"

Later on, when they passed the Tres Estrellas, Josefino made another attempt. He ran toward the lighted door of the bar, shouting:

"We finally found a place where we can drown our thirst! Come on, buddies, the drinks are on me."

But Lituma kept on walking, unmovable.

"What'll we do, José?"

"What else can we do, brother? Go to Chunga Chunguita's."

TWO

A BOAT ROARS UP TO THE DOCK and Julio Reátegui jumps out. He goes up to the square of Santa María de Nieva—a Civil Guard is throwing a stick into the air, a dog catches it in flight and brings it back—and when he reaches the level of the capirona poles, a group of people come out of the Governor's building. He raises his hand in greeting: they watch him, become excited, run to meet him, what a pleasure, what a surprise, Julio Reátegui shakes hands with Fabio Cuesta, why hadn't he told them he was coming?, with Manuel Aguila, they wouldn't forgive him, with Pedro Escabino, they would have prepared something for his arrival, with Arévalo Benzas, how long was he staying this time, Don Julio? Not long, it was a lightning visit, he would continue on his way very shortly, they all knew what his life was like. They go into the Governor's building, Don Fabio opens some beer, they drink a toast, were things going well in Nieva?, in Iquitos?, any problems with the heathens? At the doors and windows of the cabin, there are Aguarunas with wide mouths, cold eyes, and prominent cheekbones. Later on, Julio Reátegui and Fabio Cuesta come out, on the square the guard is still playing with the dog, they go up the hill toward the Mission, watched from every building, oh, Don Fabio, women, wasting a day on something like this, he would reach the camp at night, and Don Fabio what are friends for, Don Julio? He could have written a few lines and he would have taken care of everything, but of course, Don Fabio, the letter would have taken a month, and who could wait, and in the meantime Señora Reátegui. As soon as they knock, the door of the Residence opens, how are you, a greasy apron, Sister Griselda, a habit, see who's here, a red face, didn't she recognize him?, why it's Señor Reátegui, a little shout, come in, a smiling hand, come in, Don Julio, what a pleasure, and he should not be surprised that they did not recognize him the way he looked, Sister. Limping, talking without a halt, Sister Griselda guides them along a shady passageway, she opens a door for them, she points to some canvas chairs, what a pleasure for Mother Superior, and even though he was in a great hurry he had to visit the chapel, Don Julio, he would see all the changes, she would be right back. In the study there is a crucifix along with a candlestick, on the floor a chambira rug and on the wall a picture of the Virgin; sumptuous gaudy tongues of sun come through the windows and lick the beams of the ceiling. Whenever he was in a church or a convent, Julio Reátegui had strange feelings, Don Fabio, the soul, death, the kind of thoughts that kept a person awake so much as a child, and the same thing happened to the Governor, Don Julio, they would visit the sisters and come out with their heads full of deep things: and maybe underneath it all they had a touch of the mystic in them? He had thought the same thing, Don Fabio strokes his bald head, that's funny, a touch of the mystic. Señora Reátegui would laugh if she could hear them, she was always saying you'll end up in hell as a heretic, Julio, and, by the way, last year he had finally made her happy, they had gone to Lima in October, to the Procession?, yes, Our Lord of the Miracles. Don Fabio had seen photographs, but being there must have been better, is it true that all the Negroes dress up in purple? And half-breeds and whites too, half of Lima in purple, something terrible, Don Fabio, three days covered up like that, how uncomfortable and what smells, Señora Reátegui wanted him to put the habit on too, but his love didn't go that far. Voices, laughter, running invade the room and they look out the windows: voices, laughter, running. It must be recess, were there many of them now?, from the noise it sounded like a hundred, and Don Fabio around twenty. On Sunday there was a parade and they sang the national anthem, all in tune, Don Julio, in a Spanish that could not have been better. There was no doubt about it, Don Fabio was happy in Santa María de Nieva, the pride with which he spoke about things here, was this better than running the hotel?, if he had stayed on there, in Iquitos, he would have been in a good position now, Don Fabio, financially, that is. But the Governor was old now, and even though Señor Reátegui might think he was not telling the truth, he was not an ambitious man. So you weren't going to be able to stand one month in Santa María de Nieva?, Don Julio, now he could see how much he stood, and if God allowed it he would never leave the place. Why did he push so much for that appointment?, Julio Reátegui had never been able to understand it, why did he want to replace him, Don Fabio?, what was he looking for?, and Don Fabio to be—he should not laugh—respected, his last years in Iquitos had been so sad, Don Julio, no one could know the shame, the humiliations, when he brought him to the hotel he was living off charity. But he should not become sad, here in Nieva everybody loved him very much, Don Fabio, didn't he get what he was looking for? Yes, they respected him, the salary was probably nothing great, but with what Señor Reátegui gave him for his help it was enough for him to live in peace, he also owed him that, Don Julio, oh, there were no words. Between the laughter, the voices, and the running from the garden, barking, the squawking of parrots slip in. Julio Reátegui closes his eyes, Don Fabio remains thoughtful, his hand slowly affectionately passes over his bald head: by the way, did Don Julio know that Sister Asunción had died?, did he get his letter? He had got it and Señora Reátegui had written their condolences to the sisters, he added a few lines, the nun was such a good person, and Don Fabio had done something that was not entirely legal, he had flown the flag on the Governor's pole at half mast, Don Julio, to share in the mourning in some way, and Sister Angélica, is she all right?, still as strong as a rock that little old lady? Steps are heard and they stand up, go to meet the Mother Superior, Don Julio, Mother, a white hand, it was an honor for that house to have Señor Reátegui there again, how happy she was to see him, please, they should sit down and they had just been saying, Mother, remembering poor Sister Asunción. Poor? Not poor at all, she was in heaven, and Señora Reátegui, when would they see the patroness of the chapel again? Señora Reátegui was always thinking about coming, but to get here from Iquitos was so complicated, Santa María de Nieva was on the edge of nowhere, and besides wasn't it terrible traveling through the jungle? Not for Don Julio Reátegui, the Mother Superior smiles, who came and went through the Amazon country as if he were in his own home, but Julio Reátegui did not do it for pleasure, if one did not keep an eye on everything, Mother, things would go to the devil, she should excuse the expression. He had not said anything wrong, Don Julio, she too if one did not take care the devil would have a free hand, and now the pupils are singing in a chorus. Someone is leading them, at every pause Don Fabio applauds with his fingertips, smiles, approves: had the Mother received Señora Reátegui's message? Yes, last month, but she had not thought that Don Julio would take her away so soon. Usually, she preferred for them to leave the Mission at the end of the year, not in the middle of the term, but since he had taken the trouble to come personally they would make an exception, since it was a case of who it was, of course. And he, actually, was killing two birds with one stone, Mother, he had to take a look at the camp on the Nieva, the lumbermen had found rosewood, it seemed, so he took advantage to make a visit, and the Mother Superior agrees: were they going to have her take care of the girls?, Señora Reátegui said something about that. Ah, the girls, Mother, if she could only see them, they were so cute, Don Fabio figured as much, and the Mother knew them, Señora Reátegui had sent her some photographs of the children, the older one a doll and the little one such big eyes. They had to turn out like that, of course, Señora Reátegui was so beautiful, and Don Fabio said it with all due respect, Don Julio. It was some time now that their nurse had got married on them, Mother, and she could imagine how worried Señora Reátegui was, she had objections to all the girls, that they were dirty, that they might have some disease, always the worst kind, and there she was, being her own nursemaid for two months. On that count, Don Fabio sits forward in his chair, Señora Reátegui could rest easy, he slaps his leg, no one leaves here sick or dirty, wasn't that right, Mother?, he makes a bow with his head, it was a pleasure to see how clean they kept them, and Reátegui of course, Mother, Dr. Portillo's wife. Also trouble with the servants? Yes, Don Fabio, every day it was harder to find decent people in Iquitos, would it be possible to take another girl along too, Mother? Yes, it was possible, the Mother Superior tightens her lips slightly, Don Julio, but he should not look at things that way, her voice becomes thin, the Mission was not an employment agency, and now Reátegui is motionless, serious, a confused hand tapping the arm of the chair, was it possible that she had misunderstood him?, that is, the Mother Superior examines the crucifix, Don Fabio rubs his bald head, he rocks in his chair, he blinks, Mother, was it possible that she had misunderstood what Don Julio was saying? He knew where these girls came from, how they lived before they came to the Mission. Julio Reátegui assured her, Mother, there had been some mistake, she had not understood him, and after being here the girls had no place to go, the Indian villages were never in the same place, but even if they could locate their families the girls were no longer used to it, how could they go naked again?, the Mother Superior makes a friendly gesture, worship snakes?, but her smile is icy, eat lice? It was his fault, Mother, he was clumsy with his words and she saw a different meaning, but the girls could not stay at the Mission either, Don Julio, it would not be right, wasn't that true?, they had to make room for others. The idea was that they would help the sisters incorporate those girls into the civilized world, Don Julio, that they would make it easier for them to join society. It was precisely in that sense that Señor Reátegui—Mother, didn't she know him?, and in the Mission they took in those children and brought them up to gain a few souls for God, not to supply family servants, Don Julio, he should pardon her frankness. He was only too well aware of it, Mother, that was why he and his wife always cooperated with the Mission, if there was anything wrong, they would forget about it, Mother, nothing would be said, she should please not worry about it. The Mother Superior was not worrying about them, Don Julio, she knew that Señora Reátegui was very kind and that the girl would be in good hands. Dr. Portillo was the best lawyer in Iquitos, Mother, a former deputy, if it were not a question of a decent, recognized family, would Julio Reátegui have dared suggest it? He repeated to her that she should forget about it,

Mother, and the Mother Superior smiles again: was he angry with her? It was all right, everybody needed a sermon from time to time, and Julio Reátegui settles in his seat, she had boxed his ears, Mother, she had made him feel lacking, and if he guaranteed that gentleman, Don Julio, she believed him, what did it matter if she asked a few questions? Anything the Mother wished, and he could understand those precautions, quite logical, but she had to believe him, Dr. Portillo and his wife were the best of people and the girl would be very well treated, clothing, food, even a salary, and the Mother Superior did not doubt it, Don Julio. Her thin, furtive lips are tight again: and the other matter? Would they see to it that the girl would not lose what she had acquired here? They would not destroy through neglect what she had been given at the Mission? She was referring to that, Don Julio, and it was true that the Mother did not know the Portillos, Angelita organized Christmas charities for the poor every year, she herself went out collecting donations in the stores and she would distribute them in the poor neighborhoods, Mother: she could be sure that Angelita would take the girl to every Procession there was in Iquitos. The Mother Superior did not want to bother him any more, but there was something, would he take the responsibility for both of them? For any complaint or anything that happened, Mother, that's all there was to it, he would assume it and he would sign anything necessary, with great pleasure, in his name and that of Dr. Portillo. They were agreed, then, Don Julio, and the Mother Superior was going to get them; also, of course, Sister Griselda had prepared refreshments for them, it would do them good, wasn't that right?, with all the heat, and Don Fabio lifts his hands with joy: always so nice, they were. The Mother Superior leaves the room, the splashes of sun that embrace the beams are no longer brilliant but darker, in the neighboring garden the pupils are still singing, man, what did that all mean? It wasn't right, what a hard time the nun had given him, Don Fabio, and he Don Julio, nothing but a formality, the sisters loved those little orphans very much, they were sorry to see them leave, that was all, but did they ask the officers from Borja the same questions?, and those engineers who come through here, do they give them the same advice?, she should do him the favor, Don Fabio. The Governor's face is pained, the Mother was probably in a bad mood over something, he shouldn't pay any attention, Don Julio and they should not tell Reátegui that the soldier boys were going to treat them better than they would, they would make them work like animals, of course, they would not pay them a cent, certainly, did Don Fabio know the miserable pay that soldiers got? And besides they knew him only too well, if he recommended Portillo to them it meant something, Don Fabio, please, where had anyone seen such a thing? The chorus in the garden suddenly stops, and the Governor did not understand, the Mother Superior always so pleasant, always so well-mannered, it was all over now, Don Julio, he should not get angry, and he was not getting angry but injustices bothered him as much as anybody: the recess must have been over, Don Fabio's knuckles drum on the chair, the Mother made him nervous too, Don Julio, he felt he was in a confessional, they turn around and the door opens. The Mother Superior brings in a platter, a pyramid of hard-crusted cookies, and Sister Griselda an earthen tray, glasses, a pitcher full of frothy liquid, the two pupils stay beside the door, timid, shy in their cream-colored smocks: papaya juice, wonderful! That Sister Griselda, always spoiling them, Don Fabio has stood up and Sister Griselda laughs covering her mouth with her hand, she and the Mother Superior pass out the glasses, fill them. From the door, one against the other, the pupils watch out of the corners of their eyes, one has her mouth half open and shows her minute teeth, filed to a point. Julio Reátegui raises his glass, Mother, he really thanked her, he was dying with thirst, but they had to try the cookies, they bet they couldn't guess, oh?, let's see, and Don Fabio? They had no idea, Mother, so soft, corn?, too delicate, sweet potato? and Sister Griselda gives a laugh: cassava! She had invented them herself, when he brought Señora Reátegui she would give her the recipe, and Don Fabio takes a sip of his drink rolling his eyes: Sister Griselda had the hands of an angel, that was enough for her to deserve to go to heaven, and she hush, hush, Don Fabio, they should help themselves to more juice. They drink, they take out their handkerchiefs, they wipe their thin orange-colored muzzles, Reátegui has small drops of sweat on his forehead, the Governor's bald head is sparkling. Finally Sister Griselda takes away the tray, the pitcher, and the glasses, she smiles at them roguishly from the door, she goes out, Reátegui and the Governor look at the motionless pupils, the two lower their heads at the same time: good afternoon, girls. The Mother Superior takes a step toward them, come, come closer, why were they hanging back there? The one with the filed teeth shuffles over and stops without raising her head, the other one stays where she is, and Julio Reátegui you too, child, there was no reason for her to be afraid of him, he wasn't the bogeyman. The pupil does not answer and the Mother Superior suddenly adopts an enigmatic, mocking expression. She looks at Reátegui, a small excited light comes from her eyes, the Governor is indicating with his hand that the girl should come closer, and the Mother Superior, Don Julio, didn't he recognize her? She points at the one who is next to the door and her smile is accentuated, an affirmative sign, and Julio Reátegui turns toward the girl, he examines her, blinking, he moves his lips, he snaps his fingers, ah, Mother, was it her?, yes. What a surprise, it hadn't even crossed his mind, had she changed so much, Don Julio?, very much, Mother, she was coming with him, Señora Reátegui would be delighted. But they were old friends, child, didn't she remember him at all? The one with the filed teeth and the Governor are looking at each other curiously, the pupil at the door raises her head a little, her green eyes contrast with her dark skin, the Mother Superior sighs, Bonifacia: they were talking to her, what kind of manners were those. Julio Reátegui is still examining her, Mother, good gracious, it was going on four years, how time flew, child, how you've grown, she used to be such a little slip of a girl and now look at her. The Mother Superior agrees, Bonifacia, come, she should say hello to Señor Reátegui, she sighs again, she would have to respect him a great deal and his wife too, they would be very kind. And Reátegui that she should not be ashamed, child, they were going to talk for a while, she would soon be speaking Spanish very well, right? And the Governor gives a start in his seat, the one from Urakusa!, he slaps his forehead, of course, how stupid, now he could see. And the Mother Superior stop playing the boob, Don Julio was going to think that Bonifacia had her tongue cut off. But, child, she was crying, what was the matter, child, why those tears, and Bonifacia holds her head up, the tears wet her cheeks, her thick lips stubbornly closed, and Don Fabio come on, come on, silly, leaning over and compassionate, she should be very happy, she would have a home and Señor Reátegui's daughters were two wonderful girls. The Mother Superior had turned pale, this child!, her face is now as white as her hands, this silly girl!, what was she crying about? Bonifacia opens her green, wet, challenging eyes, she comes into the room, child, she kneels before the Mother Superior, silly, she grasps one of her hands, she brings it to her face, the one with the filed teeth laughs for a second and the Mother Superior babbles, looks at Reátegui, Bonifacia, calm down: she had promised her, and Sister Angélica. Her hand struggles to get away from the face that is rubbing against it. Reátegui and Don Fabio are smiling confused and benevolent, the thick lips voraciously kiss the pale and rebellious fingers and the one with the filed teeth is laughing without hiding it any more: didn't she see that it was for her own good?, where would she get better treatment? Bonifacia, hadn't she promised her less than half an hour ago?, and Sister Angélica, is that how she kept her promises? Don Fabio stands up, rubs his hands, that was the way girls were, sensitive, they cried over everything, child, she should make an effort, she would soon see how pretty Iquitos was, how good, how saintly Señora Reátegui was, and the Mother Superior, Don Julio, she begged him, she was sorry. That girl has never been difficult, she could not recognize her now. Calm down, Bonifacia, and Julio Reátegui there was nothing else to do, Mother. She had fallen in love with the Mission, there was nothing strange about that, and it was best that she not come against her will, best that she stay with the sisters. He would take the other one and Portillo could find a nursemaid in Iquitos, but above all, she should not worry about it, Mother.

1

"Look," Fats said. "The rain's stopping."

Long, blue, a few strips cut across the sky, among the gray masses the storm was still rumbling unharmoniously, and it had stopped raining. But around the Sergeant, the soldiers, and Nieves, the woods were still dripping: large hot drops were rolling off the trees, the edges of the tent, and the disorderly roots, down to the pebble beach that had become a bog, and as it received them the mud opened up small craters; it seemed to be boiling. The boat was rocking on the shore.

"Let's wait until the water goes down a little, Sergeant," Nieves the pilot said. "With the rain the rapids are probably running fast."

"Yes, of course, Don Adrián, but there's no reason why we have to stay like sardines," the Sergeant said. "Let's put up the other tent, boys. We can sleep here."

Their undershirts and pants were soaked, mud was crusted on their leggings, their skin was shining. They were rubbing their bodies, wringing out their clothes. Nieves the pilot sloshed across the beach, and when he reached the boat he looked like a tar figurine.

"It's better naked," Blondy said. "We're going to get all covered with mud."

Fats had his undershorts off and they made fun of his fat buttocks. They went out of the tent, Shorty stumbled, fell on his rear, got up cursing. They crossed the swamp with the help of their hands. Nieves was handing them the mosquito nets, the cans, the thermos bottles, they carried the bundles up to the tent on their shoulders, they came back, and suddenly they became unconstrained: they were running and shouting, they were slipping in the mud, they were kicking up balls of mud. Sergeant, there probably isn't a single dry biscuit, try this one, the anisette is probably all fucked up too, and as for Shorty he had had enough jungle, Blacky, he had it up to here. They washed the splotches of mud off in the river, they piled the cargo under a tree, and they drove in the stakes right there, stretched out the canvas, and fastened the ropes to some roots that came out of the ground, gray and twisted. Sometimes twisting rose-colored worms would appear from under a stone. Nieves the pilot prepared a bonfire.

"They set up the tent right under the tree," the Sergeant said. "It's going to rain spiders all night long."

The pile of wood crackled, it began to smoke, and a moment later a small blue flame burst forth, a red one, larger. They sat down around the fire. The biscuits were wet, the anisette hot.

"We can't get out of it, Sergeant," Blacky said. "We're going to get a good bawling out in Nieva now."

"It was crazy to go out like this," Blondy said. "The Lieutenant should have known better."

"He knew it was no use." The Sergeant shrugged. "But haven't you seen how things are between the sisters and Don Fabio? He sent us out to please them, that's all."

"I didn't join the Civil Guard to play nursemaid," Shorty said. "Don't things like this bother you, Sergeant?"

But the Sergeant had ten years in the service behind him; he was thick-skinned, Shorty, and nothing bothered him any more. He had taken out a cigarette and he was drying it over the fire, turning it around between his fingers.

"Then why did you join the Civil Guard?" Fats asked. "You're still fresh, you're wet behind the ears. All of this bustle is old stuff to us, Shorty. You'll learn soon enough."

It wasn't that, Shorty had spent a year in Juliaca, and the mountains were tougher than the jungle, Fats. The bugs and the cloudbursts didn't bother him as much as getting sent into the woods to chase kids. He was glad they hadn't caught them.

"The little snotnoses probably went back all by themselves," Blacky said. "We'll probably find them in Santa María de Nieva."

"The damned little fools," Blondy said. "They're just as apt to. I'd spank their asses."

Fats, on the other hand, would give them a hug, and he laughed, Sergeant: don't you think the older ones are just about ready? Had they seen them on Sunday when they went to bathe in the river?

"That's all you ever think about, Fats," the Sergeant said. "From the minute you get up until you go to bed, nothing but women."

"But it's true, Sergeant. They develop so fast here, at eleven they're already ripe enough for anything. Don't tell me that if you had the chance you wouldn't give them a little hug."

"Don't get my appetite up, Fats." Blacky yawned. "Remember I've got to sleep with Shorty later."

Nieves the pilot was feeding the fire with small branches. It was already getting dark. The sun was dying in the distance, fluttering among the trees like a reddish bird, and the river was a motionless, metallic sheet. In the underbrush along the bank, the frogs were croaking, and in the air there was vapor, dampness, electrical vibrations. Sometimes a flying insect would be trapped in the flames of the bonfire, devoured with a dull crackle. With the shadows, the woods sent out smells of nocturnal germination and the music of crickets to the tents.

"I don't like it. I almost got sick in Chicais," Shorty repeated with an annoyed face. "Don't you all remember the old woman with the teats? It wasn't right to snatch her children like that. I've dreamed about them twice."

"And they didn't even scratch you as much as they did me," Blondy said, laughing; but he became serious and added: "It was for their own good, Shorty. To teach them how to dress, read, and talk like Christians."

"Or would you rather they stayed savages?" Blacky asked.

"And besides they feed and vaccinate them, and they sleep in beds," Fats said. "In Nieva they live as they never have before."

"But far away from their own people," Shorty said. "Wouldn't it hurt you if you never saw your families again?"

It wasn't the same thing, Shorty, and Fats shook his head compassionately: they were civilized, and those Indian kids didn't even know how to say "family." The Sergeant raised his cigarette to his mouth, and lighted it leaning toward the fire.

"Besides, it's only bad for them at the beginning," Blondy said. "That's why the nuns are there, they're very good."

"Who knows what goes on inside the Mission," Shorty said, with a grunt. "They could just as well be very bad."

That's enough, Shorty: he should wash out his mouth before he talks about the sisters. Fats allowed anything, but not that; more respect for religion. Shorty also raised his voice: of course he was a Catholic, but he could say bad things about anybody he pleased, and did somebody want to make something out of it?

"What if I get mad?" Fats said. "What if I smack you one?"

"No fighting." The Sergeant let out a mouthful of smoke. "Stop acting like a hoodlum, Fats."

"I can understand reasons, but not threats, Sergeant," Shorty said. "Don't I have a right to say what I think?"

"Sure you do," the Sergeant said. "And I agree with you in some of it."

Shorty looked at the soldiers mockingly, did they see?, and point-blank at Fats: who was right?

"There's room for argument," the Sergeant said. "I think that if the kids ran away from the Mission, it's because they weren't used to it there."

"But, Sergeant, what's that got to do with it?" Fats protested. "Didn't you ever cut up when you were a kid?"

"Would you rather have them keep on being savages too, Sergeant?" Blacky asked.

"It's all right to educate them," the Sergeant said. "But why by force?"

"What else can the poor sisters do, Sergeant?" Blondy said. "You know what the heathens are like. They say yes, yes, but when the time comes to send their daughters to the Mission, not even a whipping is any good, and they run away."

"What if they don't want to be civilized, what business is that of ours?" Shorty said. "Everybody to his own customs and fuck it all."

"You're sorry for the kids because you don't know how they're treated in the villages," Blacky said. "They open up holes in the noses and mouths of newborn babies."

"And when the Indians get liquored they screw right in front of everybody," Blondy said. "They don't care how old the woman is, and the first one they can grab, their daughters, their sisters."

"And the old women open up the girls with their hands," Blacky said. "And then they eat the cherries so that it brings them good luck. Isn't that right, Fats?"

"Right, with their hands," Fats said. "I should know. I haven't found a virgin yet. And I've had plenty of squaws."

The Sergeant waved his hands: they were ganging up on Shorty and that wasn't right.

"Just because you're on his side, Sergeant," Blondy said.

"What happens is that I feel sorry for those kids," the Sergeant confessed. "All of them, the ones in the Mission because they must be suffering away from their people. And the others for the evil that exists in their villages."

"It's easy to see you're a Piuran, Sergeant," Blacky said. "Everybody from your home town is always sentimental."

"And proud of it," the Sergeant said. "And anybody who says anything about Piura had better watch out."

"Sentimentalists and loyal too," Blacky said. "But the Arequipans have it over the Piurans in that, Sergeant."

It was already night and the bonfire was crackling, Nieves the pilot was still throwing on small branches, dry leaves. The thermos of anisette went from hand to hand, and the soldiers had lighted up cigarettes. They were all perspiring, and in their eyes, minute, dancing, the tongues of the fire were repeated.

"But they're the cleanest people there are," Shorty said. "And, on the other hand, did any one of you ever see the sisters take a bath on that trip to Chicais?"

Fats choked: the sisters again?, he began to strangle, God damn it, are you on the sisters again?

"You insult me, but you don't answer me," Shorty said. "Is what I said true or not?"

"You're stupid," Blondy said. "Did you want the sisters to take a bath in front of us?"

"They probably took their baths hidden off somewhere," Blacky said.

"I never saw them," Shorty said. "And you people didn't see them, either."

"And you didn't see them do their duty, either," Blondy said. "That doesn't mean that they held back their crap and pee during the whole trip."

Just a minute, Fats had seen them: when everybody was asleep, they got up without making a noise, and they went down to the river like little ghosts. The soldiers laughed, and the Sergeant that Fats, was he spying on them?, did he want to see them undressed?

"Sergeant, please," Fats said, confused. "Don't say things like that, the things you can think of. The fact was I was awake and that's how I saw them."

"Let's change the subject," Blacky said. "We shouldn't be making jokes about the sisters. And besides we're never going to convince this guy. You're as stubborn as a mule, Shorty."

"And a hairy ape," Fats said. "Comparing the sisters to squaws. I feel sorry for you, I really do."

"That's all for now," the Sergeant said, cutting off Shorty, who was about to speak. "Let's go to sleep so we can get an early start."

They fell silent, staring at the flames. The thermos of anisette went around again. Then they got up, went into the tents, but a moment later the Sergeant came back out to the bonfire with a cigarette in his mouth. Nieves the pilot handed him a burning straw.

"You're always so quiet, Don Adrián," the Sergeant said. "Why didn't you get into the argument too?"

"I was listening," Nieves said. "I don't like arguments, Sergeant. And besides I'd rather not get involved with them."

"With the boys?" the Sergeant asked. "Have they done something to you? Why didn't you tell me, Don Adrián?"

"They're so proud, they look down on the ones of us who were born here," the pilot said, in a low voice. "Haven't you seen how they treat me?"

"They're stuck-up like everybody from Lima," the Sergeant said. "But you shouldn't pay any attention to it, Don Adrián. And if they ever get rude with you, tell me and I'll put them in their place."

"On the other hand, you're a good man, Sergeant," Nieves said. "I've been meaning to say that to you for a long time. The only one who treats me with respect."

"Because I think a lot of you, Don Adrián," the Sergeant said. "I've always told you that I'd like to be your friend. But you keep away from everybody, you're a loner."

"You'll be my friend now." Nieves smiled. "One of these days you'll come and eat at my house and I'll introduce you to Lalita. And to the girl who helped the kids escape."

"What? That girl Bonifacia lives with you people?" the Sergeant said. "I'd thought she'd left the village."

"She didn't have any place to go and we took her in," Nieves said. "But don't tell anyone, she doesn't want them to know where she is, because she's still half nun, she's scared to death of men."

"Have you been counting the days, old man?" Fushía asked. "I've lost track of time."

"What do you care about time? What difference does it make?" Aquilino said.

"It seems like a thousand years since we left the island," Fushía said. "Besides, I know it's a matter of opinion, Aquilino, you don't understand people. You'll see, in San Pablo they'll call the police and take away the money."

"Are you getting sad again?" Aquilino said. "I know it's a long trip, but what do you want? We have to be careful. Don't worry about San Pablo, Fushía, I've told you that I know a guy there."

"It's just that I'm all in, man, it's no joke running around like this, you've hit the jackpot with me," Dr. Portillo said. "Look at the fatigue on poor Don Fabio's face. But at least we can tell you something. In the meantime, you'd better sit down or the news will make you sit down."

"The plantings are in good shape, they look good, Señor Reátegui," Fabio Cuesta said. "The engineer is a good man and the clearing and planting is already done. They all say it's a perfect spot for coffee."

"Everything is normal on that end," Dr. Portillo said. "The weak side is the rubber and the hides. It has to do with some bandits, old friend."

"Portillo? It doesn't ring a bell, Fushía," Aquilino said. "Is he a doctor in Iquitos?"

"A lawyer," Fushía said. "The one who wins all Reátegui's lawsuits for him. A proud man, Aquilino, very vain."

"It's not the bosses' fault, Señor Reátegui, I swear," Fabio Cuesta said. "They're angrier than anybody, you can see how they've got the most to lose. It seems that there really are bandits."

Dr. Portillo too had thought, at the beginning, that the bosses were doing business behind his back, Julio, that they had invented the bandits so as not to sell the rubber to him. But they weren't, the fact is that it's getting harder and harder for them to find goods, old friend, he and Don Fabio went everywhere, they checked, there are bandits, and Don Fabio was a real gentleman, he got sick from so much traveling, and in spite of it all he went along with him, Julio, and of course it was helpful to go arm and arm with the authorities, the Governor of Santa María de Nieva inspired respect around there.

"Where Señor Reátegui is concerned, anything at all," Fabio Cuesta said. "That and much more, you know that, Don Julio. What I'm most sorry about is this bandit business, with all it cost to convince the bosses that they should sell to you instead of the bank."

"You should have seen how he treated me," Fushía said. "How long was it? Would you believe he never invited me to his house in Iquitos? You don't know how much I hated that shyster, Aquilino."

"Still full of hate, Fushía," Aquilino said. "Something happens to you and you start to hate somebody. God will punish you for that too."

"Is there more to come?" Fushía asked. "He punishes even before I do anything, old man."

"They gave us a lot of help at the Borja garrison," Dr. Portillo said. "They let us have guides, pilots. You have to thank the Colonel, Julio, drop him a note."

"A wonderful person, the Colonel, Señor Reátegui," Fabio Cuesta said. "Very helpful, very dynamic."

They could act against the bandits if they got orders from Lima, old friend, the best would be for Reátegui to run down to the capital and put some pressure on, if the soldiers intervened everything would be settled. Yes, man, it really was quite bad.

"We didn't want to believe them, Señor Reátegui," Fabio Cuesta said. "But all the bosses swore the same thing over and over again. They couldn't have got together on it."

It was very simple, old friend: when the bosses would get to the tribes, they wouldn't find anything, either rubber or hides, only redskins crying and carrying on, they robbed us, bandits, devils, etc.

"He went up the Santiago with Don Fabio, who was Governor of Santa María de Nieva, and with some soldiers from Borja," Fushía said. "Before that they'd been to the Aguarunas and the Achuals too, investigating."

"But I ran into them on the Marañón," Aquilino said. "Didn't I tell you? I was with them for two days. It was the second or third trip I was making to the island. And Don Fabio and that other one, what did you call him, Portillo?, they peppered me with questions, and I was thinking now you're going to pay for everything, Aquilino. I was scared to death."

"It's too bad they didn't come," Fushía said. "The way that shyster would have looked when he saw me and what he would have told that bastard Reátegui. And what about Don Fabio, old man? Is he still alive?"

"Yes, he's still Governor of Santa María de Nieva."

"I'm not so stupid," Dr. Portillo said. "The first thing I thought was if it's not the bosses, it must be the redskins, they're repeating that Urakusa trick, the one about the cooperative. That's why we visited the tribes. But it wasn't the redskins either."

"The women were crying when they met us, Señor Reátegui," Fabio Cuesta said. "Because the bandits hadn't only carried off the rubber, the caspi sap, and the skins, but the girls too, naturally."

It was a good piece of business, old friend: Reátegui would advance money to the bosses, the bosses would advance money to the redskins, and when the redskins came out of the jungle with the rubber and the skins, the bastards would jump them and get everything. Without having invested a penny, old friend; wasn't it a perfect way to do business? He should go to Lima and get some action, Julio, and the sooner the better.

"Why are you always looking for dirty and dangerous business?" Aquilino asked. "It's like a mania with you, Fushía."

"All business is dirty, old man," Fushía said. "What happens is that I didn't have a chunk of capital to start with, if you have money you can make the worst kinds of deal without any danger."

"If I hadn't helped you, you would have had to go to Ecuador, that's all," Aquilino said. "I don't know why I helped you. You've made me go through some terrible years. Frightened all the time, Fushía, my heart in my mouth."

"You helped me because you're a good person," Fushía said. "The best I've ever known, Aquilino. If I were rich, I'd leave you all my money, old man."

"But you're not and you never will be," Aquilino said. "And what good would your money do me if I'm about to die from one minute to the next? We're a little alike in that, Fushía, we're coming to the end just as poor as when we were born."

"There's already a regular legend about the bandits," Dr. Portillo said. "They even told us about them at the Missions. But the monks and nuns don't know much about it, either."

"In an Aguaruna village on the Cenepa, a woman told us she'd seen them," Fabio Cuesta said. "And that there were Huambisas with them. But her information wasn't worth very much. Redskins, you know, Señor Reátegui."

"There are Huambisas with them, that's a fact," Dr. Portillo said. "They all agree on that, they've recognized them by their language and the way they dress. The Huambisas are there to do damage, you know how they like to fight. But there's no way of finding out who the white men who lead them are. Two or three, they say."

"One of them is from the mountains, Don Julio," Fabio Cuesta said. "The Achuals told us, they know a little Quechua."

"But even though you can't see it, you've been lucky, Fushía," Aquilino said. "They never caught you. Without those troubles, you could have spent the rest of your life on the island."

"I owe it to the Huambisas," Fushía said; "after you, they're the ones who've helped me the most, old man. And you've seen how I've paid them back."

"But there are more than enough reasons, it isn't good for them or for you to stay on the island," Aquilino said. "You're funny, Fushía. You're sorry to leave Pantacha and the Huambisas, and, on the other hand, what you've done doesn't seem bad to you."

That was proved without a doubt too, old friend: the purchases of rubber in the region have not decreased, they have even increased in Bagua, in spite of the fact that they sold less than half of what they did before. Because the bandits were very sharp, Señor Reátegui, was he aware what they were doing? They were selling far from the scene of their robberies, doubtless by means of third parties. What did they care about selling the rubber very cheaply, since they had got it for nothing. No, no, old friend, the administrators of the Mortgage Bank had not seen any new faces, the suppliers were the same ones as always. They handled things well, the slick devils, they took no risks. They probably got hold of a couple of bosses who would buy what they stole at a low price and resell it to the bank. Since they were established, there was no way to stop them.

"Was so much danger for such little return worth it all?" Aquilino asked. "I really don't think so, Fushía."

"But it wasn't my fault," Fushía said. "I couldn't work like other people, the police weren't after them, I had to grab any deal I ran across."

"Whenever they spoke to me about you, I would break into a cold sweat," Aquilino said. "What would they have done to you if they'd caught you among the tribes, Fushía? But maybe it would have been worse if the bosses had caught you. I don't know who wanted you more."

"One thing, old man, man to man," Fushía said. "Now you can open up to me. Didn't you ever take a little commission?"

"Not a single cent," Aquilino said. "My word as a Christian."

"It's something that doesn't make sense, old man," Fushía said. "I know you're not lying to me, but I can't get it through my head, honestly. I would have done it to you, do you know that?"

"Of course I do," Aquilino said. "You would have robbed me blind."

"We've made reports to police headquarters all over the region," Dr. Portillo said. "But that's as good as nothing. Take the plane to Lima and bring in the Army, Julio. That would give them a scare."

"The Colonel said that he'd be only too glad to help, Señor Reátegui," Fabio Cuesta said. "He was only waiting for orders. And I'll help too from Santa María de Nieva in whatever way I can. By the way, Don Julio, they all remember you there with love."

"Why have you stopped?" Fushía asked. "It isn't nighttime yet."

"Because I'm tired," Aquilino said. "We'll sleep on that small beach. And besides didn't you see the sky? It's going to rain in a couple of minutes."

At the extreme north end of the city there is a small square. It is very old, and at one time its benches were of polished wood and shiny metal. The shade of a few slender carob trees fell upon them, and in the shelter the old men of the neighborhood would receive the morning heat and watch the children run about the fountain: a stone circumference which had in its center, on tiptoe, her hands held out as if about to fly, a lady wrapped in veils from whose hair the water flowed. The benches are cracked now, the fountain empty, the beautiful woman has a scar that splits her face, and the carobs are bent over, dying.

Antonia used to go to that little square to play whenever the Quirogas came to the city. They lived on La Huaca, one of the largest ranches of Piura, a broad sea at the foot of the mountains. Twice a year, at Christmas and for the June Procession, the Quirogas would travel to the city and install themselves in the large brick house that formed one of the corners of the square, which now bears their name. Don Roberto had a thick mustache, he would munch it softly when he spoke, and his manners were aristocratic. The aggressive sun of the region had respected the features of Doña Lucía, a pale and fragile woman, very religious: she herself made the wreaths that she put on the Virgin's litter when the Procession stopped at the door of her house. On Christmas night, the Quirogas gave a party attended by many important people. There were gifts for all the guests, and at midnight coins rained down from the windows on the beggars and tramps clustered in the street. Dressed in black, the Quirogas would accompany the Procession for its four long hours through the neighborhoods and the suburbs. They led Antonia by the hand, discreetly scolding her when she did not pay attention to the prayers. During their stay in the city, Antonia would appear very early in the small square, and she would play cops-and-robbers and forfeits with the neighborhood children, climb the carob trees, throw clumps of dirt at the stone lady, or bathe in the fountain, naked as a fish.

Who was that child; why were the Quirogas taking care of her? They brought her from La Huaca one June, before she could talk, and Don Roberto told a story that did not convince everybody. The dogs on the ranch had been barking one night, and when, worried, he went out into the entranceway, he found the child on the ground underneath some blankets. The Quirogas did not have any children, and their greedy relatives recommended the orphan asylum; some offered to raise her. But Doña Lucía and Don Roberto did not follow their advice, nor did they accept the offers, nor did they seem to be upset by the gossip. One morning, during a game of rocambor at the Piura Club, Don Roberto announced in an offhand way that they had decided to adopt Antonia legally.

But it did not come to pass, because at the end of that year the Quirogas did not arrive in Piura. It had never happened before: people were nervous. Fearing an accident, on the twenty-fifth of December a group of horsemen rode out on the road to the north.

They found them sixty miles from the city, there where the sand erases tracks and destroys all signs and only desolation and heat reign. The bandits had beaten the Quirogas savagely, and they had stolen their clothes, their horses, their baggage, and the two servants were lying dead too, with pestilential wounds that were writhing with maggots. The sun was still beating down on the bodies and the riders had to shoot to drive off the vultures that were pecking at the little girl. Then they found that she was alive.

"I wonder why she didn't die?" people asked. *"How could she live with her tongue and her eyes pecked out?"*

"Difficult to say," Dr. Pedro Zevallos replied, shaking his head in a puzzled way. *"Perhaps the sun and the sand cauterized the wounds and prevented hemorrhage."*

"Providence," Father García affirmed. *"The mysterious will of God."*

"An iguana must have licked her," the witch doctors in the poor districts said. *"Because its green spittle not only prevents miscarriage but can also dry up wounds."*

The bandits were never found. The best horsemen covered the desert, the most skillful trackers explored the woods, the ravines, they even reached the mountains of Ayabaca, but they could not find them. Time and again, the Chief of Police, the Civil Guard, the Army organized expeditions that searched the most remote villages and settlements. All in vain.

All the districts poured out for the procession that followed behind the caskets of the Quirogas. On the balconies of important people's houses, black crêpe was hung, and the Bishop and the authorities were present at the burial. The misfortune of the Quirogas spread all through the Department, it endured in the stories and fables of Mangachería and Gallinacera.

La Huaca was divided up into many parts and in possession of each was a relative of Don Roberto or Doña Lucía. When she left the hospital, Antonia was taken in by a washerwoman in Gallinacera, Juana Baura, who had worked for the Quirogas. When the girl appeared on the Plaza de Armas, holding a stick to detect obstacles, the women would caress her, give her candy, the men would lift her onto their horses and ride her along the Malecón. Once she was ill and Chápiro Seminario and the other ranchers who drank at the Estrella del Norte had the Municipal Band go with them to Gallinacera and play retreat across from Juana Baura's hut. The day of the Procession, Antonia would march directly behind the litter, and two or three volunteers would form a ring to isolate her from the tumult. The girl had a docile, taciturn air, which endeared her to people.

They had seen them already, Captain, Corporal Roberto Delgado points at the top of the hill, they had already gone to give the alarm: the boats land one after the other, the eleven men jump ashore, two men tie the craft to some stones. Julio Reátegui takes a drink from his canteen, Captain Artemio Quiroga takes off his shirt, sweat has soaked the shoulders, the back, and he wrings it out, Don Julio, this damned heat was going to cook their brains.

Swarms of mosquitoes besiege the group and up above they can hear barking: there they came, Captain, he should look up. They all raise their eyes: clouds of dust and many heads have appeared at the top of the hill. The outlines of pale torsos slide down now along the sandy slope, and among the legs of the Urakusas, noisy and scampering, the dogs bare their teeth. Julio Reátegui turns toward the soldiers, come on, they should wave to them and you, Corporal, lower your head, stay behind, they must not recognize you, and Corporal Roberto Delgado yes, Governor, he had already seen him, there was Jum, Captain. The eleven men wave their hands, and some smile. There are more and more Urakusas on the slope; they come down, almost squatting, gesticulating, shrieking, the women are the liveliest, and the Captain were they coming to meet them, Don Julio?, because he didn't trust them at all. No, nothing like that, Captain, couldn't he see how peacefully they were coming down? Julio Reátegui knew them, the important thing was to gain their confidence, to let them alone, Corporal, which one was Jum? The one in front, sir, the one who had his hand raised, and Julio Reátegui on guard: they would run like deer, Captain, all of them should not get away, and most of all very careful with Jum. Piled up on the edge of the drop, on a narrow flat spot, semi-naked, just as excited as the dogs who were jumping, chasing their tails, and barking, the Urakusas watch the expeditionaries, point at them, whisper. Mingled with the odors of the river, the earth, and the trees, there is now a smell of human flesh, of skins tattooed with annatto. The Urakusas beat their arms, their chests, rhythmically, and all at once a man crosses the dusty barrier, that was him, Captain, that one, and advances, strong and energetic, toward the shore. The others follow him, and Julio Reátegui that he was the Governor of Santa María de Nieva, interpreter, that he had come to talk to him. A soldier comes forward, grunts, and gestures gracefully, the Urakusas halt. The strong man assents, makes a slow circular sign with his hand, indicating to the expeditionaries that they should approach, they do so, and Julio Reátegui: Jum of Urakusa? The strong man opens his arms, Jum!, he takes a breath: Piruvians! The Captain and the soldiers look at each other, Julio Reátegui nods, takes another step toward Jum, they are a yard apart. Slowly, calmly staring at the Urakusa, Julio Reátegui unhooks the flashlight from his belt, grips it with his whole fist, raises it slowly, Jum reaches out his hand to receive it. Reátegui hits him: shouts, running, dust covering everything, the Captain's bellowing voice. Among the howling and the dust clouds, green and ochre bodies run about, fall, get up, and like a silver-plated bird, the flashlight pecks once, twice, three times. Then the breeze clears up the beach, dissolves the dust, carries away the shouts. The soldiers are deployed in a circle, their rifles pointed at a centipede of Urakusas curled together, fastened to each other. A small girl is sobbing, clinging to Jum's legs, and he is covering his face. His eyes watch the soldiers through his fingers, Reátegui, the Captain, and the wound on his forehead has begun to bleed. Captain Quiroga twirls his revolver on his finger, Governor, had he heard what he had shouted at them? Piruvians must have meant Peruvians, right? And Julio Reátegui wondered where the fellow had got that little word, Captain: the best thing would be to drive them up the hill, they would be better off in the village than here, and the Captain yes, there would be fewer mosquitoes: he had heard, interpreter, order them, make them go up. The soldier grunts and gesticulates, the circle opens, the centipede begins to walk, heavy and compact, small clouds of dust are raised again. Corporal Roberto Delgado begins to laugh: he had recognized him now, Captain, he was eating him up with his eyes. And the Captain Jum too, Corporal, what was he waiting for, he should go up. The Corporal pushes Jum, and the Urakusa advances very stiffly, his hands still over his face. The little girl is clinging to his legs, she is hindering his movements, and the Corporal grabs her by the hair, pulls, tries to separate her—let go, you—from the chief and she resists, scratches, shrieks like a little monkey, shit, the Corporal slaps her, and Julio Reátegui what the hell's the matter: was that any way to treat a child, God damn it?, what was the matter with him, God damn it? The Corporal lets her go, sir, he didn't want to hit her, just make her let go of Jum, he should not be upset, sir, and besides she had scratched him.

"You can hear the harp now," Lituma said. "Or am I dreaming, champs?"

"We can all hear it, cousin," José said. "Or maybe we're all dreaming."

Monk was listening, his head tilted, his eyes large and showing wonderment:

"What an artist! Don't you agree that he's the best there is?"

"No, it's too bad, he's too old now," José said. "His eyes aren't good any more, cousin. He never walks by himself, the Kid and Jocko have to lead him by the arm."

Chunga's house is behind the stadium, just before the vacant space between the city and the Grau barracks, not far from the underbrush of the gunnings. There, in that place, with its parched grass and soft earth, beneath the knotty limbs of the carob, drunken soldiers station themselves at dawn and at dusk. Washerwomen coming back from the river, servant girls from the Buenos Aires district on their way to market are caught by groups of soldiers and thrown down on the sand, their skirts are lifted over their heads, their legs are opened, and one after another the soldiers have them and run away. Piurans call the victim a knockdown, the operation gunning, and the resulting heir is called son of a knockdown, son of a gun, seven-creamer.

"God damn the day I went into the jungle," Lituma said. "If I'd stayed here, I would have married Lira and I would have been a happy man."

"Not that happy, cousin," José said. "You ought to see what Lira looks like now."

"A milk cow," Monk said. "A belly like a bass drum."

"And she breeds like a rabbit," José said. "She must have ten kids by now."

"One a whore and the other one a cow," Lituma said. "I sure can pick women, champ."

"Look, pal, you promised me and now you're going back on your word," Josefino said. "Piss on the past. If not, we won't go to Chunga's with you. You will take it easy, won't you?"

"Just what we said, I promise," Lituma said. "I was only kidding just now."

"Can't you see that the least little thing gets you worked up, old buddy?" Josefino said. "You've got a record now, Lituma. They'll lock you up again, and this time God knows for how long."

"You really do worry about me, Josefino," Lituma said.

Between the stadium and the empty stretch, a quarter of a mile from the road that leaves Piura and then branches into two straight black surfaces that cross the desert, one toward Paita, the other toward Sullana, there is a cluster of huts built of adobe, tin cans, and cardboard, a suburb that is not as old or as broad as Mangachería, poorer, flimsier, and it is there that Chunga's house rises up, singular and central, like a cathedral. It is also called the Green House. Tall, solid, its walls of brick and its galvanized iron roof can be seen from the stadium. On Saturday night during boxing matches, the spectators can hear Jocko's cymbals, Don Anselmo's harp, Kid Alejandro's guitar.

"I swear I used to hear it, Monk," Lituma said. "Very clear, it was enough to split my head in two. The way I hear it now, Monk."

"They must have given you an awful hard time, cousin," Monk said.

"I'm not talking about Lima, I'm talking about Santa María de Nieva," Lituma said. "Nights like death, Monk, when I was on guard duty. No one to talk to. The guys would be snoring, and all at once I wouldn't be hearing the frogs or the crickets any more, I'd hear the harp. I never heard it in Lima."

The night was cool and clear; sketched out on the sand here and there were the twisted outlines of the carob trees. They were walking in single file, Josefino rubbing his hands, the Leóns whistling, and Lituma, his head down, his hands in his pockets, would sometimes raise his face and scrutinize the sky with a kind of fury.

"Let's have a race, like when we were kids," Monk said. "Ready, set, go."

He took off, his small simian figure disappearing into the shadows. José dodged invisible objects, he began to run, he ran in front of Lituma and Josefino.

"Cane liquor is noble and pisco is tricky!" he roared. "And when are we going to sing the theme song?"

When they were already close to the place, they found Monk lying on his back, puffing like an ox. They helped him up.

"My heart's ready to burst. Jesus, I can't believe it."

"The years don't go by for nothing, cousin," Lituma said.

"But long live Mangachería," José said.

Chunga's house is like a cube and it has two doors. The main one opens into the square room, a broad dance floor whose walls are covered with names and emblems: hearts, arrows, busts, female sexes like half moons, crossed by pricks. Also photographs of actors and actresses, boxers, models, a calendar, a panoramic view of the city. The other one, a low and narrow door, opens into the bar, separated from the dance floor by a counter, behind which there is Chunga, a straw rocking chair, and a table covered with bottles, glasses, and jugs. And opposite the bar, in a corner, there are the musicians. Don Anselmo, settled on a bench, uses the wall as a back rest and holds the harp between his legs. He wears glasses, his hair falls down over his forehead, it can be seen between the buttons on his shirt, coming out of his collar, and there are gray tufts in his ears. The one who plays guitar and has such a melodious voice is the shy, laconic Kid Alejandro, who is a composer as well as a singer. The one sitting in the fibre chair and manipulating the drum and cymbals, the least artist, the most muscular of the three, is Jocko, the ex-truck driver.

"Don't hold me like that, don't be afraid," Lituma said. "I'm not doing anything, can't you see? Just looking for her. What's wrong with wanting to see her? Let go of me."

"It'll go away, cousin," Monk said. "What do you care? Think about something else. Let's have a good time and celebrate your coming back."

"I'm not doing anything," Lituma repeated. "Just remembering. Why are you holding on to me like that, champs?"

They were on the edge of the dance floor, under the thick light that was pouring out of three lamps that were covered with blue, green, and violet cellophane, facing a dense mass of couples. Hazy groups filled the corners, and shouts, laughter, the clink of glasses came from them. A motionless, transparent smoke was floating between the ceiling and the dancers' heads, and there was a smell of beer, sweat, and dark tobacco. Lituma was swaying where he stood, Josefino still holding him by the arm, but the Leóns had let go of him.

"Which table was it, Josefino? That one?"

"That's the one, old buddy. But that's all over now, you're starting a new life. Forget about all that."

"Go say hello to the harp player, cousin," Monk said. "And to the Kid and Jocko, who always remembered you with love."

"But I can't see her," Lituma said. "Why is she hiding from me? I'm not going to do anything to her, just look at her."

"I'll take care of it, Lituma," Josefino said. "I give you my word I'll get her. But you have to do your part; piss on the past. Go say hello to the old man. I'll go look for her."

The orchestra had stopped playing; the couples on the dance floor were now a dense mass, motionless and buzzing. Someone at the bar was arguing and shouting. Lituma stumbled over to the musicians, good old Don Anselmo, with his arms open, old man, harp player, escorted by the two Leóns, don't you remember me?

"He can't see you, cousin," José said. "Tell him who you are. Make a guess, Don Anselmo."

"What?" Chunga stood up with a jerk and the rocking chair kept on moving. "The Sergeant? You brought him here?"

"We couldn't get out of it, Chunga," Josefino said. "He got in today and he got stubborn, we couldn't hold him back. But he knows all about it and he doesn't give a shit."

Lituma was in Don Anselmo's arms, the Kid and Jocko were slapping him on the back, the three of them were all talking at once, and they could be heard from the bar, excited, surprised, emotional. Monk had sat down at the cymbals and was making them clang, José was examining the harp.

"Or I'll call the police," Chunga said. "Get him out of here right now."

"He's drunk as a lord, Chunga, he can hardly walk, can't you see?" Josefino said. "We'll take care of him, there won't be any trouble, I promise."

"The bunch of you are bad luck for me," Chunga said. "You most of all, Josefino. But what happened the last time won't happen again, I swear. I'll call the police."

"No trouble, Chunguita," Josefino said. "I give you my word. Is Wildflower upstairs?"

"Where else would she be?" Chunga said. "But if there's any trouble, you mother-fucker, I swear."

2

"I feel good here, Don Adrián," the Sergeant said. "This is what the nights are like where I come from. Warm and clear."

"There's no place like the jungle," Nieves said. "Paredes was in the mountains last year, and he came back saying it was too sad, not a single tree, just rocks and clouds."

The moon, very high, was lighting up the terrace, and there were many stars in the sky and on the river; behind the woods, a soft palisade of shadows, the abutments of the Andes were purple hulks. Below the cabin, among the reeds and ferns, the frogs were splashing about, and inside could be heard Lalita's voice, the crackling of the fire. In the garden plot, the dogs were barking loudly: they were fighting over rats, Sergeant, the way they hunted them, if he could only see. They would lie down under the banana trees and act as if they were asleep, and when one of them got close, voom, by the neck. The pilot had taught them that.

"In Cajamarca the people eat cavies," the Sergeant said. "They serve them with the nails, eyes, and whiskers on. They're just like rats."

"Lalita and I took a long trip through the jungle once," Nieves said. "We had to eat rats. The meat smells bad, but it's soft and white like a fish. Aquilino got poisoned, he almost died on us."

"Was the older one's name Aquilino?" the Sergeant asked. "The one with little Chinese eyes?"

"That's the one, Sergeant," Nieves said. "Do you have many local dishes in your town?"

The Sergeant raised his head, oh, Don Adrián, he looked ecstatic for a few seconds, if he were to go into a Mangache chili house and try a seco de chabelo. He would die of pleasure, his word, nothing in the world compared to it, and Nieves the pilot agreed: there was nothing like a person's home town. Didn't the Sergeant ever get an urge to go back to Piura? Yes, all the time, but a person could not do what he wanted to when he was poor, Don Adrián: had he been born here, in Santa María de Nieva?

"Farther down," the pilot said. "Where the Marañón is very wide and when there's fog you can't see the other side. But it didn't take me long to get used to Nieva."

"Dinner is ready," Lalita said, from the window. Her long hair cascaded down over the sill and her robust arms looked wet. "Would you like to eat outside there, Sergeant?"

"I would, if it's no trouble," the Sergeant said. "I feel like back home in your house, Ma'am. Except that our river is a lot smaller and it doesn't even run all the time. And instead of trees we have sand dunes."

"That doesn't sound like here at all," Lalita said, laughing. "But I'm sure that Piura must be pretty the way it is here too."

"He means that they have the same heat there, the same sounds," Nieves said. "The land doesn't mean anything to women, Sergeant."

"I was only joking," Lalita said. "But you weren't annoyed, Sergeant?"

What an idea, he liked jokes, it made people friendlier, and, by the way, the lady was from Iquitos, wasn't she? Lalita looked at Nieves, from Iquitos? and for an instant she showed her face: metallic skin, sweat, marks. The Sergeant had thought so from the way she talked, Ma'am.

"She left there a long time ago," Nieves said. "Strange that you should notice her singsong."

"I have a good ear, like all Mangaches," the Sergeant said. "I was a good singer when I was a boy, Ma'am."

Lalita had heard that northerners played the guitar well and that they were goodhearted, right?, and the Sergeant, of course: no woman could resist the songs of his people, Ma'am. In Piura, when a man fell in love, he would go get his friends, they took out their guitars, and the girl was won over with serenades. There were great musicians there, Ma'am, he knew a lot of them, an old man who played the harp, a real wonder, he composed waltzes, and Adrián Nieves indicated to Lalita the interior of the hut: wasn't she coming out? Lalita shrugged her shoulders:

"She's bashful, she doesn't want to come out," she said. "She won't pay any attention to me. Bonifacia is like a little deer, Sergeant, she pricks up her ears and gets frightened at everything."

"At least she ought to come out and say hello to the Sergeant," Nieves said.

"Leave her alone for now," the Sergeant said. "She doesn't have to come out if she doesn't want to."

"You can't change your life so fast," Lalita said. "She's only been with women, and the poor thing is afraid of men. She says they're all vipers, the sisters must have taught her that. Now she's gone off to hide in the garden."

"They're afraid of men until they try them," Nieves said. "Then they change, then they eat men up alive."

Lalita sank back into the house, and a moment later her voice came back: it hadn't happened to her, slightly annoyed, she had never been afraid of men and she did not eat them up, who was he talking about, Adrián? The pilot gave a loud laugh and leaned toward the Sergeant: she was a good woman, Lalita, but, and that was certain, she did have her ways. Small, quite thin, with light skin and large and lively eyes, Aquilino came out onto the terrace, good evening, he was bringing the lamp because it was getting dark, and he put it on the railing. After him, two other children—short pants, straight hair, barefoot—brought out a small table. The Sergeant called them over, and as he tickled them and laughed with them, Lalita and Nieves brought out fruit, smoked fish, cassavas, how good it all looked, Ma'am, some bottles of anisette. The pilot served the three boys, and they went off in the direction of the small stairs leading up to the garden plot: you've got nice churres, Don Adrián, that's what they called children in Piura, Ma'am, and the Sergeant, generally, liked kids.

"Your health, Sergeant," Nieves said. "It's good to have you with us."

"Bonifacia is afraid of everything, but she's a good worker," Lalita said. "She helps me in the garden and she knows how to cook. And she sews quite well. Did you see the boys' shorts? She made them, Sergeant."

"But you have to give her some advice," the pilot said. "Timid the way she is, she'll never get a husband. You don't know how quiet she is, Sergeant, she only opens her mouth when we ask her something."

"That sounds fine to me," the Sergeant said. "I don't like parrots."

"Well, I think you'll like Bonifacia, then," Lalita said. "She can go all day without saying boo."

"I'll let you in on a secret, Sergeant," Nieves said. "Lalita wants to marry Bonifacia off to you. That's what she's been saying to me, that's why she had me invite you. Watch out, while there's still time."

The Sergeant put on an expression that was half smiling and half nostalgic; Ma'am, he was all set to get married right away. When he joined the Civil Guard, he'd just found a woman who was in love with him, and he loved her a little too. What was her name?, Lira, what happened?, nothing, Ma'am, he was transferred out of Piura and Lira wouldn't go with him, and that was how the romance ended.

"Bonifacia would go anywhere with her man," Lalita said. "We jungle women are like that, we don't make any conditions. You have to marry someone from here, Sergeant."

"You can see now how when Lalita gets something into her head, she won't stop until she brings it off," Nieves said. "Women from Loreto are bandits, Sergeant."

"You're nice people," the Sergeant said. "They told me in Santa María de Nieva that the Nieveses keep to themselves, that they never get together with anybody. And still, Ma'am, for all the time I've been here, you're the first people who've invited me into their home."

"The fact is that nobody likes the soldiers, Sergeant," Lalita said. "Haven't you seen how abusive they are? They ruin the girls, they make love to them, they get them pregnant, and then they're ordered somewhere else."

"Then why do you want to marry Bonifacia off to the Sergeant?" Nieves asked. "The two things don't go together."

"Didn't you tell me that the Sergeant was different?" Lalita said. "But who can tell whether you're right or not?"

"It's true," the Sergeant said. "I'm a straight man, a good Christian, as they say here. And a friend like you can't find. You'll see. I'm really very grateful to you, Don Adrián, because I feel right at home in your house."

"You can come back any time you want to," Nieves said. "Come and visit Bonifacia. But don't get mixed up with Lalita, because I'm a very jealous man."

"And you should be, Don Adrián," the Sergeant said. "Your wife is so good-looking that I'd be jealous too."

"Thank you for the compliment, Sergeant," Lalita said. "But I can tell that you're just saying it to say something. I'm not good-looking any more. I used to be when I was young."

"But you're still just a girl," the Sergeant protested.

"I don't trust you any more," Nieves said. "It would be better if you came by only when I'm home, Sergeant."

In the garden, the dogs were still barking, and the boys' voices could be heard at times. Insects were flying around the resin lamp, the Nieveses and the Sergeant were drinking, chatting, joking, Pilot Nieves!, the three of them turned their heads toward the foliage on the bank: the night hid the trail that went up to Santa María de Nieva. Pilot Nieves! And the Sergeant: it was Fats, the fathead, what was the matter with him, what was he doing bothering them at this time, Don Adrián? The three boys burst out onto the terrace. Aquilino went over to the pilot and said something to him in a low voice: that he should go up there.

"It seems that we have to make a trip, Sergeant," Nieves the pilot said.

"He's probably drunk," the Sergeant said. "Don't pay any attention to Fats, when he's been drinking he gets ideas."

The staircase creaked, behind Aquilino Fats's broad outline appeared, well, Sergeant, he'd found him at last, the Lieutenant and the boys were looking for him everywhere, and good evening, everyone.

"I'm off duty," the Sergeant grumbled. "What do they want me for?"

"They've found the pupils," Fats said. "A team of lumbermen, near a camp upriver. A messenger came to the Mission a couple of hours ago. The sisters have everybody all excited, Sergeant. It seems that one of the children has a fever."

Fats was in his shirt sleeves, fanning himself with his cap, and now Lalita was bombarding him with questions. The pilot and the Sergeant had stood up, yes, what a mess, Ma'am, they'd have to go get them right away. They'd wanted to wait until tomorrow, but the nuns convinced Don Fabio and the Lieutenant, and the Sergeant were they going to leave at night? Yes, Sergeant, the sisters were afraid that the lumbermen would do something to the older ones.

"The sisters are right," Lalita said. "The poor things, so many days in the jungle. Hurry up, Adrián, get ready."

"What else can we do," the pilot said. "Have a drink with the Sergeant while I go put some gas in the boat."

"I could use one, thanks," Fats said. "What a life, right, Sergeant? I'm sorry I broke in on you in the middle of your meal."

"Did they find them all?" a voice from behind the wall said. They looked: short hair, a hazy profile, a female breast outlined beside the window. The light of the lamp barely reached in there.

"All except two," Fats said, leaning toward the window. "All except the ones from Chicais."

"Why didn't they bring them back instead of sending a message?" Lalita asked. "But at least they found them, thank God, they found them."

There was no way for them to bring them, Ma'am, and Fats and the Sergeant stretched their necks toward the wall, but the outline had disappeared, and now there was nothing but the fragment of a face, a shadow of hair. On the other side of the veranda, Adrián Nieves was giving orders and the children could be heard stirring up the water, splashing, coming and going in the ferns. Lalita served them some anisette, and they drank to his health, Sergeant, and the Sergeant better to the lady's health, you dope.

"I know already that the Lieutenant's going to give me this little job," the Sergeant said. "I suppose someone will go with me, right?, to get the kids: who's going with me?"

"Shorty and me," Fats said. "And a nun's going too."

"Sister Angélica?" the voice from the wall asked, and they turned their heads again.

"Most likely, because Sister Angélica knows something about medicine," Fats said. "She can help the one who's sick."

"Give her some quinine," Lalita said. "But one trip won't be enough, they won't all fit in the boat, you'll have to make two or three."

"It's lucky there's a moon," Nieves the pilot said, from the stairs. "I'll be ready in half an hour."

"Go tell the Lieutenant that we're coming, Fats," the Sergeant said.

Fats nodded, said good night, and went off across the terrace. When he passed by the window, the vague outline drew back, disappeared, and reappeared when Fats was already on his way down the stairs, whistling.

"Come, Bonifacia," Lalita said. "I want you to meet the Sergeant."

Lalita took the Sergeant by the arm, led him over to the door, and a few seconds later the shape of a woman emerged in the doorway. The Sergeant put out his hand, observing in confusion some motionless sparks, until a small, dark form cut the half light, fingers brushed against his, pleased to meet you, and ran away: at your orders, Miss. Lalita was smiling.

❦

"I'd thought that he was like you," Fushía said. "And now, you can see, old man, it was a terrible mistake."

"I was fooled a little too," Aquilino said. "I didn't think Adrián Nieves would do a thing like that. He never seemed worried about anything. Didn't anyone notice how it all began?"

"Nobody," Fushía said, "not Pantacha, or Jum, or the Huambisas. God damn those bastards and the day they were born, old man."

"There's hate coming back into your mouth again, Fushía," Aquilino said.

And then Nieves saw it, huddling between the clay jar and the wall: large, velvety, very dark. He got up quite slowly from beside the fire, his hand groped, clothes, some rubber shoes, a cord, gourds, a chambira basket, none of it was any good. It was still there in the corner, crouching, obviously watching him under its thin jet-black legs, its reflection like a vine on the reddish curve of the jar. He took a step, took down his machete, and it had not fled, it was lying in wait, carefully watching his every movement with its perverse little eyes, its red belly throbbing. He advanced toward the corner on tiptoe, it drew back in sudden fright, he struck, and it was like the crunch of a branch. Then there was a stripe and spots on the mat wall, black and red; the legs were intact, the fur was black and long and silky. Nieves hung up the machete, and, instead of going back to the fire, he stayed by the window, smoking. On his face he received the breath and sounds of the jungle, he took the lighted end of his cigarette and tried to burn the wings of the bats that were flying about the screen.

"Were they ever alone together on the island?" Aquilino asked.

"Once, because that son of a bitch got sick," Fushía said. "But that was still at the beginning. That business couldn't have started then, they wouldn't have dared to, they were afraid of me."

"Can you ever be afraid of anything more than of hell?" Aquilino asked. "And still people will do evil things. Fear can't stop people from everything, Fushía."

"Nobody's ever seen hell," Fushía said. "And they saw me every day."

"More than anything else, when white people get the urge there's no one who can stop them," Aquilino said. "Their bodies burn as if there was a fire inside. Hasn't it ever happened to you?"

"No woman ever made me feel like that," Fushía said. "But I do now, old man, I do now. As if I had hot coals under my skin, old man."

On the right, among the trees, Nieves could make out campfires, sudden outlines of Huambisas; on the left, however, where Jum had his hut, everything was dark. Up above, against an indigo sky, the crowns of the lupunas were swaying and the moon lit up the path that went down a slope with bushes and ferns, twisting alongside the turtle pool, and on down to the shore; the trail was probably blue, quiet, and deserted. Was the water from the pool still flowing down? Were the stakes and the net dry now? Soon the turtles would appear, stranded on the sand, their wrinkled necks stretching out up toward the sky, their eyes full of asphyxiation and rheum, and he would have to make them come out of their shells with the edge of his machete, cut the white meat into quarters, and salt them before the sun and the dampness could make them rot. Nieves threw his cigarette away and was going over to blow out the lamp when there was a knock on the wall. He lifted up the bolt of the door, and Lalita came in, wrapped in a Huambisa itípak, her hair down to her waist, barefoot.

"If I had to pick out one of them to get my revenge on, it would have to be her, Aquilino," Fushía said, "that bitch. Because she started it all, obviously, when she saw that I was sick."

"You didn't treat her right, you beat her, and besides women have their pride, Fushía," Aquilino said. "What civilized woman would have stood for it? Every trip, you brought back a woman and showed her off right under her nose."

"Do you think she was mad because of the squaws?" Fushía said. "That's foolish, old man. That bitch got hot because I couldn't make it with her any more."

"You'd better not talk about that," Aquilino said. "I know how it makes you sad."

"But that's how it all started, not being able to make it with Lalita," Fushía said. "But maybe you can't see what bad luck it was, Aquilino, how terrible it was."

"Did I wake you up?" Lalita asked, in a dreamy voice.

"No, you didn't wake me up," Nieves said. "Good evening. What can I do for you?"

He latched the door, hitched up his pants, and crossed his arms over his bare torso, but he uncrossed them at once and stood there, indecisive. Finally he pointed at the clay jar: a tarantula had got in and he had just killed it. He'd plugged up the holes only a week ago, Lalita sat down on the edge of the fireplace, but they opened up new ones every day, the tarantulas.

"They're hungry," Lalita said. "It's like that this time of year. Once I woke up and I couldn't move my leg, I tell you. There was a mark on it and then it swelled up. The Huambisas had me put my leg over some hot coals to make it sweat. I've still got the scar."

Her hands went down to the hem of the itípak, lifted it up, her thighs appeared, smooth, dull-colored, firm, and there was a scar like a small worm:

"What are you scared of?" Lalita asked. "Why are you turning away, tell me?"

"I'm not scared," Nieves said. "It's just that you're naked and I'm a man."

Lalita laughed and took off her itípak; her right foot was playing with a gourd, she caressed it distractedly with her instep, her toes, her heel.

"Bitch, whore, worse things, if you want," Aquilino said. "But I like Lalita and I don't care. She's like a daughter to me."

"Someone who does that because she can see her man dying is worse than a bitch, worse than a whore," Fushía said. "There's no word for what she is."

"Dying? In San Pablo most of them die of old age and not because they're sick, Fushía," Aquilino said.

"You're not saying that to console me, but because you don't like it when I insult her."

"He told you in front of me," Nieves whispered. "Nothing on under your itípak again and I'll let you be eaten by the taranganants; do you still remember?"

"Other times he says I'll give you to the Huambisas, I'll gouge your eyes out," Lalita said. "All the time to Pantacha I'll kill you, you're spying on her. When he makes a threat, he doesn't do anything, he just lets himself go with his words. Do you get upset when he beats me, tell me?"

"Mad too." Nieves slowly stroked the bolt on the door. "Especially when he insults you."

He was even worse when they were alone, agh, your teeth are falling out, agh, your face is all broken up, agh, you're dripping, pretty soon you'll be like an old Huambisa woman, agh, and everything else he could think of, does it upset you?, and Nieves be quiet.

"But she believed in you and she thought she knew you," Aquilino said. "I would get back to the island, and Lalita he'll take me away from here soon, if there's a lot of rubber this year we'll go to Ecuador and get married. Be nice, Don Aquilino, sell the stuff for a good price. Poor Lalita."

"She didn't take off before, because she hoped I'd get rich," Fushía said. "How dumb can you be, old man? I didn't marry her when she was nice and tight and didn't have any pimples, and she thought I was going to marry her when she wasn't able to get anybody hot any more."

"She got Adrián Nieves hot," Aquilino said. "If not, he wouldn't have run off with her."

"And is the boss going to take them to Ecuador with him too?" Nieves asked. "Is he going to marry them too?"

"I'm his woman and only me," Lalita said. "The other ones are just servants."

"Anything you say, I know how it hurts you," Nieves said. "You wouldn't have a soul if it didn't hurt you when someone brought other women home."

"He doesn't bring them home," Lalita said. "They sleep in the corral with the animals."

"But he makes it with them in front of you," Nieves said. "Don't act as if you don't know what I'm talking about."

He looked at her again and Lalita edged closer to the corner of the fireplace, she had her knees together, her eyes were lowered, and Nieves did not want to offend her, he stammered and looked out the window again, it had made him angry when she said she was going to Ecuador with the boss, the indigo skies, the campfires, the sparkling fire beetles in the ferns: he asked her to forgive him, he had not meant to offend her, and Lalita raised her eyes:

"Doesn't he give them to you and Pantacha when he doesn't like them?" she asked. "You do the same things he does."

"I'm single," Nieves babbled. "A civilized man has to have women, why compare me to Pantacha, besides I like the way you use the familiar form with me."

"Only at first, taking advantage of my trips," Fushía said. "She'd scratch them, she made one of the Achuals bleed. But then she got used to it and they got to be friends. She taught them how to talk like white people, and she had fun with them. It's not the way you think, old man."

"And you complain just the same," Aquilino said. "Everybody's dreamed about having what you've had. How many people do you know who could change off women like that, Fushía?"

"But they were only squaws," Fushía said, "squaws, Aquilino, Aguarunas, Achuals, Shapras, real dirt, man."

"And just like animals too," Lalita said, "they get their loving with me. I'm sorry because they're afraid of the Huambisas. If you were the boss, you'd be just like him; you'd even insult me."

"Do you know me well enough to judge me?" Nieves asked. "I wouldn't do that to my woman. All the less if it was you."

"Their bodies get loose so fast here," Fushía said. "Is it my fault if Lalita got old? And besides it would have been stupid for me to miss any opportunity."

"That's why you stole them so young," Aquilino said. "So that they'd be nice and tight, isn't that it?"

"Not just that," Fushía said; "I like virgins like any other man. It's just that those bastardly heathens don't let them grow up with it on, even on the youngest of them they've already broken it, that Shapra was the only one I found who still had one."

"The only thing that hurts me is remembering what I was like back in Iquitos," Lalita said. "White and even teeth, not a single spot on my face."

"You like to invent things that make you suffer," Nieves said. "Why doesn't the boss let the Huambisas get close to this side of the place? Because they all stare at you when you go by."

"Pantacha and you too," Lalita said. "But not because I'm pretty, just because I'm the only white woman here."

"I'm always on my best behavior with you," Nieves said. "Why compare me to Pantacha?"

"You're better than Pantacha," Lalita said. "That's why I've come to see you. Are you all over your fever?"

"Don't you remember that I didn't come down to the dock to meet you?" Fushía said. "That you came and got me in the rubber shack? That was it, old man."

"Yes, I remember," Aquilino said. "You seemed to be asleep when you were awake. I thought that Pantacha had given you some drug."

"And don't you remember that I got drunk on the anisette you brought?" Fushía said.

"I remember that too," Aquilino said. "You wanted to set fire to the Huambisas' huts. You were like a devil, we had to tie you down."

"It's because I'd tried for ten days and I couldn't make it with that bitch," Fushía said. "Not with Lalita or with any of the squaws either, old man, enough to drive a person crazy. I'd go off and cry all by myself, old man, I wanted to kill myself, anything. Ten days in a row and I couldn't make it with them, Aquilino."

"Don't cry, Fushía," Aquilino said. "Why didn't you tell me what was going on? Maybe you could have been cured back then. We could have gone to Bagua, the doctor would have given you some shots."

"And my legs would go to sleep, old man," Fushía said. "I would hit them and I couldn't feel anything, I'd put matches to them and it was as if they were dead, old man."

"Don't get sad now over those sad things," Aquilino said. "Look, come over here to the edge and look at all the flying fish, the electric ones. See how they follow us, the sparks look pretty up in the air and under the water."

"And later on welts, old man," Fushía said, "and I couldn't get undressed in front of that bitch any more. Having to fake all day, all night, with nobody to tell, Aquilino, having to take it all by myself."

And then there was a scratching on the wall and Lalita stood up. She went to the window, and with her face up against the screen she began to grunt. Outside someone was grunting too, softly.

"Aquilino is sick," Lalita said. "He's been vomiting up everything he eats, poor fellow. I'm going to see him. If the boss hasn't come back by tomorrow, I'll come and fix your meal."

"Let's hope he's not back," Nieves said. "I don't need your cooking, all I want is for you to come and see me."

"If I can use the familiar form with you, you can with me," Lalita said. "At least when nobody's around."

"I could catch them by the bucketful, if I had a net, Fushía," Aquilino said. "Do you want me to help you up so you can see them?"

"And then my feet," Fushía said. "Limping around, old man, and then shedding my skin like a snake, but they get a new skin and I didn't, old man, I was just one big sore. Aquilino, it's not right, it's not right."

"I know it's not right," Aquilino said. "But come over here, man, look how pretty the electric fish are."

Every day, Juana Baura and Antonia would leave Gallinacera at the same time, always following the same route. Two straight dusty blocks and they were at the market: the market women would be laying out their blankets underneath the carob trees and putting their wares in order. When they got to the store called Las Maravillas —combs, perfume, blouses, petticoats, ribbons, and earrings—they would turn left, and two hundred yards ahead there was the Plaza de Armas, an open space encircled by palm trees and tamarinds. They would arrive by the street opposite the Estrella del Norte. During their walk, one of Juana Baura's hands would be waving at friends, the other on Antonia's arm. When they reached the square, Juana looked over the wooden benches and picked the one with the most shade for the girl. If the girl seemed relaxed, the washerwoman would quietly trot back home, untie her donkey, gather together the clothes to be washed, and set out for the river. If, on the other hand, Antonia's hands were anxiously clutching hers, Juana would sit down beside her and calm her with caresses. She would repeat her silent questions until the girl let her leave. She would come back for her at noon, when the clothes had been scrubbed, and sometimes Antonia rode back to Gallinacera on a donkey. It was not unusual for Juana Baura to find the girl walking around the bandstand with some sympathetic person, or for a bootblack, a beggar, or Jacinto to tell her: they took her to So-and-So's house, to church, to the Malecón. Then Juana Baura would go back to Gallinacera alone, and Antonia would appear at dusk, led by the maid of some charitable important person.

That day they had left earlier, Juana Baura had to bring a full-dress uniform over to the Grau barracks. The market was deserted, a few buzzards were dozing on the roof of Las Maravillas. The sweepers had not come by yet and the garbage and puddles gave off a stench. A timid breeze was blowing across the empty Plaza de Armas and the sun was rising into a cloudless sky. The sand had stopped falling. Juana Baura dusted off the bench with her petticoat, saw that the girl's hands were calm, gave her a pat on the cheek, and left. On her way back, she ran into Hermógenes Leandro's wife, from the slaughterhouse, and they continued on together as the sun grew larger in the sky, it was already up to the highest roofs of the city. Juana was hunched over, rubbing her waist from time to time, and her friend you're not well, and she I've had cramps for some time now, especially during the morning. They talked about illnesses and cures, old age, what a burden life was. Then Juana said goodbye, went into her house, came out leading the donkey loaded down with dirty clothes, and under her arm the uniform, wrapped in back numbers of *Ecos y Noticias*. She went to the Grau barracks, skirting the sand, and the earth was hot, quick iguanas would suddenly run between her legs. A soldier came out to meet her, the Lieutenant would be angry, why hadn't she brought the uniform earlier. He grabbed the bundle and paid her, and then she went on to the river. Not to the Old Bridge, where she usually washed, but to a small, round beach, beyond the slaughterhouse, where she found two other washerwomen. And the three of them were there all morning, kneeling in the water, scrubbing, and chatting. Juana finished first, left, and the streets, glowing now under a vertical sun, were filled with townspeople and strangers. Antonia was not in the square, neither the beggars nor Jacinto had seen her, and Juana went back to Gallinacera, her hands would alternately beat the donkey and rub her waist. She began to hang up the clothes, halfway through the work she went to lie down on her straw mattress. When she opened her eyes, the sand was falling. Grumbling, she trotted to the back yard: some things had already been soiled. She pulled out the awning that protected the clotheslines, she finished hanging the clothes, she went back to her room, she looked under the mattress until she found the medicine. She wet a rag with the liquid, she lifted her petticoat, and she vigorously rubbed her hips and her stomach. The medicine smelled like vomit and urine. Juana held her nose as she waited for her skin to dry. She prepared some dried vegetables, and as she was eating there was a knock at the door. It was not Antonia, but a servant girl with a basket of clothes. They chatted, standing in the doorway. The small grains of sand were coming down softly and they were invisible, they could be felt on the face and arms like little spider legs. Juana was talking about cramps, about bad medicines, and the servant girl protested he should give you something else or give you your money back. Then she went away, hugging the wall under the eaves. Alone, sitting on her mattress, Juana went on I'm coming to see you on Sunday, do you think that just because I'm old you can fool me?, your medicine makes my waist shiver, you thief. Then she lay down, and when she awoke it had grown dark. She lit a candle, Antonia had not returned. She went out into the yard, the donkey pricked up his ears, he brayed. Juana took a shawl, she threw it over her shoulders, in the street now: it was dark, candles could be seen in the windows of Gallinacera, lamps, fires. She was walking very rapidly, her hair was disheveled, and near the market, out of a doorway, someone said a ghost. She trotted on, you give me some different medicine for the dream I keep on getting or you give me my money back. There were not many people in the square. She went up to all of them and nobody knew. The sand was coming down thick now, visible, and Juana covered her mouth and her nose. She went down several side streets, she knocked on several doors, she repeated the same question over and over, and when she returned to the Plaza de Armas, she ran about laboriously, she leaned against the walls. Two men in straw hats were chatting on a bench. She asked where is Antonia, and Dr. Pedro Zevallos good evening, Doña Juana, what are you doing out on the street at this hour? And the other one, who sounded like a stranger, there's so much sand that it'll split our heads open. Dr. Zevallos took off his hat, held it out to Juana, and she put it on; it was too big, it covered her ears. The Doctor said that she was so tired she couldn't speak, sit down awhile, Doña Juana, tell us all about it, and she where is Antonia. The two men looked at each other, and the other one said it would be best to take her home, and the Doctor yes, I know where it is, in Gallinacera. They took her by the arms, they almost carried her, and under the hat Juana Baura was roaring the blind girl, have you seen her?, and Dr. Zevallos calm yourself, Doña Juana, you tell us all about it when we get there, and the other one what smells so much, and Dr. Zevallos probably the remedy of some healer, poor old woman.

Julio Reátegui wipes his forehead, looks at his interpreter; he had gone against the authorities, that was not right and he would pay for it: translate it for him. The clearing at Urakusa is small and triangular, the woods encircle it closely, boughs and vines sway over the huts that are raised on pona columns and end in circles indented like a duck's tail: the interpreter grunts and gesticulates, Jum listens attentively. There are some twenty huts, identical: roofs of yarina, walls of tucuma strips held together by reeds, small stairways roughly hewn from logs. Two soldiers are chatting in front of the hut filled with Urakusa prisoners, others are raising tents near the embankment, Captain Quiroga is fighting off the mosquitoes, and the girl is quiet beside Corporal Roberto Delgado, sometimes she looks at Jum, she has light eyes and on her boyish torso there is the suggestion of two raised circles. Jum is speaking now, his purple lips explode with harsh and spitting sounds, Julio Reátegui turns aside to avoid the rain of saliva, and the interpreter Corporal stealing, that is, trying to, giving him a beating, shit, and then going away, away, never again, giving him canoe, his own canoe, Jum's canoe, and pilot going away, not seeing, he dived into water, saying, sir. And Corporal Delgado takes a step toward Jum: that's a lie, sir, he was on his way to visit his family in Bagua, would he lose time robbing things from those people?, and what could he steal from them even if he'd wanted to, Captain, couldn't he see what a miserable place Urakusa was? And the Captain: then it wasn't sure whether they killed the recruit. Was it true that he jumped into the Marañón or wasn't it? God damn it, because if he wasn't dead, he was a deserter and the Corporal crosses his fingers and kisses them: they killed him, Captain, and that business about stealing was one big lie. They'd only made a little search, but they were looking for that medicine for mosquito bites that he had told him about and they tied him up and beat him, him and the porter, and they'd probably killed the pilot and buried him so that nobody would find him, Captain. Julio Reátegui smiles at the little girl and she looks at him out of the corner of her eye, frightened?, curious? She has an Aguaruna loincloth on, and her abundant and dusty hair flows softly as she moves her head; she has no adornments on her face or arms, only on her ankles: two tiny gourds. And Julio Reátegui: why hadn't he done business with Pedro Escabino?, why didn't he sell him rubber this year like other times? He should translate that, and the interpreter grunts and gesticulates, Jum listens, his arms crossed, and the Governor motions to the girl that she should come over, she turns her back on him, and the interpreter sir, never again, saying: Escabino devil, go away, away, not Urakusa, saying: not Chicais, no Aguaruna village, boss cheating, sir, and Julio Reátegui what were the Urakusas going to do with the rubber they didn't want to sell to boss Escabino?, softly, still looking at the girl, and what about the pelts?, translate that. The interpreter and Jum grunt, spit, and wave their arms, and now Reátegui is watching them, leaning forward a little toward the Urakusa, and the girl takes a step, looks at Jum's forehead: the wound has swollen but is no longer bleeding, the chief's right eye is all inflamed, and Julio Reátegui cooperative? There was no such word in Aguaruna, boy, did he say cooperative? and the interpreter: he had said it in Spanish, sir, and Captain Quiroga yes, he had heard him. What was that all about, Señor Reátegui? Why weren't they doing business with Escabino any more? Where'd they get the idea to sell their rubber in Iquitos if they never knew there was any Iquitos? Julio Reátegui seems distracted, he shakes his head, he smooths down his hair, he looks at the Captain: for ten years Pedro Escabino had been bringing them cloth, shotguns, knives, Captain, everything they needed to go into the jungle and get rubber. When Escabino returned, they would give him the rubber they had gathered, and he would supply them with cloth, food, whatever they needed, and this year they also got advances, but they refused to sell to him: that was the story, Captain. The soldiers who have set up the tents come over, one reaches out his hand and touches the girl, who jumps, the gourds dance, a jungling sound, and the Captain: so, an abuse of trust, he hadn't known, they beat up a soldier, they cheated a civilian, most likely they had done in the recruit, and the Governor grab her, don't let her get away. Three soldiers run after the girl, who is agile, slippery. They catch her in the center of the clearing, they carry her over to the Governor, he strokes her face: she had a wide-awake look, and there was something graceful about her, didn't the Captain think so?, it was too bad the poor thing had been brought up here, and the officer: that's right, Don Julio, and her eyes were greenish. Was she his daughter?, have him ask him that, and the Captain: she didn't have a swollen belly either, and that was very common in these children, the number of parasites they swallowed, and Corporal Roberto Delgado: small and good-looking, she'd make a good company mascot, Captain, and the soldiers laugh. Was she his daughter?, and the interpreter not being, sir, not Urakusa either, but Aguaruna yes, being born in Pato Huachana, sir, saying, and Julio Reátegui calls two soldiers: they should take her to the tents and very careful not to be rough with her. A soldier takes the girl by the arm and she lets herself be led without resisting. Julio Reátegui turns toward the Captain, who is once more fighting off invisible and perhaps imaginery aerial enemies: some people who said they were teachers had been through here, Captain. They got in among the tribes with a story about teaching Spanish to the Indians, and he had already seen the results, they beat up a Corporal, they ruined Pedro Escabino's business. Could the Captain imagine what would happen if all the Indians decided to cheat the bosses who had given them advances? The Captain scratches his chin gravely: an economic catastrophe? The Governor nods: the outsiders brought on the trouble, Captain. The last time it had been foreigners, some Englishmen, with some story about botanical research; they'd gone into the jungle and come out with seeds from rubber trees, and one fine day the world was full of rubber from the British colonies, cheaper than Peruvian and Brazilian rubber, that had been the ruination of the Amazon region, Captain, and he: was it true, Señor Reátegui, that opera companies used to come to Iquitos and that rubber growers lit their cigars with banknotes? Julio Reátegui smiles, his father had a chef for his dogs, just imagine, and the Captain smiles, the soldiers smile, but Jum is still serious, his arms crossed, sometimes he glances at the hut filled with Urakusa prisoners, and Julio Reátegui smiles: they didn't have to work much then and they made a lot of money, now you had to sweat blood in order to get a few miseries in return, and you always had to fight with these people, take care of such stupid problems. The Captain is serious now, Don Julio, he should think so, life was hard for men on the Amazon, and Reátegui, his voice suddenly severe, to the interpreter: the Aguarunas could not sell in Iquitos, that they had to fulfill their commitments, that the people who came had tricked them, that there would be no business of cooperatives or tricks. Boss Escabino would come back and that they would be doing business as usual, translating that, but the interpreter very fast, sir, better repeating, and the Captain he spoke slow enough, stop fooling around. Julio Reátegui was not in a hurry, Captain, he would do what he wanted. The interpreter grunts and gesticulates, Jum listens, a light breeze blows across Urakusa, and the branches of the trees moan softly, a laugh can be heard: the girl and the soldier are playing in front of the tents. The Captain loses his patience, how long?, he shakes Jum by the shoulder, didn't he understand that time either?, was he trying to fool them? Jum raises his head, his good eye examines the Governor, his hand points at him, his mouth grunts, and Julio Reátegui what had he said?, and the interpreter: insulting, sir, you being devil, saying, sir.

There was nobody in the hallway, only the noise from the big room downstairs; the lamp hanging from the ceiling was covered with blue cellophane and a dawnish light bathed the faded wallpaper and the identical doors. Josefino went over to the first one and listened, to the second, at the third someone was panting, a cot was lightly creaking, Josefino touched with his knuckles, and the voice of Wildflower what is it?, and an unknown masculine voice what is it? He ran to the end of the hall and there it was not dawn but dusk. He remained motionless, hidden in the discreet half light, and then a lock squeaked, a black head of hair came out into the blue light, a hand was held up like a visor, green eyes glowed. Josefino showed himself, made a signal. A few minutes later a man came out in his shirt sleeves and went humming down the stairway. Josefino crossed the hall and went into the room: Wildflower was buttoning up a yellow blouse.

"Lituma got in this afternoon," Josefino said, as if he were giving an order. "He's downstairs, with the Leóns."

A quick shudder passed over Wildflower's body, her hands were motionless, stuck between the buttonholes. But she did not turn around or speak.

"Don't be afraid," Josefino said. "He won't do anything to you. He already knows and he doesn't give a damn. Let's go down together."

She still did not say anything, and she continued buttoning up her blouse, but very slowly now, clumsily twisting every button before she fastened it, as if her fingers were stiff with cold. And, nevertheless, her whole face was perspiring, and damp spots appeared on her blouse on the back and under the armpits. The room was tiny, with no windows, lighted by a single reddish bulb, and the corrugated iron roof touched Josefino's head. Wildflower put on a cream-colored skirt, struggled for a while with the zipper before it would obey her. Josefino leaned over, picked up some white high-heeled pumps from the floor, and held them out to her.

"You're sweating because you're afraid," he said. "Wipe your face. There's no reason to be scared."

He turned around to close the door, and when he turned back Wildflower was looking into his eyes, unblinking, her lips half open, her nostrils dilating rapidly, as if it were difficult for her to breath or as if she had suddenly smelled something rotten.

"Is he drunk?" she asked then, her voice fearful and hesitant as she rubbed her mouth vigorously with a towel.

"A little," Josefino said. "We were celebrating his arrival at the Leóns'. He brought some good pisco from Lima."

They went out, and in the hallway Wildflower walked slowly, one hand resting on the wall.

"It seems impossible you still haven't got used to high heels," Josefino said. "Or is it because you're upset, Wildflower?"

She did not answer. In the tenuous blue light, her straight, thick lips looked like a clenched fist, and her features were hard and metallic. They went down the stairs, and coming up to meet them were gusts of warm smoke and alcohol, the light grew dimmer, and when the dance floor rose up at their feet, shadowy, noisy, and crowded, Wildflower stopped, she stood almost doubled over the railing, and her eyes had grown large and were rolling about the vague outlines with a savage gleam. Josefino pointed to the bar:

"Next to the bar, the ones toasting. You can't recognize him because he's lost a lot of weight. Between the harp player and the Leóns, the one in the bright suit."

Rigid, hanging on to the railing, Wildflower had her face half hidden by her hair, and an anxious wheeze was coming from her chest. Josefino took her by the arm, they submerged into the dancing couples, and it was as if they had dived into muddy water or were trying to make their way through an asphyxiating wall of sweating flesh, pestilence, and unrecognizable noises. Jocko's drums and cymbals were playing a corrido, and occasionally Kid Alejandro's guitar would join in and the music would liven up, but when the strings fell silent, it was a tuneless and lugubrious martial tempo again. They came off the dance floor and over to the bar. Josefino let go of Wildflower, Chunga sat up in her rocker, four heads turned to look at them, and they stopped. The Leóns seemed very jolly and Don Anselmo had his hair disheveled and his glasses down on his nose, and Lituma's mouth, all frothy, was twisted, his hand reached for the bar to put down his glass, he did not take his small eyes off Wildflower, his other hand had begun to smooth his hair, trying to make it lie down, quickly and mechanically. Suddenly he found the bar, his free hand pushed Monk away, and his whole body lurched forward, but he took only one step and stood there wobbling like a top that is losing its momentum, his eyes rolling, the Leóns grabbed him when he began to fall. His face did not change, he kept looking at Wildflower, he was breathing heavily, and only when he advanced toward them, very slowly, with a drivel of froth and saliva on his mouth, supported by the Leóns, somewhat stubborn, did there appear, forced and painful, the replica of a smile as his lips loosened and his chin trembled. Good to see you, sweety, and a grimace came over his whole face, his small eyes showed an unbearable uneasiness now, good to see you, Lituma, Wildflower said, and he good to see you, sweety, staggering. The Leóns and Josefino got around him, suddenly there was a flash in his eyes, a kind of liberation, and Lituma leaned over, clutched Josefino, hi, old buddy, he fell into his arms, good to see you, brother. He stayed there embracing Josefino, saying incomprehensible things and at times giving a dull moan, but when he let go he seemed more peaceful, that nervous dancing in his little eyes had stopped, the grimace was gone too, and he was really smiling. Wildflower was motionless, holding her hands together on her skirt, hiding her face behind her black and shiny hair.

"Sweety, we found each other," Lituma said, barely able to stammer, his smile broader and broader. "Come over here, let's drink a toast, we have to celebrate my return, I'm champ Number Four."

Wildflower took a step toward him, her head moved, her hair parted, two small green flames were softly shining in her eyes. Lituma stretched out a hand, put it around Wildflower's shoulder, brought her over to the bar like that and to Chunga's listless and impertinent eyes. Don Anselmo had fixed his glasses, his hands searched in the air until they found Lituma and Wildflower, and he patted them lovingly, that's what I like to see, kids, paternally.

"This is meeting night, old man," Lituma said. "Now you can see how I've behaved myself. Fill up the glasses, Chunga Chunguita, and have one yourself too."

He drank his down in one gulp and stood there gasping, his face wet with beer, saliva that was dripping down onto the filthy lapels of his jacket.

"What a heart, cousin," Monk said. "As big as the sun!"

"Heart, soul, and life," Lituma said. "I want to hear that waltz, Don Anselmo. Be a good fellow, play it for me."

"Yes, don't forget the music," Chunga said. "They're complaining out there, they're calling for you."

"Let him stay here awhile, Chunguita," José's voice said, sticky, oversweet, oozing. "Let this great artist have a drink with us."

But Don Anselmo had turned halfway around and was docilely heading back to the bandstand, feeling his way along the wall, dragging his feet, and Lituma, still holding Wildflower, was drinking without looking at her.

"Let's sing the theme song," Monk said. "A heart as big as the sun, cousin!"

Chunga had begun to drink too. Indolent and opaque, half dead, her eyes went from one to another, the champs and Wildflower, the dark mass of men and residents of the house who were moving back and forth on the dance floor among murmurs and laughs, couples going up the stairs, and hazy groups in the corners. Josefino, his elbows on the bar, was not drinking, he was looking at the Leóns out of the corner of his eye as they touched their glasses. And then the harp could be heard, the guitar, the drum, the cymbals, a tremble ran over the dance floor. Lituma's eyes grew lively:

"Heart, soul, and life. Oh, those waltzes bring back memories. Let's dance, sweety."

He pulled Wildflower without looking at her, the two of them were lost among mingling bodies and shadows, and the Leóns followed the rhythm with their glasses and sang. Quiet and disagreeable, Chunga's look was fixed on Josefino now, as if she were trying to infect him with her infinite laziness.

"What a miracle, Chunguita," Josefino said. "You're drinking."

"You're even more scared," Chunga said, and for an instant a mocking glow appeared in her eyes. "You really are scared, champ."

"There's no reason to be scared," Josefino said. "And you can see that I kept my promise; there wasn't any trouble."

"You can't help being scared," Chunga said, laughing listlessly. "It makes your voice quiver, Josefino."

3

The Sergeant's bare legs were hanging over the steps of the outpost building, and all around everything was waving, the woody hills, the capironas on the square of Santa María de Nieva, even the huts were swaying like the surf with the passage of a warm and whistling wind. The town was pitch black and the soldiers were snoring, naked under their mosquito nets. The Sergeant had lit a cigarette and was taking the last drags when, unexpectedly, from behind the small clump of rushes, silently, carried along by the waters of the Nieva, the boat appeared, with its conical hut in the stern, and some figures on deck became clear. There was no mist, and from the post the dock could be seen quite clearly in the moonlight. A small figure jumped out of the boat, ran dodging the stakes along the beach, disappeared into the shadows of the square, and a moment later, quite close to the post now, it reappeared, and the Sergeant recognized Lalita's face, her resolute stride, her hair, her strong arms swinging by her sturdy hips. He stood up halfway and waited until she got to the foot of the stairs.

"Good evening, Sergeant," Lalita said. "I'm glad I found you awake."

"I'm on guard duty, Ma'am," he said. "Good evening. Please excuse the way I look."

"Because you're in your shorts?" Lalita laughed. "Don't worry about it, don't the redskins go around worse?"

"With all this heat they've got every reason to go naked." The Sergeant, almost in profile, was shielding himself behind the railing. "But the bugs have been having a banquet on me, my whole body is burning already."

Lalita had her head thrown back and the post lamp was lighting up her face, with all its innumerable bumps and blemishes, and her loose hair, which was flowing down over her shoulders like a fine Yagua blanket.

"We're going to Pato Huachana," Lalita said. "They're having a birthday party and it starts early in the morning. We couldn't get away any sooner."

"That's the way it goes, Ma'am," the Sergeant said. "Have a few drinks for me."

"We're taking the children along too," Lalita said. "But Bonifacia wouldn't come. She can't get over being afraid of people, Sergeant."

"Foolish girl," the Sergeant said. "Missing a chance like that, they don't have many parties around here."

"We'll stay till Wednesday," Lalita said. "If the poor thing needs anything, would you help her?"

"I'd be glad to, Ma'am," the Sergeant said. "Except that, you know, the three times I visited you she wouldn't even come to the door."

"Women are tricky," Lalita said. "Haven't you figured that out yet? Now that she's alone, she'll have to come out. Drop by there tomorrow."

"Absolutely, Ma'am," the Sergeant said. "Do you know that when I first saw the boat I thought it was the ghost boat? That one with the skeletons, the one that picks up sleepwalkers? I was never superstitious, but you people here have got me into it."

Lalita crossed herself, made him be quiet with her hand, Sergeant, couldn't he see that they were going to travel by night?, he shouldn't talk about such things. Till Wednesday, then, oh, and Adrián sends his regards. She left the way she had come, running, and before he went inside the post house to get dressed, the Sergeant waited to see the figure outlined again among the stakes and jumping into the boat: old buddy, they had his bed all made for him. He put on his shirt, his pants, and his shoes, slowly, surrounded by the peaceful breathing of the soldiers, and the boat must have been on its way toward the Marañón already, past the canoes and barges, and at the stern Adrián Nieves was probably lowering and raising the pole. Those jungle people, they traveled with their houses and everything, like that old man Aquilino, had he really lived twenty years on the rivers?, what a way to live. The snorting of the motor could be heard, a powerful roar that drowned out the flapping of wings and other sounds, the chirping of the crickets, and then it grew fainter, going away, and the sounds of the woods came back, one after another, and took over the night once more: now only the vegetable-animal murmur reigned. A cigarette between his lips, his shirt sleeves rolled up, the Sergeant went down the small stairway, feeling all around, and went over to the Lieutenant's cabin: a muffled breathing, almost tremulous, was coming through the screen. He went along the path, quickly, among indistinguishable croaking, the luminous eyes of hoot owls and screech owls, and the tiny, exasperated melody of the crickets, feeling furtive brushings on his skin, pricks like those of a pin, trampling young bushes that crackled, dry leaves that whispered as they fell apart under his feet. When he drew near the cabin of Nieves the pilot, he turned around: a transparent whiteness was veiling the village, but at the top of the hill the Residence of the nuns was glowing clearly with its bright walls, and the side of the chapel and its slender grayish tower could also be distinguished as it reached up into the vast blue darkness. The encircling wall of woods, agitated continuously by a soft trembling, gave off a ceaseless unchanging sound, a kind of unending guttural yawn, and in the ditch where the Sergeant's feet stood leeches with warm and gelatinous bodies rubbed furtively against his ankles. He leaned over, wet his forehead, climbed the stairs. The inside of the cabin was dark, and an intense odor, different from that of the woods, was coming from the stove, as if there were leftover food there, or a decomposing corpse, and then, in the garden plot, a dog barked. Someone might have been watching the Sergeant through the opening between the wall and the roof, two lively little lights that could have been a woman's eyes and not fireflies: was he a Mangache or not?, where had his courage gone? He tiptoed about the terrace, looking all around, the dog was still baying in the distance. The curtain was drawn and the black opening of the cabin was giving off heavy smells.

"It's the Sergeant, Don Adrián," he shouted. "I'm sorry if I woke you up."

Some bewildered thing, an immediate shuffling or a moan, and silence again. The Sergeant reached the door, he raised his flashlight and turned it on: a small round and yellow moon wandered nervously over clay jars, ears of corn, pots, a bucket of water, Don Adrián: are you there? He had to talk to him, Don Adrián, and while the Sergeant was babbling, the moon climbed over the wall, light and pale, showing shelves filled with canned goods, it crept across the boards and went avidly from an extinguished brazier to some oars, from some blankets to a coil of rope and, suddenly, a head that was in hiding, some knees, two arms clutching each other: good evening, was Don Adrián in? The moon had come to a halt on the bulk formed by the huddling woman, its faint light quivered on motionless hips. Why was she pretending to be asleep? The Sergeant was speaking to her and she was not answering him, why was she acting like that, he took two steps and the head sank a little deeper under the arms, why, Miss: her skin was as light as the disk passing over it, a natural-colored itípak covered her body from knees to shoulders. The Sergeant knew how to get along with people, why was she afraid of him, did she think he had come to steal something? The Sergeant passed his hand across his forehead and the moon quivered, went wild, the woman had disappeared, and now the yellow halo was searching for her, it revealed some feet, some ankles. She was still in the same position, but now her tensed body gave a shudder, a movement that was repeated in shortening waves. He was not a thief, a Sergeant was somebody, he had salary, room, and board, he didn't need to steal from anybody, and he wasn't sick, either. Why was she acting like that, Miss? She should get up, he only wanted to chat for a while, so they could get to know each other better, all right? He took two more steps and squatted down. She had stopped trembling and was now rigid, her breathing was inaudible, why was she afraid of him, come on, and the Sergeant reached out his hand, come on, timidly toward her hair, there was no reason for her to be afraid of him, sweety, contact with some rough filaments on the tips of his fingers and, like a whirl in the shadows, something hard rose up and struck, and the Sergeant fell into a sitting position, moving his hands in the dark. In another second, the moon outlined a silhouette crossing the threshold, on the terrace the planks groaned under the rapidly fleeing feet. The Sergeant ran out and she was at the other end, leaning against the railing, shaking her head like a crazy woman, sweety, don't try jumping into the river. The Sergeant slipped, God damn it, and kept on running, what's on your mind, come here, sweety, and she kept on dancing, bouncing against the railing, frightened like an insect caught in the chimney of a lamp. She did not jump into the river or answer him, but when the Sergeant took her by the shoulders, she turned around and faced him like a tigress, sweety, what was she scratching him for?, the wall and the railing began to creak, what was she biting him for?, the dull panting of the two struggling bodies grew less, but what was she scratching him for, sweety?, and the anxious, moaning voice of the woman. The Sergeant's skin, shirt, and pants were damp, the breeze from the woods was coming over him like a surf, wetting him, sweety. He had already managed to get hold of her hands, with his whole body he was pressing her up against the wall, and suddenly he tripped her up, he made her fall, and he fell down beside her, had she hurt herself, silly? On the floor, she defended herself weakly, but her moans were stronger, and the Sergeant seemed all aroused, sweety, sweety, he was cursing through tightened teeth, see how it was? and little by little his body was on top of hers, baby. He had only come to have a chat, and she had been a little devil, she had been carrying on like that, sweety, and her body was slippery but resigned under the Sergeant's body. She moved slightly when the Sergeant's hand grabbed her itípak and took it off, and then she was quiet as he caressed her wet shoulders, her breasts, her waist, sweety: he was mad for her, he had dreamed about her ever since that first day, why had she run away?, silly, wasn't she aroused too? She sobbed occasionally, but she was no longer struggling, and she was there, stiff and inert, or soft and inert, but she held her thighs obstinately together, silly, sweety, why was she doing that?, come on, she should hug him a little, and the Sergeant's mouth tried to separate those lips that were soldered together, and his whole body had begun to undulate, to pound against the other one, sweety, that's not nice, what was she doing, why didn't she want to, and open up her little mouth, her legs, baby: he had been dreaming about her ever since that first day. Then the Sergeant relaxed and took his mouth away from those closed lips, his body fell to one side, and he stayed there lying on his back on the planks, breathing heavily. When he opened his eyes, she was standing there looking at him, and her eyes were glowing in the half light, without hostility, with a kind of peaceful surprise. The Sergeant got up, leaning on the railing, he stretched out his hand, and she let him touch her face, sweety, she had made him have his fun in the air, she was so silly, as he hitched up his belt, she moved back, but he hugged her aggressively and kissed her. She offered no resistance, and after a moment, timidly, her hands came to rest on the Sergeant's back, weakly, as if relaxing, sweety: had she ever known a man till now, tell me? She arched a little, stood on her toes, put her mouth to the Sergeant's ear: she had never known anyone till now, boss, no.

"We were near the Apaga River, and the Huambisas found some tracks," Fushía said. "And I let myself get involved because of those bastards. We should follow them, boss, they're probably loaded down with rubber, they're probably on their way to deliver what they got during the year. I listened to them, and we followed the tracks, but those bastards weren't after any rubber, they were looking for a good fight."

"They're Huambisas," Aquilino said. "You should have known them by then, Fushía. And was that how you ran into the Shapras?"

"Yes, on the banks of the Pushaga," Fushía said. "They didn't have even one single ball of rubber, and they killed one of our Huambisas before we landed. The others went wild and we couldn't hold them back. You can imagine, Aquilino."

"I certainly can, there must have been an awful slaughter," Aquilino said. "They're the fiercest Indians there are. Did they kill many?"

"No, most of the Shapras had time to run off into the jungle,"

Fushía said. "There were only two women left when we got there. They cut the head off one, and the other one you know about. But it wasn't easy for me to bring her back to the island. I had to hold my revolver on them; they wanted to kill her too. That's how the whole business of the Shapra girl got started, old man."

Two Huambisas had come? Lalita ran to the village, Aquilino clinging to her skirt, and some of the women were weeping loudly: they had killed a man on the Pushaga, Missy, the Shapras had killed him with a poisoned arrow. And the boss and the rest of them? They were all right, they would arrive later, they were coming slowly, they were carrying a lot of things they had picked up in an Aguaruna village on the Apaga. Lalita did not go back to the cabin, she stood beside the lupunas, looking at the inlet, the channel mouth, waiting for them to appear. But she got tired of waiting and walked about the island with Aquilino still clinging to her skirt: the turtle pool, the three cabins of the white people, the Huambisa village. The Indians had by now overcome their fear of the lupunas and they were living among them, they would touch them, and the dead man's relatives were still weeping, rolling on the ground. Aquilino ran over to where some old women were cutting up ungurabi leaves. They had to make new roofs, they said, or the rains will come and will get in and wet us.

"How old was the Shapra woman when you brought her back to the island?" Aquilino asked.

"She was just a girl, she must have been only twelve years old," Fushía said. "And she was fresh, Aquilino, nobody had touched her. And she wasn't like an animal, old man, she gave back love, she was as cuddly as a kitten."

"Poor Lalita," Aquilino said. "What a face she must have put on when she saw you come back with her, Fushía."

"Don't feel sorry for that bitch," Fushía said. "What I'm sorry about is that I didn't make the ungrateful slut suffer enough."

Were the Huambisas ferocious, warlike? Maybe, but they were good to Aquilino. They taught him how to make arrows, harpoons, they let him play with the stakes they were smoothing to make their blowguns, and maybe they were no good for certain things, but hadn't they built the cabins and planted the fields and made blankets?, didn't they bring food when Don Aquilino's canned goods ran out? And Fushía even if they are Indians and enjoy their fights and raids, if he had had to share his take with them, we'd be poor, and Lalita if they got rich someday, Fushía, they'd owe it all to the Huambisas.

"When I was a boy, in Moyobamba, we used to go in groups to spy on the Lamista women," Aquilino said. "Sometimes one of them would go off by herself and we'd pull her down without looking to see whether she was young or old, pretty or ugly. But it can't be the same with a squaw as it is with a white woman."

"It was different between me and that one, old man," Fushía said. "I didn't just like to make it with her, I liked lying in the hammock with her and making her laugh too. And I used to say it was too bad I didn't know any Shapra talk, so we could speak to each other."

"Hey, Fushía, you're smiling," Aquilino said. "You think about that girl and you get happy. What did you like talking about to her?"

"Everything," Fushía said. "What's your name, lie on your back, laugh again. Or to have her ask me questions about my life and I'd give her the answers."

"Say," Aquilino said. "You fell in love with the little squaw, didn't you?"

At first it was as if they did not see her, or that she did not exist. Lalita would pass by and they would keep on cutting the chambira, taking out the fibres, and they would not raise their heads. Then the women began to turn around, laugh with her, but they would not answer her, and she couldn't they understand her? Could Fushía have forbidden them to speak to her? But they played with Aquilino, and once a Huambisa woman had run after them, caught up with them, put a necklace of seeds and shells on Aquilino, that Huambisa woman who left without a word, never came back. And Fushía that was the worst part of it, they would come when they wanted to, they would leave when they felt like it, they would return after a few months as if nothing had happened: it was rough having to deal with Indians, Lalita.

"The poor Shapra girl was frightened to death of them: when a Huambisa came over, she'd throw herself at my feet and hug me, trembling all over," Fushía said. "She was more scared of the Huambisas than of the devil himself, old man."

"The woman they'd killed on the Pushaga was probably her mother," Aquilino said. "Besides, don't all the other Indians hate the Huambisas? Because they're proud, they look down on all of them, and they're more evil than any other tribe."

"I like them better than the others," Fushía said. "Not just because they helped me. I like the way they think and act. Have you ever seen a Huambisa who was a servant or a peasant? They won't let themselves be exploited by the whites. All they want to do is hunt and fight."

"That's why they'll all disappear someday, there won't be a trace of them," Aquilino said. "But you exploited them as much as you pleased, Fushía. All the damage they did on the Morona, the Pastaza, and the Santiago was just so that you could make some money."

"I was the one who got them shotguns and took them to where their enemies were," Fushía said. "They didn't look on me as a boss, I was their ally. I wonder what they've done to the Shapra girl. They must have taken her away from Pantacha by now."

The relatives of the dead man were still crying and pricking themselves with thorns until the blood ran, Missy, to make it easier, pain and suffering go away with the bad blood, and Lalita it was probably true, one day when she suffered she would prick herself and find out. And suddenly the men and women got up and ran over to the embankment. They climbed up the lupunas, they pointed toward the channel, were they coming there? Yes, a canoe appeared at the mouth of the channel, Fushía in the lead, lots of cargo, another canoe, Pantacha, Jum, more cargo, Huambisas, and Nieves the pilot. And Lalita look, Aquilino, look at all the rubber, she had never seen so much. God had been good to them, soon they would be rich and they could go to Ecuador, and Aquilino whooped, could he have understood?, but too bad about the Huambisa who had been killed.

"Pantacha's probably been left without a woman and without a boss," Fushía said. "He must have looked all over for me, the poor guy, and he must have cried and hollered and been sorry."

"You can't feel sorry for Pantacha," Aquilino said. "There's no hope for the fellow, those potions drove him crazy. He probably hasn't even realized that you've gone. When I got to the island this last time, he didn't even recognize me."

"Who do you think fed me when those swine ran away?" Fushía asked. "He cooked for me, he used to go hunting and fishing for me. I couldn't get up, old man, and he was beside my bed all day, just like a dog. He must have cried, old man, I'd bet on it."

"I took drugs too sometimes," Aquilino said. "But Pantacha got addicted and he'll die before too long."

The Huambisas unloaded the black balls, the skins; they splashed about among the canoes. Lalita waved from the slope, and then the Shapra appeared: she was not a Huambisa or an Aguaruna, and she seemed to be dressed for a festival: green, yellow, red necklaces, a headdress of feathers, disks in her ears, and a long itípak with black designs on it. The Huambisas on shore were looking at her too, a Shapra?, a Shapra, they murmured, and Lalita took Aquilino, ran toward the cabin, and sat down on the steps. They took a long time, in the distance the Huambisas could be seen going by with the rubber on their shoulders, and Pantacha had them lay the skins out in the sun. Finally Nieves the pilot came, holding his straw hat in his hand: they'd gone a long way, Ma'am, and there'd been a lot of whirlpools, that was why the trip had taken so long, and she more than a month. A Huambisa had got killed on the Pushaga, and she already knew about it; the ones who had got in this morning had told her. The pilot put his hat on and went into his hut. Later Fushía came, and the Shapra was following him. Her face was festive too, all painted, and as she walked the disks and necklaces made noise, Lalita: he was bringing her this servant, a Shapra from the Pushaga. She was scared of the Huambisas, she didn't understand anything; Lalita would have to teach her a little white man's talk.

"You always had bad things to say about Pantacha," Fushía said. "You have a good word for everybody, old man, except for him."

"I picked him up and brought him back to the island," Aquilino said. "If it hadn't been for me, he would have been dead a long time ago. But he disgusts me. He acts like an animal, Fushía. Worse than that, he looks and he isn't looking, he listens and he isn't listening."

"He doesn't disgust me, because I know his story," Fushía said.

"Pantacha has no character, and when he dreams he feels strong and he forgets about the things that have happened to him, and about that friend of his who died on the Ucayali. Where did you find him, old man? Wasn't it somewhere around here?"

"Farther downstream, on a small beach," Aquilino said. "He was asleep, half naked, and dying of hunger. I could tell that he was running away. I made him eat something and he licked my hands, just like a dog, as you said before."

"I need a drink," Fushía said. "And then I'm going to sleep for twenty-four hours. We had a very bad trip. Pantacha's canoe tipped over before we got into the channel. And on the Pushaga we had a run-in with the Shapras."

"Give her to Pantacha or the pilot," Lalita said. "I've got enough servants already, I don't need her. Why did you bring her back?"

"So she could help you," Fushía said. "And because those bastards wanted to kill her."

But Lalita had begun to whimper, hadn't she been a good wife?, hadn't she always gone along with him?, did he think she was stupid?, hadn't she done everything he wanted?, and Fushía was getting undressed, peacefully, throwing his clothes around, who was in charge here?, since when did she argue with him? And finally oh shit: a man was different from a woman, he needed a little variety, he didn't like whining, and besides what was she complaining about, because the Shapra girl wasn't going to take anything away from her, he'd already told her, she was going to be a servant.

"You left her unconscious, all covered with blood," Aquilino said. "I got in a month later, and Lalita still had bruises all over her body."

"She told you I'd beaten her, but she didn't tell you that she'd tried to kill the Shapra girl," Fushía said. "When I was half asleep, I saw her with the revolver and I blew up. Besides, that bitch got plenty of revenge for the times I hit her."

"Lalita has a heart of gold," Aquilino said. "If she went with Nieves, she didn't do it to get even with you, but because she was in love. And if she tried to kill the Shapra, it was most likely because she was jealous, not out of any hate. Didn't she make friends with her later?"

"More than she did with the Achual women," Fushía said. "Did you notice? She didn't want her handed over to Nieves, and she said it would be better for her to stay, she helps me. And when Nieves passed her on to Pantacha, she and the Shapra girl had a cry together. She'd taught her how to talk like a white woman and everything."

"Women are funny, it's hard to understand them sometimes," Aquilino said. "Let's have a little something to eat now. Except that the matches have got wet and I don't know how I'm going to light this stove."

❂

She was already an old woman, she lived alone and her only companion was the burro, that donkey with yellowish hair and slow, pompous steps on whom every morning she loaded the baskets filled with clothes she had collected the night before at the houses of important people. As soon as the rain of sand ended, Juana Baura would leave Gallinacera, a carob staff in her hand, with which from time to time she prodded the animal. She would turn off where there was a break in the balustrade along the Malecón, bounce down a dusty slope, go under the metal supports of the Old Bridge, and settle down where the Piura has eaten into the shore and made a little inlet. Sitting on a rock in the river, the water up to her knees, she would start to scrub, and the donkey, meanwhile, just like a man who was lazy or very tired, would flop down on the soft beach, sleep, sun himself. Sometimes there were other washerwomen with whom she could chat. If she was alone, Juana Baura would wring out a tablecloth, hum, some petticoats, you thieving healer you'd like to kill me, soap a sheet, tomorrow is first Friday, Father García, I repent all of my sins. The river had whitened her ankles and her hands, had kept them smooth, fresh, and young, but time had been wrinkling and darkening the rest of her body more and more. When she went into the river, her feet were accustomed to sinking into a soft sand bar; sometimes, instead of the usual weak resistance, they would find some solid material, or something slimy and slippery, like a fish trapped in the mud: those small differences were the only things that altered the identical routine of the morning. But that Saturday she suddenly heard a sob behind her back, heart-rending and very near: she lost her balance, she sat down in the water, the basket she had on her head tipped over, the pieces of clothing were floating away. Grunting, moving her hands about, Juana got the basket back, the shirts, the shorts, the dresses, and then she saw Don Anselmo: he was holding his head in his hands, and the water along the shore was wetting his boots. The basket fell into the river again, and before the current caught it and sank it Juana was up on the beach next to him. In confusion, she stammered some words of surprise and consolation, and Don Anselmo went on weeping without raising his head. "Don't cry," Juana said as the river took charge of her articles and silently carried them off. "Good heavens, calm down, Don Anselmo, what's the matter, are you sick?, Dr. Zevallos lives across the way, do you want me to go get him?, you don't know what a fright you've given me." The donkey had opened his eyes, he was looking at them sideways. Don Anselmo must have been there for some time, his pants, his shirt, and his hair were all sprinkled with sand, and his hat, fallen by his feet, had been almost covered by earth. "By the name of the thing you love most, Don Anselmo," Juana said, "what's wrong, it must be something terribly sad to make you cry like a woman." And Juana crossed herself when he raised his head: swollen eyelids, dark rings, unshaven, and dirty. And Juana "Don Anselmo, Don Anselmo, tell me if I can help you," and he "I was waiting for you, Madam," and his voice broke. "For me, Don Anselmo?" Juana asked, her eyes opening very wide. And he nodded, put his head back into his hands, sobbed, and she "but Don Anselmo," and he wailed "Toñita is dead, Doña Juana," and she "what are you saying, my God, what are you saying?" and he "she was living with me, don't hate me for it," and his voice broke. Then, with great effort, he stretched out one of his arms and pointed to the desert: the green structure was sparkling under the blue sky. But Juana Baura did not see it. She scrambled up to the Malecón, she was running and shrieking frightfully, and as she passed by windows opened and startled faces peered out.

Julio Reátegui raises his hand: that was enough, they should let him go. Corporal Roberto Delgado straightens up, drops the whip, wipes his flushed and sweaty face, and Captain Quiroga he went too far, was he deaf or couldn't he understand orders? He goes over to the supine Urakusa, he moves him with his foot, the man moans weakly. He was faking, Captain, he liked to give it to them when they were conscious, he would see. The Corporal curses, rubs his hands, takes a step, kicks, and the second kick makes the Aguaruna spring up like a cat, by God, the Corporal was right, a tough one, and he runs rapidly away, copper-colored, crouching down, the Captain thought that he had died on them. There was only one left, Señor Reátegui, and then Jum, him too? No, they were taking that hardhead back to Santa María de Nieva, Captain. Julio Reátegui takes a drink from his canteen and spits: they should bring out the other one and get it over with, Captain, wasn't he tired? did he want a little drink? Corporal Roberto Delgado and two soldiers go over to the prisoners' hut, in the center of the clearing. A sob breaks the silence of the village, and they all look over toward the tents: the girl and a soldier are struggling near the embankment, hazy against a darkening sky. Julio Reátegui stands up, cups his hands to his mouth: what had he told him, soldier? She shouldn't see, why hadn't he kept her in the tent, and the Captain God damn it, he should play with her, he should keep her occupied. A light rain is falling on the huts of Urakusa and clouds of mist float up the embankment, the wind sends a breath of warm air to the clearing, the sky is full of stars now. The soldier and the girl disappear into a tent, and Corporal Roberto Delgado and two soldiers drag over a Urakusa, who stops in front of the Captain and grunts something. Julio Reátegui signals for the interpreter: punishment for lack of respect for the authorities, never hit soldier again, never trick boss Escabino, or they would come back and punishment would be worse. The interpreter grunts and gesticulates, and while this is going on, the Corporal takes a breath, rubs his hands, picks up the whip, sir. Translating?, yes, understanding?, yes, and the Urakusa, short, potbellied, goes from one side to the other, hops like a cricket, gives a twisted look, tries to break out of the circle, and the soldiers spin around, they are a whirlwind, they grab him, they bring him back. Finally, the man is quiet, he covers his face and hunches over. He bears it standing up for a long time, grunting with every lash, then he falls down and the Governor raises his hand: they should let him go, were the mosquito nets set up? Yes, Don Julio, everything ready, but mosquito nets or not, his face had been eaten up all through the trip, it was burning, and the Governor they should keep a sharp eye on Jum, Captain, they should not leave him alone. Corporal Delgado laughs: he couldn't escape even if he were a magician, sir, he was tied up and besides there would be a guard all night long. Sitting on the ground, the Urakusa is watching them all out of the corner of his eye. The rain has stopped, the soldiers gather some dry wood, light a campfire, tall flames break out alongside the Urakusa, who is softly touching his chest and his back. What was he waiting for, more whipping? There is laughter among the soldiers, and the Governor and the Captain look at them. They are squatting in front of the fire, the crackling reddens and distorts their faces. Why those laughs? Let's see, you, and the interpreter approaches: husband staying. Captain. The officer did not understand, he should speak more distinctly, and Julio Reátegui smiles: he was the husband of one of the women in the hut, and the Captain, oh, that was why he didn't leave, the devil, now he knew. That was right, Julio Reátegui had also forgotten about those ladies, Captain. At the same time, sneakily, the soldiers get up and come over to the Governor in a group: fixed eyes, tense mouths, aroused look. But the Governor was the authority, Don Julio, he made the decisions, the Captain simply carried them out. Julio Reátegui examines the soldiers clinging to one another; above the indistinguishable bodies the heads are craned toward him, the flames of the campfire light up their cheeks and foreheads. They are not smiling or lowering their eyes, they are waiting there without moving, their mouths half open: hell, the Governor shrugs his shoulders, if they insisted so much. Imprecise, anonymous, a murmur vibrates over the heads, the circle of soldiers breaks up into figures, shadows crossing the clearing, the sound of footsteps, the Captain coughs, and Julio Reátegui gives a discouraged look: these men were already halfway civilized, Captain, and the way they carried on over a few fleabitten scarecrows, he would never understand men. The Captain has a coughing spell, but there were so many privations in the jungle, Don Julio, and he swipes frantically about his face, there were no women in the jungle, you took what you could find, he slaps his forehead, and finally he gives a nervous laugh: the young ones had teats just like Negro women. Julio Reátegui raises his head, looks the Captain in the eye, the Captain becomes serious: naturally, Captain, that was true, he was probably getting old, if he had been younger he probably would have gone with the soldiers to where those ladies were. The Captain slaps his face now, his arms, Don Julio, he was going to bed, the bugs were eating him alive, he even thought he had swallowed one, sometimes he had nightmares, Don Julio, in his dreams great swarms of mosquitoes would attack him. Julio Reátegui pats him on the arm: he would get him some medicine in Nieva, it was worse inside than it was outside, there were so many of them at night, he should sleep well. Captain Quiroga strides off toward the tents, his cough is lost in the laughter, the cursing, and the weeping that break out in the Urakusa night like the echoes of some distant virile festivity. Julio Reátegui lights a cigarette: the Urakusa is still sitting across from him, looking at him out of the corner of his eye. Reátegui blows his smoke upward, there are many stars and the sky is a sea of ink, the smoke rises, spreads out, disappears, and at his feet the campfire is already in its final throes like an old dog. The Urakusa moves now, he drags himself off, pushing himself along with his feet, he looks as if he were swimming underwater. Later on, when the fire has gone out, a scream is heard, from the hut side?, very short, no, from the tents, and Julio Reátegui starts to run, holding down his canteen with one hand, he tosses his butt away on the run, he runs right into the tent, and the screaming stops, a cot creaks, and in the darkness there is frightened breathing: who was there? you, Captain? The girl was frightened, Don Julio, and he had come to see, it seemed that the soldier had frightened her, but the Captain had cursed him out. They go out of the tent, the Captain offers the Governor a cigarette and he rejects it: he would take care of the girl, Captain, there was no reason to worry, he should just go to bed. The Captain goes into the next tent, and Julio Reátegui feels his way toward the army cot, sits down on the edge. His hand softly touches a small, rigid body, it passes over a naked shoulder, some very dry hair: it was all right, all right, no reason to be afraid of that animal, that animal had already left, lucky that she had cried out, in Santa María de Nieva she would be very happy, she would see, the nuns would be very good, they would take very good care of her, Señora Reátegui would take care of her too. His hand caresses her hair, her back, until the girl's body relaxes and her breathing grows calm. The shouts and curses are still going on in the clearing, more heated and clownish, and there is running and sudden silences: all right, all right, poor child, she should go to sleep now, he would keep watch.

The music had stopped, the Leóns applauded, Lituma and Wildflower came back to the bar, Chunga filled up the glasses, Josefino was still drinking by himself. Under the narcotic rays of blue, green, and violet light, a few scattered couples were still on the dance floor, dancing with a mechanical and lethargic air to the rhythm of the murmurs and conversations about them. There were a few people left at the tables in the corners too; the main body of men and occupants of the house and all the merriment of the evening were concentrated at the bar. Crowding together and noisy, they were drinking beer, the laughter of Mulata Sandra was like shrieking, and a fat man with a mustache and glasses was holding his yellow glass up like a flag, he had been through the Ecuador campaign as a buck private, yes sir, and he would never forget the hunger, the lice, the heroism of the cholos, or the chiggers that got underneath your nails and wouldn't leave even if you tried to burn them out, yes sir, and Monk, suddenly, muffling his voice: hurray for Ecuador! Men and girls became silent, Monk's happy eyes distributed roguish winks right and left, and after a few seconds of indecision and stupor the fat man pushed José aside, grabbed Monk by the lapels, shook him like a rag, why was he messing with him?, he would repeat what he said if he had any guts and was a man, and Monk, with an enormous smile: hurray for Peru! They all laughed now, Sandra looked like a panther, the fat man was chewing his mustache, Josefino and José had joined the group, and Monk was adjusting his clothes.

"I just don't like jokes about patriotism, friend." The fat man was patting Monk on the back, without rancor. "You put one over on me, let me buy you a drink."

"I'm in love with life," José said. "Let's sing the theme song."

They all dissolved into a single circle and, crushing up against the bar, they clamored for more beers. Like that, exultant and gregarious, their eyes drunken, their voices shrill, damp with sweat, they drank, they smoked, they argued, and a cross-eyed young man with hair stiff as a broom was hugging Mulata Sandra, let me introduce you to my future wife, buddy, and she opened her mouth, showing her red gums, her gold teeth, shaking with laughter. Suddenly she fell on the young man like a giant cat, kissing him avidly on the mouth, and he was struggling in her dark arms, a fly in a spider's web, he protested. The champs exchanged knowing glances, mocking, they grabbed the cross-eyed man, they held him, here he was, Sandra, we give him to you, eat him up raw, she was kissing him, biting, and a kind of convulsive enthusiasm invaded the group, new couples came over, and even the musicians left their corner. Off in the distance, Kid Alejandro was smiling languidly, and Don Anselmo, followed by Jocko, was going from one side to the other, aroused, smelling out the excitement, what's up, what's going on, tell me. Sandra let go of her prey, when he passed his handkerchief over his face, the cross-eyed boy became all smeared with rouge, like a clown, they handed him a glass of beer and he poured it over his head, they applauded him, and Josefino suddenly began to search through the tumult. He stood up on his toes, he crouched down, he finally left the circle and was hunting all over the room, turning over chairs, fading away and coming back into sight in the foul and smoky air. He ran back to the bar.

"I was right all along, champ," Chunga's lipless mouth said. "You've been believing in fairy tales."

"Where are they, Chunguita? Did they go upstairs?"

"What do you care." Chunga's rigid eyes were looking him over as if he were an insect. "Are you jealous?"

"He's killing her," José said, looking like a ghost, pulling Josefino by the arm. "Hurry up."

They pushed their way through the crowd, Monk was standing by the door with his outstretched hand pointing into the darkness toward the Grau barracks. They ran out wildly among the neighborhood huts that seemed to be empty, and then they went off into the desert and Josefino tripped, fell down, got up, kept on running, and now his feet were sinking into the ground, the wind was blowing toward him with dark whirlwinds of sand, and he had to run with his eyes closed, holding his breath so that his chest would not burst. "It's their fault, the shits!" Josefino roared, "they didn't keep an eye on him," and a moment later, in a broken voice, "but how far is it, God damn it," and now a figure between the sand and the stars rose up in front of them, a strong and vengeful shadow:

"That's far enough, you bastard, you son of a bitch, you false friend."

"Monk!" Josefino shouted, "José!"

But the Leóns had turned against him too, and, like Lituma, they were unleashing their fists and their feet and their heads against him. He was on his knees and everything around him was blind and ferocious, and when he tried to get up and run away from that dizzy circle of blows, a new kick would knock him down, a punch would catch him, a hand would pull his hair, and he was forced to lift up his face and offer it to the blows and the biting of the sand that seemed to be pouring into his nose and mouth. Then there was a kind of growling, as if a vast dog pack were there, circling the conquered beast in turn, sniffing it while it was still warm, getting angry for a moment, biting it indifferently.

"He's still moving," Lituma said. "Be a man, Josefino. I want to see you, stand up!"

"He's probably seeing stars, the Marimachas, cousin," Monk said.

"Leave him alone now, Lituma," José said. "You've had your fun. What more do you want? Can't you see he could die?"

"They'd send you to jail again, cousin," Monk said. "Come on, don't be stubborn."

"Hit him, hit him." Wildflower had come up, her voice was not violent but dull. "Hit him, Lituma."

But instead of paying any attention to her, Lituma turned against her, he pushed her down onto the sand with a shove, and he was kicking her, whore, tramp, gang-bang baby, insulting her until he lost his voice and his strength. Then he dropped to the sand and began crying like a child.

"Cousin, for God's sake, take it easy."

"You're to blame too," Lituma moaned. "You all tricked me. You bastards, you double-crossers, I hope you're damned sorry."

"Didn't we get him out of the Green House for you, Lituma? Didn't we help you beat him up? You couldn't have done it all alone."

"We got you your revenge, cousin. And Wildflower too. Did you see how she was scratching him?"

"I'm talking about before," Lituma said, between hiccups and sobs. "You were all in on it, and there I was not knowing anything, like a poor, simple bastard."

"Cousin, men don't cry. Don't carry on like that. We've always loved you."

"Piss on the past, brother. Be a man, be a Mangache. Don't cry."

Wildflower had left Josefino, who was curled up on the ground and moaning weakly, and she and the Leóns were comforting Lituma, that he should show character, men get bigger when there's trouble, they were hugging him, they were brushing off his clothes, everything forgotten?, start all over again?, brother, cousin, Lituma. He was babbling, half consoled, sometimes he would get angry and kick the fallen man, then he would smile, grow sad.

"Let's get out of here, Lituma," José said. "They probably saw us from the shacks. If they call the cops, we'll be in for it."

"Let's go to Mangachería, cousin," Monk said. "We'll finish off the pisco you brought, that'll cheer you up."

"No," Lituma said. "Let's go back to Chunga's."

He began walking through the sand with long, resolute steps. When Wildflower and the Leóns caught up with him among the shacks of the settlement, Lituma had begun to whistle furiously, and Josefino could be seen in the distance, limping, moaning, and shouting.

"Things are really jumping." Monk held the door open while the others went in first. "Just waiting for us."

The fat man with the mustache came over to greet them:

"Hello, hello, my friends. Why did you disappear like that? Come on, the night's just getting started."

"Music, harp man," Lituma exclaimed. "Waltzes, tonderos, marineras."

He shoved his way over to the corner where the orchestra was, he fell into the arms of Jocko and Kid Alejandro, while the fat man and the young man with cross-eyes dragged the Leóns over to the bar and bought them beers. Sandra was fixing up Wildflower's hair, Rita and Maribel were bombarding her with questions, and the four of them were buzzing like wasps. The orchestra began to play, the bar cleared out, half a dozen couples were dancing on the floor among the halos of blue, green, and violet light. Lituma came over to the bar dying with laughter:

"Chunga Chunguita, revenge is sweet. Can you hear him? He's out there hollering but he doesn't dare come in. We left him half dead."

"I'm not interested in other people's business," Chunga said. "But you people are bad luck for me. It was your fault that I was fined the last time. This time, at least, the fight wasn't in here. What'll you have? Everybody drinks here or they can just as well leave."

"That's not a very nice answer, Chunguita," Lituma said. "But I feel good, give me anything you want to. You have one too, be my guest."

And now the fat man wanted to take Wildflower out onto the dance floor and she was resisting, showing her teeth.

"What's wrong with this one, Chunga?" the fat man asked, panting.

"What's wrong with you?" Chunga said. "They're inviting you to dance, don't be rude. Why don't you accept the gentleman's invitation?"

But Wildflower was still struggling:

"Lituma, tell him to let go of me."

"Don't let go of her, friend," Lituma said. "And you do your duty, whore."

THREE

THE LIEUTENANT STOPS WAVING GOODBYE when the boat is just a small white light on the river. The soldiers put the baggage on their shoulders, climb up from the dock, they halt on the square of Santa María de Nieva and the Sergeant points at the hills: between the dunes covered with woods some white walls were glimmering, metal roofs, that was the Mission, Lieutenant, the small rocky slope was bare, they call that the Residence, the nuns live there, sir, and the chapel is on the left. Native figures go through the village, the roofs of the huts are made of straw and look like cowls. Some women with mud-colored bodies and indolent eyes are grinding something at the base of two peeled tree trunks. The soldiers go on ahead, and the officer turns to the Sergeant: he had been only barely able to talk to Lieutenant Cipriano, why hadn't he waited at least long enough to fill him in on things? It was just that if he hadn't taken advantage of the boat he would have had to wait another month, Lieutenant, and he was set on getting away, Lieutenant Cipriano. He shouldn't worry, the Sergeant would brief him in no time at all, and Blondy sets a suitcase down on the ground and shows him the cabin: there it was, Lieutenant, the poorest Post in Peru, and Fats that one opposite would be his cabin, Lieutenant, and Shorty later on they would get him a couple of Aguaruna girls for servants, and Blacky servants were the only things that were easy to come by in this godforsaken village. As he proceeds, the Lieutenant touches the shield hanging from a beam and it gives off a metallic sound. The steps to the cabin have no railing, the planks that form the floor and walls are rough, uneven, and in the first room there are some straw chairs, a desk, a small faded flag. There is an open door in the back: four hammocks, some rifles, a stove, a garbage can, what a place. Would the Lieutenant care for a beer? They must be cold by now, they had been in a bucket of water since morning. The officer agrees, and Shorty and Blacky leave the building—was the Governor named Fabio Cuesta?, yes, a nice little old man, but he should wait until later to say hello to him, sir, this was his siesta time—and come back with glasses and bottles. They drink, the Sergeant toasts the Lieutenant, the soldiers ask him about Lima, the officer wants to know what the people in Santa María de Nieva are like, who's who, are the Mission nuns nice people?, and whether the redskins are a headache. Well, they could talk all they wanted that night, the Lieutenant wanted to get a little rest. They had told Paredes to fix a special meal, Lieutenant, to celebrate his arrival, and Blondy he was in charge of the canteen, sir, where they all ate, and Blacky he was a carpenter too, and Fats to top it all off he was half witch doctor, he would meet him later on, a good man that Paredes. The soldiers carry the suitcases into the cabin across the way, the officer follows them yawning, he goes in and falls onto the cot in the center of the room. With a sleepy voice, he dismisses the Sergeant. Without getting up, he takes off his cap, his shoes. There is a smell of dust and dark tobacco. There is not much furniture: a chest of drawers, two benches, a table, a lantern hanging from the ceiling. The windows have metal screens: the women are still grinding on the square. The Lieutenant stands up, the other room is empty and has a small door. He opens it: the ground is six feet below, hidden by the underbrush, and a few feet from the cabin the woods close in. He unbuttons his fly, urinates, and when he comes back into the front room, the Sergeant is there: that troublemaker again, Lieutenant, an Aguaruna named Jum. And the interpreter: devil saying, Aguaruna, soldier lying, and primerlima and limagovernment. Sir. Arévalo Benzas looks up shielding his eyes with his hands, he wasn't any boob, Don Julio, the Indian was trying to make them think he was crazy, but Julio Reátegui shakes his head no: that wasn't it, Arévalo, he'd been singing the same tune for so long that now he knew it by heart. Something had been put into his head, from the sound of that primer business, but who the devil could understand what he was talking about. The reddish burning sun is baking Santa María de Nieva, and the soldiers, Indians, and bosses grouped around the capironas blink, perspire, and murmur. Manuel Águila fans himself with a straw fan: was he very tired, Don Julio? Had they given him much trouble in Urakusa? A little, he would tell them all about it later, now Reátegui had to go up to the Mission for a moment, he would be right back, and they nod: they would wait for him in the Government building, Captain Quiroga and Escabino were already there. And the interpreter: running around, pilot getting away, Urakusahomeland, shit, governmentflag. Manuel Águila is using his fan as a shield against the sun, but, even so, his eyes are tearing: that he was going to get tired of so much shouting, it wouldn't do any good, the one who did it would pay for it, interpreter, translating that. The Lieutenant calmly buttons up his fly, and the Sergeant walks about the room, his hands in his pockets: it wasn't the first time he'd come, Lieutenant. Lot of times already, until one time Lieutenant Cipriano got mad, put a scare into him, and then the Indian stopped coming around. But he was a wise one, he must have found out that Lieutenant Cipriano was leaving Santa María de Nieva, and he came running to see if he could get on the good side of the new Lieutenant. The officer finishes tying his shoes, stands up. Could you at least get along with him? The Sergeant makes a vague gesture: he didn't do anything bad, but there was one thing certain, there was nobody more stubborn, a regular mule, when he got something into his skull, nobody could get it out. When had that trouble been? When Señor Julio Reátegui was Governor, before they had a Police Post in Nieva, and the Lieutenant slams the cabin door, it was the limit, he'd just arrived two hours ago and there was work to do, the redskin could have waited till tomorrow, couldn't he? And the interpreter: corporalgado devil! Captainartemio devil! Corporal. But Corporal Roberto Delgado does not get angry, he laughs, the same as the soldiers, and some Indians also laugh: he should go right on being difficult, insulting him and the Captain, he should keep it up, he would soon see who had the last laugh. And the interpreter: hungering, Corporal, sick in stomach, shit, belly dancing, Corporal, saying thirsty, would they give him water? No, he could suck him off first, and he raises his voice: whoever gave him food or water would answer to him, he should translate that for all the Indians in Santa María de Nieva, because they might look foolish and happy, but they were burning underneath it all. And the interpreter: sonsbitch, Corporal, escabinodevil, insulting. Now only the soldiers are smiling, they look at the Corporal out of the corner of their eyes, and he fine, he should insult his mother again, because he would see when they took him down. A thin, bronzed man comes over to meet them, he takes off his straw hat and the Sergeant introduces them: Adrián Nieves, Lieutenant. He could speak Aguaruna and sometimes he would act as interpreter, he was the best pilot in the region and for two months he had been working for the Police Post. The Lieutenant and Nieves shake hands and Blacky, Shorty, Fats, and Blondy move away from the desk, there he was, Lieutenant, that was the heathen—that was what they called the redskins around there—and the officer smiles: he'd thought that they let their hair grow down to their feet, he didn't expect to see a bald-headed one. A thin fuzz covers Jum's head and a straight and rosy scar divides his small forehead in two. He is of average height, stocky, wearing a tattered itípak that goes from his waist to his knees. On his hairless chest a purple triangle joins three symmetrical disks; three parallel lines cross his cheekbones. He also has tattoos on both sides of his mouth: two black "X"s, very small. His expression is peaceful, but in his yellow eyes there are restless vibrations, half fanatical. Ever since they shaved his head, he'd been shaving it himself, Lieutenant, and it was very strange, because nothing hurt them more than to have someone touch their hair. Nieves the pilot could explain it to him, Lieutenant: it was a matter of pride, they'd been talking about that very thing while they were waiting for him. And the Sergeant they should see if they could understand each other better with Don Adrián, because the last time old witch doctor Paredes acted as interpreter, and nobody could understand anything, and Fats it was because the canteen man was just pretending that he could talk Aguaruna, it wasn't true, he only knew a few words. Nieves and Jum grunt and gesticulate, Lieutenant, that he could not go back to Urakusa until they gave him back everything they'd taken away from him, but he had the urge to go back and that was why he shaved his head, so that he couldn't go back even if he wanted to, and Blondy then it wasn't because he went crazy? Yes, and now he should explain once and for all what it was they should give back to him. Nieves the pilot goes over to the Aguaruna, he grunts at him, pointing to the officer, he gesticulates, and Jum, who listens without moving, suddenly nods and spits: he should stop right there!, this wasn't a pigpen, he should not spit. Adrián Nieves puts his hat back on, it was so that the Lieutenant would see that he was telling the truth, and the Sergeant a redskin custom, someone who didn't spit when he talked was lying, and the officer that was all they needed, he was going to bathe them all in saliva. That they believed him, Nieves, that he should not spit. Jum folds his arms and the rings on his chest become deformed, the triangle becomes wrinkled. He begins to speak in a strong voice, almost without a pause, and he continues to spit all around him. He does not take his eyes off the Lieutenant, who taps his foot and watches the trajectory of each piece of phlegm with disgust. Jum waves his arms, his voice is very energetic. And the interpreter: robbing shit, Urakusarubber, girl, soldierñoreátegui, Corporal. Hothead! To protect his eyes from the sun, Corporal Roberto Delgado has taken off his cap and is holding it stretched out over his forehead: he should just keep on playing it proud, he should keep on yelling, he was bursting with laughter. And he should ask him where he learned how to be so fresh. And the interpreter: contractiscontract, smart, boss Escabino, understand, wise, taking down, Corporal. The soldiers are getting undressed and some of them are already running toward the river, but Corporal Delgado is still at the foot of the capironas: taking him down? Not on your life, he would stay there, and he should be thankful that Captain Artemio Quiroga was a nice person, because if it were up to him he'd make him remember it for the rest of his life. Why didn't he insult his mother again, come on. He should dare, he should play the brave man in front of his countrymen looking at him there, and the interpreter: all right, sonsbitch. Corporal. Again, he should say it again, that was why the Corporal had stayed there, and the Lieutenant crosses his legs and throws his head back: a wild story, no head or tail to it, what primers was this fellow talking about? Some books with drawings, Lieutenant, to teach patriotism to the Indians; there were still some left in the Government building, all dusty, Don Fabio could show them to him. The Lieutenant looks at the soldiers indecisively, and in the interval the Aguaruna and Adrián Nieves continue grunting back and forth in low voices. The officer turns to the Sergeant, was that business about the girl true? and Jum, girl!, very violently, shit!, and Fats sh-h-h, the Lieutenant was speaking, and the Sergeant shush, who could tell, they stole girls every day here, it could be true, didn't they say that those bandits on the Santiago had built themselves a whole harem? But the Indian was mixing everything together and you couldn't tell what the primers had to do with the rubber that he was asking for or with that business about a girl, my friend here had a wild tale worked out in his noggin. And Shorty if they had been Army soldiers it didn't have anything to do with them, why didn't he go complain to the Borja garrison?, they grunt and gesticulate, and Nieves the pilot: he'd already gone twice and nobody had paid any attention to him, Lieutenant. And Blondy he had to be a sorehead to keep this business alive after such a long time, Lieutenant, he should have forgotten all about it by now. They grunt and gesticulate, and Nieves: that in his village they blame him and he didn't want to go back to Urakusa without the rubber, the hides, the primers, and the girl, so they would see that Jum was right. Jum speaks again, slowly now, without raising his hands. The two tiny "X"s move with his lips, like two propellers that cannot get completely started spinning and fall back and again and fall back. What was he saying now, Don Adrián?, and the pilot: he was remembering, and insulting the ones who had hung him up, and the Lieutenant stops tapping his foot: had hung him up? Shorty points vaguely toward the square of Santa María de Nieva: from those capironas, Lieutenant. Paredes could tell him, he was there, he looked like a paiche fish he said, that was how they hung up paiches to dry them out. Jum releases a flow of grunts, this time he does not spit but makes frantic gestures: because he was telling them the truth, they hung him from the capironas, Lieutenant, and the Sergeant the same old story over and over again, and the officer the truth? and the interpreter: Piruvians! Piruvians! shit! Corporal. But Corporal Delgado already knew, he didn't need any translation for that, he might not have been able to talk Indian language, but he did have ears, did he think he was an idiot? Oh God, the Lieutenant pounds on the desk, oh God, what a mess, they'd never get to the bottom of it, did Piruvians mean Peruvians? was that the truth? And the interpreter: worse than bleeding, worse than dying, Corporal. And boninopérez and teófilocañas, he doesn't understand. Corporal. But Corporal Delgado did understand: those were the names of those subversives. That he could have fun calling for them, because they were far away, and if they came they would hang them up too. Blacky is sitting on the edge of the desk, the other soldiers are still standing, Lieutenant, it was to teach them a lesson, they said. And that all the bosses and the soldiers were furious, that they wanted to lay into him, but that the Governor at that time, Señor Julio Reátegui, held them back. And who were those guys? Had they ever come back this way? Some agitators, it seemed, passing themselves off as teachers, Lieutenant, and in Urakusa they had listened to them, the Indians got rough and cheated the boss who used to buy rubber from them, and Fats somebody called Escabino, and Jum Escabino! he roars, shit! and the officer be still, Nieves, he should have him be quiet. Where was that fellow? Was it possible to talk to him? Not so easy, Lieutenant, Escabino was dead now, but Don Fabio knew him and maybe he could talk to the Lieutenant: he would give him the details, and besides the Governor was a friend of Don Julio Reátegui. Wasn't Nieves there either when all that happened? No, he wasn't either, Lieutenant, he'd only been in Santa María de Nieva a couple of months, he'd lived a long way off before, on the Ucayali, and Blacky: they didn't only cheat their boss, there was also that business of the Corporal from Borja, the two things went together. And the interpreter: corporalgado devil! shit! Corporal Delgado uncurls all the fingers of his hands and shows them: ten insults to his mother, he'd counted them. And he could keep on having a good time at it if he wanted to, he was staying there so that he could keep on insulting her. Yes, a Corporal who was on his way to Bagua on furlough, and there were a pilot and a porter with him, and the Aguarunas attacked them at Urakusa, they beat up the Corporal and the porter, the pilot disappeared, and some people said they'd killed him and others that he'd deserted, Lieutenant, taking advantage of what was going on. And that was why they organized an expedition, soldiers from Borja and the Governor from here, and that was why they'd brought this fellow back and punished him on the capironas as an example. Wasn't that the way it was, more or less, Don Adrián? The pilot nods, Sergeant, that was what he'd heard, but since he hadn't been there, who could be sure. Oho, oho, the Lieutenant looks at Jum and Jum looks at Nieves, then he wasn't the saint he made himself out to be. The pilot grunts and the Urakusa answers, harsh and gesticulating, spitting and stamping his feet: what he was saying was quite different, Lieutenant, and the Lieutenant that was logical, what was the version of my good friend here? That the Corporal had been stealing things and that they had made him give them back, the pilot had escaped by swimming off, and the boss was cheating them on the rubber and that was why they hadn't wanted to sell it to him. But the Lieutenant does not seem to be listening, and his eyes are looking the Aguaruna over from head to toe with curiosity and a certain surprise: how long had they kept him hanging, Sergeant? They had him there for a day, and then they'd given him some lashes, Paredes the witch doctor said, and Blacky that Corporal from Borja gave them to him, and Blondy in revenge for the beating the Indians had given him in Urakusa, Lieutenant. Jum takes a step, he faces the officer, he spits. The expression on his face is almost a smile now and his yellow eyes turn malicious, a playful expression rends his lips. He touches the scar on his forehead, and slowly, ceremoniously, like a magician, he spins on his heels, shows his back: from the shoulders to the waist some furrows painted with annatto, straight, parallel, and brilliant. That was another one of his manias, Lieutenant, every time he came he would paint himself up like that, and Shorty something of his own doing, because the Aguarunas didn't usually paint their backs, and Blondy the Boras do, Lieutenant, their backs, their bellies, their feet, their rear ends, they paint their bodies all over, and Nieves the pilot so he wouldn't forget the whipping they gave him, that was the explanation he gave, and Arévalo Benzas wipes his eyes: the top of his brains had been roasted, what was he shouting? Piruvians, Arévalo, Julio Reátegui had his back against the capirona, during the whole trip he had been shouting Piruvians at them. And Corporal Roberto Delgado nods, sir, he never stopped insulting everybody, the Captain, the Governor, himself, there was no way to get him down off his high horse. Julio Reátegui looks up quickly, they would take him down soon, and when he lowers his head his eyes are wet, a little patience, Corporal, the sun was so hot, it was enough to blind a person. And the interpreter: his hair saying, primer, girl. Sir. Tricking he says, and Manuel Águila: he seemed drunk, that was the way they got delirious when they were all beered up, but maybe they should all go away, they were waiting for them, did he want him to go along with him to the sisters? No, they had no business getting involved with the sisters, Lieutenant, hadn't he seen that they were foreigners? But Paredes the witch doctor said that Sister Angélica—the oldest one at the Mission now that Sister Asunción had died—had come down at night to the square to ask them to take him down, and that she had even argued with the soldiers. The little old lady must have felt sorry for him, she was the saltiest of them all, a mass of wrinkles, and Blacky: when they were through they put hot eggs under his armpits, that Corporal, and they must have made him jump all the way up to heaven, and Jum shit! Piruvians! The Lieutenant is tapping his foot again, that wasn't the way to do things, damn it, and he raps his knuckles on the desk, they'd gone too far, except what could they do now, the whole thing was finished. What was he saying now? That they should just give him back what they took away from him, Lieutenant, and he would go back to Urakusa, and the Sergeant hadn't he told him that he was stubborn? That rubber was probably on the soles of somebody's shoes already, and the skins were probably wallets, suitcases, and who could say where the girl was: they'd explained it to him a hundred times, Lieutenant. The officer reflects, his chin on his hand: he could always write to Lima, make some requests to the Ministry, maybe the Bureau of Indian Affairs, to indemnify him, let's see, Nieves should suggest that. They grunt and suddenly Jum nods several times, governmentlima!, the soldiers smile, only the pilot and the Lieutenant are serious: limaprimer! The Sergeant unfolds his arms: couldn't he see that he was a savage, Lieutenant? How could they get things like that into his head, what did Lima or Ministry mean to him, and all the while Adrián Nieves and Jum are grunting animatedly, they exchange spits and expressions, the Aguaruna is silent at times and closes his eyes as if meditating, then he cautiously pronounces a few sentences, pointing at the officer: would he go along with him? Why, yes, he'd love to take a little trip to Lima, but it was impossible and now Jum points at the Sergeant. No, no, not the Lieutenant, or the Sergeant, or the soldiers, Nieves, they couldn't do anything, he should look for that Reátegui, he'd gone back to Borja or somewhere, the Police Post was not going to go around digging up the dead, right? fixing up trouble that had happened a long time ago, right? He was dying with fatigue, he hadn't had any sleep, Sergeant, they should get it over with once and for all. Besides, if the ones who had punished him were Army soldiers from the garrison and the authorities from here, who was going to see that he got justice? Adrián Nieves interrogates the Sergeant with his eyes, what should he tell him, then?, and to the Lieutenant: all that? The officer yawns, lazily half opens his listless mouth, and the Sergeant leans over him: best to tell him all right, Lieutenant. They would return the rubber, the skins, the primers, the girl, everything he wanted, and Fats what was wrong with him, Sergeant, who was going to give it back to him since Escabino was dead now, and Shorty it wouldn't come out of their pay, would it?, and the Sergeant to make it more official they'd give him a signed piece of paper. They'd already done it once with Lieutenant Cipriano, Lieutenant, it brought results. They'd put a stamp in the middle of the paper and all set: he should take this and go find Señor Reátegui and Escabinodevil so that they would give everything back to him. And Blacky a real cute trick, eh, Sergeant? But the Lieutenant didn't know about things like that, he couldn't sign any paper on such an old matter, and besides, but the Sergeant just a piece of newspaper, a little faked signature, and that way he'd leave and let them alone. They were stubborn, but they believed what they were told, he'd spend months and years looking for Escabino and Señor Reátegui.

All right, and now they should give him something to eat and he should leave without anyone's laying a finger on him, Captain, he should please pass it on himself. And the Captain he would be pleased to, Don Julio, he calls the Corporal: understood? The punishment was over, not another finger on him, and Julio Reátegui: the important thing was that he go back to Urakusa. No more beating soldiers, no more cheating boss, that if the Urakusas behave the white men will behave, that if the Urakusas misbehave the white men will too: he should translate that, and the Sergeant lets out a laugh that makes his whole round face happy: what had he told him, Lieutenant? Yes, they'd got rid of him, but the officer didn't like it, he wasn't used to procedures like these, and Fats the jungle wasn't Lima, sir, here you had to fight with redskins. The Lieutenant stands up, Sergeant, he was getting dizzy with all this business, they were not to wake him up even if the world was coming to an end. Didn't he want another beer before he went to sleep?, no, should they bring him a pitcher of water?, later. The Lieutenant salutes the soldiers and goes out. The square of Santa María de Nieva is filled with Indians, the women who are sitting on the ground grinding form a large circle, some have children clinging to their breasts. The Lieutenant stops in the middle of the path and, warding off the sun with his hand, he looks at the capironas for a moment: robust, tall, masculine. A skinny dog goes by and the officer follows it with his eyes, and then he sees the pilot Adrián Nieves. He comes toward him, and he shows him the black and white shreds of the piece of newspaper in his hand, Lieutenant: he wasn't as dumb as the Sergeant had thought, he'd torn up the paper and thrown it down in the square, he'd just found it.

1

"I've got a secret you couldn't even begin to guess, Sergeant," Fats said, lowering his voice. "But don't let the others hear."

Blacky, Shorty, and Blondy were talking at the bar with Paredes, who was serving them glasses of anisette. A boy went out of the canteen with three clay jars, crossed the square of Santa María de Nieva, and disappeared on his way to the Post. A strong sun was gilding the capironas, the roofs, and the walls of the huts, but it did not reach the ground, because a whitish floating mist, which seemed to be coming from the Nieva River, was keeping it away from the surface of the ground as it darkened it.

"They're not listening," the Sergeant said. "What's the secret?"

"I found out who the girl at the Nieveses' place is." Fats spat out some black papaya seeds and wiped his sweaty face with his handkerchief. "The one who got us so curious the other night."

"Oh, yes?" the Sergeant said. "Who is she?"

"The one who used to take the garbage out for the sisters," Fats whispered, looking at the bar out of the corner of his eyes. "The one they threw out of the Mission because she'd helped the pupils run away."

The Sergeant went through his pockets, but his cigarettes were on the table. He lit one and took a deep drag, he let out a mouthful of smoke: a fly flew anxiously around inside the cloud and then buzzed off.

"And how did you find out?" the Sergeant asked. "Did Nieves introduce her to you?"

By playing dumb, Sergeant, Fats used to take his walks by the pilot's cabin, and that morning he'd seen her, working in the garden with Nieves' wife: Bonifacia, that was her name. Couldn't Fats have been mistaken maybe? Why would she be with the Nieveses, wasn't she halfway to being a nun? No, since they threw her out she wasn't any more, she didn't wear her uniform and Fats had recognized her right away. A little on the chubby side, Sergeant, but she had a figure. And she must have been quite young, but, most of all, he shouldn't say anything to the others.

"Do you think I'm a gossip?" the Sergeant asked. "Keep your stupid advice."

Paredes brought over two glasses of anisette and stood next to the table while the Sergeant and Fats drank. Then he cleaned the table top with a rag and went back to the bar. Blacky, Blondy, and Shorty left the canteen, and at the door a rosy shadow lit up their faces, their necks. The mist had grown thicker, and in the distance the soldiers now looked mutilated, or like Christians walking through a river of foam.

"Don't get into any trouble with the Nieveses, they're friends of mine," the Sergeant said.

And who was going to get into any trouble with them? But it would be crazy not to take advantage of the situation, Sergeant. They were the only ones who knew, so that like good buddies, right?, Fats would do the little job for him, fifty-fifty, right?, and he'd hand her over to him, all right? But the Sergeant began to cough, he didn't like that kind of sharing, he blew smoke out of his nose, his mouth, what the hell, why should he have seconds.

"Didn't I see her first, Sergeant?" Fats said. "And find out who she was and everything. But, look, what's the Lieutenant doing over here?"

He pointed toward the square and there was the Lieutenant coming—his body half emerging from the vapor, blinking in the sun—with a clean shirt on. When he came out of the fog, the bottom half of his pants and his boots were damp.

"Come with me, Sergeant," he ordered, from the bottom of the steps. "Don Fabio wants to see us."

"Don't forget what I told you, Sergeant," Fats whispered.

The Lieutenant and the Sergeant sank into the mist up to their waists. The dock and the lower cabins around it had already been devoured by the waves of vapor, which now were attacking, tall and undulant, the roofs and the railings. At the same time, a diaphanous light was touching the hills, the Mission buildings were glowing intact, and the trees, whose trunks had dissolved into the fog, were exhibiting their clean crowns, and their leaves, their branches, and their silvery spider webs were all aglitter.

"Have you been up to the nuns, Lieutenant?" the Sergeant asked. "I bet they gave the kids a good spanking, right?"

"They've already forgiven them," the Lieutenant said. "They took them down to the river this morning. The Mother Superior told me that the sick one was better."

On the stairs leading to the Governor's cabin, they shook their wet pants and scraped their muddy soles against the steps. The square of screen that protected the doorway was so fine that it hid the inside. An old and barefoot Aguaruna woman opened the door for them, they went in, and inside it was cool and smelled of vegetables. The windows were closed, the room was in half darkness, and one could vaguely make out the bows, photographs, blowguns, and bundles of arrows hanging on the walls. Some flowery rocking chairs were placed around the chambira rug, and Don Fabio had appeared in the door of the adjoining room, Lieutenant, Sergeant, smiling and thin under his gleaming bald head, his hand outstretched: the order had just come, just imagine! He patted the officer on the back, how were they doing?, he made affable gestures, what did they think of the news?, but first some refreshments?, some beer?, didn't it seem impossible? He gave a command in Aguaruna, and the old woman brought two bottles of beer and some glasses. The Sergeant drank his glass right down, the Lieutenant passed his from one hand to the other and his eyes were wandering and worried, Don Fabio was drinking like a little bird, with tiny sips.

"Had the sisters got the message on their radio?" the Lieutenant asked.

Yes, this morning, and they had told Don Fabio right away. Don Julio had always said that Minister was sabotaging things, he's my worst enemy, he'll never leave. And it was the absolute truth, they could see it now, the Ministry changed hands and the order came flying along.

"After such a long time," the Sergeant said. "I'd even forgotten about the bandits, Governor."

Don Fabio Cuesta was still smiling: they had to leave as soon as possible so they could be on their way back before the rains came, he didn't recommend the floods of the Santiago, the debris and the whirlpools of the Santiago, how many white men had been carried off by those floods?

"We've only got four men at the post and that's not enough," the Lieutenant said. "Because, besides, one soldier has to stay here and take care of the place."

Don Fabio winked mischievously, but the new Minister was a friend of Don Julio's, a friend. He'd given them everything they needed, and they wouldn't be going alone, but with some soldiers from the Borja garrison. And they'd already received the order, Lieutenant. The officer took a drink, oh, and he nodded without enthusiasm: well, that was a different story. But he didn't understand it, and he shook his head perplexedly, this whole business was like the resurrection of Lazarus, Don Fabio. That was the way things went in our country, Lieutenant, what did he expect, that other Minister had delayed and delayed, thinking that he was harming only Don Julio, not realizing the terrible harm he was causing everybody. Better late than never, right?

"But there haven't been any new wanted notices on those thieves, Don Fabio," the Lieutenant said. "The last one was just a little while after I got to Santa María de Nieva; look how much time has gone by."

And what difference did that make, Lieutenant? There may not have been notices on this side, but there were on the other, and besides those outlaws had to pay for their debts; could he give them some more beer? The Sergeant accepted, and once more he emptied his glass with one gulp: it wasn't because of that, Governor, but because they would probably be making a useless trip, those crooks wouldn't still be there. And if the rains came early, how long would they be buried in the jungle. Not at all, not at all, Sergeant, they had to be at the Borja garrison within four days, and another thing that the Lieutenant should know: this was a matter that Don Julio took very personally. The outlaws had made him lose time and patience, something that he never forgave. Hadn't the Lieutenant said that his dream was to get out of there? Don Julio would help him if everything went well, that man's friendship was worth a million, Lieutenant, Don Fabio knew that from experience.

"Ah, Don Fabio," the officer said, smiling, "you know me too well. You put your finger right on my weak spot."

"And the Sergeant can even get something out of it," the Governor answered, clapping happily. "Of course! Didn't I tell you that Don Julio and the new Minister are friends?"

It was all right, Don Fabio, they'd do what they could. But he should give them another drink to wake them up, the news had left them half stunned. They finished their beers and they chatted and joked in the cool and fragrant shadows, then the Governor took them to the steps and waved goodbye to them from there. The mist was covering everything now, and among its veils and ambiguous dancing the huts and trees were softly floating, were growing dark and becoming clear, and there were fleeting outlines circulating through the square. A small sad voice was singing in the distance.

"First chasing after those kids and now this," the Sergeant said. "I don't think it's any fun going upstream on the Santiago at this time of year, it's going to be rough on my bones, Lieutenant. Who'll we leave behind at the post?"

"Fats, he always gets tired," the Lieutenant said. "You would have liked to stay behind, right?"

"But Fats has had a lot of experience in the jungle," the Sergeant said. "He's been here a long time, Lieutenant. Why not Shorty? He's always sick."

"Fats," the Lieutenant said. "And don't put on that face. I don't like this deal either, but you heard what the Governor said, our luck'll change all of a sudden after this expedition and we'll be able to get out of this place. Go get Nieves and bring the others over to my cabin so we can lay out a plan of action."

The Sergeant was motionless for a moment in the mist, his hands in his pockets. Then, with his head down, he crossed the square, went past the dock that was sunken in a thick coat of vapor, went onto the path, and advanced through a smoky, slippery countryside, loaded down with electricity and croaking. When he got to the pilot's cabin, he was talking to himself, his hands were squeezing his cap, and his leggings, his pants, and his shirt were speckled with mud.

"How nice to see you at this time of day, Sergeant." Lalita was brushing back her hair, leaning over the railing; her face, her arms, and her dress were dripping. "But come in, come up, Sergeant."

Indecisive, pensive, still moving his lips, the Sergeant climbed up the steps; on the terrace he shook Lalita's hand, and when he turned around, Bonifacia was next to him, soaked too. Her natural-color dress was sticking to her body, her damp hair was encircling her face like a wimple, and her green eyes were looking contentedly at the Sergeant, with no sign of embarrassment. Lalita was wringing out the hem of her skirt, had he come to visit their house guest, Sergeant?, and transparent drops were forming a circle around her feet: there she was. They had been fishing and they had gone into the river with that fog, imagine, they couldn't see where they were going, but the water was nice and warm, wonderful, and Bonifacia came forward: could she bring him something to eat? some anisette? Instead of answering, Lalita let out a laugh and went into the cabin.

"You let yourself be seen by Fats this morning," the Sergeant said. "Why did you let yourself be seen? Didn't I tell you that I didn't want you to?"

"You're getting jealous, Sergeant," Lalita said, from the window, between laughs. "What do you care if they see her? Do you want the poor girl to spend the rest of her life hiding from everybody?"

Bonifacia was scrutinizing the Sergeant's face very seriously, and there was something frightened and confused in her expression. He took a step toward her and Bonifacia's eyes became alarmed but she did not move, and the Sergeant put out an arm, took her by the shoulder, sweety, he didn't want her talking to Fats or to any other white man, Señora Lalita.

"I can't tell her not to," Lalita said, and Aquilino, who had appeared in the window, laughed. "And you can't either, Sergeant; are you her brother or something? You could only do that if you were her husband."

"I didn't see him," Bonifacia stammered. "It's not true, he couldn't have seen me, that's all I can say."

"Don't humiliate yourself, don't be silly," Lalita said. "It's better for you to make him jealous, Bonifacia."

The Sergeant pulled Bonifacia against him, better that he should never see her with Fats, and he lifts up her chin with two fingers, that he should never see her with any man, Ma'am, and Lalita let out another laugh and two more faces appeared beside Aquilino's. The three children were devouring the Sergeant with their eyes, and he should never see her with anybody, Bonifacia clutched the Sergeant's shirt and her lips were trembling: she promised him.

"You're being silly," Lalita said. "It's easy to see that you don't know white people, especially ones in uniform."

"I have to go on a trip," the Sergeant said, hugging Bonifacia. "We'll be away for three weeks, maybe a month."

"Am I going along, Sergeant?" Adrián Nieves, in his shorts, was on the steps, rubbing his bronzed and bony body with his hand. "Don't tell me that the pupils got away again."

And when he got back they would get married, sweety, and his voice broke and he began to laugh like an idiot, while Lalita shouted and burst out onto the terrace, resplendent, her arms open, and Bonifacia went to meet her and they embraced. Nieves the pilot shook hands with the Sergeant, whose voice was breaking from emotion, Don Adrián, he had got all shaken up: he wanted them to stand up with them, of course. She could see, Señora Lalita, he'd fallen into her trap, and that was that, and Lalita had known from the beginning that the Sergeant was a proper Christian, he should let her embrace him. They would have a big party, he'd see how they'd celebrate it. Bonifacia, confused, was hugging the Sergeant, Lalita, she kissed the pilot's hand, she picked up the children and held them in the air, and they would be very glad to stand up with them, Sergeant, he should stay for dinner tonight. Her green eyes were sparkling, and Lalita they would build their house right here next door, they became sad, they would help them, they became happy, and the Sergeant she would have to take very good care of her, Ma'am, he didn't want her to see anybody while he was away on the trip, and Lalita of course, she wouldn't even let her out the door, they'd tie her up.

"And where are we going this time?" the pilot asked. "With the sisters again?"

"I wish we were," the Sergeant said. "They're going to kill us, Don Adrián. What do you think? The order came through. We're going up the Santiago to look for those bandits."

"Up the Santiago?" Lalita said. Her expression had changed, she was rigid and openmouthed, and Nieves the pilot was leaning on the railing, looking at the river, the fog, the trees. The children were still playing around Bonifacia.

"With some people from the Borja garrison," the Sergeant said. "But why are you both looking like that? There's no danger, there'll be a whole bunch going. And most likely those crooks have already died of old age."

"Pintado lives down that way," Adrián Nieves said, pointing toward the river hidden in the mist. "He knows the region well and he's one of the best pilots around. You'd better tell him right away, sometimes he goes out fishing around this time."

"But what's the matter," the Sergeant said. "You don't want to come with us, Don Adrián? It'll be at least three weeks, you'll pick up a good piece of change."

"I'm sick, the fever," the pilot said. "I'm vomiting all the time and I've been getting dizzy spells."

"Come on, Don Adrián," the Sergeant said. "Don't give me that, when have you ever been sick. Why don't you want to go?"

"He's got a fever, he should be in bed right now," Lalita said. "You'd better hurry up and get Pintado, Sergeant, before he goes off fishing."

And at dusk she escaped the way he had told her to, she came down the bank, and Fushía what took you so long, quick, into the small boat. They left Uchamala with the engine off, almost in the dark, and he insisting did anybody see you, Lalita?, God help me if they saw you, I'm risking my neck, I don't know why I'm doing it and she, in the prow, watch out, a whirlpool, and rocks on the left. They finally took refuge on a beach, they hid the boat, they fell onto the sand. And he I'm jealous, Lalita, don't tell me anything about that bastard Reátegui, but he needed a boat and supplies, there are rough days ahead of us but you'll soon see, I'll make it, and she you will, I'll help you, Fushía. And he spoke about the border, they were all probably saying he went to Brazil, they'll get tired of looking for me, Lalita, who's going to think I came this way, if we get to Ecuador there won't be any problem. And suddenly take your clothes off, Lalita, and she the ants'll bite me, Fushía, and he even if they do. Then it rained all night and the wind knocked down the shelter that protected them and they took turns scaring off the mosquitoes and the bats. They left at dawn and it was a good trip until the rapids appeared: a small boat and they hid, a village, a military post, an airplane and they hid. A week went by without any rain; they were traveling from sunup to sundown, and in order to save their canned goods, they fished for anchovetas and catfish. In the afternoon they would look for an island, a sand bar, a beach, and they would sleep with the protection of a campfire. They would sneak past villages by night, with motor off, and he push, hard, Lalita, and she my arms aren't strong enough, there's a heavy current, and he hard, God damn it, it isn't much farther now. Near Barranca they ran across a fisherman and they all ate together, and they they were running away, and he can I help you?, and Fushía we want to buy some gas, I'm running out, and he give me the money, I'll go to the village and bring some back. They spent two weeks going through the gullies, then they went into channels, lagoons, and fast currents, they got lost, the boat turned over twice, they ran out of gasoline, and one day at dawn don't cry, Lalita, we're getting there, look, they're Huambisas. They remembered him, they thought he was coming as at other times to buy rubber from them. They gave him a hut, food, two fireplaces, and they spent many days like that. And he do you see what's happening to you for sticking with me?, you would have been better off in Iquitos with your mother, and she what if they kill you one of these days, Fushía?, and he you'll be the wife of a Huambisa, you'll go around with your teats out and paint yourself with indigo, rupiña, and annatto, they'll have you chewing cassava to make beer, think of what's ahead of you. She was crying, the Huambisas were laughing, and he silly, I was only teasing, you may be the first white woman they've seen, a long time back I came here with someone from Moyabamba and they showed us the head of a white man who'd gone up the Santiago looking for gold, are you frightened?, and she yes, Fushía. The Huambisas brought them strips of meat from choscas and majaz pigs, catfish, cassavas, some green worms once and they vomited, from time to time a deer, fish, like gamitanas or zúngaros. He talked with them from morning to night, and she tell me what they say, what are you asking them, what are they telling you, and he things, don't worry, the first time I came with Aquilino we won them over with liquor and we spent six months with them, we brought them knives, cloth, shotguns, anisette and they gave us rubber, hides, and even now I can't complain, they were my customers, now they're my friends, without them I'd be dead, and she yes but let's leave, Fushía, isn't the border close? And he better than the rubber men, Lalita, starting with that bastard Reátegui and just think how he treated me, I helped him earn so much dough and he refused to help me, it's the second time that the Huambisas have saved me. And she but when are we going to Ecuador, Fushía, the rains will be here soon and we won't be able to go. And he stopped talking about the border and would spend his nights awake, sitting at the fireplace, he would take walks, he would talk to himself, and she what's wrong, Fushía, let me help you, that's why I'm your wife, and he quiet he was thinking. And one morning he got up, he went down the embankment with leaps and bounds, and she from up on top don't do that, in the name of the Christ of Bagazán, Lord, Lord, and he kept using his machete on the boat until it sank, and when he came back up the bank his eyes looked happy. Go to Ecuador without any clothes, money, papers? Crazy, Lalita, the police send word from one country to another, we'll only stay a while longer here, I can get rich here, everything depends on these people and my finding Aquilino, he's the man we need, come on, I'll tell you about it, and she what have you done, Fushía, good Lord. And he nobody will come by here and when we leave they'll have forgotten about me, and besides we'll have money to shut anyone's mouth. And she Fushía, Fushía, and he I've got to find Aquilino, and she why did you sink it, I don't want to die in the jungle, and he you simpleton, he had to cover their tracks. And one day they left in a canoe, with two Huambisa paddlers, in the direction of the Santiago. They were escorted by gnats, a rain of mosquitoes, the hoarse song of the trompetero birds, and at night, in spite of the fire and the blankets, the bats would swoop over their bodies and bite into the soft spots: toes, noses, the base of the skull. And no staying too close to the river, there are soldiers around here. They went up narrow channels, dark, under arches of shaggy foliage, foul bogs, sometimes lagoons that curled with renaco trees, and also through paths that the Huambisas opened with their machetes, carrying the canoe on their shoulders. They ate what they found, roots, twigs with an acid juice, concoctions of herbs, and one day they killed a tapir, meat for a week. And she I can't make it, Fushía, my legs are worn out, my face is all scratched up, and he just a little more. Until the Santiago appeared, and there they ate chitari fish that they caught under the stones of the river and smoked over the fire, and an armadillo killed by the Huambisas, and he have you noticed that we're getting there, Lalita?, this is good country, there's food and everything's coming out right, and she my face is burning, Fushía, I tell you I can't go on. They made camp one day and then they went on, up the Santiago, stopping to sleep and eat in Huambisa villages of two or three families. And a week later they left the river and for hours they went through a narrow channel where the sun could not get in, so low that their heads touched the forest. They came out, and he Lalita, the island, look at it, the best place on earth, between the jungle and the swamps, and before landing he had the Huambisas paddle all around it, and she are we going to live here? and he it's hidden, there are tall woods on all sides, that point there is good for the dock. They landed and the Huambisas rolled their eyes, showed their fists, grunted, and Lalita what's wrong with them, Fushía, what are they so angry about, and he afraid of some nonsense, they want to go back, they're afraid of the lupuna trees. Because at the top of the embankment and all along the island, like a compact and high palisade, there were rough-barked lupunas, bulging with humps and great gnarled outcroppings that served them as seats. And she don't shout at them so much, Fushía, they'll get angry. They were arguing, grunting, and gesticulating, and finally he convinced them and they followed them into the underbrush that covered the island. And he can you hear, Lalita?, it's full of birds, there are macaws, can't you hear them?, and when they found a huancahuí bird eating a small black snake the Huambisas howled, and he the skittish bastards, and she you're crazy everything is jungle, Fushía, how are we going to live here, and he do you think I haven't thought about everything? I lived here with Aquilino and I'll live here again and I'll get rich here, you'll see how I'll keep my word. They went back to the embankment, she went down to the canoe and he and the Huambisas went back in, and suddenly above the lupunas there arose a column of leaden-colored smoke and there was the smell of burning. He and the Huambisas came running back, they jumped into the canoe, they crossed the lagoon and camped on the opposite bank, beside the mouth of the channel. And he when the burning is over there'll be a large clearing, Lalita, as long as it doesn't rain, and she I hope there won't be any wind, Fushía, so the fire won't spread over here and set the jungle on fire. It did not rain and the fire lasted almost two days, and they stayed in the same spot, getting the thick fetid smoke of the lupuna and catahua trees, the ashes that were floating about through the air, looking at the blue slender flames, the sparks that landed hissing in the lagoon, hearing the island crackle. And he there you are, the devils are all burned up, and she don't provoke them, those are their beliefs, and he they don't understand me and besides they're laughing, I cured them forever of being afraid of the lupunas. The fire was cleaning and depopulating the island: from out of the smoke there came flocks of birds, and monkeys appeared on the bank, maquisapas, frailecillos, shimbillos, pelejos, who were shrieking as they jumped onto floating logs and branches; the Huambisas went into the water, caught a lot of them, split their skulls with their machetes, and he what a banquet they would have, Lalita, they're over being mad now, and she I want something to eat too, even if it is monkey meat, I'm hungry. And when they went back to the island there were several clearings, but the embankment was still untouched and in many places closed redoubts of thick jungle survived. They began cleaning up, all day long they threw dead logs, charred birds, snakes into the lagoon, and he tell me that you're happy, and she I am, Fushía, and he do you believe in me?, and she yes. And then there was a stretch of flat land, and the Huambisas cut down some trees and tied the logs together with vines, and he look, Lalita, it's just like a house, and she not really but it's better than sleeping out in the jungle. And on the following morning, when they woke up, a paucar had made its nest across from the cabin, its black and yellow feathers shone among the leaves, and he good luck, Lalita, those birds like people, if he came here it's because he knows we're going to stay.

And on that same Saturday some people picked up the body of Antonia and took it wrapped in a sheet to the washerwoman's shack. The wake brought together many men and women from Gallinacera in Juana Baura's yard, and she wept all night, time and again she would kiss the dead girl's hands, eyes, feet. At dawn some women took Juana out of the room, and Father García helped put the remains in the coffin that had been bought with a general collection. That Sunday, Father García said the mass in the chapel near the market, and he led the funeral procession, he returned from the cemetery to Gallinacera with Juana Baura: the people watched him cross the Plaza de Armas surrounded by women, pale, his eyes flashing, his fists clenched. Beggars, bootblacks, and tramps joined the cortege, and when it reached the market, it filled the whole street. There, standing on a bench, Father García began to shout, and all around windows were opened, vending women left their stands to listen to him, and two policemen who tried to clear the area were insulted and stoned. Father García's shouts could be heard at the slaughterhouse, and at the Estrella del Norte people from out of town were quiet, startled: where was all that noise coming from and where were so many women going? Secret, feminine, persistent, a voice ran through the city, and all the while, under a sky of sombre vultures, Father García was still speaking. Whenever he fell silent, Juana Baura's wails could be heard as she knelt at his feet. Then the women began quietly to move about and mutter. And when the Civil Guards arrived with their staffs, an enraged sea rose up to meet them, Father García in the lead, wrathful, a crucifix in his right hand, and when they tried to block the women's way, there was a rain of stones, threats: the guards retreated, took refuge in the houses, others fell and the sea attacked them, submerged them, left them behind. The infuriated waves went into the Plaza de Armas, roaring, fierce, armed with sticks and stones, and as it passed, doors were barred, gates were closed, the important people ran into the cathedral, and the strangers, taking refuge in doorways, witnessed the advance of the torrent with astonishment. Had Father García fought the police? Had they attacked him? His torn cassock showed a thin and milk-white chest, long bony arms. He was still holding up the crucifix and shouting. And the torrent passed by the Estrella del Norte, a volley of stones and the windows of the bar fell into pieces, and when the women went onto the Old Bridge the aged skeleton creaked, staggered like a drunkard, and when they passed the Río Bar and reached Castilla many women were holding torches in their hands, they were running, people poured out of the mouths of the chicha bars, more shouts, more torches. They reached the desert and a whirlwind arose, a gigantic, weightless top, golden, and in the heart of the spiral could be seen faces of women, fists, flames.

Huddled under the snow-white blinding glare of noon, its doors and windows closed, the Green House looked like a deserted mansion. The hedges sparkled softly in the sunlight, grew hazy at the corners with a kind of timidity, and, like a wounded deer, there was something defenseless about the peacefulness of the place, docile and fearful as it faced the mob that was drawing near. Father García and the women reached the doors, the shouting ceased, and there was a sudden lack of movement. But then shrieks were heard, and just as ants desert their labyrinths when flooded by the river, the occupants poured out, pushing and howling, painted and half dressed, and Father García's voice rose, thundered out over the sea, and innumerable tentacles reached out from among the waves and the surf, caught the occupants, pulled them down, and beat them on the ground. And then Father García and the women flooded into the Green House, filled it in a few seconds, and from the interior there came the loud noise of destruction: glasses and bottles being smashed, tables being broken, sheets and curtains being torn. From the first floor, the second, and the tower room, a small domestic flood poured out. Through the baking air flew flower pots, chamber pots, chipped washbasins and trays, plates, torn mattresses, cosmetics, and a salvo of cheers would greet each projectile as it described an arc and came to rest in the sand. Many men and women bystanders were arguing over the objects and articles of clothing, and there were confrontations, disputes, violent conversations. In the midst of the disorder, beaten, voiceless, still trembling, the occupants stood up, some fell into the arms of others, wept and consoled each other. The Green House was on fire: purple, sharp, and leaping, the flames could be seen amidst the ash-colored smoke that was slowly circling up toward the Piuran sky. The mob began to draw back, the shouts died down: out the doors of the Green House came the invading women and Father García on the run, shaking with coughs, weeping from the smoke.

From the balustrade of the Old Bridge, from the Malecón, the church towers, the roofs and balconies, clusters of people were watching the fire: a hydra with blood-red and celestial heads crackling beneath a blackish canopy. Only when the slim tower fell and, impelled by a light breeze, coals, shreds, and ashes rained down for a time on the city did the Civil Guards and the police appear. They mingled with the women, impotent and tardy, confused and fascinated like everyone else by the spectacle of the fire. And suddenly there was shoving, movement; women and beggars were whispering, saying *"There he comes, here he is."*

He was coming across the Old Bridge: Gallinazo women and bystanders turned to look at him, they got out of his way, no one stopped him, and he went forward, rigid, his hair messy, his face dirty, his eyes incredibly frightened, his mouth trembling. They had seen him the night before, drinking in a chicha bar in Mangachería, where he had appeared at dusk, his harp under his arm, weepy and red-faced. And he spent the night there, singing between hiccups. The Mangaches went over to him: *"What was it all about, Don Anselmo?, what happened?, is it true that you were living with Antonia?, that you had her in the Green House?, is it true that she's dead?"* He moaned, he sobbed, and finally he rolled on the floor, drunk. He slept, and when he woke up he asked for another drink, he kept on drinking, plucking his harp, and that was what he was doing when a child came into the bar: "The Green House, Don Anselmo! They're burning it down! The women from Gallinacera and Father García, Don Anselmo!"

Some men and women confronted him on the Malecón, "You

kidnapped Antonia, you killed her," and they tore his clothes, and when he fled they stoned him. Only when he got to the Old Bridge did he start to shout and beg, and the people he's making it up, he's afraid they'll lynch him, but he kept on shouting, and the frightened occupants with their heads yes, it was true, she must have been inside. He knelt on the sand, he begged, he took heaven as his witness, and then a kind of unrest broke out among the people, the guards and the police interrogated the Gallinazo women, contradictory voices arose, and what if it was true?, they should go see, they should move, they should call Dr. Zevallos. Wrapped in wet burlap, some Mangaches dived into the smoke and came out moments later, suffocated, defeated, you couldn't get in, it was hell inside there. Men and women attacked Father García, and what if it was true?, Father, Father, God would punish him. He looked from one to the other, wrapped up in himself; Don Anselmo was arguing with the guards, give him a piece of burlap, he'd go in, they should have mercy. And when Angélica Mercedes appeared and they all knew it was true, the baby was there, unharmed, in the arms of the cook, and they saw how the harp player was moved, how he thanked heaven and kissed Angélica Mercedes on the hands, many women softened. With loud voices they pitied the baby, consoled the harp player, or turned their wrath on Father García and reproached him. Stupefied, relieved, moved, the crowd surrounded Don Anselmo, and no one, either the occupants or the Gallinazo women or the Mangaches, noticed the Green House any more, the great fire that was consuming it, or that the punctual rain of sand was beginning to put it out, giving it back to the desert on which it had had a fleeting existence.

The champs came in as always: opening the door with a kick and singing their theme song: they were the champs, work wasn't for them, they lived off the rest, they emptied their glasses, and now they were ready to wiggle their asses.

"I can only tell you what I heard that night, girl," the harp player said. "You must have noticed that I can barely see anything. That was what saved me from the police, they left me alone."

"The milk's getting hot," Chunga said, from the bar. "Give me a hand, Wildflower."

Wildflower got up from the musicians' table, went over to the bar, and she and Chunga brought a pitcher of milk, bread, instant coffee, sugar. The lights in the room were still on, but day was already coming in through the windows, hot and bright.

"The girl doesn't know how it happened, Chunga," the harp player said, taking small sips of his milk. "Josefino didn't tell her."

"I ask him and he changes the subject," Wildflower said. "Why are you so interested, he says, stop it, you're making me jealous."

"And a cheat, a hypocrite, and a cynic," Chunga said.

"There were only two customers when they came in," Jocko said. "At that table. One of them was Seminario."

The Leóns and Josefino had settled down at the bar and they were shouting and jumping, very turned on: we love you, Chunga Chunguita, you're our queen, there's nobody sweeter, Chunga Chunguita.

"Quit your nonsense and have something to drink or I'll throw you out," Chunga said. The orchestra came over: "Why aren't you playing?"

"We couldn't," Jocko said. "The champs were making so much noise. They seem to be having a good time."

"They're loaded with dough tonight," Chunga said.

"Look, look here." Monk showed her a fan made out of pound notes and he was sucking on his fingers. "Guess how much?"

"You sure are greedy, Chunga, you ought to see your face," Josefino said.

"You stole it, of course," Chunga replied. "What can I get you?"

"They were probably drunk," Wildflower said. "That always makes them crack jokes and sing."

Drawn by the noise, three occupants appeared on the stairway: Sandra, Rita, Maribel. But when they saw it was the champs, they looked cheated, they stopped their elegant posing, and Sandra's great laugh could be heard, it was them, what a bunch, but Monk opened up his arms to them, they should come down, they should order anything they wanted, and he showed them the bills.

"Give the musicians a drink too, Chunga," Josefino said.

"Very nice boys," the harp player said, smiling. "They were always inviting us. I knew Josefino's father, girl. He was a boatman and he used to ferry across the cattle that came from Catacaos. Carlos Rojas, a very nice fellow."

Wildflower refilled the harp player's cup and put some sugar in it. The champs sat down at a table with Sandra, Rita, and Maribel, and they were talking about a game of poker they had just had at the Reina. Kid Alejandro was drinking his coffee lazily: they were the champs, work wasn't for them, they lived off the rest, they emptied their glasses, and now they were ready to wiggle their asses.

"We won it clean, Sandra, I swear. Luck was on our side."

"Three ace-high straights in a row; did you ever see anything like it?"

"The champs taught the theme song to the girls," the harp player said, in a friendly and kindly voice. "And then they came over to where we were and asked us to play their theme song for them. I would have done it, but first they had to ask Chunga's permission."

"And you gave us the sign that it was O.K., Chunga," Jocko said.

"They were buying as they never had," Chunga explained to Wildflower. "Why shouldn't I keep them happy?"

"That's how trouble starts sometimes," the Kid said, with a melancholy gesture. "Over a song."

"Sing, so they can pick up the tune," the harp player said. "Let's go, Kid, Jocko, keep your ears open."

While the champs were singing the theme song together, Chunga was rocking in her chair like a peaceful housewife, and the musicians were keeping time with their feet and whispering the lyrics. Then they all sang it out loud, accompanied by guitar, harp, and cymbals.

"That's enough," Seminario said. "Enough singing and cheap tricks."

"He hadn't paid any attention to the noise until then, and he'd been very quiet, talking to his friend," Jocko said.

"I saw him get up," the Kid said. "He was furious. I thought he was going to attack us."

"He didn't sound drunk," the harp player said. "We did what he said, we stopped, but that didn't calm him down. How long had he been here, Chunga?"

"Quite a while. He'd come right from his ranch, with his boots, riding breeches, and pistol."

"A bull of a man, that Seminario," the Kid said. "And mean-looking. You're stronger, you're meaner."

"Thank you, brother," Jocko said.

"You're an exception, Jocko," the Kid said. "The body of a prize fighter and the soul of a lamb, as the maestro says."

"Don't be like that, Señor Seminario," Monk said. "We were only singing our theme song. Let us buy you a beer."

"But he was in a bad mood," Jocko said. "Something was bothering him and he was looking for a fight."

"So you're the banty roosters who start fights in the street?" Seminario said. "Think you want to start one with me?"

Rita, Sandra, and Maribel tiptoed over to the bar, and the Kid and Jocko used their bodies to shield the harp player as he sat on the bench with a peaceful look and proceeded to tune his harp. And Seminario went on, he was a son of a bitch too, swaggering, and he knew how to have fun, pounding his chest, but he worked for a living, plowed his land, he didn't like bums, fat and loquacious under the violet light, loafers, nuts.

"We're young, sir. We weren't doing anything wrong."

"We know you're strong, but that's no reason to insult us."

"Is it true that once you picked up a man from Catacaos and threw him up onto a roof? Is that true, Señor Seminario?"

"Did they go on like that with him?" Wildflower asked. "I wouldn't have believed it of them."

"They are afraid of me." Seminario was laughing, appeased. "They are buttering me up."

"Men always forget their pride when it's important," Chunga said.

"Not everybody, Chunga," Jocko protested. "If he'd messed with me, I'd have given him an answer."

"He had a gun and the champs had a right to be scared," the Kid said softly. "Fear is like love, Chunga, it's a human thing."

"You think you're such a wise man," Chunga said. "But your philosophy won't work with me, in case you didn't know."

"Too bad the boys didn't leave then and there," the harp player said.

Seminario had gone back to his table, and the champs too, without any signs of the jollity of a moment before: let him get drunk and he'd see, but no, he had a gun on, better let it go for another time, and why not set fire to his pickup truck?, it was just outside, next to the Club Grau.

"Maybe we should leave and lock him up here and set the Green House on fire," Josefino said. "All it takes is a couples of matches and a can of kerosene. The way Father García did."

"It would burn like dry straw," José said. "The whole neighborhood too, all the way to the stadium."

"Maybe we ought to burn all Piura down," Monk said. "A great big fire that they could see clear off in Chiclayo. The whole desert would turn black."

"And the ashes would fall as far away as Lima," José said. "But there's just one thing, we'd have to save Mangachería."

"Naturally; that would be all we needed," Monk said. "We'd find a way."

"I was five years old when the fire happened," Josefino said. "Do you guys remember anything?"

"Not of the beginning," Monk said. "We went out there the next day with some kids from the block, but the cops chased us. They say that the ones who got there first stole a lot of things."

"I can only remember the smell of something burned," Josefino said. "And that you could see smoke, and that a lot of carob trees got singed."

"Let's have the old man tell us about it," Monk said. "We'll buy him some beers."

"We're they lying?" Wildflower asked. "Or were they talking about the other fire?"

"Piuran ways, girl," the harp player said. "Never believe anything they say when they talk about that. Nothing but lies."

"Aren't you tired, maestro?" the Kid said. "It's going on seven, we ought to be leaving."

"I don't feel sleepy yet," Don Anselmo said. "Let me digest my breakfast first."

Leaning on the bar, the champs were trying to convince Chunga: that she should let him stay awhile, what would it cost, let him talk to them a little bit, Chunga Chunguita shouldn't be mean.

"They all love you a lot, Don Anselmo," Wildflower said. "Me too, you remind me of a little old man back home called Aquilino."

"So generous, so nice," the harp player said. "They took me over to their table, they bought me a beer."

He was perspiring. Josefino put a glass in his hand, he drank it down and smacked his lips. Then, with his colored handkerchief, he wiped his forehead, his thick white eyebrows, and blew his nose.

"A favor for some good friends, old man," Monk said. "Tell us about the fire."

The harp player's hand searched for his glass and, instead of his own, he took Monk's; he downed it. What were they talking about, what fire, and he blew his nose again.

"I was just a kid and I saw the flames from the Malecón. And people running with pieces of burlap and pails of water," Josefino said. "Why won't you tell us, harp man? What harm is there after such a long time?"

"There never was any fire, any Green House," the harp player declared. "People made it all up, boys."

"Why are you kidding us?" Monk said. "Come on, harp man, tell us about it, even if it's only a few things."

Don Anselmo raised two fingers to his mouth and imitated smoking. The Kid gave him a cigarette and Jocko lit it. Chunga had turned out the lights in the main room, and the sun was pouring into the place through the windows and the chinks in the wall. There were yellow splotches on the walls and on the floor, the metal of the roof reflected the light. The champs were insisting, was it true that the occupants had got burned?, was it really the women from Gallinacera who'd set it on fire?, was he inside?, did Father García do it out of pure meanness or for some religious reason?, was it true that Doña Angélica had saved Chunguita from being burned to death?

"Just a tale," the harpist assured them, "foolishness of the people who want to get Father García angry. They ought to leave him alone, poor old man. And now I have to get back to work, boys, excuse me."

He got up, and with short little steps, holding his hands in front of him, he went back to the orchestra corner.

"You see? He's playing dumb, the way he always does," Josefino said. "I could see it was no use."

"Your brain gets soft when you get that old," Monk said. "Maybe he's forgotten everything. We ought to ask Father García about it, but who'd dare."

And then the door opened and the patrol came in.

"Those sly buggers," Chunga muttered. "They've come to do me out of a drink."

"The patrol, I mean Lituma and two other cops, Wildflower," Jocko said. "They used to drop by every night."

2

Under the curved shade of the banana trees, Bonifacia stood up and looked toward the village: men and women were running across the square of Santa María de Nieva, waving their hands excitedly, toward the dock. She bent down over the straight furrows, but a moment later she stood up again: the people were still pouring down, all excited. She took a peek at the Nieveses' cabin; Lalita was humming inside, gray smoke was snaking its way up among the roof poles, the pilot's boat had still not appeared on the horizon. Bonifacia twisted her head, went into the bushes on the shore, and with the water over her ankles she headed toward the village. The treetops were blending with the clouds, their trunks with the ochre outcroppings along the bank. The flood season had begun, the river was pulling along parasitic currents of redder or darker waters, and also bushes, decapitated flowers, lichens, and forms that could have been clods, animal dung, or dead rodents. Looking all around, slowly, cautiously, like a tracker, she went through a clump of reeds, and when she came around a bend she could see the dock: the people were motionless among the stakes and the canoes, and a raft was halted a few yards from the floating wharf. The sunset was turning the Aguaruna women's itípaks and faces blue, and there were men there too, their pants rolled up to their knees, torsos naked. She could see the rope that would tighten up and slacken with the motion of the newcomer's raft, the brace in the prow, and, quite clearly, the hut built on the stern. A flock of herons flew over the grove and Bonifacia could hear the flapping of their wings close by, she raised her head and saw their thin white necks, their pink bodies, as they went off into the distance. Then she continued on ahead, bending far over and not along the riverbank but through the underbrush, scratching her arms, her face, and her legs on the edges of the leaves, the thorns, and the rough vines, among buzzing sounds, feeling slimy caresses on her feet. Almost where the woods ended, a little way from the people gathered there, she stopped and squatted down: the vegetation closed in over her and now she could look through a complicated green geometry of rhombuses, cubes, and unlikely angles. The old man was in no hurry; he was walking very calmly about the raft, carefully setting up the boxes and merchandise for the onlookers, who were whispering and showing signs of impatience. The old man went into the hut and came out with a bolt of cloth, some shoes, a string of chaquira seed, necklaces, and seriously, carefully, as if with a mania, he put them in order on top of the boxes. He was very thin, when the wind filled out his shirt he looked slightly hunchbacked, but suddenly the front and the back would sink in until they almost touched, and his real figure would be revealed, slim and very narrow. He was wearing short pants, and Bonifacia could see his legs, as thin as his arms, his face of tanned skin that was almost black, and the fantastic, silky hair that flowed down over his shoulders. The old man took a long time, still bringing out household utensils and multicolored adornments, piling them up ceremoniously on the printed cloth. The whispering would mount whenever the old man took something out of the hut, and Bonifacia could see the interest of the women, Indian and white, their fascinated, greedy looks at the beads, combs, mirrors, bracelets, and tinsel, and the eyes of the men fixed on the bottles lined up in a corner of the raft, alongside canned goods, belts, and machetes. The old man looked over his work for a moment, he turned toward the people, and they ran over in a tumult, splashed all around the raft. But the old man shook his white mane and held them back by waving his hands. Holding up his rudder pole like a lance, he made them go back, come aboard in order. The first one was Paredes' wife. Fat, clumsy, she was unable to climb on board, the old man had to help her, and she went about touching everything, smelling the flasks, nervously fingering the cloth and the soap, and the people muttered and protested until she went back onto the dock, the water up to her waist, holding up a flowered dress, a necklace, some white shoes. So they went climbing up onto the raft, one after the other, the women. Some were slow and not sure about what to choose, others kept on challenging the prices endlessly, and there were those who would weep or make threats as they asked for discounts. But they all came back from the raft with something in their hands, some white men with bags of provisions, and some Indians with only a small bag of beads to be strung. When the dock was empty, night was coming on: Bonifacia stood up. The Nieva was at full flood, curly white-haired waves ran under the foliage and finished at her knees. Her body was stained with mud, pieces of grass were sticking to her hair and dress. The old man was taking care of his merchandise, methodically and precisely, he was placing the boxes in the prow, and the sky over Santa María de Nieva was a constellation of pitch and owl eyes, but across the Marañón, over the dusky fortress of the horizon, a blue strip was still resisting night, and the moon was coming up behind the Mission buildings. The old man's body was a dirty blotch, his hair was sparkling in the half light with the silver of a fish. Bonifacia looked toward the village: there were lights in the Government building, in Paredes' bar, and some lanterns were glimmering on the hillside in the windows of the Residence. The darkness was slowly gobbling up the cabins on the square, the capironas, the upper path. Bonifacia left her refuge and ran, hunched over, to the dock. The mud on the shore was soft and warm, the water in the inlet seemed motionless, and she felt it rise up over her body, and just a few yards from the bank the current began, a moderate and obstinate force that made her move her arms so as not to lose her direction. The water was up to her chin when she grasped the raft, and she saw the old man's white pants, the circle of his hair: it was late, she should come back tomorrow. Bonifacia pulled herself up a little along the edge, she leaned on her elbows, and the old man, leaning toward the river, looked her over: could she talk white man's talk? did she understand?

"Yes, Don Aquilino," Bonifacia said. "Good evening."

"It's time to go to bed," the old man said. "The store's closed, come back tomorrow."

"Be nice," Bonifacia said. "Let me come up for just a little while."

"You've sneaked some money away from your husband and that's why you're showing up at this time," the old man said. "And what if he asks for it back tomorrow?"

He spat into the water and laughed. He was squatting, his hair was falling down all frothy and free around his face, and Bonifacia could see his dark forehead, free of wrinkles, his eyes that were like two small glowing animals.

"What do I care," the old man said. "All I do is run my business. Come on, climb aboard."

He stretched out a hand, but Bonifacia had already climbed up, lithely, and once on deck, she wrung out her dress and rubbed her arms. Necklaces? Shoes? How much money do you have? Bonifacia began to smile timidly, couldn't you use some work, Don Aquilino?, and her eyes were anxiously watching the old man's mouth, could she cook for him while he was in Santa María de Nieva?, could she pick him some fruit?, could she clean up the raft when it needed it? The old man came over to her, where did he know her from?, and he looked her up and down: he'd seen her somewhere before, right?

"I'd like a piece of cloth," Bonifacia said, and she bit her lips. She pointed to the hut, and her eyes lighted up for an instant. "That yellow cloth you put away last. I can pay for it with some work, you tell me what it is, and I'll do it."

"No work," the old man said. "Don't you have any money?"

"I need it for a dress," Bonifacia whispered, soft and insistent. "Can I bring you some fruit for it? Would you rather I did some fishing for you? And I'll pray so that nothing will happen to you on your trips, Don Aquilino."

"I don't need any prayers," the old man said. He looked at her closely, and suddenly he snapped his fingers. "Hah, now I remember you."

"I'm going to get married, don't be mean," Bonifacia said. "I could make a dress out of this cloth. I know how to sew."

"Why aren't you dressed up like a nun?" Don Aquilino asked.

"I'm not living with the sisters any more," Bonifacia said. "They put me out of the Mission and now I'm going to get married. Let me have this piece of cloth and I'll do some work for you and the next time you come I'll pay you in soles, Don Aquilino."

The old man put a hand on Bonifacia's shoulder, he made her stand back so that the moon lit up her face, he slowly examined her green and urgent eyes, the small dripping body: she was a woman now. Had the sisters thrown her out because she'd got involved with a white man? With the one she was going to marry? No, Don Aquilino, she'd got involved afterward, and nobody knew about it in the village where she was, where was she staying?, the Nieveses had taken her in, could she do some small job for him, please?

"Are you living with Adrián and Lalita?" Don Aquilino asked.

"They introduced me to the man who's going to be my husband," Bonifacia said. "They've been very good to me, just like my own parents."

"I'm going over to the Nieveses' now," the old man said. "Come along."

"What about the cloth?" Bonifacia asked. "Don't make me beg so much, Don Aquilino."

The old man jumped noiselessly into the water. Bonifacia saw his hair floating over to the dock, saw it come back. Don Aquilino climbed up with the rope on his shoulder, he rolled it up, and with the rudder pole he pushed the raft up toward shore. Bonifacia lifted up the other pole, and with her foot on the nearby bank she imitated the old man, who was dipping and pulling out the pole with skill, without any effort. Alongside the clump of rushes, the current was stronger, and Don Aquilino had to maneuver so that the raft would not leave the shore.

"Don Adrián left early to go fishing, but he must be back by now," Bonifacia said. "I'll invite you to the wedding, but please give me the cloth, Don Aquilino, all right? I'm going to marry the Sergeant, do you know him?"

"A cop? Then I won't give it to you," the old man said.

"Don't talk like that, he's a good man," Bonifacia said. "Ask the Nieveses, they're friends of the Sergeant's."

Some lamps were burning in the pilot's cabin, and there were figures outlined along the railing. The raft was hooked up by the stairway, there were shouts of greeting, and Adrián Nieves went into the water to grab the rope and fastened it to a mooring nail. Then he climbed up onto the raft and he and Don Aquilino embraced each other, and then the old man came up onto the terrace, and Bonifacia saw him grab Lalita by the waist and give her his face, and she saw that he kissed her several times on the forehead, had he had a good trip?, on her cheeks, and the three children had grabbed the old man by the legs, shouting, and he rubbed their heads, a little rain, yes, it was a bit early this year, devilish.

"Oh, there you are," Lalita said. "We were looking all over for you, Bonifacia. I'm going to tell the Sergeant that you went into town and looked at the men."

"Nobody saw me," Bonifacia said. "Except for Don Aquilino."

"It doesn't matter, we'll tell him just to make him jealous," Lalita said, laughing.

"She came to see what I had to sell," the old man said. He had picked up the two youngest children and they were both rumpling his hair. "I'm tired, they had me going all day long."

"Let me get you a drink while dinner is getting ready," the pilot said.

Lalita brought out a chair onto the terrace for Don Aquilino, she went back inside, the crackling of the brazier could be heard along with the smell of frying. The children climbed up the old man's legs and he played with them as he toasted Adrián Nieves. They had finished the bottle when Lalita came over, drying her hands on her skirt.

"Your hair is getting so pretty," she said, stroking Don Aquilino's head. "Whiter and softer all the time."

"Do you want to make your husband jealous too?" the old man said.

Dinner would be ready soon, Don Aquilino, she had prepared things that he would like, and the old man shook his head, trying to get away from Lalita's hands: if she wouldn't leave him alone, he'd cut off his hair. The children were grouped in front of him now, looking at him silently and with restless eyes.

"I know what you're waiting for," the old man said. "I didn't forget, I've got presents for all of you. A man's suit for you, Aquilino."

The slanted eyes of the oldest boy lighted up, and Bonifacia leaned on the railing. From there she watched the old man stand up, go down the stairs, come back to the terrace with packages which the children snatched out of his hands, and then she watched him go over to Adrián Nieves. They began to talk in low voices, and from time to time Don Aquilino would look at her out of the corner of his eye.

"You were right," the old man said. "Adrián says that the Sergeant is a good Christian. Go get the cloth, it's a wedding present."

Bonifacia wanted to kiss his hand, but Don Aquilino held her back with a gesture of weariness. And while she was going back to the raft, digging among the boxes and taking out the cloth, she could hear the old man and the pilot whispering mysteriously, and she could see them, their two faces close together, talking and talking. She went up onto the terrace and they fell silent. Now the night smelled of fried fish, and a rapid breeze was making the woods tremble.

"It's going to rain tomorrow," the old man said, sniffing the air. "Bad for business."

"They must be at the island by now," Lalita said later, while they were eating. "They left more than ten days ago. Did Adrián tell you?"

"Don Aquilino met them on the way," Nieves the pilot said. "Besides the Civil Guards, there were some soldiers from Borja. What the Sergeant said was true."

Bonifacia could see that the old man was glancing at her without stopping his chewing, as if uneasy. But a moment later he was smiling again and telling stories about his trips.

The first time they went on an expedition, they were away for two weeks. She was on the embankment, the sun was turning the inlet red, and suddenly, at the mouth of the channel: one, two, three canoes appeared. Lalita jumped up, she had to hide, but then she recognized them: in the first one Fushía, in the second Pantacha, in the third Huambisas. Why had they returned so soon when he had said a month? She ran down to the dock, and Fushía had Aquilino come, Lalita?, she not yet, and he God damn that old man and his mother to hell. All they were bringing back was a few alligator skins. Fushía was furious, we'll starve to death, Lalita. The Huambisas were laughing as they unloaded, their women were milling around among them, talkative, grunting, and Fushía look how happy they are, those bastards, we got to the village and the Shapras weren't there, these guys burned everything, they cut the head off a dog, nothing, a complete waste of time, a worthless trip, not a single ball of rubber, just those hides that aren't worth anything and these guys so happy. Pantacha was wearing shorts, scratching his armpits, we have to go farther in, boss, the jungle is big and full of riches, and Fushía fool, to go farther in we need a pilot. They went to the cabin, they ate some bananas and fried cassavas. Fushía talked all the time about Don Aquilino, I wonder what happened to the old man, he never let me down before, and Lalita it's been raining a lot the past few days, he may have holed up somewhere so that the things we told him to bring won't get wet. Pantacha, lying in the hammock, was scratching his head, his legs, his chest, and what if his boat got sunk in the rapids, boss?, and Fushía then we would be screwed, I don't know what we'd do. And Lalita don't get nervous, silly, the Huambisas have planted all over the island, and they've even built small corrals, and Fushía that's a crock of shit, that won't go very far, and redskins can live off cassava but not a white man, we'll wait two more days and if Aquilino doesn't come I'll have to do something. And a while later Pantacha closed his eyes, began to snore, and Fushía shook him, the Huambisas should lay out the skins before they get drunk, and Pantacha first a little nap, boss, I'm all beat from so much rowing, and Fushía, stupid, can't you understand?, leave me alone with my woman. Pantacha, his mouth open, you've got it made, you've got a real woman, boss, his eyes were sad, it's been years since I knew what a white woman is like, and Fushía beat it, scram, get out. Pantacha went off weeping, and Fushía there he goes, he's going off to have some of his dreams, hurry up and get undressed, Lalita, what are you waiting for, she it's my period and he what does it matter. And at dusk, when Fushía awoke, they went to the village, which smelled of cassava beer, the Huambisas were falling down drunk, and Pantacha was nowhere around. They found him at the other end of the island, he had taken his camp stove over to the edge of the inlet, and Fushía what did I tell you, he's having his dreams as large as life. He was mumbling, his face hidden in his hands, the fire was still burning under a small pot of herbs. Some beetles were crawling on his legs, and Lalita he doesn't even feel them. Fushía put out the fire, kicked the pot into the water, let's see if we can wake him up, and between the two of them they shook him, pinched him, slapped him, and he, muttering, he was only from Cuzco by accident, his soul had been born on the Ucayali, boss, and Fushía hear him?, she I heard him, he's acting crazy, and Pantacha his heart was sad. Fushía shook him, kicked him, God damned hillbilly, this is no time for dreaming, we've got to stay awake, we're going to starve to death, and Lalita he can't hear you, he's in a different world, Fushía. And he, mumbling, twenty years on the Ucayali, boss, he was crazy about paiches, his body was as tough as a tucuma tree, the gnats couldn't dent it. He was waiting for the bubbles, the paiches were coming up for air, hand me the harpoon, Andrés, hard, strong, tie it up, I'll hitch it, boss, he was sleeping like the paiches with the first push of the pole and the canoe tipped over on them on the Tamaya, he got out and Andrés didn't, you drowned, brother, the mermaids dragged you down to the bottom, now you're married to them, why did you have to die, Iquitos boy, Andrés. They sat down to wait for him to wake up completely, and Fushía it'll take a while, I can't lose this cholo, an addict maybe, but he's useful to me, and Lalita why is he always mixing up his drugs, and Fushía so he won't feel alone. Cockroaches and beetles were crawling over the stove and his body, and why had he become a lumberman, boss, it's a rough life in the jungle, the rivers and the paiches are better, I know what malaria is, Pantacha, that shaking, you come with me, I'll pay you more, have some cigarettes, have a drink, you're the man for me, take me to where there are cedars, rosewood, get me some land titles, balsa wood, and he would go with them, boss, how much of an advance will you give me, and he wanted to have a house, a wife, children, live in Iquitos like a white man. And suddenly Fushía, Pantachita, what happened on the Aguaytía?, tell me, I'm your friend. And Pantacha opened his eyes and closed them, they were red, like a monkey's behind, and, muttering, that river flowed with blood, boss, and Fushía whose blood, cholo?, and he hot, thick, like the rubber that comes out of the cuts in the trees, and the channels, the lagoons around there, one big wound, boss, you don't have to believe me, and Fushía of course I believe you, cholo, but so much hot blood from where?, and Lalita leave him alone, Fushía, don't ask him any more questions, he's suffering, and Fushía shut up, whore, come on, Pantachita, who was bleeding?, and he, muttering, that sneaky Bákovic, that Yugoslavian who'd tricked them, worse than a devil, boss, and Fushía why did you kill him, Pantacha?, and how, cholo, how did you do it, and he he didn't want to pay them, there isn't enough cedar, let's go farther in, and he took his Winchester and he killed a porter who stole a bottle from him too. And Fushía you shot him, cholo?, and he with my machete, boss, his arm had gone numb from hitting him, and he began to kick and weep, and Lalita look at what's happened to him, Fushía, he's all stirred up, and Fushía I got a secret out of him, now I know that he was on the run when Aquilino found him. They sat down again beside the stove, they waited, he calmed down and finally woke up. He staggered to his feet, scratching himself furiously, boss, don't be mad, and Fushía those concoctions are going to drive you crazy, and one day he'd kick him out, and Pantacha he didn't have anyone, his life was so sad, boss, you have your wife, and the Huambisas have theirs too, and even the animals, but he was all alone, you should not get mad, boss, you either, Ma'am.

They waited for two more days, Aquilino had not come, the Huambisas went as far as the Santiago to check, and they came back without any news. Then they looked for a place to dig the pool, and Pantacha the other side of the dock, boss, the bank is lower there, and the water off the lupunas would flow into it there, and the heads of the Huambisas yes, and Fushía all right, let's build it there. The men cut down the trees, the women cleared away the grass, and when there was a clearing the Huambisas cut stakes, sharpened them, and drove them in in a circle. The ground was black on the surface, red on the inside, and the women picked it up in their itípaks, threw it into the inlet, while the men dug the hole. Then it rained and in a few days the pool was full, ready for the charapa turtles. They left at dawn, the channel had risen, roots and vines came up to scratch them, and on the Santiago Lalita began to tremble, she had a fever. They traveled for two days, Fushía how long, and the Huambisas pointed ahead. Finally a sandbank, and Fushía said there, I hope, and they landed, hid themselves among the trees, and Fushía don't move, don't breathe, if they hear you they won't come, and Lalita I feel sick to my stomach, I think I'm pregnant, Fushía, and he shit, shut up. The Huambisas had turned into plants, motionless among the branches, their eyes were shining, and that was how it got dark, the crickets began to chirp, the frogs to croak, and a big, fat hualo toad came over to Lalita's foot, such an urge to squash it, its slime, its whitish belly, and he don't move, the moon had already come out, and she I can't stay here playing dead any more, Fushía, I feel like crying out. The night was clear, warm, there was a light breeze, and Fushía they've screwed us, there isn't a single one, those bastards, and Pantacha quiet, boss, can't you see them?, they're coming out now. With the small waves of the river they were coming like round mats, dark, huge, they ran aground, and suddenly they moved, slowly advanced, and their shells gleamed with golden lights, two, four, six, coming closer, crawling along the sand, their heads out, wrinkled, wriggling, do you think they can see us, smell us?, and some of them were already digging their nests, others were coming out of the water. And then, silently, swift copper-colored silhouettes arose from among the trees, and Fushía let's go, run, Lalita, and when they reached the beach, Pantacha watch out, boss, they can bite, they almost took my finger off, the females are the worst. The Huambisas had turned several over and were grunting happily. On their backs, their heads sunken in, the turtles were moving their flippers, and Fushía count them, she eight of them, and the men were cutting holes in their shells, they tied them together with reeds, and Pantacha let's have one to eat, boss, the waiting had made him hungry. They slept there, and the next day they set out again and at night another small beach, five turtles, another string, and they slept, they traveled, and Fushía it's lucky it's the laying season, and Pantacha is what we're doing illegal, boss?, and Fushía life was made up of illegal things, cholo. The return was very slow, the canoes were going upstream, towing the strings, and the turtles resisted, slowing them down, and Fushía what are you doing, you bastards, don't hit them, you'll kill them, and Lalita did you hear me?, pay some attention to me, I've been vomiting, Fushía, I'm going to have a child, and he the worst things always happen to you. In the channel, the turtles got caught on the roots on the bottom and they had to keep stopping, the Huambisas would jump into the water, the turtles would bite them, and they would climb back grumbling into the canoe. When they got to the inlet, they saw the boat, and Don Aquilino was on the dock, waving to them with his handkerchief. He'd brought canned goods, pots, machetes, anisette, and Fushía you wonderful old man, I thought you'd drowned, and he he'd run into a boatload of soldiers and he'd gone along with them to cover up. And Fushía soldiers?, and Aquilino there was some trouble in Urakusa, the Aguarunas had beaten up a corporal, it seemed, and killed a pilot, the Governor of Santa María de Nieva went with them to settle accounts, they were going to teach them a good lesson if they didn't run away. The Huambisas brought the turtles up to the pool, they gave them leaves, rinds, and ants to eat, and Fushía so that bastard Reátegui is in these parts?, and Aquilino the soldiers wanted me to sell them the canned goods, I had to lie to them, and Fushía hadn't they said that that bastard Reátegui had gone back to Iquitos and given up the Governorship?, and Aquilino yes, he says that after he gets through with this business he's going back, and Lalita I'm glad you got here, Don Aquilino, I wouldn't have wanted to eat turtle all winter long.

And so Don Anselmo ended up as a Mangache. But it was not overnight, as when a man chooses a place, builds his house, and settles down; it was slow, imperceptible. In the beginning he would appear in the chicha bars, his harp under his arm, and the musicians (almost all of them had played for him at one time or another) accepted him into their groups. People liked to listen to him, they applauded him. And the bar women, who were fond of him, would feed him and give him drinks and, when he was drunk, a mat, a blanket, a corner to sleep in. He was never seen in Castilla or crossing the Old Bridge, as if he had decided to live far from his memories and the desert. He would not even frequent the neighborhoods near the river, Gallinacera, the slaughterhouse, only Mangachería: the city stood between him and his past. And the Mangaches adopted him, along with the hermetic Chunga, who, huddled in a corner, her chin on her knees, would stare shyly off into space while Don Anselmo played or slept. The Mangaches talked about Don Anselmo, but to his face they called him harp player, old man. Because since the fire he had grown old: his shoulders were stooped, his chest was sunken in, wrinkles had broken out on his skin, his stomach was swollen, his legs were bowed, and he had become dirty, sloppy. He would still drag along in the boots left over from his good days, dusty, run down, his pants were in tatters, his shirt had lost all its buttons, his hat was full of holes, his fingernails were long and black, his eyes were bloodshot and bleary. His voice had grown hoarse, his manners had grown softer. At first, certain important people would hire him to play at birthday parties, baptisms, and marriages; with the money he earned, he convinced Patrocinio Naya to put him and Chunga up at his place and give them one meal a day. Chunga was just beginning to speak. But he was always so ragged and drunk that white people stopped calling on him and he earned his living as best he could, helping people move, carrying bundles, or cleaning doorways. He would appear in the chicha bars in the evening, all at once, dragging Chunga along with one hand, his harp in the other. He was a popular figure in Mangachería, the friend of everybody and no one, a solitary figure who would tip his hat in greeting to half the world but would barely exchange a single word with people, and his harp, his daughter, and alcohol seemed to dominate his life. Of his former habits, only his hatred for buzzards survived: when he saw one, he would look for stones and throw them at it and curse it. He drank a lot, but he was a discreet drunkard, never looking for a fight, not at all rowdy. One could tell when he was drunk from his walk, not zigzagging or staggering, but ceremonious: his legs apart, his arms rigid, his face grave, his eyes staring at the horizon.

His pattern of life was simple. At noon he would leave Patrocinio Naya's shack and, sometimes leading Chunga by the hand, sometimes alone, he plunged into the street with a kind of urgency. He would go all through the Mangache maze, walking briskly, coming and going through the twisting, crooked paths, and in that way he came to the southern boundary, where the desert stretched out toward Sullana, or he would go down to the edge of the city, that row of carob trees with a spring that flowed out from among their roots. He would go, return, go back, with short pauses at the chicha bars. He would enter without the slightest hesitation and, quiet, silent, serious, wait for someone to offer him a glass of light chicha, a shot of pisco: he would thank him with a nod and then leave to continue his march or walk or penance, always with the same feverish rhythm, until the Mangaches saw him stop somewhere, drop down under the shade of an eave, make himself comfortable on the sand, cover his face with his hat, and remain like that for hours, oblivious of the chickens and goats who would sniff his body, rub their feathers or whiskers against him, shit on him. He did not hesitate to stop passers-by and ask them for a cigarette, and when they refused he did not get angry: he continued on his way, proud and solemn. At night he returned to Patrocinio Naya's for his harp and went back to the chicha bars, but this time to play. He would spend hours tuning the strings, stroking them delicately, and when he was very drunk, his hands would not obey him and the harp got out of tune, he began to mutter, his eyes grew sad.

Sometimes he would go to the cemetery, and there it was that people saw him angry for the last time, one November 2nd, when the police stopped him at the gate. He cursed, he struggled with them, he threw stones at them, and finally some people convinced them to let him in. And it was in the cemetery, on another November 2nd, that Juana Baura saw Chunga, who must have just turned six, dirty, ragged, playing among the graves. She called her over, petted her. From then on, the washerwoman would come to Mangachería from time to time, driving her donkey loaded down with clothes, and would ask about the harp player and Chunga. She would bring her food, a dress, shoes, and him cigarettes and a few coins, which the old man ran off to spend in the nearest chicha bar. And one day Chunga was no longer seen in the alleys of Mangachería, and Patrocinio Naya said that Juana Baura had taken her away to Gallinacera for good. The harp player went on with his life, his walks. Every day he grew older, dirtier, and shabbier, but everyone had become accustomed to the sight of him, no one would look the other way when he met him, calm and stiff, or when he had to step aside so as not to step on his body stretched out on the sand, beneath the sun.

Only years later did the harp player begin to venture outside the limits of Mangachería. The streets of the city were growing, changing, becoming solid, with paving stones and raised sidewalks, bedecked with brand-new houses, and were becoming noisy, with children running after automobiles. There were bars, hotels, and strange faces, a new highway to Chiclayo, a railroad with gleaming tracks that joined Piura and Paita, passing through Sullana. Everything was changing, the Piurans too. They were no longer seen on the streets wearing boots and riding breeches, but with suits and even ties, and the women, who had given up the dark-colored skirts that reached down to their ankles, were dressing in bright colors, they were no longer escorted by servants, hidden in veils and cloaks, but they appeared alone, their faces exposed, their hair loose. Every day there were more streets, taller houses, the city was spreading out and the desert was retreating. Gallinacera had disappeared and in its place there arose a wealthy neighborhood. The shacks clustered behind the slaughterhouse burned one day at dawn; municipal guards, police, with the Mayor and Chief of Police in the lead, arrived, and with trucks and clubs they drove everybody out, and the following day they began to lay out straight streets, blocks, to build two-story houses, and in a short time no one could have guessed that peasants had once lived in that well-kept neighborhood inhabited by whites. Castilla was growing too, was becoming a regular small city. Streets were paved, movie theatres appeared, schools were opened, avenues, and the old people felt transported into a different world, they would protest against inconveniences, indecencies, attacks.

One day, his harp under his arm, the old man set out toward that renovated city, he reached the Plaza de Armas, sat down under a tamarind tree, and began to play. He returned the following afternoon, and many others after that, especially on Thursdays and Saturdays, when there were band concerts. Piurans would flock to the Plaza de Armas to listen to the band from the Grau barracks, and he would begin earlier; he would give his own concert an hour before, pass the hat, and as soon as he had a few soles, go back to Mangachería. That district had not changed, nor had the Mangaches. There were still adobe huts there, tallow candles, goats, and, in spite of progress, no patrols of the Civil Guard ventured into its harsh streets. And the harp player doubtless felt that he was a real Mangache, because the money he earned giving concerts on the Plaza de Armas he always spent back in the district. At night he would still play in the places run by Tula, Gertrudis, or Angélica Mercedes, his former cook, who now had her own chicha bar. No one could imagine Mangachería without him any more, no Mangache could conceive of not seeing him the next morning wandering hieratically through the alleys, stoning buzzards, coming out from among the huts with a red flag, sleeping in the sun, of not hearing his harp, in the distance, in the darkness. Even in his manner of speaking, the few times that he did speak, any Piuran could recognize a Mangache in him.

"The champs called him over to their table," Chunga said. "But the Sergeant pretended that he hadn't seen them."

"Always such a gentleman," the harp player said. "He came over to say hello and give me an embrace."

"With all their tricks, those bums are going to make my men lose their respect for me, old man," Lituma said.

The two soldiers had stayed at the bar while the Sergeant talked to Don Anselmo; Chunga served them beer and the Leóns and Josefino kept right on.

"Maybe we ought to stop, Wildflower's getting sad," the Kid said. "Besides, it's getting late, maestro."

"Don't be sad, girl." Don Anselmo's hand hovered over the table, knocking over a glass, and he patted Wildflower on the back. "Life's like that and nobody's to blame."

Those double-crossers, they'd put on a uniform and they wouldn't think of themselves as Mangaches any more, they wouldn't say hello, they didn't even want to look at a person.

"The soldiers didn't know that it was meant for the Sergeant," Chunga said. "They were drinking their beer as peaceful as you could ask for, talking to me. But he knew, he was blistering them with his eyes, and with his hand wait, shut up."

"Who invited those soldier boys in here?" Seminario asked. "Come on, it's time they left. Chunga, please throw them out."

"That's Señor Seminario, the rancher," Chunga said. "Don't pay any attention to him."

"I already recognized him," the Sergeant said. "Don't look at him, boys, he's probably drunk."

"Now he's butting in with the cops," Monk said. "He's getting tougher, this guy."

"Our cousin could answer him back, he ought to use his uniform for something," José said.

Kid Alejandro was sipping his coffee:

"He was quiet enough when he got here, but after two drinks he got mad. He must have had something terrible on his mind, and he was getting rid of it that way, cursing and insulting."

"Don't be like that, sir," the Sergeant said. "We're just doing our work; that's what they pay us for."

"You've seen enough already, you've seen that everything is all right," Seminario said. "Now get out of here and let decent people enjoy themselves in peace."

"Don't worry about us," the Sergeant said. "You just keep right on enjoying yourself, sir."

Wildflower's face was getting more and more troubled, and at his table Seminario was seething with rage, the cop was backing down too, there weren't any real men left in Piura any more, what had they done to the place, God damn it, it just wasn't right. And then Hydrangea and Poppy went over to him and they calmed him down a little by petting him and making jokes.

"Hydrangea and Poppy," Don Anselmo said. "The names you give them, Chunguita."

"And what did they do?" Wildflower asked. "Did what he said about Piura make them mad?"

"Their eyes were burning," Jocko said. "But what could they do, they were scared to death."

They hadn't thought that Lituma was so soft, he was armed and he should have stood up to him, Seminario was carrying on, a person shouldn't look for three legs on a cat when he knows it has four, and Rita not so fast because now she was going to hear it all, and Maribel there was going to be a fight, and Sandra with her loud laughter. And after a while the patrol left, the Sergeant went to the door with the two soldiers and came back alone. He went over to sit down at the champs' table.

"He should have left too," Jocko said. "The poor guy."

"Why poor?" Wildflower protested vehemently. "He's a man, he doesn't need anyone feeling sorry for him."

"But you're always calling him poor fellow, Wildflower," Jocko said.

"I'm his wife," Wildflower explained, and the Kid hid a trace of a smile.

Lituma was lecturing them, why were they making fun of him in front of his men?, and they you have two faces, you act serious in front of them and then you send them away so you can have your own good time. They felt sorry for him in uniform, he was a different person, and he felt sorrier for them, and after a bit they were friends again and they sang: they were the champs, work wasn't for them, they lived off others, they emptied their glasses, and now they were ready to wiggle their asses.

"Having a song all their own," the harp player said. "There's nobody like these Mangaches."

"But you're not one any more, cousin," Monk said. "You let yourself be beaten."

"I don't know why your face hasn't fallen off you, cousin," José said. "There's never been a Mangache who was a cop."

"They were most likely telling jokes or talking about their drinking," Chunga said. "What else was there to talk about."

"Ten years, buddy." Lituma sighed. "It's horrible how life goes by."

"Here's to life as it goes by," José proposed, raising his glass.

"Mangaches get a little philosophical when they're drunk. They probably got it from the Kid," the harp player said. "They were more likely talking about death."

"Ten years, it doesn't seem like it," Monk said. "Do you remember Domitila Yara's wake, cousin?"

"The day after I got back from the jungle, I ran into Father García and he wouldn't answer my hello," Lituma said. "He's never forgiven us."

"Not a philosopher, maestro," the Kid said, blushing. "Just a plain musician."

"They more likely were remembering things," Wildflower said. "Whenever they got together, they'd start talking about what they did when they were churres."

"You're already talking like a Piuran, Wildflower," Chunga said.

"Haven't you ever felt sorry about it, cousin?" José asked.

"Cop or anything else, who cares." Lituma shrugged his shoulders. "Lots of fun and lots of carousing as a champ, but lots of hungry days too, buddies. Now, at least, I can eat well, morning, noon, and night. That's something all by itself."

"I'd like to have a little more milk if I can," the harp player said.

Wildflower got up, Don Anselmo: she would fix it.

"The only thing I'm jealous about is the way you've been around, Lituma," Josefino said. "We'll end up dying without ever having got out of Piura."

"Speak for yourself," Monk said. "Nobody's going to bury me before I get to Lima."

"Good girl," Anselmo said. "Always so obliging in everything. So helpful, so pleasant. Is she pretty?"

"Not so much, quite chubby," Jocko said. "And when she has high heels on it makes you laugh to watch her walk."

"But she has beautiful eyes," the Kid affirmed. "Green, very big, mysterious. You'd like them, maestro."

"Green?" the harpist asked. "I certainly would like them."

"Who would have thought that you'd end up married and a cop," Josefino said. "And pretty soon a father, Lituma."

"Is it true that women are easy to make in the jungle?" Monk asked. "Are they as hot as people say?"

"A lot more than they say," Lituma said. "You have to keep fighting them off. If you don't watch out, they'll squeeze you to death. I don't know why I didn't come back with my lungs full of holes."

"Then you can have anyone you want," José said.

"Especially if you're from the coast," Lituma said. "Coast people drive them crazy."

"She may be a good person, but I wonder about her feelings," Jocko said. "Whoring for her husband's friend, and poor Lituma in jail."

"Don't be so quick to judge, Jocko," the Kid said, upset. "You ought to find out what really happened. It's never easy to know what goes on behind things. Never throw the first stone, brother."

"And then he says he's not a philosopher," the harp player said. "Listen to him, Chunguita."

"Were there many females in Santa María de Nieva, cousin?" Monk insisted.

"You could change off every day," Lituma said. "Lots of them, and all of them hotter than anything you ever saw. All kinds, and wholesale, white ones, dark ones; all you had to do was reach out your hand."

"And if they were so good-looking, why did you marry that one?" Josefino laughed. "Because—don't tell me, Lituma—she's nothing but a pair of eyes, the rest of her isn't worth anything."

"He gave a pound on the table that you could hear in the cathedral," Jocko said. "They were arguing about something, and it seemed that Josefino and Lituma were going to explode."

"Just flashes, little matches, they light up and they go out, they never stay mad," the harp player said. "Piurans are all goodhearted people."

"Can't you take a joke any more?" Monk asked. "You sure have changed, cousin."

"She's like a sister to me, Lituma," Josefino exclaimed. "Did you really think I meant what I was saying? Sit down, buddy, have a drink on me."

"It's just that I'm in love with her," Lituma said. "That's no sin."

"I'm glad you love her," Monk said. "Bring us some more beer, Chunga."

"The poor thing isn't used to anything, she's scared of so many people around," Lituma said. "It's not like where she comes from, you have to understand her."

"Of course we understand her," Monk said. "Come on, let's drink to our cousin-in-law."

"She's awfully nice the way she takes care of us, the big meals she gives us," José said. "All three of us love her very much, cousin."

"Is it all right, Don Anselmo?" Wildflower asked. "It isn't too hot, is it?"

"Very good, delicious," the harp player said, tasting it. "Do you really have green eyes, girl?"

Seminario had spun around toward them, chair and all, what was all that racket, couldn't a person have a quiet talk?, and the Sergeant, with all due respect, he was going too far, nobody was bothering him, he shouldn't butt in on them, sir. Seminario raised his voice, who were they to answer him like that, and he certainly would butt in on them, the four of them and the whores that gave them birth, understand?

"He insulted their mother?" Wildflower asked, blinking.

"Several times that night, that was the first time," Jocko said. "Those rich people think they can insult everybody's mother just because they own land."

Hydrangea and Poppy came running back, and from the bar Sandra, Rita, and Maribel were stretching their necks. The Sergeant's voice was husky with rage; his family had nothing to do with this, sir.

"If you don't like it, come on over and we'll talk about it, boy," Seminario said.

"But Lituma didn't," Chunga said. "Sandra and I held him back."

"Why talk about mothers when the fight's between men?" the Kid asked. "A person's mother is the most sacred thing there is."

And Hydrangea and Poppy had gone back to Seminario's table.

"I didn't hear them laugh or sing their song again," the harp player said. "They were depressed by that insult to their mothers, the boys were."

"They consoled themselves by drinking," Chunga said. "There wasn't room for any more bottles on their table."

"That's why I believe that the troubles a person carries around inside of himself explain everything," the Kid said. "That's why some people end up as drunkards, others as priests, others as murderers."

"I'm going to wet my head," Lituma said. "That guy ruined the night for me."

"He was right to get mad, Josefino," Monk said. "Nobody likes to hear his wife called ugly."

"I'm sick of his being so stuck-up," Josefino said. "I've tasted over a hundred females, I know half of Peru, I've been around. He spends all his time needling us about his famous travels."

"Underneath it all, you're mad at him because his wife won't pay any attention to you," José said.

"If he knew you were after her, he'd kill you," Monk said. "He's in love with his woman like a puppy."

"It's his fault," Josefino said. "Why does he brag so much? 'She's a devil in bed, she moves this way, that way.' Screw him. I want to see if all those great things are true."

"You want to bet a couple of libras that you don't make it, brother?" Monk asked.

"We'll see," Josefino said. "The first time she tried to slap me, the second time she only insulted me, and the third time she didn't even act resentful and I was able to pet her a little. She's softening up; I know my people."

"If you get her, you know," José said, "where one champ goes, all three go, Josefino."

"I don't know why I want her so much," Josefino said. "She really isn't worth anything."

"Because she comes from someplace else," Monk said. "A person always likes to find out secrets, what habits she brought with her from where she comes from."

"She's like a little animal," José said. "She doesn't understand anything, she spends her time asking why this, why the other thing.

I wouldn't want to be the first one to try. What if she told Lituma about it, Josefino?"

"She's timid," Josefino said. "I spotted her right away. She's got no personality, she'd die of shame before she told him. It's just too bad he knocked her up. Now I've got to wait until she gives birth before I can do that little job."

"Then they began to dance very nicely," Chunga said. "It appeared that everything was all over."

"Trouble comes all of a sudden, when you least expect it," the Kid said.

"Who was he dancing with?" Wildflower asked.

"With Sandra." Chunga was looking at her with her dull eyes, and she was speaking slowly. "Very tight. And they were kissing each other. Are you getting jealous?"

"I was just asking," Wildflower said. "I'm not the jealous kind."

And Seminario, all of a sudden, firmly, they should leave, disagreeably, or all by himself, roaring, he would throw the four of them out together.

3

"Not a sound all night long, no lights either," the Sergeant said. "Doesn't that strike you as funny, Lieutenant?"

"They must be on the other side," Sergeant Roberto Delgado said. "It looks like a big island."

"It's starting to get light," the Lieutenant said. "Have them bring up the boats, but no noise."

Between the trees and the water, the uniforms looked like vegetables. Crowded into their narrow redoubt, soaked to the skin, their eyes drunk with fatigue, guards and soldiers were hitching up their pants, tying their leggings. They were wrapped in a greenish light that filtered through the labyrinth of branches, and among the leaves, limbs, and vines, many of the faces showed purple bites and scratches. The Lieutenant went over to the bank of the inlet, he pushed the foliage aside with one hand, with the other he raised his binoculars and studied the island: a steep bank, lead-colored slopes, trees with stout trunks and leafy crowns. The water was showing reflections, the singing of the birds could be heard now. The Sergeant went over to the Lieutenant, crouching down, the woods crackled under his feet. Behind them, the hazy outlines of the guards and the soldiers were barely moving in the entanglement as they quietly uncorked their canteens and lit cigarettes.

"They've stopped arguing," the Lieutenant said. "No one would believe that they spent the whole trip fighting."

"The bad night made them all friends," the Sergeant said. "Tired, uncomfortable. There's nothing like that to make men come to an understanding, Lieutenant."

"Let's put the squeeze on them before it gets completely light," the Lieutenant said. "We'll have to deploy a patrol on the opposite bank."

"Yes, but to do that we'll have to cross the inlet," the Sergeant said, pointing at the island. "It's about three hundreds yards, sir. We'll be sitting ducks."

Sergeant Roberto Delgado and the others had come over. The mud and the rain had made their uniforms all look alike, and only the caps and the helmets showed who were police and who were Army men.

"Let's send them a messenger, Lieutenant," Sergeant Roberto Delgado said. "There's no way out for them except to surrender."

"They must have seen us by now," the Sergeant said. "Huambisas have good ears, like all redskins. They may be zeroing in on us right now from the lupuna trees."

"I see them there and I still can't believe it," Sergeant Delgado said. "Indians living near lupunas, the way they're so scared of them."

Soldiers and police were listening: livid skins, small abcesses of coagulated blood, dark circles under their eyes, restless pupils. The Lieutenant scratched his cheek, they'd have to see, beside his temple three pimples formed a purple triangle, were the two Sergeants scared shitless?, and a lock of dirty hair fell over his forehead, which was half hidden by his visor. What? Maybe his police might be afraid, Lieutenant, Sergeant Roberto Delgado didn't know how they were going to take all this. A muttering broke out and, with a single movement that shook the foliage, Shorty, Blacky, and Blondy drew away from the soldiers: it was an insult, Lieutenant, they wouldn't stand for it, what right did he have?, and the Lieutenant tapped his cartridge belt: maybe he'd pay for it, if they weren't on a mission, he'd show him.

"It was only a joke, sir," Sergeant Roberto Delgado stammered. "In the Army we kid officers and they never get mad. I thought it was the same in the police."

A noise of agitated water drowned out their voices, and the careful splashing of oars, a slipping along, could be heard. The boats appeared from under the cascade of vines and reeds. Pintado the pilot and the soldier who was helping him bring them up were smiling, and neither their expressions nor their movements showed fatigue.

"Actually, it might be best to ask them to surrender," the Lieutenant said.

"Of course, Lieutenant," Sergeant Roberto Delgado said. "I didn't suggest it because I was afraid, but as a bit of strategy. If they try to escape, we can have target practice with them from here."

"On the other hand, if we go over there, they could make duck soup out of us while we're crossing the inlet," the Sergeant said. "There are only ten of us and God knows how many of them there are. Or what weapons they've got."

The Lieutenant turned around, and guards and soldiers became tense: which one's been in the longest? An anxious look on all the faces now, tightened mouths, alarmed eyes, and Sergeant Roberto Delgado pointed to a short, copper-colored soldier, who took a step forward: Private Hinojosa, Lieutenant. Very well, Private Hinojosa would take the men from Borja to the other side of the lagoon and dig in across from the island, Sergeant. The Lieutenant would stay here with the guards, watching the channel mouth. And what had Sergeant Delgado come for, then, Lieutenant? The officer took off his cap, what for? he smoothed his hair with his hand, he would tell him, and when he put his cap back on, the lock on his forehead had disappeared: the two Sergeants were going to demand their surrender. The bandits were to take off their weapons and stand out on the bank with their hands held on top of their heads, Sergeant, Pintado would take them across. The Sergeants looked at each other without speaking, soldiers and guards, mingling again, were whispering, and in their eyes there was no longer fear, but relief, flashes of mockery. Following Hinojosa, the soldiers got into one of the boats, which rocked and sank down a little. The one acting as pilot lifted the rudder pole, and a slight crackling, the vibration of the branches again, the helmets disappeared under the ferns and reeds, and the Lieutenant examined the guards' shirts, Shorty, he should take his off: his was the whitest. The Sergeant would tie it to his rifle, and he knew, of course, if they acted up, shoot, without thinking twice.

The Sergeants were in the boat, and after Shorty gave them his shirt, Pintado pushed the boat off with his pole. He let it float slowly through the foliage, but as soon as they got into the lagoon, he started the motor, and with the monotonous sound the air was filled with birds fleeing noisily from the trees. An orange glow was growing larger behind the lupunas, and in the thickness round about were reflected the first rays of the sun, and the water of the inlet was clear and quiet.

"Oh, brother, I was getting ready to get married," the Sergeant said.

"Hold that rifle higher," Sergeant Delgado said, "so they'll be sure to see the shirt."

They crossed the lagoon without taking their eyes off the embankment and the lupunas. Pintado steered with one hand and with the other he was scratching his head, his face, his arms, struck by a sudden and generalized itching. Now they could make out a narrow, muddy beach, with peeled trees and some floating logs that must have served as a dock. On the opposite bank, the boat with the soldiers landed, and they jumped out, took up positions in the open, and aimed their rifles at the island. Hinojosa had a good voice, those mountain huaynos he sang in Quechua last night were good, right? Yes, but what was going on, why hadn't they seen them, why weren't they coming out? The Santiago was full of Huambisas, buddy, the ones who saw them coming must have told them, and they had plenty of time to get away through the channels. The boat headed for the dock. Tied together with thick reeds, the floating logs were covered with moss, fungus, and lichens. The three men looked at the almost vertical embankment, the curved and lumpy lupunas: there was nobody there, Sergeants, but he'd really been scared. The Sergeants jumped out, slogged through the mud, began to climb up, their bodies hugging the slope. The Sergeant was holding up his rifle, a hot breeze was making Shorty's shirt wave, and when they got to the top, a blazing sun made them close their eyes and rub them. Braids of vines covered the spaces between one lupuna and another, a thick, putrid smell would bathe their faces each time they peered into the underbrush. Finally they found an opening, they advanced, up to their waists in wild and noisy grass, then they followed a path that went ahead, winding and narrow, between rows of trees, that disappeared and reappeared beside a thicket or a clump of ferns. Sergeant Roberto Delgado was getting nervous, God damn it, he should keep that rifle up high so they would see that they were coming under a white flag. The treetops formed a compact dome that only small threads of sunlight could penetrate here and there, golden openings that quivered, and there were voices of invisible birds everywhere. The Sergeants protected their faces with their hands, but they still got jabs, stinging scratches. The path suddenly came to an end in a clearing that had a smooth and sandy surface, clear of grass, and they saw the huts: hey, buddy, look at that. Tall, solid, they were already half devoured by the woods. One had lost its roof, and a hole that looked like a round wound marked its front; a tree was coming out of the other one, impetuously thrusting its hairy branches through the windows, and the walls of both of them had disappeared under crusts of ivy. There was tall grass all around; the stairs had fallen apart, imprisoned by climbing vines, and they were the resting place for stalks and roots, and nests could also be seen on the steps and supports, swollen anthills. The Sergeants stalked around the huts, stretched out their necks to look inside.

"They didn't leave last night, they left a long time ago," Sergeant Delgado said. "The jungle's practically swallowed up these huts already."

"These aren't Huambisa huts, they were built by white men," the Sergeant said. "Indians don't make them so big, and besides they always carry their huts off with them when they move."

"There used to be a clearing here," Sergeant Delgado said. "The trees are young. Quite a few people used to live here, buddy."

"The Lieutenant's going to be mad," the Sergeant said. "He was so sure that he'd catch some of them."

"Let's give him a signal," Sergeant Delgado said; he aimed his rifle at a hut and pulled off three shots, and the echo repeated them far away. "They'll think the crooks are giving us trouble."

"Frankly, I'm glad there wasn't anybody here," the Sergeant said. "I'm getting married and I'm not ready to lose my head yet, not at my age."

"Let's take a look around before the others get here," Sergeant Delgado said. "Maybe there's something worth taking."

All they found were the remains of rusty objects, converted into spider nests, and the worm-eaten boards, chewed up by termites, would sink under their feet and softly give way. The men came out of the huts, they covered the island, and here and there they would come across charred pieces of wood, rusty cans, pieces of crockery. In one low-lying spot there was a pool of stagnant water, and amidst the putrid smell that it gave off there were clouds of mosquitoes. It was surrounded by two circles of stakes, a kind of net, and what the devil was that, Sergeant Roberto Delgado had never seen anything like it. What could it be, some redskin kind of thing, but they'd better get away from there, it stank and there were so many mosquitoes. They went back to the huts, and the Lieutenant, the guards, and the soldiers were wandering around in the clearing like sleepwalkers, roaming among the trees, restless and perplexed.

"A ten-day trip!" the Lieutenant shouted. "All that stupid trouble just for this! How long ago do you think they left?"

"I'd say months ago, Lieutenant," the Sergeant said. "Maybe over a year."

"There weren't just two, there were three huts, Lieutenant," Blacky said. "There was another one over here, a windstorm must have blown it down. You can still see the foundation, look."

"I'd say several years, Lieutenant," Sergeant Delgado said. "From that tree that's grown up inside there."

After all, what difference did it make, the Lieutenant smiled, disappointed, a month, ten years, tired: they'd been screwed just the same. And Sergeant Delgado, all right, Hinojosa, make a thorough search, and they should pack up anything that could be eaten, drunk, or worn, and the soldiers spread out through the clearing and were lost in the trees, and Blondy should make some coffee so they could get the bad taste out of their mouths. The Lieutenant squatted down, began to scratch on the ground with a small branch. The Sergeants lit cigarettes; swarms of insects buzzed over their heads as they chatted. Pintado the pilot cut some dry branches, made a campfire, and after a while the men were flinging bottles, clay jars, tattered blankets out of the cabins. Blondy warmed up the contents of a thermos bottle, served steaming coffee in brass cups, and the Lieutenant and the Sergeants were finishing theirs when they heard shouting, what was up?, and two soldiers appeared on the run, a guy?, the officer jumped up, what?, and Private Hinojosa: a dead man, Lieutenant, they'd found him on a small beach down there. A Huambisa? a white man? Followed by guards and soldiers, the Lieutenant was running now, and for a few moments all that was heard was the crunch of foliage as it was being trampled, the soft murmur of the grass as the bodies ran it down. Quickly and all together, they dodged around the stakes, slid down the embankment, ran around a gulley spotted with stones, and when they got to the beach, they stopped short around the man stretched out there. He was lying face up, his tattered pants barely covering his greasy, shriveled legs, his dark skin. His armpits were two tight, blackish thickets, and his fingernails and toenails were very long. Scabs and ulcers were devouring his torso, his shoulders, a piece of whitish tongue was hanging out of his wrinkled lips. Guards and soldiers were examining him, and suddenly Sergeant Roberto Delgado smiled, squatted down, and breathed in, his nose alongside the mouth of the man. Then he let out a little laugh, stood up, kicked the man in the ribs: listen here, fool, he shouldn't kick a dead man like that, and Sergeant Roberto Delgado, kicking again, he was as dead as he was, couldn't the Lieutenant smell it? They all leaned over, smelled the rigid and indifferent body. Nothing dead about him, Lieutenant, my old buddy here was having himself a good dream. With a kind of increasing and furious joy, he kicked him again, and the man contracted, something hoarse and deep came out of his mouth, by God: it was true. The Lieutenant clutched the man's hair, pulled it, and once more, weakly, that interior snore. The son of a bitch had taken something, and the Sergeant that was right, look, there was his brew. Next to the silvery ashes and kindling for a fire, there was a clay jar, scorched, filled with herbs. Dozens of curhuinse ants, with their long mandibles and black bellies, were crawling all over him as others, in a circle, protected the attack. If he'd been dead, the bugs would have eaten him already, Lieutenant, there wouldn't be anything left but bones, and Blondy but they'd already started on his legs. Some of the curhuinses were climbing up the leathery soles of his feet as others investigated his insteps, his toes, his ankles, they were touching his skin with their thin antennae, and behind them they were leaving a trail of purple spots. Sergeant Roberto

Delgado kicked him again in the same place. There was a swelling along the ribs of the man, an oblong tumulus with a dark vertex. He was still motionless, but from time to time he would give that hollow snore, and his tongue was slowly awakening as he licked his lips with difficulty. He was in paradise, the bastard, he couldn't feel anything, and the Lieutenant water, quick, and they should clean off his feet, God damn it, the ants were eating him up. Shorty and Blondy squashed the curhuinses; two soldiers brought some water from the lagoon in their helmets and washed the man's face. He was trying to move his limbs now, his face stiffened, his head moved from right to left. Suddenly he belched, and one of his arms folded over slowly, clumsily, his hand stroked his body, he touched the swelling, caressed it. Now he was breathing anxiously, his chest was full, his stomach distended, and his tongue was sticking out, white, with spots of green saliva. His eyes were still sealed, and the Lieutenant to the soldiers more water: he was halfway between, boys, they had to wake him up. Soldiers and police went to the lagoon, they came back and they poured water over the man, and he opened his mouth to receive it, his tongue eagerly, noisily sucking in the drops. His moaning was more normal now, and continuous, and the contractions of his body too seemed free of the invisible bonds.

"Give him some coffee, bring him to any way you can," the Lieutenant said. "And keep pouring water on him."

"I don't think he'll make it to Santa María de Nieva, the shape he's in, Lieutenant," the Sergeant said. "He'll die on us on the way."

"I'll take him to Borja, it's closer," the Lieutenant said. "You take the boys back to Nieva right now, and tell Don Fabio that we caught one of them. It won't be long before we get the others. I'll go to the garrison with the soldiers and I'll have the doctor there take a look at him. I'll be God damned if this one's going to die on me."

A few yards away from the group, the Lieutenant and the Sergeant were smoking. Guards and soldiers were working on the man, shaking him, and he seemed to be using his tongue cautiously, his voice, he was trying hard to make some new movements and sounds.

"What if he doesn't belong to the gang, Lieutenant?" the Sergeant asked.

"That's why I'm taking him to Borja," the Lieutenant said.

"They've got Aguarunas there from villages that were looted by the bandits, we'll see if they recognize him. Tell Don Fabio that he should notify Reátegui."

"The guy's beginning to talk, Lieutenant," Shorty shouted. "Come and listen."

"Could you make out what he said?" the Lieutenant asked.

"Something about a river that was bleeding, about a white man who died," Blacky said. "Things like that, Lieutenant."

"All we need is for him to be crazy, it'd be just my luck," the Lieutenant said.

"Their minds always wander when they're on the dream," Sergeant Roberto Delgado said. "He'll come out of it afterward, sir."

Night was coming on, Fushía and Don Aquilino were eating some roast cassava, drinking cane liquor out of the bottle, and Fushía it's getting dark, Lalita, light the lamp, she squatted down and oh my God, the first pains, she was unable to get up, she fell sobbing onto the floor. They raised her up, they put her into the hammock. Fushía lit the lamp, and she I think it's my time, I'm afraid. And Fushía I never saw a woman die of childbirth, and Aquilino me either, don't be frightened, Lalita, he was the best midwife in the jungle, could he touch her, Fushía? he wouldn't be jealous?, and Fushía you're too old for me to be jealous, go ahead, touch her. Don Aquilino had lifted up her skirt, he was kneeling down to look and Pantacha came running in, boss, they were fighting, and Fushía who, and Pantacha the Huambisas with that Aguaruna that Don Aquilino had brought back with him, Don Aquilino with Jum?, Pantacha's eyes were opened wide, and Fushía slapped him, you son of a bitch, looking at someone else's woman. He was rubbing his nose, he was sorry, boss, he'd only come to warn him, the Huambisas wanted Jum to leave, you know how they hate the Aguarunas, they'd got all worked up and he and Nieves couldn't hold them back, was the boss lady sick? And Don Aquilino you'd better go see, Fushía, they shouldn't kill him with all the work it took me to get him to the island, and Fushía God damn it to hell, we've got to cool them off, have them all get drunk together, they'll either kill each other off or get to be good friends. They left and Don Aquilino went over to Lalita, he massaged her legs, so that the muscles would soften up, her belly, and the child would come out easily, you'll see, and she laughing crying, she was going to tell Fushía that he was taking advantage of it to pet her, he was laughing, and oh my God, again, on her shoulder blades, oh my God, they must have been breaking apart, and Don Aquilino take a drink to calm yourself down, she took it, vomited, and sprayed it on Don Aquilino, who was rocking the hammock, easy, easy, Lalita, pretty girl, and the pain was passing. Some red lights were dancing around the lamp, look, Lalita, the fireflies, the ayañahuis, when a person dies his soul becomes a little moth, did she know that?, and they travel about at night, lighting up the jungle, the rivers, the inlets, when he died, Lalita, she would always have an ayañahui next to her, and he would be her lamp. And she I'm afraid, Don Aquilino, don't talk about death, and he don't be afraid, he was rocking the hammock, it was to distract her, with a damp rag he was mopping her forehead, nothing's going to happen to you, he'll be born before sunup, when I touch you I can see that it's going to be a boy. The hut was filled with the smell of vanilla, and the damp wind was bringing jungle whispers too, the sound of locusts, dogs barking, and the shouts of an agitated quarrel. And she your hands are so soft, Don Aquilino, that relaxes me a little, and what a wonderful smell, but don't you hear the Huambisas?, go take a look, Don Aquilino, what if they kill Fushía?, and he that was the one thing that wouldn't happen, Lalita, don't you know what a devil he is? And Lalita how long have you known each other, Don Aquilino, and he it's going on ten years, he's never come out on the short end, even when he looks for the worst kind of trouble, Lalita, terrible things, he can get away from his enemies like a river snake. And she did you get to be friends in Moyobamba?, and Don Aquilino I was a water vendor, he set me up in a business, and she water vendor?, and Don Aquilino from house to house, with his donkey and his buckets, Moyobamba is poor, everything a person makes goes to buy methylene to make the water better, and if not you get fined, and one morning Fushía arrived, he went to live in a shack next to mine, and that was how we became friends. And she what was he like then, Don Aquilino?, and he where are you from, they'd ask him, and he was all mystery and lies, he could barely talk like one of us, Lalita, he'd mix it all up with Brazilian. And Fushía come on, man, you're living a dog's life, haven't you had enough of it?, let's go into business, and he was right, a dog's life. And Lalita what did the two of you do, Don Aquilino?, and he a big raft, and Fushía would buy bags of rice, cotton cloth, percale, and shoes, the raft would sink under so much weight, and what if they rob us, Fushía?, and Fushía, oh, shut up, I've bought a revolver. And Lalita is that how you got started, Don Aquilino?, and he we used to go to the camps and among the rubber men, the woodcutters, and gold prospectors, bring us this and that on your next trip, and they would bring it, and then they went in among the Indians. Good business, the best there was, beads for balls of rubber, mirrors and knives for skins, and that was how we got to know these people, Lalita, they became great friends of Fushía's, you've seen how they help him, he's a god to the Huambisas. And Lalita you made out very well, then, and he it would have been better if Fushía hadn't been such a devil, he robbed everybody, and finally they were after him from the camps, and the police were on his trail, they had to separate, and he came to Huambisa country for a while, and then he went to Iquitos, and there he started to work for Reátegui, was that where you met him, Lalita? And she what did you do, Don Aquilino?, and he that free kind of life had got into his blood, Lalita, that business of carrying his home on his back like a knapsack, with no special place, and he kept on doing business by himself, but in an honest way. And Lalita you went everywhere, didn't you, Don Aquilino?, and he on the Ucayali, the Marañón, and the Huallaga, and at first he didn't go on the Amazon because of the bad reputation Fushía had left behind him, but after a few months he went back, and one day, in a camp on the Itaya, he couldn't believe his eyes, he saw Fushía, Lalita, turned into a businessman, with paymasters, and he told me there about his business with Reátegui. And Lalita how happy you must have been to see each other again, Don Aquilino, and he we wept, we got drunk remembering old times, Fushía, fortune's smiled on you, use your head, be clean, don't get into any more trouble, and Fushía you stick with me, Aquilino, it's like a lottery, I hope the war never gets over, and he so the rubber's for smuggling?, and Fushía wholesale, man, they come to pick it up in Iquitos, they take it away in crates marked tobacco, Reátegui's going to be a millionaire and so am I, I won't let you go, Aquilino, I'm hiring you, and she why didn't you stay with him?, and he he was already getting old, Fushía, he didn't want any scares or going to jail, and oh my God, I'm dying, my back, it's coming now, she shouldn't be frightened, was there a knife around?, and he was heating it on the lamp when Fushía came in. Don Aquilino had they done anything to Jum?, and Fushía they're all drinking together now, and Pantacha and Nieves too. He wouldn't let them kill him, he needed him, he'd be a good contact with the Aguarunas, but what had they done to him, who burned his armpits?, they were dripping pus, old man, and the scabs on his back, too bad if they got infected and he died of tetanus, and Don Aquilino in Santa María de Nieva, the soldiers and the bosses there, and the one who split his forehead was your friend Reátegui, did he know that he finally went back to Iquitos? And Fushía they shaved his head too, and he was uglier than a renaco, and oh my God, my bones, strong, strong, and Don Aquilino they really gave it to him, and he told the boss who bought their rubber no, we're going to go to Iquitos and sell it ourselves, a man called Escabino, it seemed, and on top of it all, they beat up a corporal who came to Urakusa, and they killed his pilot, and Fushía don't be a fool, he's alive and kicking, he's Adrián Nieves, the one I picked up last month, and Don Aquilino I know, but that's what they say, and she I'm breaking in half, give me something, Fushía, for the love of God. And Fushía does he hate white people?, so much the better, he can convince the Aguarunas to give their rubber to me, big plans, old man, in a couple of years he'd go back to Iquitos a rich man, you'll see how the people who turned their backs on me will treat me, and Don Aquilino, boil some water, Fushía, help me, you wouldn't think you were the father. Fushía filled the pot, lit the stove, and she they're getting stronger, one right after the other, she was choking as she breathed, her face was puffy, and her eyes looked like those of a dead fish. Don Aquilino knelt down, massaged her, she was opening up a little now, Lalita, it was coming, don't be impatient.

And Fushía take a lesson from the Huambisa women, they go off into the jungle all by themselves and come back after they've given birth. Don Aquilino was heating the knife, and the shouts outside were being swallowed up by crackling and whistling, and Fushía see?, they're not fighting any more, they're good friends, and the old man it would be a boy, Lalita, what did he tell her, she should listen, the capironas were singing, he was never wrong. And Fushía he doesn't say very much, and Don Aquilino but he keeps his place, he helped him during the whole trip, he said that two white men had ruined Urakusa with their tricks, and Fushía old man, on your next trip you'll make a mint, and Don Aquilino when will you stop dreaming, and he hadn't he come a long way since the first time? And Aquilino he wouldn't have come back to the island if it hadn't been for you, Lalita, he'd taken a liking to her, and she when you got here we were starving to death, Don Aquilino, do you remember how I cried when I saw all the canned goods and the noodles?, and Fushía what a banquet, old man, they all got sick because they weren't used to it, and how I had to beg you, why didn't he want to help him?, because you'll earn money too. And the old man but it's stealing, Fushía, they'll put me in jail, I can't sell that rubber and those skins for you, and Fushía everybody knows you're honest, don't the rubber men, the woodcutters, and the redskins pay you in hides, rubber, and gold nuggets? If they asked him, he could say it's what I've earned, and the old man I never got so much, and Fushía you don't have to take it all on one trip, little by little, and oh my God, again, Don Aquilino, my legs, my back, Fushía, oh my God. And Don Aquilino I don't want to, the redskins would complain sooner or later, the police would come, and the bosses wouldn't stand around scratching their balls while he got the jump on them in their business, and Fushía Shapras, Aguarunas, and Huambisas all kill each other, didn't they hate each other?, it would never occur to anyone that there were white men mixed up in it, and the old man no, I won't do it, and Fushía he could take the goods far away, well hidden, Aquilino, you'll sell them to the same rubber men cheaper and they'll be happy. And the old man finally accepted, and Fushía that was the first time something like that had ever happened, Lalita, trusting the honesty of a white man, if the old man wants to cheat me, he could sell everything and pocket the dough, he knows I'm trapped here, and he could even double it by telling the police the guy you're looking for is on an island up the Santiago. He was more than two months overdue, and Fushía sent canoes to the Marañón, and the Huambisas came back they couldn't find him, he isn't there, he's not coming, that bastard, and one afternoon he appeared out of a cloudburst at the mouth of the channel, and he had clothes, food, machetes, and five hundred soles. And Lalita could she hug him and kiss him like her father?, and Fushía he'd never seen anything like it, old man, what an honest man, he wouldn't forget it, Aquilino, the way you treat me, in his place he would have run off with the money, and the old man you don't have any heart, friendship for him was worth more than business, gratitude, Fushía, because of you I stopped living a dog's life in Moyobamba, a person's heart can never forget, oh my God, oh my God, and Don Aquilino it was really starting now, Lalita, push, push so he won't strangle coming out, push with everything you've got, yell. He had the knife in his hand, and she pray, oh my God, Fushía, and Don Aquilino was going to massage her, but push, push, Fushía brought the lamp closer and watched, the old man comfort her a little, hold her hand, man, and she they should give her some water, she was breaking in two, would the Virgin help her, would the Christ of Bagazán help her, oh Lord, oh Lord, she'd promised him, and Fushía here's some water, don't yell so much, and when Lalita opened her eyes, Fushía was looking down at the mat, and Don Aquilino I'm getting the legs out, Lalita, it's all over, see how quick it was? And Fushía yes, old man, it's a boy, but is he alive?, he's not moving or breathing. Don Aquilino squatted down, lifted him off the mat, and he was dark and greasy like a little monkey, and he slapped him and he cried, Lalita, look at him, you were so scared and look at what a joy you've got now, and she should go to sleep, and she I would have died without you, she wanted her son to be named Aquilino, and Fushía all right, out of friendship, but what an ugly name, Don Aquilino what about Fushía? And he it's funny being a father, old man, they would have to have a little celebration, and Don Aquilino rest, girl, did she want to hold him?, here he is, he was dirty, clean him off a little.

Don Aquilino and Fushía sat down on the floor, they drank some cane liquor out of the bottle, and outside the noise was still going on, the Huambisas, the Aguaruna, Pantacha, Nieves the pilot were vomiting, and the room was lighted up by little moths, fireflies bouncing off the walls, who would have thought that he would have been born so far away from Iquitos, in the jungle like a papoose.

The orchestra had its beginning at Patrocinio Naya's. Kid Alejandro and Jocko, the truck driver, used to have lunch there; they would find Don Anselmo, who was getting up, and while Patrocinio was cooking, the three would chat. People say that the Kid was the first one to make friends with him; someone who was just as lonely as Don Anselmo, sad, and a musician too, probably saw a kindred soul in the old man. He most likely told him the story of his life, his troubles. After they ate, Don Anselmo would pick up his harp, Kid Alejandro would take his guitar, and they would play: Jocko and Patrocinio would listen, be moved, applaud. Sometimes the truck driver would accompany them on the box drum. Don Anselmo learned the Kid's songs, and started saying, "He's a real artist, the best songwriter in Mangachería," and Alejandro, "There's nobody can play the harp like the old man, nobody better," and he called him maestro. The three became inseparable. Word soon spread through Mangachería that there was a new orchestra, and around noontime the girls would come to stroll in front of Patrocinio Naya's shack and listen to the music. They would all look at the Kid with languid eyes. And one day the news was that Jocko had left the Feijó Enterprises, where he had been a driver for ten years, to become a musician just like his companions.

At that time Alejandro really was a kid, his hair was black, quite long, curly, his skin pale, his eyes deep and unconsoled. He was as thin as a reed, and the Mangaches would say, "Better not bump into him, he'll be dead the minute you touch him." He spoke slowly and sparingly, he was not a Mangache by birth, but by choice, like Don Anselmo, Jocko, and so many others. He came from a good family, born on the Malecón, educated in the Salesian school, and he was all ready to leave for Lima and the University there when a girl from a good family ran off with a stranger who had been passing through Piura. The Kid slashed his wrists and was in the hospital for several days between life and death. He came out disillusioned with the world and a bohemian: he would spend his nights awake, drinking and playing cards with the worst kind of people. Until his family got sick of it and threw him out, and, like so many desperate people, he came to rest in Mangachería and there he stayed. He began to earn his living playing guitar in the chicha bar owned by Angélica Mercedes, who was a relative of Jocko's. That was how he met the truck driver, that was how they became brothers. Kid Alejandro drank a lot, but alcohol would not get him to fight or make love, only to write songs and poetry that always referred to deception and spoke of women as ingrates, treacherous, ambitious, and creatures who punished men.

After he became friends with Jocko and Kid Alejandro, the harp player changed his habits. He became a gentle man, and his life seemed to have become orderly. He no longer wandered about the whole day through like a lost soul. At night he went to Angélica Mercedes', the Kid would urge him to play, and they would play duets. Jocko would entertain the customers with stories about his travels, and between numbers the old man and the guitar player would join Jocko at a table and have a drink and a chat. And when Jocko got tight, his eyes would glow and he would sit down by a box or take a plank and keep time for them, he would even sing with them, and his voice, even though husky, did not sound so bad. He was a huge man, Jocko was: a prize fighter's shoulders, enormous hands, a tiny forehead, a mouth like a funnel. In Patrocinio Naya's shack, Don Anselmo and the guitarist taught him how to play, they tuned up his ear and his hands. The Mangaches used to peek through the wall boards, they would watch the harp player get furious when Jocko lost the beat, forgot the lyrics, or hit a sour note, and they would listen to Kid Alejandro as he sadly taught the truck driver the mysterious lines of his songs: eyes like the break of day, the soft glow as dawn is on its way, the poison that your love poured, mean and evil, into my aching heart.

It was as if the closeness between those two young men had

given the enjoyment of life back to Don Anselmo. No one found him sleeping stretched out on the sand any more, he no longer wandered about like a sleepwalker, and even his hatred for buzzards had abated. The three went everywhere together, the old man between the Kid and Jocko, with their arms around each other like kids. Don Anselmo looked less dirty, less ragged. One day the Mangaches saw him wearing some new white pants, and they thought it was a present from Juana Baura or one of those old personages who would embrace him and invite him to have a drink when they found him in a chicha bar, but it had been a Christmas gift from Jocko and the Kid.

It was around that time that Angélica Mercedes hired the orchestra on a regular basis. Jocko had got hold of a drum and some cymbals, he played them with skill, and he was unflagging: when the Kid and the harp player left the corner to wet their lips and relax their bodies, Jocko would stay there playing by himself. He may have been the least inspired of the three, but he was the merriest, the only one who would take the liberty of a humorous song from time to time.

At night they would play at Angélica Mercedes', in the morning they would sleep, they ate together at Patrocinio Naya's house, and they rehearsed there during the afternoon. In the hot summers they went up river toward El Chipe, they swam and talked over the Kid's latest songs. They had won everybody over, the Mangaches used the familiar form when they talked to them, and they addressed large and small in the familiar. And when Señorita Santos, the midwife and abortionist, married a city policeman, the orchestra was at the party, playing for nothing, and Kid Alejandro sang for the first time a pessimistic waltz that dealt with marriage, which insults love, dries it up, and burns it. And ever since, at every Mangache baptism, confirmation, wake, or engagement party, the orchestra inevitably played and for nothing. But the Mangaches would reward them with gifts, invitations, and women would name their children Anselmo, Alejandro, and even Jocko. The orchestra's fame was established, and the ones who called themselves the champs spread it throughout the city. Important people, outsiders came to Angélica Mercedes', and one afternoon the champs brought over a white man dressed in white silk who wanted to give a serenade. He came to get the orchestra in a truck which raised the dust. But a half an hour later the champs came back alone: "The girl's father got mad, he called the cops, they've taken them off to the police station." They held them overnight, and the next morning Don Anselmo, the Kid, and Jocko came back happy; they had played for the police, and they had been given coffee and cigarettes. And a while later that same white man eloped with the girl of the serenade, and when he came back to get married to her he hired the orchestra to play at the wedding. Mangaches came from all their shacks to Patrocinio Naya's so that Don Anselmo, the Kid, and Jocko could go off well-dressed. Some loaned shoes, others shirts, the champs supplied them with suits and ties. Since then, it became customary for the white people to hire the orchestra for their parties and serenades. Lots of Mangache groups would break up and form again later on with new personnel, but this one continued on the same, it did not grow and it did not shrink, and Don Anselmo's hair grew white, his shoulders became stooped, and he dragged his feet, and the Kid had ceased to be a kid, but their friendship and their closeness were still intact.

Years later, Domitila Yara, the holy woman who lived across from Angélica Mercedes' chicha bar, died, Domitila Yara the church biddy, always dressed in black, with her face veiled and her dark stockings, the only holy woman who had ever been born in the district. Domitila Yara would pass by, and Mangaches would kneel down and ask for her blessing: she would mumble some prayers and make the sign of the cross on their foreheads. She had a picture of the Virgin, with pink, blue, and yellow ribbons that served as hair, and wrapped in cellophane. Flowers made of wire and confetti hung from the image, and beneath the lacerated heart one could see a prayer written out in longhand enclosed in a tin frame. The image would swing at the end of a broomstick, and Domitila Yara always carried it with her, holding it up like a banner. Wherever there was a birth, a death, an illness, a misfortune, the holy woman would appear with her image and her prayers. A rosary with enormous cockroach-like beads hung down from her parchment fingers to the ground. They said that Domitila Yara had performed miracles, that she could speak to the saints, and that she would flagellate herself at night. She was a friend of Father García, and they used to stroll together, slowly and gravely in the Plazuela Merino and along the Avenida Sánchez Cerro. Father García came to the holy woman's wake. He was unable to get in, he had to push the Mangaches clustered in front of the shack aside, and he was already cursing when he managed to get to the door. Then he saw the orchestra, playing sadly alongside the dead woman. He went berserk: he kicked in Jocko's drum, and he also tried to break the harp and pull the strings out of the guitar, and all the while saying to Don Anselmo, "curse of Piura," "sinner," "get out of here." "But, Father," the harpist stammered, "we were playing in her honor," and Father García "profaning an honest house," "leave the dead woman in peace." And the Mangaches ended up getting angry, it wasn't right, insulting the old man for no reason, they would not allow it. And finally the champs came in, lifted Father García up bodily, and the women sin, sin, all the Mangaches would end up in hell. They carried him all the way to the avenue as he struggled in the air like a tarantula, and the urchins were shouting firebug, firebug, firebug. Father García never set foot in Mangachería again, and ever since that time, from the pulpit, he would speak of the Mangaches as evil examples.

The orchestra stayed at Angélica Mercedes' for a long time. No one would have believed that one day it would leave to play in the city. But that was what happened, and at first the Mangaches were displeased with that desertion. Then they came to understand that life was not like Mangachería, it changed. As houses of prostitution began to be opened, offers rained down on the orchestra, and there are certain temptations that one cannot resist. Besides, even though they went into Piura to play, Don Anselmo, the Kid, and Jocko continued living in the district and playing for nothing at all Mangache celebrations.

This time it really got ugly: the orchestra stopped playing, the champs stood motionless on the dance floor, holding on to their partners, looking at Seminario, and Kid Alejandro said:

"That's when the trouble really started, that was when the pistols came out."

"Drunkard!" Wildflower shouted. "He was provoking them all the time. I'm glad he's dead. Troublemaker!"

The Sergeant let go of Sandra, took a step forward, did he think that he was talking to one of his servants, sir?, and Seminario, choking, so you like to answer back too, he also took a step, you son of a!, another one, his formidable silhouette wavered on the boards that were bathed in blue, green, and violet light, and he stopped suddenly, his face full of surprise. Sandra's laugh turned into a shriek.

"Lituma was pointing his pistol at him," Chunga said. "He drew it so fast that nobody had noticed, like those young fellows in cowboy movies."

"He had every right to," Wildflower babbled. "He couldn't lower himself any more."

Champs and girls had run over to the bar, the Sergeant and Seminario were sizing each other up with their eyes. Lituma didn't like bullies, sir, they weren't doing anything to him, and he was treating them like servants. He was sorry, but he couldn't act that way, sir.

"Stop blowing smoke in my face, Jocko," Chunga said.

"And did he draw his gun too?" Wildflower asked.

"He only put his hand on his belt," the Kid said. "He was petting it like a puppy."

"He was scared!" Wildflower exclaimed. "Lituma had shown him up."

"I thought that there weren't any men left in my home town," Seminario said. "That all Piurans had turned into sissies and fairies. But we've still got this half-breed. Now all you need to see is who Seminario is."

"Why do they always have to fight, why can't they live in peace and enjoy things together," Don Anselmo said. "Life could be so nice."

"Who can tell, maestro," the Kid said. "It might be even more boring and sad than it is now."

"You've shown him up, cousin," Monk said. "Bravo!"

"But don't trust him, buddy," Josefino said. "The minute you look away, he'll go for his gun."

"You don't know who I am," Seminario repeated. "That's why you're being so brave, boy."

"You don't know who I am either," the Sergeant said, "Señor Seminario."

"If you didn't have that pistol, you wouldn't be so brave, boy," Seminario said.

"But the fact is that I do have it," the Sergeant said. "And nobody can treat me like his servant, Señor Seminario."

"And then Chunga came running over and stepped in between. You were the bravest of them all!" Jocko said.

"And you people, why didn't you hold her back?" the harpist's hand tried to touch Chunga, but she drew back in her chair and the old man's fingers only brushed her. "They were armed, Chunguita, it was dangerous."

"Not any more it wasn't, because they'd begun to argue," Chunga said. "A person comes here to have a good time, not to get into fights. The two of you make up, come on over to the bar and have a beer on the house."

She made Lituma put his revolver away, she made them shake .ands, and she brought them over to the bar, taking them by the arms, they ought to be ashamed of themselves, behaving like a couple of kids, did they know what they were?, a pair of boobs, come on, come on, why didn't they take out their silly pistols and shoot her, and they laughed, Chunga Chunguita, little mother, little treater, the champs were singing.

"Did they start drinking together even after the insults?" Wildflower asked, surprised.

"Are you sorry they didn't shoot each other down?" Jocko said. "The way you women like to see blood."

"Chunga had invited them," the harp player said. "They couldn't make her mad, girl."

They were leaning on the bar and drinking, good friends, and Seminario pinched Lituma on the cheek, he was the last male in the land, boy, the rest were all cream puffs, cowards, the orchestra started playing a waltz, and the human cluster at the bar broke up, champs and girls went back to the dance floor, Seminario had taken off the Sergeant's cap and was trying it on, how did he look, Chunga?, not as horrible as this half-breed here, of course, but he shouldn't get mad.

"He may be a little fat, but he's not horrible," Wildflower said.

"When he was young, he was as skinny as the Kid," the harpist remembered. "And a regular devil, even worse than his cousins."

"They put three tables together and they all sat down," Jocko said. "The champs, Señor Seminario, his friend, and the girls. It looked as if everything had been settled."

"You could see that it was forced and that it wasn't going to last long," the Kid said.

"Not forced at all," Jocko said. "They were having a good time, and Señor Seminario even sang the champs' theme song. Then they danced and told jokes."

"Was Lituma still dancing with Sandra?" Wildflower asked.

"I don't remember why, but they started arguing again," Chunga said.

"That business about who was more of a man," Jocko said. "Seminario was still on it, that there weren't any men left in Piura any more, and all about his wonderful uncle."

"Don't say anything bad about Chápiro Seminario; he was a great man, Jocko," the harp player said.

"In Narihualá he took care of three thieves with his bare fists, and he brought them back to Piura with their necks tied together," Seminario said.

"He made a bet with some friends that he could still do it, and he came here and won the bet," Chunga said. "At least that's what Poppy said."

"I'm not saying anything against him, maestro," said Jocko. "But it was getting to be too much."

"A Piuran just as great as Admiral Grau," Seminario said. "Go to Huancabamba, Ayabaca, Chulucanas, and there are peasant women all over the place who were proud to have slept with my Uncle Chápiro. He had at least a thousand illegitimate children."

"Was he a Mangache maybe?" Monk asked. "There are a lot of types like that in the district."

And Seminario frowned, your mother's the Mangache, and Monk naturally and very proud of it, and Seminario furious, Chápiro was gentry, he only went to Mangachería once in a while, to have a drink of chicha and to lay some half-breed, and Monk hit the table with his fist: he was insulting again, sir. Everything had been going along fine, like among friends, and all of a sudden he was starting to insult the Mangaches, sir, people who said bad things about Mangachería would be sorry.

"He always used to come over to where you were, maestro," the Kid said. "The feeling he used to show when he embraced you. It looked like the meeting of two brothers."

"We'd known each other for such a long time," the harp player said. "I loved Chápiro, I was terribly broken up when he died."

Seminario stopped, euphoric: Chunga should lock the door, that night they'd be in charge, his cotton fields were full, the harp player should come over and talk about Chápiro, what were they waiting for, loaded with cotton, they should lock the door, he was paying.

"And customers who knocked at the door were sent away by the Sergeant," Jocko said.

"That was the big mistake; they shouldn't have stayed alone," the harp player said.

"I'm not a fortune-teller," Chunga said. "When customers pay, they get what they want."

"Of course, Chunguita," the harpist apologized. "I wasn't saying it because of you, but for all of us. Naturally nobody could have guessed."

"Nine o'clock, maestro," the Kid said. "It won't be good for you; let me get a taxi."

"Is it true that you and my uncle used the familiar form with each other?" Seminario asked. "Tell these people about that great Piuran, old man, that man who had no equal."

"The only men left are the ones in the Civil Guard," the Sergeant stated.

"He'd caught Seminario's disease with all the drinks," Jocko said. "He began to talk about maleness too."

The harpist cleared his throat, it was dry, they should give him a drink. Josefino filled a glass and Don Anselmo blew off the foam before he drank. He stayed with his mouth open, breathing heavily: what people noticed most was Chápiro's energy. And that he was so honest. Seminario grew happy, he embraced the harpist, they should see, they should listen, what had he told them?

"He was a bully and a sad devil, but he had family pride," the Kid conceded.

He used to come in from the country on his horse, the girls would go up to the tower to look at him and they were not allowed up there, but Chápiro drove them half crazy, and Don Anselmo took another small drink, and in Santa María de Nieva Lieutenant Cipriano drove the squaws crazy too, and the Sergeant took a small drink too.

"When the beer got to him, he used to start talking about that Lieutenant," Wildflower said. "He admired him a lot."

The big show-off would come along raising the dust, he would rein in his horse and make it kneel in front of the girls. Life arrived with Chápiro, the ones who were sad became happy, and the happy ones got even happier; and such endurance, he would go upstairs, come down, some more gambling, more drinking, upstairs again, with one girl, with two, and all night like that, and at dawn he would go back to his ranch to work without having slept a wink, he was made of iron, and Don Anselmo asked for more beer, and once he played Russian roulette, the Sergeant pounded his chest and looked around as if waiting for applause. The only one, besides, who always paid his bills, the only one who paid right down to the last cent, money is meant to be spent, he used to say, he was always buying drinks for other people, and on the streets and squares the same tune: Anselmo was the one who brought civilization to Piura. But it wasn't because of any bet, just because he was bored, Lieutenant Cipriano was fed up with the jungle.

"But I heard it was all a lie," Wildflower said, "that his revolver was empty, and that he only did it so the soldiers would respect him more."

And the best of friends, he ran into him in the doorway of the Reina, he embraced him, he'd found out too late, brother, if he'd been in Piura they wouldn't have burned it, Anselmo, he would have put the priest and those Gallinacera women in their place.

"What trouble was Chápiro talking about, harp player?" Seminario asked. The thing that happened to you?"

It was raining cats and dogs, and he it's impossible to live like a human here, no women, no movies, if you fell asleep in the woods a tree would grow out of your belly, he was from the coast, they should stick the jungle someplace where the sun didn't shine, they could have it, he couldn't take it any more, and he drew his revolver, he spun the chamber twice, and holding it against his head, he pulled the trigger, Fats said that there weren't any bullets in it, that's a lie, there were and he knew it: the Sergeant pounded his chest again.

"Trouble, Don Anselmo?" Wildflower asked. "Did something happen to you?"

"We were talking about a wonderful fellow, girl," Don Anselmo said. "Chápiro Seminario, an old man who died three years ago."

"Come on, harp player, are you getting to be a fibber?" Monk said. "You wouldn't tell us about the Green House before, and now you are. Go ahead, what was the fire like?"

"Oh, you boys," Don Anselmo said. "Nonsense, foolishness."

"You're turning stubborn on us again, old man," José said. "Just now you were talking about the Green House. Where was it Chápiro was arriving with his horse, then? Who were those girls who came out to see him?"

"He was getting back to his ranch," Don Anselmo said. "And the ones who came out to see him were cotton pickers."

He pounded on the table, the laughter stopped, Chunga brought another round of beer, and Lieutenant Cipriano blew on the barrel of his pistol as peaceful as you want, they saw him and they didn't believe him, and Seminario threw a glass against the wall: Lieutenant Cipriano was a mother-fucker, he wasn't going to let that half-breed keep on interrupting.

"Did he insult his mother again?" Wildflower asked, blinking rapidly.

"Not his, but that Lieutenant's," the Kid said.

"You in the name of that Chápiro guy and me in the name of Lieutenant Cipriano," the Sergeant proposed very calmly. "A game of Russian roulette, let's see who's more of a man, Señor Seminario."

4

"Do you think the pilot's run away, Lieutenant?" Sergeant Roberto Delgado asked.

"Naturally; he isn't that dumb," the Lieutenant said. "Now I know why he played sick and didn't come with us. He must have run off the minute he saw us leave Santa María de Nieva."

"But we'll catch him sooner or later," Sergeant Delgado said. "The damned fool didn't even change his name."

"The one I'm interested in is the other one," the Lieutenant said. "The big fish. What's his name? Tushía? Fushía?"

"He most likely doesn't know where he is," Sergeant Delgado said. "Maybe he got swallowed by a real boa."

"Well, let's get on with it," the Lieutenant said. "O.K., Hinojosa, go get the guy."

The soldier, who was dozing off in a squatting position, huddled against the wall, stood up like an automaton, without blinking or answering, and went out. As soon as he crossed the threshold, he felt the rain, he raised his hands, he went ahead, slipping on the mud. The downpour was lashing the villages savagely, and among the rush of water and the gusts of whistling wind, the Aguaruna huts looked like animals in wait, Sergeant. In the jungle, the Lieutenant had become a fatalist, every day he was expecting a jergón snake to bite him, or for the fever to lay him low. Now he was thinking that the damned rain would keep up and they would be there for a month like rats in a cave. Oh, everything was going to pot with that waiting, and when his gruff voice stopped, the crackling noise of the cloudburst in the woods could be heard again, the steady dripping from trees and cabins. The clearing was a great ash-colored pool, dozens of rivulets were flowing toward the embankment, the air and the woods were steaming, stinking, and there came Hinojosa, leading a stumbling and moaning shape by a rope tied around his neck. The soldier bounded up the steps into the cabin, the prisoner fell prone in front of the Lieutenant. His hands were tied behind him, and he got up with the help of his elbows. The officer and Sergeant Delgado, sitting on a plank between two sawhorses, continued chatting for a while without looking at him, and then the Lieutenant signaled to the soldier: coffee and a drink, was there any left?, yes, and he should go join the others, they would question him alone. Hinojosa went out again. The prisoner was dripping, just like the trees, there was already a small lake around his feet. His hair covered his ears and his forehead, fox-like rings encircled his eyes, two mistrusting coals that were protruding. Strips of livid and scratched skin could be seen among the folds of his shirt, and his pants were also in tatters, leaving one buttock exposed. Trembling shook his body, Pantachita, and his teeth were chattering: he had no reason to complain, they'd taken care of him like a newborn baby. First they'd cured him, right?, then they'd protected him from the Aguarunas, who wanted to cut him up into little pieces. Let's see if they could get along any better today. The Lieutenant had been very patient with you, Pantachita, but there was no reason for abuses, either. The noose hung around the prisoner's neck like a string of beads. Sergeant Roberto Delgado leaned over, grabbed the end of the rope, and made Pantacha take a step closer to the plank.

"In the Sepa you'll be well fed and you'll have a place to sleep," Sergeant Delgado said. "It's not like other prisons, it doesn't have any walls. You might even be able to escape."

"Isn't that better than getting shot?" the Lieutenant said. "Isn't it better to be sent to the Sepa than having us tell the Aguarunas here's Pantachita, take it all out on him for what the thieves did to you? You've seen how much they'd like to have you. So don't play crazy today."

Pantacha, his look evasive and burning, was trembling very strongly, his teeth were chattering furiously, and he had hunched over and was pulling in and letting out his stomach. Sergeant Delgado smiled at him, Pantachita, he wouldn't be so stupid as to take the blame on himself for all that was stolen and all those dead redskins, would he? And the Lieutenant smiled too: the best thing was for them to get it all over as fast as they could, Pantachita. Then they'd give him some of those herbs he liked and he could make himself one of his stews, what did he say? Hinojosa came into the cabin, left a thermos of coffee and a bottle on the plank, ran out. The Lieutenant uncorked the bottle and held it out to the prisoner, who brought his face close to it, mumbling. The Sergeant pulled hard on the rope, simple bastard, and Pantacha fell down between the Lieutenant's legs: not yet, first the talking, then the guzzling. The officer took the rope, made the prisoner's head turn toward him. The mat of hair shook, the eyes remained fixed on the bottle. He stank worse than the Lieutenant had ever known, the smell was making him sick, and now he was opening his mouth, a little drink?, and panting hoarsely, sir, for the cold, he was freezing inside, sir?, he just wanted one little one, and the Lieutenant all right, except that it would be little by little, where had that Tushía hidden?, everything in due time, or Fushía?, where was he? But he'd already told him, sir, trembling from head to foot, he'd run off into the darkness and they didn't see him, and it looked as if his teeth were going to break, sir: he should ask the Huambisas about it, the Yacumama probably came at night, they said, and it probably got in and carried him off to the bottom of the channel. It was because of the bad things he'd done, sir.

The Lieutenant was looking at the prisoner, his forehead wrinkled, his eyes sunken. Suddenly he turned, his boot hit the exposed buttock, and Pantacha dropped with a groan. But from the floor he continued looking obliquely at the bottle. The Lieutenant tugged on the rope, the hairy head struck twice against the floor, Pantachita, he was all over his foolishness now, right? Where had he gone? and by his own effort Pantacha into the darkness, sir, he groaned and his head hit the floor again: it must have come slowly, it must have climbed up the embankment and got into his cabin, it must have covered his mouth with its tail, sir, and that was how it must have carried him off, poor fellow, and would they give him just a sip, sir. That was what the Yacumama was like, quiet, and the inlet must have opened up, and the Huambisas said it would come back and swallow us and that was why they left too, sir, and the Lieutenant kicked him. Pantacha stopped speaking, knelt: he'd been left there all alone, sir. The officer drank from the thermos and ran his tongue over his lips. Sergeant Roberto Delgado was playing with the bottle, and Pantachita wanted them to send him to the Ucayali, sir, he was groaning again and his cheeks were sunken in from the effort, where his friend Andrés had died. He wanted to die there too.

"So the Yacumama carried off your boss," the Lieutenant said, with a calm voice. "So the Lieutenant is a bumpkin and Pantachita can tell him anything he feels like. Oh, come on, Pantachita."

Untiring, fervent, Pantacha's eyes were contemplating the bottle, and the rain outside had become stronger, in the distance there was thunder, and from time to time flashes of lightning would illuminate the roofs that were being beaten by the water, the trees, the mud of the village.

"He left me all alone, sir," Pantacha shouted, and his voice grew angry, but his look was still quiet and shy. "I fed him, and he never got out of his hammock, poor fellow, and he left me behind, and the others went away too. Why don't you believe me, sir?"

"That business about his name is probably a lie," Sergeant Delgado said. "I don't know of anybody in the jungle called Fushía. Doesn't this guy get on your nerves with his craziness? I'd shoot him and get it over with, Lieutenant."

"What about the Aguaruna?" the Lieutenant asked. "Did the Yacumama carry Jum off too?"

"He left, sir," Pantacha said, with a groan, "didn't I tell you? Or maybe he was carried off too, sir, who can tell."

"I had that Jum from Urakusa right in front of me for a whole afternoon," the Lieutenant said, "and that other slippery article was acting as interpreter, and I listened to them and swallowed their stories. Oh, if I only could have guessed. He was the first redskin I ever had dealings with, Sergeant."

"It's the fault of that fellow who was Governor of Nieva, Lieutenant, that Reátegui," Sergeant Delgado said. "We didn't want to let the Aguaruna go. But he gave the orders, and now you can see."

"The boss left, Jum left, the Huambisas left," Pantacha sobbed. "All alone with my sadness, sir, and these terrible chills I feel."

"But Adrián Nieves, I swear I'll catch him," the Lieutenant said. "He's been laughing in our faces, he's been living off what we've been paying him."

And they all had their women there. The tears were flowing through his hair and he was giving deep sighs, sir, with great feeling, and all he'd wanted was a white woman, even if it was just to talk to her, just one, and they'd even carried off the Shapra woman too, sir, and the boot came up, struck, and Pantacha huddled up, groaning. He closed his eyes for a few seconds, opened them, and meekly now he looked at the bottle: just a little one, sir, for the cold, he was freezing inside.

"You know this country, Pantachita," the Lieutenant said. "How long is this damned rain going to last; when will we be able to leave?"

"It'll clear up tomorrow, sir," Pantacha babbled. "Pray to God and you'll see. But have pity on me, just give me a little one. For the cold, sir."

There wasn't anybody who could stand it, God damn it, there wasn't anybody who could stand it, and the Lieutenant lifted up his boot, but this time he did not kick, he pressed it on the prisoner's face until Pantacha's cheek touched the floor. Sergeant Delgado took a swig from the bottle, then from the thermos. Pantacha had opened his lips and his tongue, pointed and reddish, was licking, sir, delicately, just a little one, the sole of the boot, for the cold, sir, the tip, sir, and something lively and servile was boiling in the rolling coals, just one?, while his tongue was wetting the dirty leather, sir?, for the cold and he kissed the boot.

"You know all the tricks," Sergeant Delgado said. "When you're not trying to work morality on us, you're playing crazy, Pantachita."

"Tell me where this Fushía is and I'll give you the whole bottle," the Lieutenant said. "And besides that I'll let you go. And on top of it all, I'll give you some money. Hurry up and answer before I change my mind."

But Pantacha had begun whimpering again, and his whole body was clinging to the floor, looking for warmth, and it was shaken by brief spasms.

"Take him away," the Lieutenant said. "His craziness is catching, I'm beginning to feel like vomiting, I'm starting to see the Yacumama, and the rain's coming down as pretty as ever, mother-fucker."

Sergeant Roberto Delgado grabbed the rope and ran, Pantacha went behind him on all fours like a leaping dog. At the steps, the Sergeant shouted and Hinojosa appeared. He took Pantacha away, jumping over streams of water.

"What if we start out in spite of the rain?" the Lieutenant said. "After all, the garrison isn't so far away."

"We'd tip over in the first two minutes, Lieutenant," Sergeant Delgado said. "Haven't you seen what the river's like?"

"I mean on shanks' mare, through the jungle," the Lieutenant said. "We'd get there in three or four days."

"Don't worry, Lieutenant," Sergeant Delgado said. "The rain'll be over soon. It's useless, convince yourself of that, we can't move in this weather. That's the way the jungle is, you have to be patient."

"It's going on two weeks, God damn it!" the Lieutenant said. "I'm missing out on a transfer, a promotion, don't you realize that?"

"Don't get mad at me, sir," Sergeant Delgado said. "It's not my fault that it's raining, Lieutenant."

❧

She was always alone, always waiting, what was the use of counting the days, it will rain, it won't rain, will they come back today, not yet, it's too soon. Will they bring any goods? May they bring, Christ of Bagazán, Lord, Lord, a lot, rubber, skins, may Don Aquilino come with clothes and food, how much did he sell?, and he quite a bit, Lalita, at a good price. And Fushía wonderful old man. Let them become rich, Holy Virgin, holy, holy, because then they would leave the island, they would go back to where there were white people, and they would get married, right, Fushía?, right, Lalita. And let him change and love her again and at night in your hammock?, yes, naked?, yes, should she suck him?, yes, did he like it?, yes, more than with the Achual women?, yes, than with the Shapra woman?, yes, yes, Lalita, and that they should have another child. Look at him, Don Aquilino, doesn't he look like me?, look how he's grown, he talks Huambisa better than white man's talk. And the old man are you suffering, Lalita?, and she a little because he doesn't love her any more, and he is he very bad with you?, are you jealous of the Achual women, the Shapra?, and she terribly angry, Don Aquilino, but they were the only company she had, she had no girl friends, did he understand?, and she was sorry to see them passed on to Pantacha, Nieves, or the Huambisas, will they come back today? But that afternoon it wasn't they who came, but Jum, and it was siesta time when the Shapra came shouting into the cabin, she shook the hammock, and her bracelets were dancing, her little mirrors and bells, and Lalita have they come?, and she no, the Aguaruna who ran away came back. Lalita went out to look for him and there he was by the turtle pool, salting some catfish, and she Jum, where did you go, why, what had he been doing for such a long time, and he silent, they thought that you wouldn't come back, and he respectfully, Jum, he held out the catfish to her, I've brought you these. He came back the same as when he had left, his head shaved, annatto stripes that were like lash marks, and she they went off on an expedition, they needed him so much, for up there, why didn't you say goodbye?, toward Lake Rimachi, did he know the Rimache?, are they fierce?, would they fight with the boss, or would they give him their rubber willingly?, Jum. The Huambisas went to look for him, and Pantacha they probably killed him, boss, they hate him, and Nieves the pilot I don't think so, they've become friends, and Fushía they're capable of it, those bastards, and Jum they didn't kill me, I went back there and now I'm here, was he going to stay?, yes. The boss would scold him, but don't leave, Jum, he would get over it soon, and besides, deep down, didn't he like him?, and Fushía a little crazy, Lalita, but useful, he was a good convincer. White men really devils, Aguaruna agh?, would he talk to them?, Jum, boss tricking, lying, agh?, Lalita, if you could see how he works with them, he shouts at them, begs them, dances for them, and they yes, yes, Aguaruna agh, with their hands and their heads, agh, and always they are willing to give them the rubber. What do you tell them, Jum, tell me how you convince them, and Fushía but someday they'd kill him and who the fuck would take his place. And she are you sure you don't want to go back to Urakusa?, do you really hate white men so much?, us too?, and Pantacha yes, Ma'am, because they beat him, and Nieves then why doesn't he kill us in our sleep, and Fushía we're his revenge, and she is it true they hung him from a capirona?, and he he's crazy, Lalita, not stupid, did you scream when they burned you?, and very good at making traps, there's nobody better at hunting and fishing, did he have a wife?, did they kill her?, and if there's no food Jum goes into the woods and comes back with cashew birds, wild turkeys, partridges, did you paint yourself up to remind yourself of the whipping?, and once they saw him kill a chuchupe snake with his blowgun, Lalita, he knows those people are his enemies, right, Jum?, the ones that Fushía leaves without any goods, don't think that he's helping me because of my pretty face. And Pantacha today I watched him by the embankment, he touched the scar on his forehead, he was talking to the wind, and Fushía it's better for me that he works that way, revenge doesn't cost me a cent, and he in Aguaruna I didn't understand him. Because when Don Aquilino's boat was arriving, the Huambisas fell from the lupunas onto the dock like a rain of howler monkeys, and, hooting and jumping, they got their rations of salt and anisette, and the axes and machetes that Fushía was handing out to them reflected eyes drunk with happiness, and Jum went away, where?, out there, I've come back now, didn't he want anything?, no, a shirt?, no, some cane liquor?, no, a machete?, no, salt?, no, and Lalita the pilot will be happy to see you back, Jum, he really is your friend, isn't he?, and he yes, and she thank you for the fish but it's too bad that you salted them. And Nieves the pilot didn't know their names, Ma'am, he hadn't told him, just two white men, they made him hate the bosses and said that they were doing bad things to him, and she did they trick you?, did they rob you?, and he they told me what we should do, and she I would like us to talk, Jum, why did he turn his back on her when she called him?, and he silent, was he ashamed?, and he I brought it for you and the Huambisas were bleeding it, and she a deer?, and he a deer, respectfully, yes, and Lalita come on, they would eat it, wood should be cut, and Jum are you hungry?, and she very, very hungry, since they left I haven't eaten any meat, Jum, and then they come back and she goes into the cabin, look at Aquilino, hasn't he grown, Jum?, and he yes, and he spoke Indian better than white man's talk, and he yes, and did Jum have any children?, and he he used to but not any more, and she many?, and he only a few, and then it began to rain. Thick, dark clouds, motionless over the lupunas, dumped down black water for two successive days, and the whole island became a muddy puddle, the inlet a roiled cloud, and a lot of birds fell down dead at the door of the cabin, and Lalita poor men, they were probably on the river, they should cover the skins, the rubber and Fushía hurry up, God damn it, the bastards, he was sick of them all, on that small beach, look for a dry place, a cave where they could make a fire, and Pantacha cooking his herbs and Nieves the pilot chewing tobacco like the Huambisas. And Lalita would he bring her something this time?, necklaces?, bracelets?, feathers?, flowers?, did he love her?, and she if the boss knew, and he even if he knew, did he think about her at night?, and he it's nothing bad, just a little present because you were good when I was sick, and she he's so clean, so well-bred, he takes off his hat when he meets me, and Fushía shouldn't insult me so much, was she pimply?, Fushía was capable of getting even, the pilot's eyes get hot when I pass close by, was he dreaming about her?, did he want to touch her?, embrace her?, get undressed, get into my hammock, should she kiss him?, on the mouth?, on the back?, holy, holy, I only hope they come back today.

❧

They first appeared during that millionaire year: the planters would celebrate their twelve loads of cotton morning and night, and at the Piura Club and the Club Grau they would toast with French champagne. In June, for the anniversary of the city, and during Independence Day celebrations, they had floats, popular dances, and half a dozen circuses put their tents up in the desert. The rich people brought orchestras from Lima for their dances. It was also a year of many events: Chunga had begun to work in Doroteo's little bar, Juana Baura and Patrocinio Naya died, the Piura was flowing full, and there were no epidemics. Voracious, in swarms, traveling salesmen and cotton brokers fell upon the city, crops changed hands in bars. Stores, hotels, residential neighborhoods appeared. And one day the news went around: *"Near the river, in back of the slaughterhouse, a house with girls."*

It was not a house, just a filthy alley closed to the outside by a garage door, with small adobe rooms around the edges; a red bulb lit up the front. In the back, on planks set up across two barrels, was the bar, there were six inmates: old, flabby, from out of town. *"They've come back,"* the jokesters said, *"they're the ones who didn't get burned."* From the beginning, the house near the slaughterhouse did a very good business. Its surroundings became masculine and alcoholic, and in *Ecos y Noticias, El Tiempo,* and *La Industria* allusions, letters of protest, appeals to the authorities appeared. And then, unexpectedly, a second house of girls arose, right in the middle of Castilla; it was not an alley, but a chalet with a garden and balconies. Demoralized, the parish priests and ladies who had been collecting signatures demanding the closing of the house near the slaughterhouse gave up. Only Father García, from his pulpit in the church on the Plaza Merino, hoarse and tenacious, continued demanding sanctions and predicting catastrophes: *"God has given them a good year; now the time of the lean cow is on its way for Piurans."* But that was not the way it was, and the following year the cotton crop was as good as the year before. Instead of two, there were four houses of girls, and one of them, a few blocks from the cathedral, was luxurious, more or less discreet, with white women, not past their prime, and evidently from the capital.

And that same year Chunga and Doroteo had a fight with bottles, and at the police station, papers in hand, she proved that she was the sole owner of the little bar. What story was there behind it all, what mysterious trafficking? In any case, from then on Chunga was the proprietor. She ran the place warmly but firmly, she knew how to make herself respected by the drunks. She was a shapeless young woman, with scant humor, and with rather dark skin and a steely heart. She could be seen behind the bar, her black hair struggling to escape from its tight net, her lipless mouth, her eyes that watched everything with an indolence that could make merriment dissolve. She wore flat-heeled shoes, short socks, a shirt that looked like a man's, and she never used lipstick or nail polish, nor did she use any rouge on her cheeks, but in spite of her dress and her ways, there was something very feminine about her voice, even when she was mouthing obscenities. Her thick, square hands were equally facile at lifting tables and chairs, uncorking bottles, or slapping fresh people.

They said that she was harsh and hardhearted because of the advice she had received from Juana Baura, who had probably indoctrinated her with a mistrust of men, a love for money, and the habit of being alone. When the washerwoman died, Chunga gave her an expensive wake: good liquor, chicken stew, coffee, all night long and anything that the mourners wanted. And when the orchestra came into the house, led by the harpist, those who were sitting up with Juana Baura stole glances at them, rigid, their eyes full of malice. But Don Anselmo and Chunga did not embrace, she put her hand out to him the same as she did to Jocko and the Kid. She had them come in, she took care of them with the same distant courtesy that she showed the others, she listened attentively as they played their sad songs. It was obvious that she was in control of herself, and her expression was severe but quite relaxed. The harp player, on the other hand, seemed melancholy and confused, he was singing as if he were praying when an urchin came to tell him that they were getting impatient at the house near the slaughterhouse, the orchestra was supposed to have started at eight and it was after ten. With Juana Baura dead, the Mangaches said, Chunga will come to live with the old man in Mangachería. But she moved into the bar; they say that she slept on a straw mattress underneath the counter. During the time when Chunga and Doroteo split up and she became the proprietor, Don Anselmo's orchestra was no longer playing at the house by the slaughterhouse, but at the one in Castilla.

There were swift improvements in Chunga's bar. She painted the walls herself, she decorated them with photographs and prints, she covered the tables with flowered oilcloths, and she hired a cook. The bar was transformed into a restaurant for workers, truck drivers, icemen, and policemen. Doroteo, after the split, went off to live in Huancabamba. Years later he returned to Piura, and, *"the way things happen in this life,"* people said, he ended up as a customer at the bar. He must have suffered when he saw the improvements in the place that had once belonged to him.

But one day the restaurant-bar closed its doors and Chunga disappeared. A week later she returned to the settlement at the head of a team of workmen, who knocked down the adobe walls and built new ones of brick, put on a metal roof, and opened up some windows.

Active, smiling, Chunga was on the job all day, she helped the workmen, and old men, all excited, would exchange knowing and retrospective glances: *"She's bringing it back to life, brother," "Like father, like daughter," "You can't beat heredity."* At that time the orchestra was no longer playing at the Castilla House, but at the one in the Buenos Aires district, and when they went there the harp player asked Jocko and Kid Alejandro to stop by the settlement. They went through the desert, and, looking at the work, the old man, almost blind now, how is it coming?, have they put up the doors?, does it look good from close up?, what does it look like? His anxiety and his questions betrayed a certain pride, which the Mangaches stimulated with their jokes: *"How about Chunguita, harp player, she's getting rich on us; did you see the house she's building?"* He would smile with pleasure but, on the other hand, when the salacious old men would run across him, *"Anselmo, she's bringing it back to life for us,"* the harp player would act puzzled, mysterious, not understanding, I don't know what you're talking about, I have to go now, what are you talking about, what Green House.

With a decided and prosperous air, firm steps, one morning Chunga appeared in Mangachería, and she went along the dusty alleys asking for the harp player. She found him sleeping in the shack that had belonged to Patrocinio Naya. Stretched out on a cot, his arm twisted over his face, the old man was snoring and the white hair on his chest was wet with perspiration. Chunga went in, closed the door, and in the meantime the news of her visit was spreading. The Mangaches had seen her walking through the district, they peeped through the stakes that formed the wall, they put their ears to the door, they passed their discoveries on. A while later the harp player came out into the street with a thoughtful, nostalgic look on his face, and he asked some urchins to go get Jocko and the Kid; Chunga had sat down on the cot and was smiling. Then the old man's friends arrived, the door was closed again, *"She's not visiting him as a father, but as a musician,"* the Mangaches whispered, *"Chunga wants something from the orchestra."* They stayed in the shack for more than an hour, and when they came out many of the Mangaches had left, tired of waiting. But they watched them from their shacks. The harpist was ambling like a sleepwalker again, stumbling, weaving, openmouthed. The Kid seemed drunk and Chunga was giving her arm to Jocko, and she looked content and talkative. They went to Angélica Mercedes', where they ate some spicy tidbits, then the Kid and Jocko played and sang some sad songs. The harp player was looking at the ceiling, he was scratching his ears, his face was changing continuously, he would smile, become sad. And when Chunga left, the Mangaches surrounded them, avid to find things out. Don Anselmo was still bemused, stupefied, and the Kid shrugged his shoulders, only Jocko answered their questions. *"You've got no cause to complain, old man,"* the Mangaches said, *"it's a good deal, and besides you'll get all kinds of breaks working for Chunguita; is she going to paint it green too?"*

"He was drunk and we weren't taking him seriously," Jocko said. "Señor Seminario was laughing, trying to tease him."

But the Sergeant had taken out his gun again, he held it by the barrel and the butt and was struggling to open it. Everybody around him began to look at each other and laugh nervously, to move in their seats, suddenly uncomfortable. Only the harp player kept on drinking, Russian roulette?, between sips, what kind of a thing was that, boys.

"Something to prove whether men are men," the Sergeant said: "you'll see in a minute, old man."

"I could tell that Lituma was serious by his calmness," the Kid said.

His face leaning toward the table, Seminario was silent and still, and his eyes, still quarrelsome, seemed concerned now too. The Sergeant finally got his revolver open, and his fingers were taking out the bullets, standing them up among glasses, bottles, and ashtrays filled with butts. Wildflower sobbed.

"Me, on the other hand, I was taken in by how calm he was," Chunga said; "or else I would have grabbed his pistol away while he was unloading it."

"What's the matter with you, cop," Seminario said, "what kind of joke is this?"

His voice was broken, and the Kid agreed, yes, that time he had lost all his push. The harpist put his glass down on the table, sniffed the air, restless, were they really getting ready to fight, boys? They shouldn't do that, they should keep on talking in a friendly way about Chápiro Seminario. But the girls were running away from the table, Rita, Sandra, Maribel, jumping, Poppy, Hydrangea, squealing like birds, and, huddled by the staircase, they were whispering, their eyes wide, very frightened. Jocko and the Kid took the harp player by the arms, almost carried him to the orchestra corner.

"Why didn't they talk to him," Wildflower stammered. "If you talk to him in a nice way, he understands. Why didn't they try at least."

Chunga tried, he should put that pistol away, who was he trying to scare.

"You heard how he insulted my mother before, Chunguita," Lituma said, "and Lieutenant Cipriano's too, and he doesn't even know him. Let's see if people who go around insulting mothers have cold blood and a steady hand."

"What's the matter, cop," Seminario roared. "Why all the theatrics."

And Josefino interrupted him: it was no use hiding it, Señor Seminario, why act drunk?, he should admit that he was afraid, and he was telling him with all due respect.

"And his friend tried to hold them back too," Jocko said. " 'Let's get out of here, brother, don't get mixed up in any fights.' But Seminario had already got his dander up, and he gave him a slap."

"And me another one," Chunga protested. " 'Let me go,' and a dirty word, shit on his mother, 'let me go!' "

"You fucking dike," Seminario said. "Get away from me or I'll put a hole in you."

Lituma was holding the revolver with the tips of his fingers, the fat-bellied chamber with five openings in front of his eyes, his voice was sparse, didactic: first you looked to make sure that it was empty; that is, that there wasn't any bullet left inside.

"He wasn't talking to us, he was talking to his gun," the Kid said. "That's the impression he gave, Wildflower."

And then Chunga got up, ran across the dance floor, and outside, slamming the door behind her.

"When you need them, they're never around," she said; "I had to go all the way to the Grau monument before I could find a pair of cops."

The Sergeant took a bullet, lifted it delicately, held it up to the light of the blue bulb. You had to pick up the round and insert it in the weapon, and Monk lost control, cousin, enough already, they should go back to Mangachería right now, cousin, and José the same, almost weeping, he shouldn't play around with that pistol, they should do what Monk said, cousin, they should leave.

"I can't forgive them for not telling me what was going on," the harp player said. "The shouting of the Leóns and the girls had me all nervous, but I never imagined, I thought they were mixing it up."

"Who could have guessed anything, maestro," Jocko said. "Seminario had taken his gun out too, he was waving it in Lituma's face, and we were waiting for it to go off at any minute."

Lituma, still so calm, and Monk don't let them, stop them, there was going to be trouble, you, Don Anselmo, he'd listen to you. Like Wildflower, Rita and Maribel were weeping, Sandra he should think about his wife, and José about the child she was expecting, cousin, don't be stubborn, let's go to Mangachería. With a dry sound, the Sergeant brought barrel and butt together: you closed the weapon, calmly, confidently, and everything is all set, Señor Seminario, why was he taking so long in getting ready.

"Like people in love who you talk and you talk to, and it's no use because their heads are in the clouds," the Kid said, with a sigh. "Lituma was fascinated by his pistol."

"And he had all of us fascinated," Jocko said, "and Seminario obeyed him as if he were his peasant. As soon as Lituma said that to him, he opened his pistol and took out all the bullets except one. The poor fellow's fingers were shaking."

"Something inside him probably told him he was going to die," the Kid said.

"That's the way, now put your hand on the chamber without looking and give it a spin, so you won't know where the bullet is, spin it fast, like a roulette wheel," the Sergeant said. "That's why they call it that, harp player, do you see now?"

"Enough talking," Seminario said. "Let's get started, you fucking half-breed."

"That's the fourth time you've insulted me, Señor Seminario," Lituma said.

"It made me shiver to see the way they spun the chambers," Jocko said. "They looked like two kids spinning tops."

"Now you can see what Piurans are like, girl," the harp player said. "Gambling away their lives out of pure pride."

"What do you mean pride," Chunga said. "It was because they were drunk and they had to screw up my life."

Lituma took his hand off the chamber, you were supposed to draw lots to see who began, but what difference did that make, he'd invited him, so he raised the pistol, put the mouth of the barrel to his temple, you close your eyes, and he closed his eyes, and you shoot, and he squeezed the trigger: click, and a chattering of teeth. He turned pale, they all turned pale, and he opened his mouth and they all opened their mouths.

"Shut up, Jocko," the Kid said. "Can't you see she's crying."

Don Anselmo petted Wildflower's hair, he handed her his colored handkerchief, girl, she shouldn't cry, it was all over now, what difference did it make, and the Kid lit a cigarette and offered it to her. The Sergeant had put the revolver down on the table and was drinking slowly from an empty glass, but nobody laughed. His face looked as if he had just come out of the water.

"Nothing happened, don't get worried," the Kid begged. "It won't be good for you, maestro. I swear that nothing happened."

"You made me feel something I've never felt before," Monk stammered. "Now I'm begging you, cousin, let's leave."

And José, as if waking up, that was enough, cousin, he'd done something tremendous, from the stairway the buzzing of the girls rose, Sandra was howling, the Kid and Jocko take it easy, maestro, easy, and Seminario pounded the table, quiet, wrathful, God damn it, it's my turn, quiet. He lifted up his revolver, he put it to his temple, he did not close his eyes, his chest puffed up.

"We heard the shot as we were coming into the neighborhood with the cops," Chunga said. "And the shouting. We kicked at the door, the police knocked it down with their rifles, and you didn't open it for us."

"A guy had just been killed, Chunga," the Kid said. "Who was going to be thinking about opening up the door."

"He fell forward on top of Lituma," Jocko said, "and the force knocked them both down onto the floor. The friend started shouting for them to call Dr. Zevallos, but everybody was paralyzed with fright. And besides it wouldn't have done any good."

"What about him?" Wildflower asked, in a very low voice.

He was looking at the blood that had spattered him, and he was touching himself all over thinking that it must have been his blood, and it did not occur to him to get up, and he was still sitting down feeling himself when the cops came in, holding their rifles, nobody move, keeping everybody covered, nobody move, if anything had happened to the Sergeant, they'd pay for it. But nobody paid any attention to them, and the champs and the girls were running and stumbling over chairs, the harpist was lurching about, he grabbed someone, which one was it, he shook him, another, which one had died, and a cop stood in front of the stairway and made those who wanted to get away come back. Chunga, the Kid, and Jocko leaned over Seminario: face down, still holding his revolver in his hand, and a sticky stain was spreading in his hair. His friend, on his knees, was covering his face with his hands, Lituma was still feeling himself.

"The guards asked, 'What happened, Sergeant; did he give you some trouble and you had to shoot him?' " Jocko said. "And he looked sick to his stomach, saying yes to everything."

"The man committed suicide," Monk said. "We didn't have anything to do with it, please let us leave, our families are waiting for us."

But the guards had bolted the door and were guarding it, their fingers were on the triggers of their rifles, and they were being abusive with their mouths and eyes.

"Be reasonable, be human, please let us leave," José repeated. "They were having their fun, we weren't mixed up in it. Who do you want us to swear it to?"

"Bring a blanket from upstairs, Maribel," Chunga said. "To cover him with."

"You didn't lose your head, Chunga," the Kid said.

"I had to throw it away later, there was no way to get the stains out," Chunga said.

"Funny things can happen," the harp player said. "They live differently, they die differently."

"Who are you talking about, maestro?" the Kid asked.

"The Seminarios," the harpist said. His mouth was open, as if he were going to say something else, but he said nothing.

"I don't think Josefino is going to pick me up," Wildflower said. "It's getting very late."

The door was open and the sun was coming through it like a hungry fire, all the corners of the large room were aglow. Above the roofs of the neighborhood, the sky appeared very high, cloudless, very blue, and the golden rump of the desert could be seen too, and the squat, sparse carob trees.

"We'll take you, girl," the harp player said. "That way you'll save yourself taxi fare."

FOUR

SILENTLY, PUSHED ALONG BY THE RUDDER POLES, the canoes reach the shore, and Fushía, Pantacha, and Nieves jump out. They go into the underbrush for a few yards, they crouch down, and they speak in low voices. In the meantime, the Huambisas beach the canoes, hide them under the branches, rub out the footsteps in the mud of the bank, and in turn go into the woods. They are carrying blowguns, axes, bows, bundles of darts hanging around their necks, and at their waists knives and the tar-covered curare tubes. Their faces, torsos, arms, and legs are hidden under their war paint, and, as they do for big celebrations, they have also stained their teeth and their nails. Pantacha and Nieves carry shotguns, Fushía only a revolver. A Huambisa exchanges some words with them, then he crouches down and lithely disappears into the woods. Did the boss feel better? The boss had never been sick, who invented that. But the boss should not raise his voice, the men were getting nervous. Silent figures, scattered among the trees, the Huambisas peer right and left, their movements are sober, and only the sparkle of their eyes and the furtive contractions of their lips reveal the anisette and the brews that they were drinking all night long around the campfire on the sandbank where they spent the night. Some dip the cotton-wrapped tips of the arrows in curare, others blow on their blowguns to get rid of what has been left inside. Silently, without looking at each other, they wait for a long time. When the Huambisa who left rises up among the trees like a quiet cat, the sun is already high, and its yellow tongues are melting the traces of black huiro dye and annatto on the naked bodies. There is a complex geography of lights and shadows, the color of the thickets stands out more, the barks seem thicker, rougher, and from up above there comes a deafening sound of birds. Fushía stands up, speaks with the one who has just returned, goes back to Pantacha and Nieves: the Muratos are out hunting in the jungle, there are only women and children there, there are no hides or rubber to be seen. Is it worth going in anyway? The boss thinks so, you never know, those bastards may have hidden them. The Huambisas are talking now, gathered around the one just back. They question him slowly, with monosyllables, and he answers in a low voice, backing up his words with gestures and slight movements of his head. They divide up into three groups, the boss and the white men take the lead, and they go forward like that, unhurriedly, parallel, preceded by two Huambisas who open up a trail with their machetes. The earth murmurs slightly under their steps, and at the contact of their bodies the tall grasses and the branches bend aside with a uniform scratching sound, then straighten up and come back together behind them. They continue their march for a long time, and suddenly the light is clearer and closer by, the rays slant across the vegetation, which has become sparser and shorter, less monotonous, more open. They stop, and in the distance one can now see the edge of the jungle, a vast clearing, some huts, and the calm waters of the lake. The boss and the white men take a few more steps and watch. The huts are gathered together on a rise of bald and grayish earth a short distance from the lake, and behind the village, which looks deserted, a smooth ochre beach stretches out. On the right flank, an arm of the woods emerges and comes almost up to the huts: over there, Pantacha should let himself be seen, and the Muratos would flee in this direction. Pantacha turns around, explains, makes some gestures, surrounded by Huambisas, who listen to him and nod. They go off in Indian file, crouching down, pushing the vines away with their hands, and the boss, Nieves, and the others turn their eyes toward the village again. Now it is showing signs of life: figures can be made out among the cabins, movements, and some of the figures are slowly heading toward the lake, in formation, with bundles on their heads which must be either carrying pads or pitchers, escorted by tiny shadows, dogs perhaps, perhaps children. Does Nieves see anything? He doesn't see any rubber, boss, but those things stretched out on forked sticks could be hides drying in the sun. The boss can't understand it, there are rubber trees in the area, could the rubber bosses have come already to pick it up? Those Muratos are a lazy lot, it would be hard for them to die from overwork. The talk of the Huambisas is getting hoarser and hoarser, more energetic. Squatting down, or standing, or up in the trees, they stare at the huts, the hazy outlines on the beach, the shadows that follow, and now their eyes are no longer docile, but fearless, and there is something in them of the greedy boldness that dilates the pupils of a hungry otorongo cat, and even their tense skins have taken on the lustrous smoothness of a jaguar. Their hands show their impatience, they clutch their blowguns, touch their bows, their knives, they slap their thighs, and their teeth, daubed with huiro, filed to a point, chatter or bite into reeds, pieces of tobacco. Fushía goes over to them, talks to them, and they grunt, spit, and their expressions are smiling, belligerent, aroused, all at the same time. Next to Nieves, with one knee on the ground, Fushía is watching. The figures are coming back from the lake, they move languidly, heavily, among the huts, and in one place they have lighted a campfire: a small gray tree climbs up toward the bright sky. A dog barks. Fushía and Nieves look at each other, the Huambisas lift up their blowguns, and, peeping from the edge of the woods, their eyes search, but the dog does not appear. He barks from time to time, invisible, safe and sound. And what if one day they went in and there were soldiers waiting for them in the huts? Hadn't the boss ever thought of that? He'd never thought of that. What he had thought of, on the other hand, and on every trip, was that when they got back to the island soldiers would be covering them from the embankment. They would find everything burned, the Huambisa women dead, and the boss lady carried off. It scared him a little at first, not now, no more nerves. Had the boss ever been scared? He never had been, because poor people who are scared will be poor all their lives. That wasn't it, boss, Nieves had always been poor, and being poor didn't take away his fear. Just that Nieves went along and the boss didn't. He'd had bad luck, but it would go away, sooner or later he'd take his place alongside rich people. Who ever doubted it, boss, he always got what he wanted. And an explosion of shouting shakes the morning: howling, sudden, naked, they emerge from the tongue of woods and run toward the village, gesticulating, they go up the rise, and among the fast, distant bodies, Pantacha's white shorts can be seen, his shouts can be heard, reminding one of the sarcastic laugh of the chicua bird, and now a lot of dogs are barking, and the huts are ejecting shadows, shrieks, and a tenacious agitation, a kind of boiling, moves along the slope as they flee, tripping, rebounding, bumping against each other, figures that come toward the woods and can finally be distinguished clearly: they are women. The first of the painted bodies have reached the top. Behind Nieves and Fushía, the Huambisas are yelling, jumping, all the foliage is shaking and the birds can no longer be heard. The boss turns around, points to the clearing and the fleeing women: they can go. But they stay where they are for a few seconds more, stimulating themselves with shouts, panting and kicking, and suddenly one raises his blowgun and starts to run, he crosses the narrow strip of underbrush that separates them from the clearing, and when he reaches the open, the rest run too, their throats bursting with the shouting. The pilot and Fushía follow them, and in the clearing the women raise their arms, look at the sky, turn around, scatter into groups, and the groups into solitary figures that jump, come and go, fall to the ground, and then disappear one after another, sunken under skins that glow with black and red colors. Fushía and Nieves go forward, and the shouts precede and follow them, seem to be coming out of the luminous dust that surrounds them as they climb up the rise. In the Murato village, the Huambisas are fluttering among the huts, they kick the thin walls into dust, they use their machetes to knock down the yarina roofs, one is throwing stones into space, another puts out the fire, and they are all staggering, drunk? stupefied? dead tired? Fushía goes after them, he shakes them, he questions them, he gives orders, and Pantacha, sitting on a jar, sweaty, his eyes bulging, openmouthed, points to a hut that is still untouched: there was an old man in there. Yes, no matter how much he told them, boss, they cut it off. Some of the Huambisas have calmed down and are scratching around here and there, they pass by loaded down with skins, balls of rubber, blankets, which they pile up in the clearing. The shouting has become concentrated now, it comes from the women penned in between a row of stakes and three Huambisas who are guarding them, expressionless, a few feet away. The boss and Nieves go into the hut, and there on the floor between two kneeling men are a pair of short and wrinkled legs, a sex hidden by a wooden box, a stomach, a thin and hairless torso with ribs that protrude in the earthen-colored skin. One of the Huambisas turns around, he shows them the dripping head, recent, garnet spots. On the other side, the mouth that had been opened between the bony shoulders is still pouring out, those bastards, intermittent spurts of thick blood, which could be seen on their faces. But Nieves has left the hut, running backward like a crab, and the two Huambisas show no enthusiasm and their eyes look numb. They listen, mute, impassive, to Fushía, who shouts, gestures, and waves his revolver, and when he quiets down they leave the hut, and there is Nieves, leaning against the wall, vomiting. It was a lie, he still hadn't lost his fear, but he shouldn't be ashamed, it was enough to turn anybody's stomach, those bastards. What was Pantacha good for? What good did it do for the boss to give orders? And they'd never learn, God damn it, someday they'd cut their heads off too. But even if he had to shoot them, God damn it, kick their asses in, God damn it, those pricks would obey him. They go back to the clearing and the Huambisas step back, and everything has been laid out on the ground: skins of alligators, deer, snakes, and huangana pigs, gourds, necklaces, rubber, bunches of barbasco bush. Still huddling together and noisy, the women roll their eyes, the dogs are barking, and Fushía holds the hides up to the light, calculates the weight of the rubber, and Nieves drops back, sits down on a fallen log, and Pantacha comes over beside him. Did he think he was the medicine man? Who could tell, but one thing sure, he didn't try to escape, and when they went in he was sitting there burning some herbs. Did he cry out? Who could tell, he didn't hear him, and at first he tried to stop them, and then he tried to get away, and he left, and his legs were shaking, and he was shitting his pants and he didn't notice he was shitting. One thing was sure, the boss was furious, not so much because they'd killed him, because hadn't they obeyed him?, yes. But there was practically nothing, those skins were damaged, and the rubber was of the worst quality, he would get into a rage. But why was he hiding it? Wasn't he sick too? They were white men, on the island you forgot that redskins were redskins, but now you understood, you couldn't live like that, if he had some masato beer he'd get drunk. And besides, he should notice, they were arguing with the boss, he would get furious, furious. Hidden by the Huambisas surrounding him, Fushía's voice roars dully in the sunny morning, and they roar back vehemently, shake their fists, spit, quiver. Over their straight hair, the hand of the boss appears, holding his revolver, he aims at the sky and shoots, and the Huambisas murmur for a moment, quiet down, another shot, and the women are quiet too. Only the dogs are still barking. Why did the boss want to leave right away? The Huambisas were tired, Pantacha was tired too, and they all wanted to celebrate, it was right, they were not going to work hard for the rubber or the skins just for the fun of it, one day they'd get all heated up, they'd kill them. The boss was sick, Pantacha, he wanted to hide it, but he couldn't. Didn't he used to get into a good mood? Didn't he used like to celebrate too? Now he didn't even look at the women, and he was always raging around. Could it be that he was going crazy because he wasn't getting rich the way he wanted to? Fushía and the Huambisas are talking back and forth now with animation but without violence, there are no roars, but a lively, nervous whispering goes around, and some of the faces look jovial. The women are quiet, pressed up against each other, hugging their children and their dogs. Sick? Of course, the night before Jum left the island, Nieves went in and he saw him, the Achual women were rubbing his feet with resin, and he, God damn it, get out, he was furious, he didn't want them to know he was sick. Fushía gives instructions, the Huambisas roll up the skins, they put the balls of rubber on their shoulders, they trample and destroy everything that the boss has no use for, and Pantacha and Nieves approach the group. They were getting worse by the day, those bastards, they didn't want to obey, they talked back to him, God damn it, but he'd teach them. They wanted to celebrate, boss, and besides there were so many women. Why didn't the boss let them? God damned fool, him too?, wasn't the region full of soldiers?, dumb hillbilly, if they got drunk they'd be there two days, boob, he was getting started now, the Muratos might come back, the soldiers might take them by surprise. The boss didn't want any trouble for such a small amount, they should take the goods to the river, boob, and be quick about it. Several Huambisas are already going down the hill, and Pantacha goes behind them, scratching himself, egging them on, but the men are walking slowly and unwillingly, in silent and glum columns. The ones who stay in the village are muttering, wandering confusedly from one side to another, they avoid Fushía, who watches them, revolver in hand, from the center of the clearing. Finally, walls begin to burn. The Huambisas stop moving, they wait as if contented as the flames embrace the village in a single whirlwind. Then they start back. As they go down the grassy slope, they turn around to look at the women, who, back on the slope, are throwing handfuls of earth on the burning hut. They reach the woods, and once more they have to open a trail with their machetes and advance through a narrow, precarious, shady passageway among trunks, reeds, vines, and small pools. When they come out onto the beach, Pantacha and his men have taken the canoes from among the branches and loaded them. They embark, they leave, the pilot's canoe in front goes along testing the depth of the bottom with the rudder pole. They row all afternoon, with a short stop to eat, and when it gets dark they stop at a beach half hidden by chambiras that are fuzzy and spiny. They light a campfire, take out their food, roast some cassavas, and Pantacha and Nieves call the boss: no, he doesn't want to eat. He has stretched out on his back on the sand, using his arms as a pillow. They eat and lie down next to each other, they cover themselves with a Murato blanket. There was something funny about how the boss had changed, he not only didn't eat, he didn't talk either. Could it be that business about his legs, had he noticed?, he walked as if it was all he could do and he always fell behind. They must have been hurting him, sure, and besides he never took off his pants or his boots for anything. The whispering crossed and recrossed in the blackness, it ran in all directions: voices of insects, voices of the river as it beat against the rocks, the grass, and the earth of the shore. In the shadows all around, the fireflies glowed like a will-o'-the-wisp. But Pantacha had seen him when he took out that Murato headdress, that akítai, it was the prettiest-looking thing yet, more colors than the ones the Huambisas made, he'd seen him when he was hiding it in his pants. Oh, yes? And why did Pantacha think Jum had run away from the island? He should not change the subject, was he taking the akítai back to the Shapra woman?, had he fallen in love with her? How was he going to fall in love with her if he couldn't even understand her, if he really didn't like her very much? Would he give her to him then? When they got back? That same night? Yes, that same night if he wanted her. Who was that akítai for, then? For one of the Achual women? Was the boss going to give him one of the Achuals? For nobody, just for himself, he liked things with feathers, and besides it was a souvenir.

1

Bonifacia waited below the cabin for the Sergeant. The wind was raising her hair up like a crest, and she also looked like a small rooster because of her satisfied attitude, the way her legs were planted in the sand, her firm and bulging little behind. The Sergeant smiled, stroked Bonifacia's bare arm, honest to God, he'd got all worked up when he saw her in the distance, and the green eyes dilated a little, the sun was being reflected in each pupil like the vibration of small darts.

"You've polished your boots," Bonifacia said. "Your uniform looks like new."

A pleased smile rounded out the Sergeant's face and almost hid his eyes:

"Señora Paredes washed it," he said. "I was afraid that it would rain, but what luck, not a cloud in the sky. It's like a day in Piura."

"You haven't even noticed," Bonifacia said. "Don't you like my dress? It's new."

"I really hadn't noticed," the Sergeant said. "It looks good on you, yellow is a good color for dark girls."

It was a sleeveless dress, with a square neck and a full skirt. The Sergeant was examining Bonifacia with a smile on his face, his hand was still stroking her arm, and she was not moving, her eyes on the Sergeant's. Lalita had lent her some white shoes, she had tried them on the night before and they hurt, but she would wear them to church, and the Sergeant looked at Bonifacia's feet, bare, sunken in the sand: he didn't like her going around naked. It didn't make any difference here, sweety, but when they left she'd have to wear shoes all the time.

"I have to get used to them first," Bonifacia said. "Didn't you know that in the Mission I only wore sandals? They're not the same, they don't pinch."

Lalita appeared on the porch: what news did he have of the Lieutenant, Sergeant. A ribbon held her long hair in, and around her neck a necklace of chaquira seeds was shining. She was wearing lipstick, how pretty the lady was, rouge on her cheeks, the Sergeant would just as soon marry her, and Lalita hadn't the Lieutenant come back?, what had they found out?

"No news," the Sergeant said. "Except that he hasn't reached the Borja garrison yet. It seems that it's raining hard, they got stuck halfway there. But why are you so worried, it isn't as if the Lieutenant was your son."

"Go away, Sergeant," Lalita said, in an annoyed way. "It's bad luck to see the bride before the wedding."

"Bride?" Sister Angélica exploded. "You mean concubine, mis- ss."

"No, Sister," Lalita insisted, with a humble voice. "The bride of the Sergeant."

"The Sergeant?" the Mother Superior said. "Since when? How did it happen?"

Incredulous, surprised, the nuns leaned toward Lalita, who had assumed a reserved look, her hands together, her head lowered. But she was peeking at the sisters out of the corner of her eye, and her half smile was deceptive.

"If it doesn't work out for me, you and Don Adrián will be to blame," the Sergeant said. "You got me into this, Ma'am."

He was laughing, with his mouth open, very strongly, and his body was celebrating too, shaking from head to toe. Lalita was making signs with her fingers to ward off bad luck, and Bonifacia had walked off a little with the Sergeant.

"Go up to the church," Lalita said. "You're making trouble for yourself and for her too. It's no use. What did you come here for?"

Why did she think, Ma'am, and the Sergeant stretched his hands out toward Bonifacia, to see his sweety, and she ran, he just felt like it, and the same as Lalita, she crossed her fingers and exorcised the Sergeant, who, in a mood that was getting better and better, witches, witches, was laughing loudly: oh, if the Mangaches could only see you two witches. But they didn't think so, and the small, shaking fist of Sister Angélica came out of her sleeve, hit the air, and disappeared into the folds of her habit: she would not set foot in that place. They were in the courtyard, opposite the Residence, and in the background the pupils were running about among the trees in the orchard. The Mother Superior seemed softly distant.

"You're the one who is acting the strangest, Sister Angélica," Lalita said. " 'I'm luckier than anybody else,' she says, 'I've got a lot of mothers,' she says, and the first one is her Mama Angélica. She believed that instead of this you'd help me convince the Mother Superior, Sister."

"She's a devil, full of tricks and evil arts," the fist appeared and disappeared. "But she's not going to put it over on me just like that. Let her go off with her Sergeant if she wants, but she won't set foot in here."

"Why didn't she come herself instead of sending you?" the Mother Superior asked.

"She was ashamed, Mother," Lalita said. "She wasn't sure whether you'd receive her or throw her out again. Just because she was born a heathen doesn't mean that she hasn't got any pride. Forgive her, Mother, remember that she's going to get married."

"I was about to go get you, Sergeant," Nieves the pilot said. "I didn't know you were here."

He had come out onto the porch and was leaning on the railing next to Lalita. He was wearing rough cotton pants and a long-sleeved shirt without a collar. He had no hat on, and was wearing thick-soled shoes.

"Both of you get out of here right now," Lalita said. "Adrián, take him away at once."

The pilot went down the stairs, his legs as stiff as clubs, the

Sergeant saluted Lalita and winked at Bonifacia. They went off in the direction of the Mission, not along the path by the river, but through the trees on the hillside. How did the Sergeant feel? How long had the bachelor party at Paredes' lasted? Until two o'clock, and Fats had got drunk and jumped into the water with his clothes on, Don Adrián, he'd been a little tight too. Had they heard anything more from the Lieutenant? You too, Don Adrián? They didn't know anything, the rain had probably caught them, and he must have been foaming at the mouth. Lucky he hadn't stayed with him. Yes, it would probably pin them down for a while, they said that there was a real flood along the Santiago. Come on, give him an honest answer, was he happy getting married, Sergeant?, and the Sergeant smiled, his eyes wandered for a few moments, and suddenly he pounded his chest: that woman, she'd got in here, Don Adrián, that was why he was marrying her.

"You've handled yourself like a good Christian," Adrián Nieves said. "The only people who ever get married here are old couples, the sisters and Father Vilancio harp on it all the time, but nothing happens. But you, on the other hand, here you are taking her to the church up there on your own volition, and she isn't even pregnant. The girl is very happy. Last night she said she was going to be a ›od wife."

"Where I come from, they say that the heart never plays tricks," the Sergeant said. "And my heart tells me that she'll be a good wife, Don Adrián."

They went ahead slowly, avoiding puddles, but the Sergeant's leggings and the pilot's pants had become splattered. The trees on the hill were filtering the light of the sun, giving it a certain freshness and making it quiver. Below the Mission, Santa María de Nieva lay quiet and golden between the rivers and the woods. They jumped over a hummock, they climbed up the stony path, and there above, at the door of the chapel, a group of Aguarunas came to the edge of the slope to watch them: women with drooping breasts, naked children, men with shifty eyes and long hair. They drew apart to let them through, and some children stretched out their hands and grunted. Before going into the church, the Sergeant brushed off his uniform with his handkerchief and straightened his cap; Nieves rolled down the cuffs of his pants. The chapel was full, it smelled of flowers and resin lamps, the bald head of Don Fabio Cuesta was shining in the darkness like a fruit. He had put a necktie on, and from his pew he waved at the Sergeant, who brought his hand up to his cap. Behind the Governor, Fats, Shorty, Blacky, and Blondy were yawning, their mouths sour and their eyes bloodshot, and the Paredeses and their children took up two pews: innumerable children with wetted-down hair. On the other side, behind a grating, where the half darkness grew into darkness, a formation of smocks and identical heads of hair: the pupils. Kneeling, motionless, their eyes, like a cloud of fireflies, curiously followed the Sergeant, who, on tiptoe, was shaking hands with those present, and the Governor touched his bald spot, Sergeant, he had to take his hat off in church and keep his head uncovered, the way he was. The soldiers smiled, and the Sergeant smoothed his hair, which had become rumpled from the quickness with which he had removed his cap. He went up to sit down in the first row, next to Nieves the pilot. They'd fixed the altar up nice, right? Very nice, Don Adrián, the sisters were very nice. The red clay vases were aglow with flowers, and there were also orchids tied together in garlands that reached down from the wooden crucifix to the floor; on both sides of the altar, pots with tall ferns were lined up in double rows all the way to the walls, and the chapel floor had been scrubbed and was shining. From the lighted candelabra, curls of transparent and fragrant smoke rose up into the dark air and helped feed the dense cloak of vapor that hung under the ceiling: they were there now, Sergeant, the bride and the matron of honor. There was a murmur, heads turned toward the door. Up on her white high-heeled shoes, Bonifacia was just as tall as Lalita now. A black veil covered her hair, her eyes passed over the pews, wide and alarmed, and Lalita was whispering to the Paredeses, her flowered dress dominating that part of the chapel with an airy and young vivacity. Don Fabio leaned over to Bonifacia, he said something in her ear and she smiled, poor thing: his sweety was frightened, Don Adrián, look at her timid face. They'd give her a drink afterward and she'd cheer up, Sergeant, it's because she's scared to death at meeting the sisters, she thought they were going to scold her, doesn't she have pretty eyes, Don Adrián? The pilot put a finger to his lips, and the Sergeant looked at the altar and crossed himself. Bonifacia and Lalita sat down beside them, and a moment later Bonifacia knelt down and started to pray, her hands together, her eyes closed, her lips moving slightly. She was still like that when the grating creaked and the sisters came into the chapel, the Mother Superior in front. Two by two, they went up to the altar, knelt down, crossed themselves, went to their pews without a sound. When the pupils began to sing, everyone stood up, and Father Vilancio came in, his bright red beard like a bib over his purple robe. The Mother Superior signaled to Lalita that she should go up to the altar, and Bonifacia, still kneeling, was drying her eyes with her veil. Then she arose and went toward the altar between the pilot and the Sergeant, very erect, without looking to the side. And all during the mass she was stiff, her gaze fixed on a point between the altar and the garlands of orchids, while the sisters and the pupils prayed aloud and the others knelt, sat, and stood up. Then Father Vilancio went over to the bride and groom, the Sergeant stood at attention, the red beard was only inches away from Bonifacia's face, he asked the Sergeant, who clicked his heels and gave an energetic yes, and Bonifacia, but her answer could not be heard. Now Father Vilancio was smiling cordially and he held out his hand to the Sergeant and to Bonifacia, who kissed it. The atmosphere of the chapel seemed to lighten, the pupils stopped singing, and there were whispered conversations, smiles, movements. Nieves the pilot and Lalita embraced the newlyweds, and in the circle formed around them Don Fabio was joking, the children were laughing, Fats, Shorty, Blacky, and Blondy waited one after the other to congratulate the Sergeant. But the Mother Superior scattered them, gentlemen, they were in church, quiet, they should go out into the courtyard, and her voice dominated the others. Lalita and Bonifacia opened the grating, then the guests, finally the sisters, and Lalita silly, she should let go of her, Bonifacia, the sisters had set up a table with a white cloth full of juices and pastries, she should let go of her, everybody wanted to congratulate her. The stones of the courtyard were sparkling, and on the white walls of the Residence, spotted by the sun, there were shadows that looked like climbing vines. How ashamed she was among them, sisters, she didn't even dare look at them, and habits, whispering, laughs, uniforms hovering around Lalita. Bonifacia was still hugging her, her head hidden in the flowered dress, and in the meantime the Sergeant was giving and receiving embraces: she was crying, sisters, silly girl. Why was she acting like that, Bonifacia? It was because of all of you, sisters, and the Mother Superior, ninny, don't cry, come, let me give you a hug. Abruptly Bonifacia let go of Lalita, turned and fell into the arms of the Mother Superior. Now she was going from one nun to the other, she had to pray all the time, Bonifacia, yes, Missy, be a good Christian, yes, not forget them, she would never forget them, and Bonifacia was hugging them tightly, and they very tightly, and thick, involuntary, uncontainable tears were running down Lalita's cheeks, they were smearing her rouge, yes, yes, she would always love them, and they were revealing the blemishes on her skin, she had prayed for them so much, pimples, marks, scars. There was nobody like these sisters, Father Vilancio, look at all they'd prepared. But, come, the chocolate was getting cold, and the Governor was hungry. Could they begin, Sister Griselda? The Mother Superior rescued Bonifacia from the arms of Sister Griselda, of course they could, Don Fabio, and the circle opened: two pupils were fanning the table loaded with plates and pitchers, and between them there was a dark figure. Who had prepared all this for her, Bonifacia? She had to guess, and Bonifacia was whimpering, Mother, tell me that you've forgiven me, she was tugging on the Mother Superior's habit, she should please give her that wedding present, Mother. Thin, pink, the Mother Superior's index finger pointed toward the sky: had she asked forgiveness from God? had she repented? Every day, Mother, then he had forgiven her, but she would have to guess, who had it been? Bonifacia was moaning, who else could it have been, her eyes were searching among the sisters, where was she, where had she gone? The dark figure pushed the two pupils apart and came forward, hunched over, dragging her feet, her face more withdrawn than ever: she finally remembered her, that ingrate, that thankless one. But now Bonifacia had run forward, and in her arms Sister Angélica was swaying, the Governor and the others had begun to eat pastries, and she had been the one, her Missy, and Sister Angélica she had never come to see her, devil, but she had dreamed about her, thought about her Missy day and night, and Sister Angélica she should have one of these, one of those, she should have some juice.

"She wouldn't even let me into the kitchen, Don Fabio," Sister Griselda was saying. "This time you have to compliment Sister Angélica. She prepared everything just the way her favorite wanted it."

"What haven't I done for this one," Sister Angélica said. "I've been her nurse, her servant, and now her cook."

Her face was trying hard to keep on being sulky and cross, but her voice had broken now, she was grunting like an Indian, and suddenly her eyes watered, her voice became twisted, and she broke into sobs. Her old curved hand was clumsily patting Bonifacia, and the sisters and the guards passed the pitchers, filled up the glasses, Father Vilancio and Don Fabio were laughing loudly, and one of the Paredes children had climbed up onto the table, his mother was spanking him.

"The way they love her, Don Adrián," the Sergeant said. "The way they spoil her."

"But why so much crying?" the pilot asked, "when underneath it all they're so happy."

"Can I get them something, Missy?" Bonifacia asked. She was pointing at the pupils, lined up in three rows in front of the Residence. Some were smiling, others were waving timidly at her.

"They have their special meal too," the Mother Superior said. "But go give them a hug."

"They've made some gifts for you," Sister Angélica said, with a grunt, her face deformed by the tears and the pouting. "So have we, I made a little dress for you."

"I'll come and see you every day," Bonifacia said. "I'll help you, Missy. I'll still take out the trash for you."

She left Sister Angélica and she went to the pupils, who broke ranks and came to meet her, in the midst of a great shouting. Sister Angélica opened a way among the guests, and when she got to the Sergeant her face was less pale, stern again.

"Are you going to be a good husband?" she said, shaking him by the arm. "God help you if you beat her, if you look at another woman. Will you behave with her?"

"Of course I will, sister," the Sergeant replied, confused. "I love her so much."

❦

"Ah, you're awake now," Aquilino said. "It's the first time you've slept since we left. Up till now, you were the one looking at me when I opened my eyes."

"I had a dream about Jum," Fushía said. "I was seeing his face all night long, Aquilino."

"I heard you complain every so often, and once I even thought you were crying," Aquilino said. "Was that why?"

"It's funny, old man," Fushía said. "I wasn't in the dream at all, just Jum."

"And what was your dream about the Aguaruna?" Aquilino asked.

"That he was dying on that little beach where Pantacha used to cook up his herbs," Fushía said. "And somebody came over to him and said, 'Come with me,' and he said, 'I can't, I'm dying.' The whole dream was like that, old man."

"Maybe it was really happening," Aquilino said. "Maybe he died last night and was saying goodbye to you."

"The Huambisas have probably killed him, they hated him so much," Fushía said. "But wait a minute, don't be like that, don't leave."

"It's no use," Lalita said, panting, "you call me over and every time it's no use. Why do you make me come to you if you can't do it, Fushía?"

"I can, I can!" Fushía screamed. "It's just that you want to come right away, you don't even give me time and then you get mad. Of course I can, you whore."

Lalita moved over and lay on her back in the hammock, which creaked as it rocked. A blue clearness was coming into the cabin through the door and the cracks, along with the hot vapors and the nighttime murmurs, but it did not reach the hammock; the murmurs did.

"You think you can trick me," Lalita said. "You think I'm dumb."

"I've got worries in my head," Fushía said. "I have to forget about them, but you don't give me any time. I'm a man, not an animal."

"It's all because you're sick," Lalita whispered.

"It's all because your pimples disgust me!" Fushía shouted. "What's happened is that you've got old. You're the only one I can't make it with, with anybody else I can do it as many times as I want."

"You may hug and kiss them, but you can't make it with them, either," Lalita said, very slowly. "The Achual women told me."

"You talked about me with them, you whore?" Fushía's body was infecting the hammock with an anxious and continuous trembling. "You talk about me with the Indians? Do you want me to kill you?"

"Do you know where he used to go every time he disappeared from the island?" Aquilino asked. "To Santa María de Nieva."

"To Nieva? What was he doing there?" Fushía asked. "How do you know that Jum went to Santa María de Nieva?"

"I found out a little while back," Aquilino said. "Wasn't the last time he ran away eight months ago?"

"I just can't keep track of time, old man," Fushía said. "But you're right, about eight months ago. Did you run into Jum and did he tell you?"

"Now that we're so far away, it's time you found out," Aquilino said. "Lalita and Nieves are living there. And a little while after they arrived at Santa María de Nieva, Jum showed up."

"You knew where they were?" Fushía roared. "You helped them, Aquilino? Are you a bastard too? You double-crossed me too, old man?"

"That's why you're ashamed, and you hide and you don't get undressed in front of me," Lalita said, and the hammock stopped creaking. "Don't you think I can smell how you stink? Your legs are going to rot, Fushía, that's worse than my pimples."

The swinging of the hammock was active again, and again the poles creaked, slowly, but he was not the one trembling now, it was Lalita. Fushía had doubled himself up, and he was a rigid form between the blankets, as if he had been drugged, a red throat trying to speak, and in the shadow that covered his face there were two lively and startled little lights at eye level.

"You insult me too," Lalita babbled. "And if anything happens to you, I'm to blame, you called me over just now, and still you get mad, I'm mad too, and I say the first thing that comes into my head."

"It's the mosquitoes, you whore." Fushía moaned softly, and his naked arm hit out weakly. "They've bitten me and they've infected me."

"Yes, the mosquitoes, and it's a lie that it makes you stink; you'll be cured soon," Lalita sobbed. "Don't be like that, Fushía, when people get mad they don't think, they say anything that comes into their heads. Can I get you some water?"

"They're building themselves a house?" Fushía said. "Are they going to settle down in Santa María de Nieva, those bastards?"

"They've hired him as pilot, the Civil Guard there," Aquilino said. "A new lieutenant has come, younger than the one named Cipriano. And Lalita is expecting a child."

"I hope it dies in her belly and that she dies too," Fushía said. "But tell me, old man, wasn't that where they hung him up? What did Jum go to Santa María de Nieva for? Was he out to get his revenge?"

"It was that same old story," Aquilino said. "Claiming the rubber that Señor Reátegui took away from him when he went to Urakusa with the soldiers. They didn't pay any attention to him, and Nieves realized that it wasn't the first time he'd gone there to claim it, that all his running away had been because of that."

"He was claiming something from the police while he was working for me?" Fushía said. "Didn't he realize? He could have screwed us all up, old man, that simple son of a bitch."

"I'd say he was crazy," Aquilino said. "Following the same line after so many years. He could be dying right now and he still couldn't get what happened to him out of his head. I've never met an Indian as stubborn as Jum, Fushía."

"They bit me when I jumped into the inlet to take out that dead turtle," Fushía said, moaning. "Mosquitoes, water spiders. But the wounds are healing up, you dummy, can't you see that when you scratch they get infected? That's why they smell."

"They don't smell, they don't smell," Lalita said. "I was just angry, Fushía. You used to love me all the time before, and I had to invent things, it's my period, I can't. Why have you changed, Fushía?"

"You're not tight any more, you're an old woman, a man can only make it with a tight woman," Fushía shouted and the hammock began to jump. "This doesn't have anything to do with the mosquito bites, you bitch."

"I wasn't talking about mosquito bites," Lalita whispered, "because I can tell that they're going away. But my body gets sore at night. Why call me, then, if I'm the way I am? Don't make me suffer, Fushía, don't make me come to your hammock if you can't do it."

"I can do it!" he shrieked. "When I want to, I can, but I don't want to with you! Get out of here, talk to me about mosquitoes and I'll give you a shot where it hurts you the most. Beat it, get out of here!"

He continued shouting until she moved aside the mosquito netting, got up, and went over to lie down in the other hammock. Then Fushía became quiet, but the poles went on creaking at regular intervals with violent shaking, as if attacked by fever, and only much later was the hut peaceful, wrapped in the nocturnal murmurings of the woods. Lying on her back, her eyes open, Lalita stroked the chambira cords of the hammock with her hands. One of her feet got out of the mosquito netting, and tiny winged enemies attacked her by the dozen, voraciously lighted on her toenails and her toes. They poked at her skin with their thin weapons, long and buzzing. Lalita hit her foot against the pole and they fled, startled. But they were back a few seconds later.

"Then that bastard Jum knew where they were," Fushía said. "And he didn't tell me anything, either. They all turned against me, Aquilino. Pantacha probably knew too."

"It means that he hadn't got used to things, and that everything he did was so he could get back to Urakusa," Aquilino said. "He must miss his village a lot, he must love it very much. Was it true that when he went out with you he talked to the Indians?"

"He used to convince them to give me their rubber without a fight," Fushía said. "He'd get all worked up, and he always told them the story about those white men. Did you know them, old man? What were they up to? I was never able to find out."

"The ones who went to live in Urakusa?" Aquilino asked. "Once I heard Señor Reátegui talk about that. They were foreigners who had come to make the redskins rise up and kill all the white men in the region. Jum's mistake was paying any attention to them."

"I don't know whether he hated them or liked them," Fushía said. "Sometimes he would say 'Bonino' and 'Teófilo' as if he wanted to kill them, and other times as if they were friends of his."

"Adrián Nieves said the same thing," Aquilino said. "That Jum was always changing his mind about those white men, and that he was still deciding, one day they were good, and the next day bad, cursed devils."

Lalita tiptoed across the cabin and went out, and outside the air was loaded with a vapor that wet her skin, and when it got into her mouth and nose it made them numb. The Huambisas had put out their campfires, their huts were black pouches, very thick, motionless, on the island. A dog came over to rub against her feet. In the lean-to beside the corral, the three Achual women were sleeping under the same blanket, their faces shining with resin. When Lalita came to the front of Pantacha's cabin and spied, her itípak, wet with perspiration, was sticking to her body: a muscular leg emerged from the shadows, between the smooth and hairless thighs of the Shapra woman. She was watching, the anxious breathing, the half-opened mouth, a hand on her breast. Then she ran to the next cabin and pushed on the reed door. In the dark corner where Adrián Nieves had his cot, there was a sound. The pilot must have waked up already, he must have recognized her outline on the threshold against the night, the two rivers of hair that framed her body down to her waist. Then the boards creaked and a white triangle advanced toward her, good evening, the outline of a man, what was up?, a sleepy and surprised voice. Lalita did not say anything, she was only panting and waiting, exhausted, as if it were the end of a long race. There were still many hours before trills and happy noises would replace the nocturnal croaking, and birds would fly about on the island, colored butterflies, and the clear light of dawn would illuminate the leprous trunks of the lupunas. It was still the time of the fireflies.

"But I'm going to tell you something," Fushía said. "What hurts me most of all, Aquilino, what weighs on me most, is having had such bad luck."

"Cover up, don't move," Aquilino said. "There's a boat coming; you'd better hide."

"Make it quick, old man," Fushía said. "I can't breathe in here, I'm suffocating. Get by it quick."

It is clear the way it is in summer, the sun spreads out its rays, and tears come to people's eyes when they look at it. And you can feel this heat in your heart, try to cross the street, go under the tamarinds, go sit on her bench. Get right up, what good is a bed if sleep doesn't come, a sand as fine as her hair falling on the Old Bridge, go sit down at the Estrella del Norte, lower your hat, wait for her, she'll be along soon. Don't be so impatient, and Jacinto the empty city is so sad, look, Don Anselmo, the sweepers have gone by and the sand has dirtied it up all over again. Look at the market corner, a donkey loaded down with baskets is arriving there, isn't this the moment when the city awakens? There she is, light, silent, she goes into the square as if she were sliding, see how she takes her over to the bandstand, sits her down, touches her hands, her hair, and she docile, her knees together, her arms crossed: there's your reward for so much waiting. And there goes the Gallinacera woman off, whipping her donkey, sit up straight in the saddle, get set better, keep on looking at her. Does love show its face when it comes, head in the air, does it come in disguise? And you it's pity, tenderness, compassion, the wish to give her something. Drop the reins and let him go wherever he wants, walking, trotting, galloping, he knows where, it's early. And in the meantime you have made some bets: so much if she's wearing white, so much if yellow, so much for a hair ribbon, I'll see her ears, so much for no ribbon, her hair loose, I won't see them today, so much for sandals, so much for barefoot. And if you win it will be Jacinto who will win, and he why such a big tip today and yesterday only half if you had the same to drink, how did he know? He didn't really know, you look sleepy, don't you ever sleep, Don Anselmo?, you it's an old habit, not going to bed without breakfast, the air of the dawn wakes up the brain, everything back there smells of fun, smoke, and alcohol, now I'll go back and my night will start. And he I'll come by and visit you soon, good boy, come see me, we'll have a drink, your credit is good, you know that. But now that he's going away, stay alone, nobody should take your table, because morning will soon be on its way, people will come, a white woman will come up to her, she'll make her turn around, take her to the Estrella del Norte and invite her to have something sweet. And there, again, sadness, rage in his heart, time has not lessened them. And then, bring a coffee, Jacinto, a short drink, and then another, and finally a bottle of the best. And at noontime Chápiro, Don Eusebio, Dr. Zevallos we have to get him up on his horse, it'll take him to the desert, the girls will put him to bed. Grab the saddle horn, then, roll your head around in the sand dunes, turn over on the ground like a bundle, crawl into the main room, and they let him go to sleep right there, he's too heavy to carry up to the tower, bring him a basin, he's vomiting, bring down a mattress, take off his boots. And there, harsh, bitter, the heaving, the streams of bile and alcohol, the itching of his eyelids, the smell, the drunken relaxation of his muscles. Yes, it came in disguise, at first it seemed like pity: she couldn't have been more than sixteen, the thing that had happened to her, the darkness of her life, the silence of her life, her little face. Try to imagine: what it must have been like, the screams she gave, the terror that she must have felt, and the fear that must have been in her eyes. Try to see: the dead bodies, the bubbling up of blood, the wounds, the worms, and then Dr. Zevallos tell me again, it can't be, it's too terrible, had she passed out?, how did she ever survive? Try to guess: first circles in the air, blackish among the dunes and the clouds, shadows reflected on the sand, then clumps of feathers on the sand, curved beaks, acid croaks, and then you take out your revolver, kill it, and there's another one over there, and kill it, and the girls what's wrong, boss, why do you hate buzzards so much, what have they done to you, and you shoot them, God damn it, shoot them, fill them full of holes. Disguised as sorrow, as compassion. You go up too, what's wrong, buy her custard, molasses candy, caramels. Close your eyes, and there again the swarming of your dreams, you and she in the tower, it must be like playing the harp, bring the tips of your fingers together and touch her, but she must have been softer still than silk or cotton, like a song, don't open your eyes yet, keep on touching her cheeks, don't wake up. First curiosity, then something seemed like pity, and suddenly afraid to ask. They talk, the bandits from

Sechura, they attacked them and they killed them, the wife was naked when they found her, suddenly they talk about her, they say poor thing, and out there that violent heat, the babbling tongue, what's happening to me, the girls are going to suspect, what's wrong with me. Or perhaps an important person at the Estrella del Norte brings her over, orders a soda for her, asphyxiation, envy, I have to go, goodbye, the desert, the green gate, a bottle of cane liquor, bring the harp up to the tower, play it. Compassion, pity? It was already taking off its disguises. And that morning is, as now, so bright. She's old, don't take her, probably sick, let Dr. Zevallos examine her first, you what did you say your name was?, you have to change your name, not Antonia. And she whatever you say, boss, did you love somebody with that name?, and there, again, the blushing, the warm flow beneath the skin, and, untimely, the truth. The night is lazy, insomniac, a single spectacle from the window: up above the stars, in the air the slow rain of sand, and on the left Piura, many lights, in the shadow the white shapes of Castilla, the river, the Old Bridge, like a great lizard between the two banks. But may the noisy night pass by quickly, let it dawn, he picks up the harp, don't go downstairs, no matter how much they call you, play for her in the darkness, sing low to her, softly, very slowly, come Toñita, I'm serenading you, can you hear it? The Spaniard is not dead, there he is on the corner by the cathedral, his blue kerchief around his neck, his buttons like mirrors, his vest underneath his white jacket, the heat again, the waves that make the veins fat, the active pulse, the alert look, is he heading toward the bandstand?, yes, is he going toward her?, yes, is he smiling at her?, yes. And she again, taking the sun, motionless, unaware, very quiet, bootblacks and beggars all around, Don Eusebio in front of her bench. Now she knows, she can feel a hand on her chin, has she raised herself up on her seat?, yes, is he talking to her?, yes. Invent what he is saying to her: good morning, Toñita, a beautiful morning, the sun warms without burning, a pity that the sand is falling, or if you could only see the light there is, how blue the sky is, just like the ocean at Paita, and there, the beating of the temples, the waves crashing down, the open-mouthed heart, the interior sunstroke. Are they coming together?, yes, to the terrace?, yes, is he holding her arm?, yes, and Jacinto don't you feel well, Don Anselmo?, you look pale, a little tired, bring me another coffee and a shot of pisco, right over to your table?, yes, hold on, shake hands, Don Eusebio how are you, he old friend, this young lady and I will keep you company, may we? There she is now, next to you, look at her without fear, that is her face, those small birds are her eyebrows, and behind her closed lids the darkness reigns, and behind her closed lips there is also a small dark and deserted dwelling place, that is her nose, those are her cheekbones. Look at her long tanned arms, and the ends of the light hair that hangs in waves across her shoulders, and her forehead, which is smooth and sometimes wrinkles for a moment. And Don Eusebio, let's see, let's see, some coffee with milk?, but you've already had breakfast, something sweet maybe, that's what young people like, how about something sweet?, let's say a quince, and some papaya juice, let's see, Jacinto. Sit down, agree, something sweet, that slim column is her neck, hide your joy, yawn, smoke, those slender-stemmed flowers her hands, and the brief shadows that seem blond as they receive the sun her eyebrows. And talk to him, smile at him, so you finally bought the house next door, so you're going to enlarge your business and take on more help, get interested and pester him, will you open branches in Sullana?, and in Chiclayo?, you're so glad, say something and take a look, really, it's a long time since you've come to see me, her expression is far away and serious, it is concentrated on the drink, some drops of orange light in her mouth, and in the meantime, work is like that, obligations, family, but get away from it, Don Eusebio, an outlet once in a while, her fingers open up, they pick up a quince, they hold it up, how are the girls?, do they miss him, asking about you, come whenever you want and I"ll take care of you, watch her bite now, see how ravenous and clean her teeth are. And then the donkey and the baskets, take off your hat, smile, keep on talking, and there is the Gallinacera woman taking her leave, you're so good. Toñita, shake hands with the gentlemen, I thank them for you, and there again the fleeting freshness, five soft touches on your hand, something that gets into your body and calms it down. How calm it is now, isn't it?, such peace, and look, Don Eusebio, that's the reason and you didn't know, you didn't even know when you died. And he I can't have any more, I'm ashamed, Anselmo, let me buy one round at least, you don't know what it makes me feel like. You never, not a cent, everything here is yours, this is your house, you took away my fear, you sat her down at any table and people didn't look askance or pay any attention. And that was the exaltation. Now, yes, take a chance, go to her bench every morning, touch her hair, buy her some fruit, take her to the Estrella del Norte, stroll with her under the burning sun, love her as much as in those days gone by.

"The donkeys," Bonifacia said. "They go by the house all day, and I never get tired of watching them."

"Don't they have any burros in the jungle, cousin?" José asked. "I thought that animals were what they had most of there."

"But not donkeys," Bonifacia said. "Only once in a while, never the way it is here."

"Here they come," Monk said, from the window. "Your shoes, cousin."

Bonifacia put her shoes on rapidly, her left foot wouldn't go in, darn it, she stood up, went to the door, unsure, fearful on the high heels, opened it, and Josefino held out his hand to her, a breath of boiling air, Lituma, a surge of light. The room dark again, Lituma was taking off his tunic, he was half dead, cousins, his cap, they should have a drink of algarrobina. He dropped into a chair and he closed his eyes. Bonifacia went into the next room, and Josefino, stretched out on a mat beside José, this damned heat that dulls your brain. Prisms of light filtered in through the shutters, dotted with particles and insects, and outside everything seemed silent and uninhabited, as if the sun had dissolved the urchins and the street dogs in its white acid. Monk left the window, they were the champs, work wasn't for them, they lived off the rest, they wiggled their asses, and now they were ready to empty their glasses, but they only sang it after the first glass of algarrobina.

"We were talking about Piura with our cousin-in-law," Monk said. "What strikes her most is the donkeys."

"And so much sand and so few trees," Bonifacia said. "In the jungle everything is green, and here everything is yellow. And the heat is very different too."

"What's different is that Piura is a city with buildings, cars, and movies," Lituma explained, yawning. "And Santa María de Nieva is a miserable little village with naked savages, mosquitoes, and rain that rots everything, starting with the people."

Two little animals crouched behind the strands of loose hair, and, green, hostile, they peeped out. Bonifacia's left foot, halfway out of her shoe, was struggling to get back in.

"But in Santa María de Nieva there are two rivers that have water all year round and lots of it," Bonifacia said softly, after a moment. "The Piura doesn't have very much, and only in the summertime."

The champs let out a laugh, two and two three, three and two four, and Bonifacia got angry now. Sweaty, without opening his eyes, fat, Lituma was slowly rocking in his chair.

Four and two are five, five and two are six, and cousin Lituma answered now. The foot had made it into the shoe the hard way, with a savage stamp of the heel.

"You're not used to civilization," he said finally, with a sigh. "Wait a little while and you'll see the difference. And you won't want to hear about the jungle any more and you'll be ashamed to say 'I'm from the jungle.' "

"I'll never be ashamed," Bonifacia said. "No one should ever be ashamed of where they come from."

"We're all Peruvians," Monk said. "Why don't you give us another algarrobina, cousin?"

Bonifacia stood up and very slowly went from one to the other, filling up their glasses again, barely lifting her feet from the slippery floor that the humiliated little animals were observing from up above with mistrust.

"If you'd been born in Piura, you wouldn't be going around as if you were walking on eggs." Lituma laughed, opening his eyes. "You'd be used to wearing shoes."

"Don't tease our cousin-in-law any more," Monk said. "Don't get so impatient, Lituma."

The golden little drops of algarrobina were falling on the hostile floor, not into Josefino's glass, and Bonifacia's mouth and nose, like her hands, had also begun to tremble, but it was no sin, and even her voice: God had made her that way.

"Of course it's no sin, cousin, who ever said it was," Monk said. "Mangache women aren't used to high heels, either."

Bonifacia put the bottle on a shelf, sat down, the little animals became calm, and suddenly, silently, rebellious, very quick, helping each other, her feet freed themselves of the shoes. She leaned over without haste, pushed them under the chair, and now Lituma had stopped rocking, the champs were no longer singing, and a lively, belligerent agitation was coming over the dark green figures that were showing themselves boldly.

"This one still doesn't know me, she doesn't know who she's dealing with," Lituma said to the Leóns; and he raised his voice: "You're not a squaw any more, you're the wife of Sergeant Lituma. Put your shoes back on!"

Bonifacia did not answer, nor did she move when Lituma stood up, his face wet and angry, nor did she dodge the slap that gave a brief, whistling sound, and the Leóns jumped up and intervened: it wasn't that important, cousin. They held Lituma, he shouldn't act like that, and they controlled him with jokes, he should keep that Mangache blood in check. The humidity had stained the front and back of his khaki shirt, which was still light-colored only on the arms and shoulders.

"She has to learn," he said, rocking again, but more rapidly, in time with his voice. "In Piura she can't go around like a savage. And besides who wears the pants in this house."

The little animals were peeping out through Bonifacia's fingers, almost invisible, teary?, and Josefino poured himself a little algarrobina. The Leóns sat down, there's no love without blows, people said, and the Chulucanas peasant women the more my husband hits me, the more he loves me, but maybe in the jungle women had different ideas and one two and three, his cousin should forgive him, she should lift up her little face, she should be good, a little smile. But Bonifacia kept her face hidden and Lituma stood up, yawning.

"I'm going to take a little nap," he said. "You guys hang around, finish off that bottle, then we'll go over there." He looked at Bonifacia out of the corner of his eye, gave a virile tone to his voice: "If there's no love at home, you have to find it outside."

He winked indifferently at the champs and went into the other room. Some whistling was heard, some springs creaked. They kept on drinking, one glass, silence, two glasses, and at the third the snoring began: deep, methodical. There were the little animals again, dry and tight behind the hair.

"Those night shifts put him in a bad mood," Monk said. "Don't pay any attention to him, cousin."

"What kind of a way to treat a woman is that," Josefino said, searching for Bonifacia's eyes, but she was looking at Monk. "He's nothing but a cop."

"But you know how to treat them, cousin, don't you?" José said, glancing at the door: prolonged, grave snoring.

"Of course I do." Josefino was smiling and sliding on the mat toward Bonifacia. "If she was my wife, I'd never lay a hand on her. I mean to hit her, only to make love to her."

Timid now, skittish, the little animals were examining the faded walls, the beams, the blue flies buzzing by the window, the gold nuggets immersed in the prisms of light, the veins in the hardwood floor. Josefino stopped, his head was touching the bare feet, which drew back, and the Leóns you're the original worm-man, and Josefino the serpent that tempted Eve.

"In Santa María de Nieva the streets are different from here," Bonifacia said. "They're dirt, and it rains so much they're nothing but mud. High heels would sink in and women wouldn't be able to walk."

"Walking on eggs, what a stupid insult," Josefino said. "And a lie besides. I think she's pretty when she walks; lots of girls wish they could walk like her."

The heads of the Leóns were moving in a synchronized way toward the door: one would go, the other one would come back. Bonifacia was trembling again, thanks for what he said, her hands, her mouth, but she knew it was just to say something, that was all, and especially her voice, he didn't really think so deep down inside. And her feet drew back. Josefino put his head under the chair, and his voice came out slowly and as if asphyxiated, he meant it with all his heart, slow words, light, filled with honey, and a thousand other things he would tell her if there weren't people present.

"Don't trouble yourself on my account, champ," Monk said.

"You're in your own home here and the only people with you are a pair of deaf-mutes. If you want, we'll go see if it's raining. Whatever you two say."

"Go ahead, go on," overnice, musical, "leave me with Bonifacia so I can console her a little."

José coughed, stood up, and tiptoed over to the door. He came back smiling, he was really done in, he was sleeping like a marmot, and the curious, restless little animals tirelessly explored the shelves, the legs on the chairs, the edge of the mat, the long body lying there.

"Our cousin doesn't like flirting," Monk said. "She's turned red, Josefino."

"You still don't know Piurans, cousin," José said. "You shouldn't think it's anything bad. That's the way we are, women loosen our tongues."

"Go ahead, Bonifacia," Josefino said. "Tell them to go see if it's raining."

"She'll tell Lituma if you keep it up," Monk said. "And cousin will get mad."

"Let her tell him," sticky, warm, "I don't care. You know me well enough; if I like a woman, I say so, I don't care who she is."

"The algarrobina's got you," José said. "Speak lower."

"And I like Bonifacia," Josefino said. "Let her know it once and for all."

Bonifacia's hands closed over her knees and her face rose: her lips were smiling heroically under the frightened little animals.

"The way you run on, buddy!" Monk said. "Champion of the hundred-yard dash."

"Don't keep at it that way," José said. "You're frightening her."

"If he heard it, he'd get angry," Bonifacia stammered; she looked at Josefino, he blew her a kiss, and she the ceiling, the shelf, the floor. "If he found out, he'd get angry."

"Let him, so what," Josefino said. "You want to know something, boys? Bonifacia can't get out of being my woman someday."

Now the floor, fixedly, and her lips murmured something. The Leóns were coughing, they did not take their eyes off the next room: a pause, a snore, another one, longer, tranquilizing.

"That's enough, Josefino," Monk said. "She's not a Piuran, she barely knows us."

"Don't be upset, cousin," José said. "Follow his line or give him a slap."

"I'm not upset," Bonifacia whispered, "it's just that if he found out, and besides if he heard . . ."

"Ask her to forgive you, Josefino," Monk said. "Tell her it's just a joke, look at the state she's in."

"It was just a joke, Bonifacia." Josefino laughed, sliding back. "I swear. Don't act like that."

"I won't," Bonifacia stammered. "I won't."

2

"Why so careful, when did the people around here get so prissy?" Blondy said. "Why not bust in all together and haul him out whatever way we can?"

"The Sergeant's bucking," Shorty said. "Haven't you seen how he's been following the rulebook? He wants everything done the way it's supposed to be. Marriage must have spoiled him, Blondy."

"And Fats is dying with envy over that marriage," Blondy said. "It seems that last night he got tight at Paredes', and he was cursing himself for not having moved faster, 'I've lost my last chance of ever finding a woman again.' The kid has her good points, but Fats exaggerates."

They were stationed in the reeds and they had their rifles aimed at the pilot's cabin, hanging over the branches, a few yards away from them. A weak, oily glow was growing inside, and it managed to light up a corner of the porch. Had anyone come out, boys? A figure leaned over Blondy and Shorty: no, Sergeant. And Fats and Blacky were on the other side; he could escape only by flying. But they were not going to lose their heads, boys, the Sergeant was speaking slowly, if he needed them, he'd call them, his movements were calm too, and up above some thin clouds were filtering the light of the moon without hiding it. In the distance, bordered by the shadows of the woods and the soft reflection of the rivers, Santa María de Nieva was a cluster of lights and furtive bits of brightness.

Without hurrying, the Sergeant opened his holster, took out his revolver, snapped off the safety catch, whispered something else to the guards. Still slow, calm, he went off in the direction of the cabin, disappeared, swallowed up by the vines and the night, and a short time later he reappeared beside the lighted corner of the porch, his face showing up for a second in the weak glow that was escaping through the wall.

"Have you noticed the way he walks and talks?" Blacky asked. "He's half dopey. Something's wrong with him, he didn't used to be like that."

"The squaw is squeezing him like a lemon," Fats said. "I'll bet he goes to bed with her three times during the day and three times at night. Why do you think he makes up any excuse he can think of to leave the post? To go to bed with the squaw, naturally."

"They're on their honeymoon and it's only right," Blacky said. "You're dying with envy, Fats, don't try to hide it."

They were lying prone on a small stretch of beach behind a parapet of thickets, very close to the water. They had their rifles in their hands, but they were not aiming at the cabin, which from there looked slanted, tall in the shadows.

"He's got stuck-up," Fats said. "Why didn't we go drag Nieves out as soon as the Lieutenant's order arrived, I wonder? Let's wait till it gets dark, we have to make a plan, we'll surround the house, where have you heard so much nuttiness all at the same time. To make an impression on Don Fabio, Blacky, to make himself important, that's all."

"The Lieutenant kept right on it, they'll give him another stripe," Blacky said. "And nothing for us, you'll see. Couldn't you see that when the message from Borja came? The Governor saying the Lieutenant here, the Lieutenant there, and weren't we the ones who found the crazy guy on the island?"

"The squaw's probably given him a love potion, Blacky," Fats said. "She's probably driving him crazy with something. That's why he goes around so tired, why he sleeps like a log."

"Damn it all, damn it all," the Sergeant said. "What are you doing here, what's the matter with you?"

Lalita and Adrián Nieves were watching him, motionless, from beside the stove. At their feet, an earthen plate was overloaded with bananas, the lamp was giving off white and smelly smoke, and at the threshold the Sergeant's astonished blinking continued under his visor, hadn't Aquilino told him?, his voice was worried, two hours ago, Don Adrián, he'd told the kid, run, it's a matter of life and death, and his hand moved his revolver in disbelief, damn it all, damn it all. Yes, he'd given him the message, Sergeant, the pilot was talking as if he were chewing: he'd sent the children to a friend's, on the other shore. From the edges of his mouth two channels were advancing gravely toward his cheeks. What about now? Why hadn't he taken off too? It wasn't the kids who had to hide, only he, Don Adrián: the Sergeant slapped his thigh with the revolver. He'd held off for a few hours, Ma'am, taking a risk himself, what more did they want him to do?, he'd given him more than enough time, Don Adrián.

"They're parleying," Shorty said. "Now he'll probably tell Don Fabio, 'I went in alone, I took him all by myself.' He wants to share the credit with the Lieutenant. He's working like a dog to get his transfer, the Piuran."

Along with the light, a whispering was coming out of the cabin now, it barely moved the night, it floated in it without breaking it, like a solitary wave on still waters.

"But when the Lieutenant gets back, we'll talk to him," Blondy said. "They can send us to Iquitos with the prisoners. That way at least we can get a few days of furlough."

"She may be something of a witch and a little chubby and anything else you say," Blacky said. "But don't tell me, Fats, anyone would have been glad to have done the squaw that little favor, and you first of all. Because every time you get drunk, all you talk about is her, man."

"I would have laid her, naturally," Fats said. "But would you have married an Indian? Never in my life, brother."

"He's capable of killing him and saying he turned on me and I had to shoot him," Shorty said. "He's capable of anything just to get his medal, the Piuran."

"And what if they turn out to be fairy tales?" Blondy said. "When the message came from Borja and I read what the Lieutenant said,

I couldn't believe it, Shorty. Nieves doesn't look like a bandit and he always seemed like a nice fellow."

"Bah, nobody looks like a bandit," Shorty said. "Or maybe everybody looks like a bandit. But I was surprised too when I read the order. How many years will they give him?"

"Who can tell," Blondy said. "A long sentence, naturally. They've robbed everybody, and the people here have sworn to get them. You've seen how they've been badgering us for so long to look for them, even though they haven't been doing any more stealing."

"What I can't believe is that this guy was the boss," Shorty said. "Besides, if he stole as much as they say, he wouldn't be so broke."

"Nobody said he was the boss," Blondy said. "But that doesn't matter; if the others don't show up, they'll make Nieves and the crazy guy take the rap for all of them."

"I've cried, Sergeant, I've begged him," Lalita said. "Ever since you all went to the island, I cried, let's run away, let's hide, Adrián. And now when you warned us, the boys picked some fruit, we packed his things, Aquilino begged him too. But he wouldn't listen, he won't pay any attention to anyone."

The light of the lamp was falling full on Lalita's face, it was lighting up the harsh surface of her cheekbones, the boils, the craters on her neck, and the waving tangles of hair that covered her mouth.

"Even though you're wearing a uniform, you've got a good heart," Adrián Nieves said. "That's why I agreed to be your best man."

But the Sergeant was not listening to him. He had turned around and was scrutinizing the terrace, his finger to his lips, Don Adrián, he should sneak out right now, the railing, without making any noise, the river, he would count to ten, the sky, and he would shoot into the air, run out, boys, he got away through here, and he would lead the guards toward the woods. He should push the boat off in the darkness, Don Adrián, and not turn the motor on until he got to the Marañón, and then he should run like the devil was after him and not let himself get caught, Don Adrián, especially that, he could get screwed up too, he shouldn't let himself get caught, and Lalita yes, yes, she would untie the boat, get out the oars, she would go with him, and the words stumbled on her lips, her forehead became tight and there was an unusual and quick rejuvenation of her skin, Adrián, your clothes are ready, and food, there was nothing missing, and they would row, and before they got to the garrison they would go into the woods. And the Sergeant, wait, peering outside: they should flatten themselves out on the bottom of the boat, if the boys saw them they'd shoot, and Shorty never missed.

"Thank you very much, but I've already thought a lot about it, and I can't escape along the river," Adrián Nieves said. "No one can get past the Pongo now, Sergeant; not even a magician. You saw how the Lieutenant was stuck on the Santiago, and that's a creek compared to the Marañón."

"But, Don Adrián," the Sergeant said. "What do you want, then, I don't understand."

"The only way is through the woods, the way I did the last time," Nieves said. "But I don't want to, Sergeant. I've got tired thinking about it, ever since you all went to the island. I'm not going to spend what life I've got left running through the jungle. I was just his pilot, I only ran his boat, that's all, the way I do for you; they can't do anything to me. I've always behaved myself here and everybody can vouch for that, the sisters, the Lieutenant, the Governor too."

"They're not fighting," Shorty said. "You would have heard shouting, they seem to be talking."

"He probably found him asleep and he's waiting for him to put his clothes on."

"Or he's screwing Lalita," Fats said. "He's probably tied Nieves up and he's laying her in front of him."

"The things you think of, Fats," Blacky said. "I think somebody must have given you a dose of Spanish fly, you're hot in the pants night and day. Besides, who'd want to lay Lalita with all her pimples?"

"But she's a white woman," Fats said. "I'd rather have a white woman with pimples than a squaw without them. It's only her face that's like that, I've seen her taking a bath, she has nice legs. Now she's going to be all alone and she'll need someone to comfort her."

"You're crazy because you haven't got a woman," Blacky said. "It happens to me too sometimes."

"What do you use your brains for, Don Adrián," the Sergeant said. "If you don't dive into the water now, you're screwed, don't you see that they'll blame you for everything? The Lieutenant's message says that the crazy man is dying, don't be stubborn."

"They'll lock me up for a few months, but after that I'll be able to live in peace and come back here," Adrián Nieves said. "If I go into the jungle, I'll never see my wife and children again, and I don't want to live like an animal until I die. I never killed anybody, Pantacha can vouch for that, so can the Indians. I've behaved like a good Christian here."

"The Sergeant's telling you for your own good," Lalita said. "Listen to him, Adrián. For the love you have for me, for the children, Adrián."

She scratched on the floor, she fingered the bananas, she lost her voice, and Adrián Nieves had begun to get dressed. He was putting on a rumpled shirt that had no buttons.

"You don't know how sorry I am," the Sergeant said. "You're still my friend, Don Adrián. And the way Bonifacia is going to feel. She thought you were far away by now, as I did."

"Take them, Adrián," Lalita sobbed. "Put them on too."

"I don't need them," the pilot said. "Keep them for me until I get back."

"No, no, put them on," Lalita insisted, shouting. "Put your shoes on, Adrián!"

An expression of embarrassment came over the face of the pilot for a second: he looked confusedly at the Sergeant, but he squatted down and put on his heavy shoes with thick soles, Don Adrián: he would do the best he could to look after the family, at least he didn't have to worry about that. He was standing up now, and Lalita had come over and was holding his arm. She wasn't going to cry, was she? They'd been through so many things together and she never cried, there was no reason to cry now either. They'd let him out soon, then life would be more peaceful, and in the meantime she should take good care of the children. She nodded like an automaton, old again, her face twisted and her eyes like dishes. The Sergeant and Adrián Nieves went out onto the terrace, they went down the stairs, and when they stepped into the first reeds, a woman's shriek rang out in the night, and in the shadows on the right, aha! the bird was coming out! Blondy's voice. And the Sergeant, God damn it, hands on your head: go quietly or he'd let him have it. Adrián Nieves obeyed. He was going in front, his arms in the air, and the Sergeant, Blondy, and Shorty were following him, walking slowly among the furrows of the small field.

"What took you so long, Sergeant?" Blondy asked.

"I was questioning him a little," the Sergeant said. "And I let him say goodbye to his wife."

When they got to the clump of rushes, Fats and Blacky came out to meet them. They joined the group without saying anything, and that way, in silence, they went along the path to Santa María de Nieva. Whispering could be heard in the hazy huts as they passed, among the capironas too, and under the eaves people were watching. But no one came over or asked them anything. Opposite the dock, the sound of running bare feet could be heard close by, Sergeant: it was Lalita, she was wild, she was going to give them trouble. But she panted through the guards and only stopped for a few seconds beside Nieves the pilot: he'd forgotten the food, Adrián. She handed him a package and ran off the same way she had come, her steps were lost in the darkness, and from far off, as they were arriving at the post, a lament like that of an owl was heard.

"See what I told you, Blacky?" Fats said. "She still has a good dy. Better than any squaw's."

"Come on, Fats," Blacky said. "That's all you ever think about. Jesus, are you screwed up."

"With good weather, tomorrow afternoon, Fushía," Aquilino said. "I'll go first and check. There's a place near there where you can hide in the boat."

"And what if they don't take me, old man?" Fushía asked. "What'll I do, what'll become of my life, Aquilino?"

"Everything in its own time," Aquilino said. "If I find that fellow I know, he'll help us. Besides, money fixes everything up."

"Are you going to give them all the money?" Fushía asked. "Don't be foolish, old man. Keep some for yourself, at least what you need for your business."

"I don't want your money," Aquilino said. "I'll go back to Iquitos afterward to pick up some merchandise, and I'll do a little business in the region. When I've sold everything, I'll come to San Pablo and visit you."

"Why don't you talk to me?" Lalita said. "Did I eat the canned goods? I gave them all to you. It's not my fault that they're gone."

"I don't feel like talking," Fushía said. "And I don't feel like eating either. Throw that out and call the Achual women."

"Do you want them to heat some water for you?" Lalita asked. "They're already doing that, I told them to. At least have some fish, Fushía. It's shad, Jum brought it just now."

"Why didn't you give me that pleasure?" Fushía asked. "I wanted to see Iquitos from the distance, even if it was just the lights."

"Are you crazy, man?" Aquilino said. "What about the naval patrols? Besides, everybody knows me around here. I want to help you, but I don't want to go to jail."

"What's San Pablo like, old man?" Fushía asked. "Have you been there many times?"

"A few times, passing through," Aquilino said. "It doesn't rain much there, and there aren't any swamps. But there are two San Pablos, I was only in the Colony, doing business. You'll be living on the other side. It's about a mile and a quarter away."

"Are there many white people?" Fushía asked. "Around a hundred, old man?"

"There must be more," Aquilino said. "They go naked on the beach when the sun's shining. The sun must do them good, or maybe it's to attract the boats that go by. They shout for food and cigarettes. If a person doesn't pay any attention to them, they curse him, throw stones."

"You act disgusted when you talk about them," Fushía said. "I bet you'll leave me in San Pablo and I'll never see you again, old man."

"I gave my word," Aquilino said. "Haven't I always kept it with you?"

"This'll be the first time you won't keep it," Fushía said. "And the last time too, old man."

"Do you want me to help you?" Lalita asked. "Let me take off your boots."

"Get out of here," Fushía said. "Don't come back till I call you."

The Achuals came in, silently, carrying two large, steaming basins. They put them down next to the hammock, without looking at Fushía, and went out.

"I'm your wife," Lalita said. "Don't be ashamed. Why do I have to leave?"

Fushía turned his head, looked at her, and his eyes were two fiery slits: Loreto whore. Lalita turned, left the cabin, and it had grown dark. The heavy atmosphere seemed close to breaking out into thunder, rain, and lightning. In the Huambisa village the bonfires were crackling, their light was burning among the lupunas and revealed a growing agitation, motion, shrieks, hoarse voices. Pantacha, sitting on the porch of his cabin, was swinging his legs in the air.

"What's going on?" Lalita asked. "Why so many fires? Why are they making so much noise?"

"The ones who went hunting have come back, Ma'am," Pantacha said. "Didn't you see the women? They spent all day making masato beer, they're going to have a celebration. They want the boss to come too. Why is he so worked up, Ma'am?"

"Because Don Aquilino hasn't come," Lalita said. "The canned goods have run out and he's running out of liquor too."

"It's been around two months since the old man came last," Pantacha said. "This time he really isn't coming, Ma'am."

"It's all the same to you now, right?" Lalita said. "Now that you've got a woman, nothing bothers you."

Pantacha let out a laugh, and the Shapra woman appeared at the cabin door loaded with adornments: a crown, bracelets, ankle hoops, tattoos on her cheekbones and her breasts. She smiled at Lalita and sat down on the porch next to her.

"She's learned to talk white man's talk better than I do," Pantacha said. "She likes you a lot, Ma'am. Now she's afraid because the Huambisas who went hunting have come back. She's never stopped being afraid of them, no matter what I do."

The Shapra pointed at the brush that hid the embankment: Nieves the pilot. He was coming with his straw hat in his hand, shirtless, his pants rolled up to the knees.

"I haven't seen you all day," Pantacha said. "Were you fishing?"

"Yes, I went down as far as the Santiago," Nieves said. "But I didn't have any luck. There's going to be a storm and the fish were running away or going down deeper."

"The Huambisas have come back," Pantacha said. "They're going to have a celebration tonight."

"That's probably why Jum left," Nieves said. "I saw him going out the channel in his canoe."

"He'll stay away two or three days," Pantacha said. "That Indian hasn't stopped being afraid of the Huambisas, either."

"It isn't that he's afraid, it's just that he doesn't want them to cut off his head," the pilot said. "He knows that when they're drunk the hate they have for him comes out."

"Are you going to celebrate with the Indians too?" Lalita asked.

"I'm tired from so much rowing," Nieves said. "I'm going to bed."

"It's prohibited, but sometimes they leave," Aquilino said. "When they want something. They make canoes, they launch them, and they anchor off the Colony. 'Give us what we want or we'll come ashore,' they say."

"Who lives in the Colony, old man?" Fushía asked. "Are there any police?"

"No, I haven't seen any," Aquilino said. "The families are there. The wives and children. They've built themselves little farms."

"Are their families so disgusted by them?" Fushía said. "Even though they're relatives?"

"There are some cases where being family doesn't count," Aquilino said. "They probably haven't got used to it, they're probably afraid of catching it."

"But then nobody goes to visit them," Fushía said. "So visitors must be prohibited."

"No, not at all, there are a lot of visitors," Aquilino said. "You have to get into a boat before going in, and they give you some soap to bathe with, and you have to take your clothes off and put on a robe."

"Why are you trying to make me think you'll come and visit me, old man?" Fushía asked.

"You can see the houses from the river," Aquilino said. "Good houses, some like the ones in Iquitos, brick. You'll be better off here than on the island, man. You'll have friends and nothing will bother you."

"Leave me on some small beach, old man," Fushía said. "You'll come by from time to time and bring me food. I'll live in hiding, nobody'll see me. Don't take me to San Pablo, Aquilino."

"If you could only walk, Fushía," Aquilino said. "Don't you realize, man?"

"And why did you let the Huambisa medicine man cure your fever if you're still so much afraid of them?" Lalita asked. The Shapra smiled without answering.

"I brought him even though she didn't want me to, Ma'am," Pantacha said. "He sang over her, danced around her, spit tobacco juice on her nose, and she didn't open her eyes. She was trembling more from fear than from fever. I think she was cured by the fright."

The thunder rolled, it began to rain, and Lalita took refuge under the roof. Pantacha stayed on the porch, letting the water wet his legs. Moments later, the rain stopped and the clearing filled with vapor. The pilot's cabin still showed no light, Ma'am, he must have been asleep already, and that was just a warning, the real cloudburst would come down on the Huambisas in the middle of their celebration. Aquilino was probably frightened by the thunder, and Lalita jumped down the steps, went to see him, crossed the clearing, and entered the cabin. Fushía had his legs submerged in the basins, and the skin on his thighs was rosy and scabby, like the clay of the receptacles. He was grabbing the mosquito netting and looking steadily at her, Fushía, why was he ashamed?, and he pulled it off and covered himself, and now he was groaning, what was wrong with her seeing him?, and, doubled over, he was trying to reach his boot, Fushía, she didn't care, and finally he got it and threw it without taking aim: it went by Lalita, it hit the cot, and the child did not cry. Lalita went out of the cabin again. A soft rain was falling now.

"And what about the ones who die, old man?" Fushía said. "Do they bury them right there?"

"Right there, of course," Aquilino said. "They're not going to throw them into the Amazon; it wouldn't be Christian."

"Are you always going to be traveling back and forth along the rivers, Aquilino?" Fushía said. "Haven't you thought that someday you might die in your boat?"

"I'd like to die in my village," Aquilino said. "I don't have anybody in Moyobamba any more, either family or friends. But I'd like to be buried in the cemetery there, I don't know why."

"I'd like to go back to Campo Grande too," Fushía said. "To find out what happened to my relatives, to the friends I had when I was a boy. Someone must still remember me."

"Sometimes I'm sorry I don't have a partner," Aquilino said. "A lot of people have offered to work with me, put up a little capital for a new boat. They're all tempted to spend their lives traveling around."

"And why haven't you accepted?" Fushía asked. "Now that you're old, you'd have some company."

"I know people," Aquilino said. "I would have got along with the partner as long as I was showing him the business and introducing him to the customers. Then the other fellow would have thought why go on dividing up such a small amount of money. And since I'm old, I would have been the one sacrificed."

"I'm sorry that we won't be staying together, Aquilino," Fushía said. "I've been thinking about that all during the trip."

"It wasn't any business for you," Aquilino said. "You're too ambitious, you wouldn't be satisfied with the little you make at this."

"You can see how far ambition got me," Fushía said. "Ending up a thousand times worse off than you, and you never had any ambitions."

"God didn't help you, Fushía," Aquilino said. "Everything that happens depends on that."

"And why didn't he help me and he did help others?" Fushía said. "Why did he screw me up and help Reátegui, for example?"

"Ask him yourself when you die," Aquilino said. "How should I know, Fushía?"

"Let's go for just a little while before the cloudburst comes, boss," Pantacha said.

"All right, but just for a while," Fushía said. "So those bastards won't get resentful. Isn't Nieves coming?"

"He was fishing on the Santiago," Pantacha said. "He's already gone to sleep. He turned his lamp out a while back."

They went away from the cabins toward the reddish and glowing spots of the Huambisa village, and Lalita waited, sitting by the dripping eaves of the cabin. The pilot appeared a little while afterward, wearing pants and a shirt: everything was ready now. But Lalita didn't want to; tomorrow, there was going to be a storm now.

"Not tomorrow, right now," Adrián Nieves said. "The boss and Pantacha will be celebrating, and the Huambisas are already drunk. Jum is in the channel waiting for us, he'll take us as far as the Santiago."

"I can't leave Aquilino here," Lalita said. "I don't want to abandon my child."

"Nobody said he was going to stay behind," Nieves said. "I want us to take him along too."

He went into the cabin, came out with a bundle in his arms, and without saying anything to Lalita, began walking toward the turtle pool. She followed him, whimpering, but then, at the embankment, she calmed down and took the pilot's arm. Nieves waited for her to get into the canoe first, he handed her the child, and in a few moments the boat cut softly across the dark surface of the inlet. Behind the sombre palisade of the lupunas, the light from the bonfires peeped through weakly and singing could be heard.

"Where are we going?" Lalita asked. "You don't tell me anything, you do everything by yourself. I don't want to go with you any more. I want to go back."

"Quiet," the pilot said. "Don't talk until we get out of the inlet."

"It's dawn already," Aquilino said. "We haven't shut our eyes, Fushía."

"It's the last night we'll be together," Fushía said. "I can feel fire here inside, Aquilino."

"I can feel it too," Aquilino said. "But we can't stay here any longer, we have to keep going. Aren't you hungry?"

"A small beach, old man," Fushía said. "In the name of our friendship, Aquilino. Not to San Pablo, leave me anywhere. I don't want to die there, old man."

"Be brave, Fushía," Aquilino said. "Just think, I was figuring. It's just thirty days since we left the island."

Things are the way they are, reality and desire become mingled, and if not, why had she come that morning. Did she recognize your voice, your smell? Speak to her, see how something smiling and anxious rises up in her face, hold on to her hand for a few seconds and discover underneath her skin that discreet fear, the delicate alarm of her blood, see how she tightens her lips, how she moves her eyelids. Did she want to know? Why are you holding my arm like that, why are you playing with my hair, why is your hand on my waist, and when you speak your face is so close to mine. Explain it to her: so that you will not confuse me with the others, because I want you to recognize me, Toñita, and that breeze and those sounds from my mouth are the things that I am telling you. But be prudent, alert, watch out for people, and now there is no one around, take her hand, let go of it at once, you're frightened, Toñita, why have you started to tremble?, ask her to forgive you. And there, again, the sun that gilds her lashes, and she, surely thinking, doubting, imagining, you it's nothing wrong, Toñita, don't be afraid of me, and she darkly making an effort, inventing, why, how, and the others there, Jacinto is cleaning off the tables, Chápiro is talking about cotton and cockfights and the peasant women he has had, some women offer her creamcakes, and she eagerly, anxiously scratching in the mute shadows, why, how. You I'm crazy, it's impossible, I'm making her suffer, be ashamed of yourself, jump on your horse, the desert again, the downstairs room, the tower. Draw the curtains, have Butterfly come up, have her get undressed without opening her mouth, come, don't move, you're a little girl, kiss her, you love her, her hands are flowers, she what beautiful things, boss, do you really like me that much? She should get dressed, go back to the main room, why did you have to talk, Butterfly, she you're in love and you want me to take her place, you go on, beat it, no girl in the house will ever come back to the tower. And solitude again, the harp, the cane liquor, get drunk, stretch out on the bed, and you stir too, dig in the darkness, is it right for people to love?, do I have the right to love her?, would I care if it were a sin? The night is slow, sleepless, empty without her presence, which kills doubt. They laugh downstairs, toast and joke, among the noisy guitars the thin whistle of a flute can be made out, they become aroused, dance. It was a sin, Anselmo, you're going to die, repent, you it wasn't, Father, I won't repent for anything except that she died. It was done with evil intent, by force, you it was not done with evil intent, we understood each other without her seeing me, we loved each other without her talking to me, things were the way they were. God is great, Toñita, isn't it true that you recognize me? Prove it, squeeze her hand, count to six, does she squeeze?, to ten, can you see that she doesn't let go of your hand?, to fifteen, and there it is in yours, confident and soft. And in the meantime the sand has stopped falling, a cool wind is coming up from the river, come to the Estrella del Norte, Toñita, we'll have something, and what arm was her hand looking for?, on whom did she lean to cross the square?, you mine and not Don Eusebio's, on me and not on Chápiro, does she love you, then? Feel what you were feeling; the adolescent and tanned flesh, the thin fuzz on her arm, and under the table her knee next to your knee, is the canistel juice delicious, Toñita?, and her knee still, and then pretend and enjoy, so Don Eusebio's affairs are going well, so the store he opened in Sullana is making the most money, so Arrese died on us, Dr. Zevallos, what a misfortune for Piura, he was a very educated man, and there, delightfully, the slight heat between veins and muscles, a small flame in the heart, another in the temples, two small craters throbbing under the wrists. Not just her knee now, her foot too, it must look small and defenseless next to your thick boot, and her ankle, her slim thigh alongside yours, you God is great, but perhaps he doesn't realize, could it be chance? Make another test, press, does she draw back?, does she stay close to you?, does she press too?, you are you playing, girl?, what do you feel for me? There, again, the strong desire: to be alone sometime, not here but in the tower, not during the day but at night, not dressed but naked, Toñita, don't draw away, keep on touching me. And there, the suffocating summer morning, the bootblacks, the beggars, the vendor women, the people coming out of church, the Estrella del Norte with its men and its conversations, cotton, floods, the barbecue on Sunday, and suddenly feel her hand as it searches, as it finds and grasps yours, watch out, careful, don't look at her, don't move, smile, cotton, gambling, hunting, tough venison, and devilish agricultural diseases, and in the meantime listen to her hand in yours, its mysterious message, decipher that voice of secret pressures and soft pinches, and all the time Toñita, Toñita, Toñita. Enough of doubting now, tomorrow even earlier, hide in the cathedral and spy, listen to the tiny song of the sand on the crests of the tamarind trees, wait there, tense, your eyes fixed on the corner half hidden by the bandstand and the trees. And there, again, time held back there, under the dome and the arches, the severe surface, the empty pews, and the implacable will, and a cold secretion on your back, the sudden emptiness in your stomach: the donkey, the Gallinacera woman, the baskets, a figure floating forward. Let no one come, let him go away quickly, do not let the priest come out, and now, quick, running, the outside light, the front of the church, the broad steps, the sidewalk, the shadowy square. Open your arms, receive her, see how her head leans on your shoulder, caress her hair, clean the blond sand off it, and, at the same time, careful, the Estrella del Norte will open and Jacinto will appear, yawning, local people and outsiders will arrive, go ahead. No tricks, kiss her, and while her face grows warm, don't be frightened, you're pretty, I love you, don't cry, feel your mouth on her cheek and notice, her blush is going away, her posture is docile again, and the surface that yields beneath your lips is like the fragrance of a hot summer's day, as when the rainbow lights up the sky. And then steal her away: we can't go on like this, come with me, Toñita, you will take care of her, you will spoil her, she will be happy with you, after a little while you will both leave Piura, you will live out in the open. Run with her, the eaves are still dripping sand, the people are asleep or stretching in their beds, but look, look all around, give her your hand, put her up on your horse. Don't be nervous, speak to her slowly: hold on to my waist, tight, just for a little while. And once more the sun is taking its place up above the city, the temperate air, the deserted streets, the furious urgency, and suddenly see how she is holding on, clutching your shirt, how her body clings to yours, see that flame in her face: does she understand?, hurry, so they don't see us?, let's go?, I want to go with you?, you Toñita, Toñita, do you realize where we're going, why we're going, what we are? Cross the Old Bridge and don't go into early-rising Castilla, go quickly past the carob trees on the bank, and now, yes, the desert, spur as if with hatred, make him jump, make him gallop, make his hoofs beat along the smooth back of the desert, and make him raise a protective cloud of dust. There, the whinnying, the animal's fatigue, her arm on your waist, and at times the taste of her hair, which the wind blows into your mouth. Keep on spurring, you're getting there now, use the whip, and, once more, breathe in the smell of that morning, the dust and mad excitement of that morning. Go in without making any noise, pick her up, go up the narrow stairs to the tower, feel her arms around you like a living necklace, and there the groaning sounds, the anxiety that separates her lips, the flash of her teeth, you nobody can see us, people are asleep, calm down, Toñita. Tell her their names: Firefly, Froggy, Flower, Butterfly. And what's more: they're worn out, they've been drinking and making love, and they can't hear us, and they won't say anything, you will explain it all to them, they'll understand things. But go on, what they call them, inmates. Tell her about the tower and the view, paint the river for her, the cotton fields, the brown profile of the distant mountains, and the reflections on the roofs of Piura at noon, the white houses of Castilla, the immensity of the desert and the sky. You I'll see for you, you'll lend her your eyes, everything I have is yours, Toñita. She will be able to imagine when the river starts to rise: those thin serpents that one December day come creeping through the river bed, and how they come together and grow, and their color, you greenish brown, and keep on growing and stretching out. She will hear the tolling of the bells, and guess how many people are going out to see it, the kids who shoot off fireworks, the women who sprinkle maslin and confetti, and the Bishop's garnet cassock as he blesses the meandering waters. Tell her how they kneel along the Malecón and describe the fair to her—the booths, the awnings, the ice cream, the vendors' cries—name for her the fortunate important people who ride their horses fast along with the current and shoot into the air, and also the people from

Gallinacera and Mangachería who go swimming in their shorts, and the brave ones who dive off the Old Bridge. And tell her how the river is a river now, and how day and night it goes along its way toward Catacaos, thick and dirty. Also who Angélica Mercedes is, who will be her friend, and the dishes she will make for her, you what you like most, Toñita, spicy things, thick soup, spiced meat and bananas, and even light chicha, but I don't want you to get drunk. And don't forget the harp, you every night a serenade, just for you. Speak into her ear, sit her on your knees, don't force her, be patient, only caress her, or, better still, smell her without touching her, slowly, softly, wait for her to seek your lips. And keep on talking to her, in her ear, with tenderness, the weight of her body is light, and a warm perfume comes from her skin, touch the fuzz on her arms the way you do the strings of the harp. Talk to her, whisper to her, take her shoes off delicately, kiss her feet, and there, again, lightly and slowly, the curve of her arch, her little toes in your mouth, her fresh smile in the darkness. Laugh too, shall I tickle you?, keep kissing her, there, her ankles, so thin, and her hard, round knees. Stretch her out then, carefully, make her comfortable, and very slowly, very sweetly, open her blouse and touch her, does her body stiffen?, let her go, touch her again, and talk to her, you love her, you will spoil her like a child, you will live for her, don't bruise her, don't bite her, just hold her tightly, guide her hand to her skirt, she should unbutton it herself. You I'll help you, Toñita, I'll take it off for you, sweet girl, and lie down beside her. Tell her what you feel, what her breasts are like, you two little bunnies, kiss them, you love them, you would see them in your dreams, at night they would come into the tower, white and hopping, you tried to catch them and they got away, you but they're softer and more alive, and there, the discreet half shadow, the flapping of the curtains, the hazy outline of objects, and the stiffness, and the motionless glow of her body. Keep on caressing her, and tell her your knees are, and your hips are, and your shoulders are, and what you feel, and that you love her, always that you love her. You Toñita, little girl, child, and hold her tightly to you, now, yes, find her thighs, separate them, timidly, be careful, be obedient, don't hurry her, kiss her and draw back, kiss her again, calm her, and, all the while, feel how your hand grows moist and her body abandons itself and unfolds, the lazy drowsiness that invades her, and how her breath grows active and her arms call you, feel how the tower begins to move, grows warm, disappears among the hot dunes. Tell her you're my wife, don't cry, don't hug me as if you were going to die, tell her you're beginning to live, and now distract her, play with her, dry her cheeks, sing to her, rock her, tell her to sleep, you I'll be your pillow, Toñita, I'll watch over your sleep.

"They took him to Lima this morning," Bonifacia moaned. "They say for a long time."

So? Wasn't the jail in Piura worse than a pigsty?, Josefino took a few steps around the room, the people lived in filth, he leaned on the window sill, they starved them to death, in the weak light from a street lamp the San Miguel School, the church, and the carob trees on the Plaza Merino looked like dreams, and the ones who talk back get crap instead of food, and Lituma talked back, and God help them if they didn't swallow it: it was better for him to be sent to Lima.

"They wouldn't even let me say goodbye to him," Bonifacia said. "Why didn't they tell me they were taking him away."

Weren't goodbyes sad? Josefino went over to the couch where she had just sat down, Bonifacia's feet took off their shoes with rage, her body was undergoing a sudden shaking. It was better that way, for Lituma too, because he would have got sad, and she where would she get the money from, the trip was very expensive, they had told her at the Roggero Enterprises. Josefino ran his hand over her shoulders. What would the poor thing do in Lima? She would stay here, in Piura, and he would look after her, and he would make her forget everything.

"He's my husband, I have to go," Bonifacia moaned. "Even if it's just to visit him every day. I'll bring him food."

But in Lima it was different, how silly, they fed them well and they treated them well. Josefino closed his arms around Bonifacia, she resisted for a moment, gave in, and now he was getting hot, wasn't that cop a brute?, and she that's a lie, didn't he give her a bad life?, and she that's not true, but she let herself go up against him, and she began to weep again. Josefino stroked her hair. And besides, so what, it was luck, take things the way they came, Wildflower: they'd got free of him.

"I'm bad, but you're worse than I am," Bonifacia whimpered. "Both of us are going to hell, and why do you call me Wildflower when you know I don't like it, you see, you see how bad you are?"

Josefino pushed her away gently, stood up, and that was too much, wouldn't she have starved to death without him?, wouldn't she have had to beg for a living? He felt through his pockets, leaning on the window, everything like a dream, and to top it off she came and cried over the cop in front of him, took out a cigarette and lit it: a man had his pride, what the hell.

"You've been using the familiar form with me," he said suddenly, turning toward Bonifacia. "Before, only in bed and always the formal afterward. You're funny, Wildflower."

He returned to her side and she began to turn away, but she let herself be hugged and Josefino laughed. Was she ashamed? Things that the nuns in the village had put in her noggin? Why only familiar in bed?

"I know it's a sin, and just the same I keep on with you," Bonifacia sobbed. "You don't realize it, but God's going to punish me, and you too, and it's all your fault."

What a hypocrite she was, she was like the Piurans in that, all the women, what a hypocrite she was, lovey, did she or didn't she know that she was going to be his woman that night he brought her home?, and she I didn't know, making a face, I wouldn't have come, I didn't have anyplace to go. Josefino spat the cigarette onto the floor, and Bonifacia was huddled up against him, and Josefino was able to speak into her ear. But he would have liked for her to be sincere, Wildflower, to confess just once, slowly, just to him alone, sweety, did she like it or didn't she?, lovey.

"I liked it because I'm bad," she whispered. "Don't ask me, it's a sin, don't talk about it."

Better than with the cop?, she should swear, no one would hear her, he loved her, was it true that she liked it better?, he kissed her on the neck, he bit her ear, underneath her skirt everything was tight, tense, and warm, was it true that the cop never made her shout?, and she, with a distant voice, yes, the first time, from pain mostly, was it true that he had made her shout when he wanted to?, and just out of pleasure, right?, and she he should be still, Josefino, God is listening, and he I touch you and you change, right there you change, I like you when you're hot. He let go of her, she stopped making her cooing sound, and a moment later she was weeping again.

"He was throwing you away, Wildflower," Josefino said; "you were wasting your time with the cop. Why do you feel so sorry for him?"

"Because he's my husband," Bonifacia said. "I have to go to Lima."

Josefino leaned over, picked up the butt from the floor, lit it, and some urchins were playing around the Plaza Merino, one had climbed up on the statue, and the windows in Father García's house were lighted, it couldn't be so late, did she know that yesterday he pawned his watch?, he forgot to tell her, Wildflower, and of course, of course, what a head: everything was all set with Doña Santos, early tomorrow.

"I don't want to now," Bonifacia said. "I don't want to, I'm not going."

Josefino threw the butt toward the Plaza Merino, but it didn't even reach the Avenida Sánchez Cerro, and he came away from the window, and she was tense, and he what's wrong with you, was she trying to kill him with her look?, he already knew that she had pretty eyes, why open them so wide, and what was that all about. Bonifacia was not crying, and she had an aggressive look, a resolute voice: she didn't want to, it was her husband's child. And what was she going to feed her husband's child with? And what was she going to eat until her husband's child was born? And what was Josefino going to do with a stepchild? The worst of everything was that people never thought about things, what did they do with the noggin that God had put on top of their necks, what the fuck did they use it for.

"I'll work as a servant," Bonifacia said. "And then I'll take him to Lima."

As a servant, fat belly? She was dreaming, nobody would hire her, and if someone happened to they'd put her to work scrubbing floors, and her husband's child would come tumbling out or be born dead, or a monster, she should ask a doctor, and she let him die by himself, but she didn't want to kill him: it was the way she wanted it.

She began to whimper again, and Josefino sat down beside her and put his arm over her shoulders. She was ungrateful, an ingrate. Did he treat her well, yes or no? Why had he brought her to his house?, because he loved her, why had he fed her?, because he loved her, and in exchange, and to top it all off, and in spite of that, a stepchild so that people could laugh at him? God damn it, a man wasn't a clown. And besides how much was the Santos woman going to charge? A wild amount, a whole lot of dough, and instead of thanking him she was crying. Why was she like that with him, Wildflower? It looked as if she didn't love him, and he loved her so much, sweety, and he pinched her on the neck and blew behind her ear, and she moaned, her village, the sisters, she wanted to go back, even if it was redskin country, even if there weren't any buildings or cars, Josefino, Josefino, she wanted to go back to Santa María de Nieva.

"You need more money to go back home than to build yourself a house, lovey," Josefino said. "You go on talking without knowing what you're saying. There's no reason to act that way, love."

He took out his handkerchief and wiped her eyes and kissed them, and turned her body toward him, and he hugged her passionately, he was worried about her, why?, in everything he did he thought about what was good for her, why, God damn it, why?: because he loved her. Bonifacia sighed, the handkerchief at her mouth: how could it be good for her if he wanted to kill her husband's child?

"It's not killing, silly, has it been born yet maybe?" Josefino said. "And why do you talk so much about your husband if he isn't your husband any more?"

Yes he was, they were married in the church, and for God that was the only kind that counted, and Josefino you've got a mania, why bring God into everything?, Wildflower, and she you see, you see?, and he lovey, silly, he should give her a kiss, and she no, and he what would he do if he didn't love her so much, rocking her, looking for her armpits, preventing her from getting up, silly, stubborn, his little Wildflower, you see, you see?, and between a hiccup and a sob she was laughing, and for a moment her mouth was quiet and he managed to kiss it. Did she love him?, once, only once, silly, and she I don't love you, and he but I love you a lot, Wildflower, just that you get stuck-up and you take advantage of me because of it, and she you say it, but you don't love me, and he she should touch his heart and see how it was beating for her, and besides if she loved him, he would make her happy in everything, and underneath her skirt everything was tight, warm, slippery, the same as under her blouse, and on her back too, warm, dry, and thick, and Josefino's voice began to vacillate and become, like hers, very low, she wouldn't go to Señora Santos's even if he wanted her to, and contained, even if he killed her she wouldn't go, and lazy, but she did love him, and uneven and hot.

3

"What a face you've put on," the Sergeant said, "you look as if they were carrying you away from here by force. Why aren't you happy?"

"I am," Bonifacia said. "It's just that I feel a little sorry for the sisters."

"Don't put that suitcase so close to the edge, Pintado," the Sergeant said, "and the boxes aren't tied down tight enough, they'll fall overboard with the first bounce."

"Think about us when you're in heaven, Sergeant," Shorty said. "Write to us, tell us what city life is like. If they still have cities."

"Piura is the liveliest city in Peru, Ma'am," the Lieutenant said. "You're going to like it a lot."

"I think so, sir," Bonifacia said. "If it's so lively, I'm going to like it."

Pintado the pilot had already put all the baggage in the boat, and now he was inspecting the motor, kneeling between two gasoline cans. A soft breeze was blowing, and the waters of the Nieva, grape-colored, were going forward toward the Marañón, stirred up with small waves, rising and falling, and brief whirlpools. The Sergeant was going back and forth through the boat, diligent, smiling, checking the bundles, the lashing, and Bonifacia seemed interested in that bustle, but sometimes her eyes would leave the dock and take a peep at the hills: under the clean sky, the Mission was now shining among the trees, its metal roofs and its walls gave off soft reflections of the clear light of dawn. The rocky path, on the contrary, was hidden by threads of mist that floated almost at ground level, unbroken: the woods turned aside the breeze that would have broken them up.

"Isn't it true that we're itching to get to Piura, sweety?" the Sergeant asked.

"That's right," Bonifacia said. "We want to get there as soon as possible."

"It must be a long way off," Lalita said. "And life must be so different from here."

"They say it's a hundred times bigger than Santa María de Nieva," Bonifacia said, "with houses like the ones you see in the magazines the sisters get. There aren't many trees, they say, and sand, lots of sand."

"I'm sorry to see you go, but I'm glad for you," Lalita said. "Do the sisters know yet?"

"They've given me lots of advice," Bonifacia said. "Sister Angélica cried. She's got so old she can't hear what you're saying any more, I had to shout at her. She can barely walk, Lalita, her eyes seem to be moving all the time. She took me to the chapel and we prayed together. I'll never see her again, I'm sure of that."

"She's an evil and mean old woman," Lalita said. "You didn't sweep there, you didn't wash the pots, and she scares me talking about hell, every morning, have you repented for your sins? And she says terrible things to me about Adrián too, that he's a bandit, that he tricked everybody."

"She has a bad temper because she's old," Bonifacia said. "She must realize that she's going to die soon. But she's good to me. She loves me and I love her too."

"Carob trees, donkeys, and tonderos," the Lieutenant said. "And you'll get to know the ocean, Ma'am, it isn't far from Piura. That's better than swimming in the river."

"And besides they say they've got the prettiest women in Peru there, Ma'am," Fats said.

"Come on, Fats," Blondy said. "What does the lady care about there being pretty women in Piura?"

"I'm telling her so she can keep an eye on the Piuran women," Fats said. "So they won't leave her without a husband."

"She knows I'm serious," the Sergeant said. "All I'm thinking about is seeing my friends, my cousins. As far as women are concerned, mine's enough for me."

"Oh, you sly cholo." The Lieutenant laughed. "Keep a close watch on him, Ma'am, and if he runs off on you give him a whack."

"If it's possible, wrap up a Piuran girl and mail her to me, Sergeant," Fats said.

Bonifacia was smiling at them all, but at the same time she was biting her lips, and at regular intervals a different expression would come back to her face and sadden it; for a few seconds her look would be clouded over, and a slight tremor would agitate her lips, and then it would disappear and her eyes would be smiling again. The village was waking up now, white people were gathering in Paredes' store, Don Fabio's old servant was sweeping the porch of the Government house, and underneath the capironas young and old Aguarunas were heading in the direction of the river, carrying poles and harpoons. The sun was lighting up the yarina roofs.

"We'd better leave right away, Sergeant," Pintado said. "It's best to get past the Pongo now, there might be more wind later on."

"Listen to me first, and then you can say no," Bonifacia said. "Let me explain it to you at least."

"It's better never to make plans," Lalita said. "Afterward, if they don't work out, it's worse. Just think about what's happening at the moment, Bonifacia."

"I've already told him and he agrees," Bonifacia said. "He'll give me one sol every week, and I'll do work for people, you know that the sisters taught me how to sew. But do you think somebody will steal it? It has to go through so many hands, it probably won't ever reach you."

"I don't want you to send anything," Lalita said. "What do I need money for?"

"I have an idea," Bonifacia said, touching her head. "I'll send it to the sisters; who would ever dare steal it from them? And the sisters will pass it on to you."

"No matter how much a person wants to leave, it's always sad," the Sergeant said. "It's come over me a little too right now, boys, for the first time. A person gets to like places, even though they're not worth much."

The breeze had turned into a wind, and the tops of the taller trees were bending their crests, swaying them over the smaller ones. Up above, the door of the Residence opened, the dark figure of a sister hurried out, and while she was crossing the courtyard in the direction of the chapel, the wind puffed up her habit, wrinkled it like a wave. The Paredeses had come out the door of their cabin and, leaning on the railing, they were looking at the dock, they were waving goodbye.

"It's only human, Sergeant," Blacky said. "So much time here, and besides being married to someone from here. It's easy to see how you must feel a little sad. You must feel even sadder, Ma'am."

"Thank you for everything, Lieutenant," the Sergeant said. "If I can do anything for you in Piura, you know that I'm at your disposal. When will you be in Lima?"

"Within a month or so," the Lieutenant said. "I have to go to Iquitos first and close up this affair. I hope it all goes well for you back home, cholo; maybe I'll drop in on you one of these days."

"Take care of your money for when you have children," Lalita said. "Adrián used to say we'll start next month, and six months later he had to buy a new motor. And we never saved a cent. But he almost never spent anything, everything was for food and the children."

"And then you'll be able to go to Iquitos," Bonifacia said. "Have the sisters hold the money I send you until there's enough for the trip. Then you can go see him."

"Paredes told me I'll never see him again," Lalita said. "And that I'll die here working for the sisters. Don't send me anything. You'll need it there, you need money in the city."

Could he, cholo? The Sergeant nodded, and the Lieutenant embraced Bonifacia, who was blinking and moving her head as if puzzled, but her lips and her eyes, although moist, were still smiling doggedly, Ma'am: now it was their turn. Fats embraced her first, and Blacky darn it, how long was he going to take, and he Sergeant, don't get angry, it was a friendly embrace, Blondy, Shorty. Pintado the pilot had cast off the lines and was holding the boat alongside the dock, bent over the rudder pole. The Sergeant and Bonifacia got on board, settled down among the bundles, Pintado lifted up the pole, and the current took the boat off, began to rock it, to carry it along slowly toward the Marañón.

"You have to go see him," Bonifacia said. "I'll send it even if you don't want me to. And when he gets out, you'll both come to Piura; I'll help you the way you helped me. Nobody knows Don Adrián there, and he can find some kind of work."

"You'll change your expression when you see Piura, sweety," the Sergeant said.

Bonifacia had one hand outside the boat, her fingers were touching the roily water and opening straight, short-lived wakes that disappeared in the frothy confusion that the propeller was spreading. Sometimes, under the opaque surface of the river, a brief, quick fish could be seen. Above them the sky was clear, but in the distance, toward the Andes, there were fat clouds floating and the sun was slicing them like a knife.

"Are you only sad about the sisters?" the Sergeant asked.

"About Lalita too," Bonifacia said. "And I think about Sister Angélica all the time too. Last night she held on to me, she didn't want to let me go, and she was so sad the words wouldn't come out."

"The nuns have been very nice," the Sergeant said. "All the presents they gave you."

"Will we come back someday?" Bonifacia asked. "Even if only once, on vacation?"

"Who can tell," the Sergeant said. "But it's a little far to come for a vacation."

"Don't cry," Bonifacia said. "I'll write to you and I'll tell you everything I'm doing."

"Ever since I left Iquitos, I've never had any girl friends," Lalita said. "Since I was a girl. There on the island, the Achual and Huambisa women spoke almost no white man's talk, and we couldn't understand each other except in certain things. You've been my best girl friend."

"And you mine too," Bonifacia said. "More than a friend, Lalita. You and Sister Angélica are the ones I love most here. Come on, don't cry."

"Why didn't you come back, Aquilino?" Fushía asked. "Why didn't you come back, old man?"

"I couldn't come any quicker, man, calm down," Aquilino said. "The fellow was asking me all sorts of questions, and he talked about the nuns, and the doctor, and I couldn't convince him. But I did convince him, Fushía, it's all arranged."

"The nuns?" Fushía asked. "Are there nuns here too?"

"They're like nurses, they take care of the people," Aquilino said.

"Take me somewhere else, Aquilino," Fushía said. "Don't leave me in San Pablo, I don't want to die here."

"The fellow kept the money, but he promised me all sorts of things," Aquilino said. "He'll get you papers, he'll fix everything up so that nobody will know who you are."

"You gave him everything I put together over all these years?" Fushía asked. "So many sacrifices, so much struggling for that? So that just anybody ends up with it?"

"I had to keep raising it little by little," Aquilino said. "First five hundred and no, then a thousand and no, he refused to bargain, he said that jail was more expensive. He also promised me that he'll give you better food, better medicine. What can we do, Fushía, it would have been worse if he hadn't accepted."

It was raining hard, and the old man, soaked to the skin, cursing the weather, brought the boat out of the channel by pushing with the rudder pole. Near the dock now, he could make out some naked figures on the embankment. He shouted in Huambisa for them to come down and help him, and they disappeared behind the lupunas that were being shaken by the wind, and they reappeared, reddish-colored, taking little leaps, sliding down the muddy slope. They moored the boat to some stakes and, splashing under the large raindrops that were spattering on their backs, they carried Don Aquilino ashore. The old man began to take his clothes off as he climbed up the embankment. When he reached the top, he had taken off his shirt, and at the village, without answering the friendly signs the women and children were making to him from the cabins, he took off his pants. In that way, with only his straw hat and abbreviated shorts on, he went through the brush toward the white men's clearing, and there something simian and stumbling swung down from a railing, Pantacha, he embraced him, you're in one of your dreams, and he babbled sluggishly in his ear, choked up with herbs, and you can't even talk, let go of me. Pantacha's eyes were tormented, and threads of drool were coming out of his lips. Very agitated, he was making signs, pointing at the cabins. The old man saw the Shapra woman on the porch, sullen, motionless, her neck and arms hidden by strings of necklaces and bracelets, her face all painted.

"They ran away, Don Aquilino," Pantacha finally grunted, rolling his eyes. "And the boss is in a rage, shut up in there for months, he won't come out."

"Is he in his cabin?" the old man asked. "Let go of me, I've got to talk to him."

"Who are you to give me orders," Fushía said. "Go back, have the fellow give you the money back. Take me to the Santiago, I'd rather die among people I know."

"We have to wait till nighttime," Aquilino said. "When they're all asleep, I'll take you as far as the boat where they make the visitors bathe, and the fellow will pick you up there. Don't carry on like that, Fushía, try to get a little sleep now. Or do you want something to eat?"

"The way you're treating me is the way they'll treat me there," Fushía said. "You don't even listen to me, you decide everything, and I have to obey. It's my life, Aquilino, not yours; I don't want to, don't leave me in this place. Have some pity, old man, let's go back to the island."

"I couldn't do it even if I wanted to," Aquilino said. "Upstream to the Santiago and hiding all the time would take months of traveling, and there's no gas left, or any money to buy it with. I've brought you here out of friendship, so that you can die among white men, and not like an Indian. Listen to me, get a little sleep."

His body barely filled out the blankets that were covering him up to his chin. The mosquito netting protected only half the hammock, and a great disorder reigned all around: scattered tin cans, rinds, gourds with leftover masato, the remains of meals. There was a strange smell of pestilence and many flies. The old man touched Fushía on the shoulder, he snored, and then the old man shook him with both hands. Fushía's eyelids parted, two bloody embers fastened on Aquilino's face with effort, went out, and lighted up several times. Fushía rose up on his elbows a little.

"The rain caught me in the middle of the channel," Aquilino said. "I'm soaked."

He was talking and wringing out his shirt and pants, he was twisting them furiously; then he hung them on the cord of the mosquito netting. Outside it was still raining very hard, a muddy light fell on the puddles and the ash-colored mud of the clearing, the wind was roaring against the trees. Sometimes a multicolor zigzag would light up the sky, and seconds later the thunder could be heard.

"The whore ran off with Nieves," Fushía said, his eyes closed. "They ran away together, those two bastards, Aquilino."

"And what do you care if they've gone?" Aquilino said, drying his body with his hand. "Bah, a person's better off alone than with a bad companion."

"I don't care about that whore," Fushía said. "But I do care that she ran off with my pilot. She'll have to pay me for that."

Without opening his eyes, Fushía turned his face, spat, man, raised the blankets up to his mouth, he'd better watch where he was spitting, it just missed him.

"How many months has it been since you left?" Fushía said. "I've been waiting for you for years."

"Do you have much of a load?" Aquilino asked. "How many balls of rubber? How many skins?"

"We had bad luck," Fushía said. "We found only empty villages. I don't have any goods this time."

"Because you couldn't go on the trips, because your legs aren't any good for going through the jungle any more," Aquilino said. "To die among people you know! Do you think the Huambisas would have stayed with you? They were ready to take off at any time."

"I could have given orders from the hammock," Fushía said. "Jum and Pantacha would have taken them where I ordered."

"Don't be foolish," Aquilino said. "They hate Jum and they haven't killed him so far because of you. And Pantacha is off his nut with his brews, he could barely talk when we left him. It was all over, man, don't fool yourself."

"Did you get good prices?" Fushía asked. "How much money did you bring me?"

"Five hundred soles," Aquilino said. "Don't make a face, what I had wasn't worth any more, and I had to fight to get that. But what's happened?, it's the first time you haven't had any goods."

"The region is finished," Fushía said. "Those bastards are wise to us and they hide. I'll go farther away, even if it's near the cities, I'll go way in, but I'll find rubber."

"Did Lalita steal all your money?" Aquilino asked. "Did she leave you any?"

"What money?" Fushía was clutching the blankets next to his mouth; he had huddled up more. "What money are you talking about?"

"What I've been bringing you, Fushía," the old man said. "What you made from your robberies. I know that you had it hidden. How much have you got left? Five thousand soles? Ten thousand?"

"Neither you nor your mother nor anybody else is going to take what's mine," Fushía said.

"Don't make me feel any more sorry than I already do," Aquilino said. "And don't look at me that way, your eyes don't scare me. Just answer my question."

"Do you think they were so afraid of me, or was it because they were in such a hurry they forgot to steal my money?" Fushía said. "Lalita knew where I kept it."

"It could also be that they felt sorry for you," Aquilino said. "They might have said he's all through, he's going to be alone, at least we can leave him the money so he can get some comfort out of it."

"It would have been better if the bastards had stolen it," Fushía said. "Without any money, this fellow wouldn't have taken me. And you, with your good heart, you wouldn't have thrown me out into the jungle. You would have taken me back to the island, old man."

"Fine, you're finally calming down," Aquilino said. "Do you know what I'm going to do? Chop up some plantains and boil them. From tomorrow on, you'll be eating like a white man; this will be your farewell to Indian food."

The old man laughed, fell into the empty hammock, and began to rock, pushing himself with one foot.

"If I was your enemy, I wouldn't be here," he said. "I still have those five hundred soles, I would have kept them. I was sure that you wouldn't have any cargo this time."

The rain was sweeping the porch, it was crackling dully on the roof, and the warm air that was coming from outside was lifting up the mosquito netting, it was making it flap like a white stork.

"You don't have to cover up so much," Aquilino said. "I know that the skin is falling off your legs, Fushía."

"Did that whore tell you about the mosquitoes?" Fushía muttered. "I scratched myself and it got infected, but it's going away now. They think that because I'm this way I won't track them down. We'll see who has the last laugh, Aquilino."

"Don't change the subject," Aquilino said. "Are you really getting better?"

"Give me a little more, old man," Fushía said. "Is there still some left?"

"Take mine, I don't want any more," Aquilino said. "I like it too. I'm like a Huambisa in that, every morning when I wake up I chop up some plantains and boil them."

"I'm going to miss it more than Campo Grande, more than Iquitos," Fushía said. "I think the island is the only home I've ever had. I'm even going to miss the Huambisas, Aquilino."

"You're going to miss all of them, but not your son," Aquilino said. "He's the only one you haven't talked about. Doesn't it matter to you at all that Lalita took him away?"

"He probably wasn't my son," Fushía said. "That bitch probably . . ."

"Quiet, quiet, I've known you for years, and it's hard for you to fool me," Aquilino said. "Tell me the truth, are they getting better or are they worse than before?"

"Don't talk to me in that tone," Fushía said. "I won't stand for it, God damn it to hell."

His voice, which lacked conviction, was extinguished in a kind of howl. Aquilino got out of the hammock, went over to him, and Fushía covered his face: he was a timid, shapeless little bundle.

"Don't be ashamed with me, man," the old man whispered. "Let me see."

Fushía did not answer, and Aquilino took a corner of the blanket and raised it. Fushía had no boots on, and the old man stood there looking, his hand clutching the blanket like a claw, his forehead gnawed by wrinkles, his mouth open.

"I'm very sorry, but it's time now, Fushía," Aquilino said. "We have to go."

"Just a little while longer, old man," Fushía moaned. "Look, light me up a cigar. I'll smoke it and then you take me to the guy. Just ten minutes, Aquilino."

"But smoke it fast," the old man said. "The fellow must be waiting already."

"Look at all of it once and for all," Fushía said with a moan, under the blanket. "Even I haven't got used to it, old man. Look farther up."

His legs were doubled up, and when he stretched out the blankets fell to the floor. Now Aquilino could see too, the translucent thighs, the groin, the bald pubis, the small hook of flesh that had been his sex, and his stomach: there the skin was intact. The old man bent over hurriedly, he took the blankets, he covered the hammock.

"Did you see, did you?" Fushía sobbed. "Did you see that I'm not a man any more, Aquilino?"

"He also promised me that he'll give you cigars whenever you want," Aquilino said. "You know, when you feel like smoking, just ask him."

"I'd like to die right now," Fushía said, "without knowing what was going on, all at once. You'd wrap me up in a blanket and hang me from a tree, like a Huambisa. Except that nobody would cry for me every morning. What are you laughing at?"

"The way you're smoking, so the cigar will last longer and time will go by," Aquilino said. "But since we have to go in any case, what difference do two minutes or so mean to you, man."

"How am I going to travel there, Aquilino," Fushía said. "It's a long way off."

"It's better for you to die there than here," the old man said. "They'll take care of you there and the disease will stop climbing up. I know a fellow, with the money you have he'll take you in without asking for papers or anything."

"We won't get there, old man, they'll grab me on the river."

"I promise that we'll get there," Aquilino said. "Even if we have to travel only at night, looking for side channels. But we have to leave today, without being seen by Pantacha or the Indians. No one has to know, it's the only way you'll be safe there."

"The police, the soldiers, old man," Fushía said. "Can't you see that they're all looking for me? I can't leave here. There are too many people out to get even with me."

"San Pablo is a place where they'll never go hunting for you," the old man said. "Even if they knew you were there, they wouldn't go. But nobody's going to know."

"Old man, old man," Fushía sobbed. "You're good, I beg you, do you believe in God?, do it for God, Aquilino, try to understand me."

"Of course I understand you, Fushía," the old man said, getting up. "But it's been dark for quite a while now, I have to take you over right now, the fellow's going to get tired of waiting for us."

❦

It is night again, the ground is soft, their feet sink in up to the ankles, and the places are always the same: the bank, the path that winds among the farm plots, a small carob grove, the desert. You this way, Toñita, never that way, so they won't see them from Castilla. The sand is falling mercilessly, cover her with the blanket, put your hat on her, she should lower her head if she doesn't want her face to burn. The same sounds: the purring of the wind in the cotton fields, guitar music, singing, clapping, and, at dawn, the deep lowing of the cattle. You come, Toñita, let's sit down here, they will rest awhile and then continue walking. The same images: a black cupola, stars that blink, shine steadily, or go out, the desert with its folds and blue dunes, and in the distance the erect, solitary building, its livid lights, shadows that come out, shadows that go in, and sometimes, in the early morning, a horseman, some peasants, a herd of goats, Carlos Rojas's boat, and, on the other bank of the river, the gray doors of the slaughterhouse. Speak to her about the dawn, you are you listening to me, Toñita?, did you fall asleep?, how one can make out the belfries, the tile roofs, the balconies, whether it is going to rain and whether there is a mist. Ask her if she's cold, if she wants to go back, cover her legs with your jacket, she should lean on your shoulder. And there, again, the unexpected excitement, the strange galloping of that night, the surprise of her body. Stand up, look, who is racing?, a bet?, Chápiro, Don Eusebio, the Temple twins? You let's hide, let's crouch down, don't move, don't be frightened, there are two horses, and there, in the darkness, who, why, how. You they passed close by and on wild horses, who are those madmen, they go to the river, now they're coming back, don't be afraid, sweet, and there her face turning, asking, her anxiety, the trembling of her mouth, her nails like sharp tacks, and her hand why, how, and her breathing next to yours. Now calm her down, you I'll explain it for you, Toñita, they've gone now, they were going so fast I couldn't see their faces, and she tenacious, thirsting, searching in the blackness, who, why, how. You don't get that way, who they were, what does it matter, what a little silly. A trick to distract her: get under the blanket, hide, let her cover you up, there they come, there are a lot of them, if they see us they'll kill us, feel her agitation, her fury, her terror, have her come closer, have her hug you, have her sink into you, you more, Toñita, come closer, and tell her now that it's all a lie, nobody's coming, give me a kiss, I was teasing you, sweet. And today don't speak to her, listen to her beside you, her silhouette is a ship, the desert is a sea, she is sailing, she tranquilly avoids dunes and bushes, don't interrupt her, don't step on the shadow she casts. Light a cigarette and smoke, think that you are happy and that you would give anything to know whether she is happy too. Chat with her and joke, you I'm smoking, you'll teach her when she grows up, young girls don't smoke, she would choke, laugh, she should laugh, beg her, you don't always be so serious, Toñita, by what you love most. And there, again, the unsureness, that acid that wears life away, you I know, she's so bored, the same voices, closed in, but wait, a little while, they'll travel to Lima, a house for just the two of them, they won't have to hide, you'll buy her everything, you'll see, Toñita, you'll see. Feel that bitter emotion again, you never get angry, sweet, she should be different, she should get angry sometimes, she should break things, cry loudly, and there, distant, identical, the expression on her face, the soft pounding of her temples, her fallen eyelids, the secret of her lips. Now only memories and a little melancholy, you that's why they take such good care of you, the way they've behaved, they didn't say anything, they bring you candy, they dress you, they comb your hair, they seem like different people, they fight so much among themselves, the bad things they do, so good with you, and so helpful. Tell them I brought her, I stole her, you love her, she's going to live with you, they have to help you, and there, again, their excitations, their protestations we promise, we swear, we'll live up to your confidence, their whispering, their running about, look at them, emotional, curious, smiling, feel their desperation to go up to the tower, to see her and talk to her. And again she and you they all love you, because you're young?, because you can't speak?, because you make them feel pity? And there, that night: the river is flowing darkly and in the city there are no lights left, the moon is barely lighting up the desert, the planted fields are vague splotches, and she is far away and unprotected. Call her, ask her, Toñita, can you hear me?, what do you feel?, why does she pull your hand that way, she's frightened by the sand that is falling so strongly. You come, Toñita, cover up, it will stop soon, do you think it's going to cover us up, that it's going to bury us alive? what are you trembling about, what do you feel, is it hard to breathe?, do you want to go back?, don't breathe like that. And you didn't realize, you I'm so stupid, how terrible not to understand, sweet, never knowing what's going on with you, unable to guess. And there, again, your heart like a fountain, and the questions, her sparkling, what do you think I'm like, and the inmates, and their faces, and the ground you're walking on, where does what you hear come from, what are you like, what do those sounds mean, do you think that everybody is like you?, that we hear and do not answer?, that somebody feeds us, puts us to bed, and helps us upstairs? Toñita, Toñita, what do you feel for me?, do you know what love is?, why do you kiss me? Make an effort now, don't let her catch your anguish, lower your voice and tell her softly that it doesn't matter, my feelings are your feelings, you want to suffer when she suffers. She should forget those sounds, you never again, Toñita, I got nervous, tell her about the city, about the poor Gallinacera woman who is weeping for her, about the donkey and the baskets, and what people are saying at the Estrella del Norte, you they're all asking questions, Toñita, they're looking for you. They're in mourning, poor thing, could she have been killed?, did a stranger carry her off?, the things they're inventing, their lies, their rumors. Ask her if she remembers, would she like to go back to the square?, sit in the sun near the bandstand?, whether she misses the Gallinacera woman, you would you like to see her again?, shall we take her to Lima? But she cannot hear or she doesn't want to hear, something isolates her, torments her, and there, still, her hand, her trembling, her fright, you what's wrong, does something hurt?, do you want me to massage you? Do what she wants, touch her where she shows you, don't lean too hard, stroke her stomach, pet the same spot, ten times, a hundred times, and all the while, now I know, it hurts, the food, do you want to peepee?, help her, cacky?, she should squat down, she should not worry, you will be an awning for her, open the blanket, keep the rain off her head, make the sand leave her alone. But it's no use and now her cheeks are moist, the alarm of her body has grown, the wrinkling of her face, and knowing that she is crying and not being able to guess is terrible. Toñita, what can you do, what does she want you to do. Carry her in your arms, run, kiss her, you we're getting there, it's close now, she'll have a *mate*, you'll put her to bed, and next morning she'll wake up all right, and she shouldn't cry, for the sake of God she shouldn't cry. Call Angélica Mercedes, she should cure her, she it's a stomachache, boss, you some hot tea?, gas?, she it's nothing serious, don't be frightened, you yerbaluisa?, camomile?, and her hand there, feeling, warming, caressing the same spot, and how stupid, how stupid, you didn't realize. And there, the inmates, their joy, their bodies that fill up the tower, their odors, creams, talcum, vaseline, their shrieks and leaps, the boss didn't realize, how innocent, just like a kid. Look at them all grouped together, notice, they surround her, they play with her and they tell her things. Let them amuse her and go downstairs to the main room, open a bottle, fall into an easy chair, toast yourself, feel the confused, excited perturbation, close your eyes and try to hear them: two at least, Butterfly three, Firefly four, and could he be that stupid, what were you thinking about, boss, she wasn't bleeding? when did she stop, boss?, that way we'll know exactly. Feel the alcohol, its softening effervescence that weakens your legs and the remorse, how she was getting restless, and you I never realized. What did it matter to you, what does it matter whether it's born tomorrow or in eight months, Toñita will get fat, and afterward that will keep her happy. Kneel down next to her bed, you it wasn't anything, let's celebrate, you'll be proud of him, you'll change his diapers, and if it's a girl it should look like her. And the women should go to Don Eusebio's tomorrow, they should buy what's needed, and naturally the clerks will make fun of them, who's going to give birth?, and by whom?, and if it's a boy we'll call him Anselmo. Go to Gallinacera, get the carpenters, have them bring boards, nails, and their hammers, they should build a small room, make up any old story for them. Toñita, Toñita, have some whims, vomiting, bad moods, be like the rest, can you touch it?, is it moving already? And one last time ask yourself if it was better or worse, whether life should be like that, and what would have happened if she no, if you and she, if it was a dream or if things are always different from dreams, and one more final effort, and ask yourself if you ever became resigned, and if it's because she died or because you're old that you accept the idea of dying yourself.

"Are you going to wait for him, Wildflower?" Chunga asked. "He's probably out with another woman."

"Who is it?" the harp player asked, his white eyes turned toward the stairs. "Sandra?"

"No, maestro," Jocko said. "The one who started the day before yesterday."

"He was going to pick me up, Ma'am, but maybe he forgot," Wildflower said. "I'll just go."

"Have some breakfast first, girl," the harp player said. "Come on, Chunga, invite her."

"Yes, of course, get a cup," Chunga said. "There's warm milk in the teapot."

The musicians were having breakfast at a table near the bar, in the light of the violet bulb, the only one that was still lit. Wildflower sat down between Jocko and Kid Alejandro: until now they had scarcely heard her voice, she was so quiet; like that in her village, all the women? Through the windows the neighborhood could be seen, in the shadows, and up above three weak stars, the Marimachas? No, Ma'am, they talk and talk, they were like parrots. The harp player was nibbling on a slice of bread, parrots?, and she yes, little creatures they had in her village, and he stopped chewing, what?, girl, she hadn't been born in Piura? No, sir, she came from far away, from the jungle. She didn't know where she'd been born, but she'd always lived in a place called Santa María de Nieva. Small, sir, no cars or buildings or movies like Piura, did he know? The harpist continued chewing, the jungle?, parrots?, his head tall, surprised, and suddenly he put his glasses on quickly, girl: he'd already forgotten that all that existed. What river was Santa María de Nieva on?, near Iquitos?, far away?, the jungle, that's strange. Identical and continuous, as they came out of the Kid's mouth, the smoke rings were growing, losing shape, breaking up on the dance floor. He would have liked to have known the Amazon region too, listen to the music of the redskins. It wasn't anything like white men's music, right? Not at all, sir, people up there didn't sing very much, and their songs weren't happy like the marinera or the waltz, mostly sad, and very strange. But the Kid liked sad music. And what were the words to the songs like? Very poetical? Because she must have been able to understand the language, wasn't she? No, she couldn't speak their language, and she lowered her eyes, the redskins', she stammered, a word here and there, that was all, from hearing it so much, you know. But they shouldn't think, there were whites there too, a lot of them, and the redskins aren't seen very much, because they stick to the woods.

"And how did you ever fall into that guy's hands?" Chunga asked. "Have you ever seen a sadder devil than Josefino?"

"What does it matter, Chunga," the Kid said. "They're questions of love, and love doesn't listen to any reason. And it won't accept any questions or give any answers, as a poet once said."

"Don't be frightened." Chunga laughed. "I was just asking for the fun of it, as a joke. Everybody's life just slides off my back, Wildflower."

"What's the matter, maestro? Why did you get so thoughtful?" Jocko asked. "Your milk's getting cold."

"Yours too, Miss," the Kid said. "Hurry up and drink it. Do you want some more bread?"

"How long are you going to use the formal address with the girls?" Jocko said. "You're funny, Kid."

"I treat all women the same," the Kid said. "Inmates or nuns, there's no difference for me, I respect them all the same."

"Then why do you insult them so much in your songs?" Chunga asked. "People would think you were a fairy."

"I don't insult them, I sing the truth to them," the Kid said. And he smiled, weakly, blowing one last ring, white and perfect.

Wildflower stood up, Ma'am, she was rather tired, she was going . .w, and thank you very much for the breakfast, but the harp player grabbed her arm, girl, shaking her arm, she should wait. Was she going to the champ's house, over there by the Plaza Merino? They would take her and Jocko should go get a taxi, he was sleepy too. Jocko got up, went out, and a trail of cool air reached the table as he closed the door: the neighborhood was still in darkness. Did they notice how fickle the Piura sky was? Yesterday at this time, the sun was high and burning, no sand was falling, and the shacks looked as if they had been scrubbed. And today the lazy night would not leave, why should it go, it should stay on forever, and the Kid pointed to the small square of sky showing in the window: as far as he was concerned, he'd be happy, but a lot of people wouldn't like it. Chunga touched her temple: the things that worried this guy, what a screwball. Was it six o'clock?, Wildflower crossed her legs and put her elbows on the table, in the jungle dawn came very early, by this time everybody was up, and the harp player yes, yes, the sky would become pink, green, blue, all colors, and Chunga what, and the Kid what, maestro, did he know the jungle? No, things like that occurred to him, and if there was any milk left in the teapot he would like to have some. Wildflower served him and put sugar in for him, Chunga was looking at the harpist with mistrust, and now her expression was stern. The Kid lit another cigarette, and once more transparent, ephemeral, floating gray hoops came out of his mouth in the direction of the small black square that was the window, they caught up with each other halfway there, and the opposite happened to him compared to other people as far as light was concerned, they mixed and were like small clouds, other people got happy and optimistic with the sun, and the night made them sad, and finally they became so thin that they were invisible, and he on the other hand felt bitter during the day and only at dusk did his spirits pick up. They were nocturnal animals, Kid, like foxes and owls: Chunguita, Jocko, he, and now she too, girl, and the sound of a door was heard. On the threshold, Jocko was holding Josefino by the waist, they should see who he'd found, Wildflower got up, talking to himself on the highway.

"You're having a real good time, Josefino," Chunga said. "You're falling all over the place."

"Good morning, lad," the harp player said. "We thought you weren't coming for her. We were going to take her home ourselves."

"No use talking to him, maestro," the Kid said. "He's on his last legs."

Wildflower and Jocko brought him over to the table, and Josefino was not on his last legs, rubbish, the last round was on him, nobody move, and Chunguita should get some beer. The harp player stood up, boy, he thanked him for the kindness, but it was late and the taxi was waiting, Josefino was making faces, euphoric, everybody was going to get tight, shouting, drinking milk, kids' food, and Chunga yes, all right, so long, they should take him away. They went out, and over toward the Grau barracks a small blue bar of sky was already showing, and in the neighborhood sleepy figures were moving about behind the wild cane stalks, the crackle of a brazier could be heard, and the air was carrying rancid odors. They crossed the sand, the harpist holding on to the arms of Jocko and the Kid, Josefino leaning on Wildflower, and at the highway they all got into a taxi, the musicians in back. Josefino was laughing, Wildflower was jealous, old man, she asked him why do you drink so much and where were you, and who were you with, she was trying to get a confession out of him, harp player.

"Well done, girl," the harp player said. "The Mangaches are the worst there are, never trust him."

"What's going on here?" Josefino said. "Right in front of my eyes? Boy, oh boy. Don't touch her, buddy, somebody might get hurt, buddy, boy, oh boy."

"I'm not bothering anybody," the driver said. "It's not my fault if the car is narrow. Did I touch you maybe, Miss? I do my job and I don't go around looking for trouble."

Josefino laughed with his mouth open, he didn't understand jokes, buddy, loudly, he could touch her if he felt like it, he had his permission, and the driver laughed too, Mister: he'd really believed him. Josefino turned to the musicians, it was Monk's birthday, they should come with them, they would all celebrate together, the Leóns loved him so much, old man. But the maestro was tired and he had to get some rest, Josefino, and Jocko patted him on the back. Josefino began to get weary. He swallowed and yawned and closed his eyes. The taxi went by the cathedral and the street lights on the Plaza de Armas were out now. The earthen-colored contours of the tamarinds stiffly surrounded the circular bandstand with its cured roof that was like an umbrella, and Wildflower that he shouldn't be like that, wicked, she'd asked him so many times. Green, large, frightened, her eyes were looking for those of Josefino, and he held out a hand mockingly, he was wicked, he would eat them raw and in one mouthful. He had a laughing attack, the driver glanced at him: he went down the Calle Lima, between *La Industria* and the grillwork of the City Hall. She didn't feel like it, but Monk was a hundred years old yesterday, and he was expecting her, and the Leóns were his brothers and he tried to please them every way he could.

"Don't bother the girl, Josefino," the harp player said. "She must be tired, leave her alone."

"She doesn't want to come to my house, harp player," Josefino said. "She doesn't want to see the champs. She says that she's ashamed, just imagine. Stop here, buddy, this is where we get out."

The taxi stopped, the Calle Tacna and the Plaza Merino were in the shadows, but the Avenida Sánchez Cerro was lit up with a caravan of trucks heading toward the New Bridge. Josefino jumped out, Wildflower did not move, they began to struggle, and the harpist don't fight, boy, make up, and Josefino they should come, and the driver too, Monk was very old, he was a thousand years old. But Jocko said something to the driver and they left. Now the avenue was in the shadows too and the trucks were a few red and roaring winks going off toward the river. Josefino began to whistle through his teeth, he took Wildflower by the shoulder, and now she offered no resistance and walked along peacefully by his side. Josefino opened the door, he closed it behind them, and there, doubled up in an easy chair, his head beneath a floor lamp, was Monk, snoring. A thin, biting smoke was drifting about the room over empty bottles, glasses, butts, and the remains of a meal. They had quit, were those the Mangaches?, Josefino jumped about, the Mangache champs?, and an incoherent voice arose in the next room: José had got into his bed, he'd kill him. Monk sat up, shaking his head, who the fuck had quit, and he smiled and his eyes shone, but my God, and his voice rose, look who's here, and he got up, it's been such a long time, and he stumbled forward, but how glad he was to see her, cousin, pushing the chairs aside with his hands, the bottles on the floor with his feet, he'd been wanting to see her again so much, and Josefino did I do what I promised or didn't I?, and his word as good or not as good as that of a Mangache? His arms open, his hair mussed, a broad smile on his face, Monk advanced, weaving, such a long time, and besides what a good-looking girl you've got to be, and why did you hide, cousin, she had to congratulate him, didn't she know it was his birthday?

"That's right, he just turned a million," Josefino said. "Don't be so bashful, Wildflower, give him a hug."

He dropped into an easy chair, he grabbed a bottle, raised it to his mouth, and drank, and the slap resounded like a stone falling into the water, naughty cousin, Josefino laughed, Monk let himself be slapped again, naughty cousin, and now Wildflower was going back and forth, glasses were breaking, Monk behind her, slipping and laughing, and in the next room they were the champs, work wasn't for them, they lived off the others, and José's voice was coming out and Josefino was humming too, curled up under the floor lamp, the bottle was slowly slipping out of his hand. Now Wild-flower and Monk were motionless in a corner, and she was still slapping him, naughty cousin, it was really hurting, why was she hitting him?, and he was laughing, she ought to be kissing him, and she was laughing too at Monk's clowning, and even the invisible José was laughing, pretty little cousin.

EPILOGUE

THE GOVERNOR GIVES THREE SOFT RAPS with his knuckles, the door of the Residence opens: Sister Griselda's ruddy face tries hard to smile at Julio Reátegui, but her eyes turn away, very restless, toward the square of Santa María de Nieva and her mouth trembles. The Governor enters, the little girl follows him docilely. They advance along a dark passageway to the Mother Superior's study, and the shouting in the village is now muffled and distant, like the hubbub on Sundays when the pupils go down to the river. In the study, the Governor drops into one of the canvas chairs. He sighs with relief, he closes his eyes. The girl remains in the doorway, her head to one side, but a moment later when the Mother Superior enters, she runs to Julio Reátegui, Mother, who has stood up: good morning. The Mother Superior replies with a glacial smile, motions with her hand for him to sit down again, and she remains standing by the desk. It had pained him to see her turned into a little savage in Urakusa, Mother, with the intelligent eyes that she had, Julio Reátegui thought that in the Mission they would be able to educate her, had he done the right thing? Yes, indeed, Don Julio, and the Mother Superior speaks the way she smiles, cold and distant, without looking at the girl: that was what they were there for. She didn't understand any Spanish at all, Mother, but she would learn fast, she was very quick, and she hadn't been any trouble to them at all on the trip. The Mother Superior listens to him attentively, as motionless as the wooden crucifix nailed to the wall, and when Julio Reátegui is silent, she neither agrees nor asks any questions, she waits with her hands folded over her habit and her mouth slightly tightened, Mother: then he would leave her. Julio Reátegui stands up, he had to go now, and smiles at the Mother Superior. That whole business had been very upsetting, very troublesome, they had rain and all sorts of inconveniences, and he still couldn't go to bed, as he would have liked to, his friends had prepared a luncheon in his honor, and if he didn't go they would be upset, people's feelings got hurt so easily. The Mother Superior stretches out her hand, and at that instant the noise grows in volume; for a few seconds it sounds very close, as if the exclamations and shouts were not rising up from the square but were coming from the orchard, from the chapel. Then the noise diminishes and continues as before, moderated, diffuse, inoffensive, and the Mother Superior blinks once, stops before reaching the door, turns toward the Governor, Don Julio, without smiling, pale, her lips moist: the Lord would take into account what he was doing for that child, her voice pained, she only wanted to remind him that a Christian should know forgiveness. Julio Reátegui nods, tilts his head a little, crosses his arms, his posture is at once grave, peaceful, and solemn, Don Julio: he should do it for God. The Mother Superior is speaking heatedly now, and for his family too, and her cheeks have reddened, Don Julio, for his wife, who was so kind and merciful. The Governor nods again, wasn't he just a poor man, an unfortunate being?, his face more and more worried, had he ever had any education?, his left hand strokes his cheek, did he know what he was doing?, and wrinkles have appeared on his brow. The girl is looking at them furtively, her eyes are shining through her hair, frightened, green, and savage: it hurts him more than anybody, Mother. The Governor speaks without raising his voice, it was something that went against his nature and against his ideas, with a certain sorrow, but it wasn't a question of himself alone, he would soon be leaving Santa María de Nieva, but of the ones who were staying, Mother, Benzas, Escabino, Águila, she, the pupils, and the Mission: didn't she want the region to be habitable, Mother? But a Christian had other weapons to correct injustices with, Don Julio, she knew that he had good feelings, he couldn't be in agreement with those methods. He should try to make them listen to reason, they all obeyed him here, that they should not do that to the poor unfortunate. He was going to disappoint her, Mother, he was very sorry, but he too thought that it was the only way. Other weapons? Those of the missionaries, Mother? How many centuries had they been there? How far had they got with those weapons? It was simply a question of avoiding trouble in the future, Mother, that outlaw and his people had brutally beaten a corporal from Borja, killed a recruit, tricked Don Pedro Escabino, and suddenly the Mother Superior no, she shakes her head angrily, no, no, she raises her voice: vengeance was inhuman, it was something that savages practiced, and that was what they were doing to the poor man. Why didn't they give him a trial? Why not put him in jail? Didn't he realize that it was horrible, that one did not treat a human being like that? It wasn't vengeance, it wasn't even punishment, Mother, and Julio Reátegui lowers his voice, and with the tips of his fingers he strokes the girl's dirty hair: it was a matter of a warning. He was sad at going away and leaving that bad memory at the Mission, Mother, but it was necessary for the good of all. He had a warm spot for Santa María de Nieva, the Governorship had made him neglect his affairs, lose money, but he wasn't sorry, Mother, wasn't it true that he had brought some progress to the village? Now there were authorities, soon they would set up a Civil Guard post, the people would be able to live in peace, Mother: all that could not be destroyed. The Mission was the first to thank him for what he had done for Santa María de Nieva, Don Julio, but what Christian could understand why they were killing a poor unfortunate? What blame did he have, since no one had ever taught him the difference between right and wrong? They weren't going to kill him, Mother, nor were they going to send him to jail, he was certain that he himself liked this better than being locked up. They had no hatred for him, Mother, they just wanted the Aguarunas to learn precisely that, the difference between right and wrong, if that was the only way they understood it, it was not their fault, Mother. They remain silent for a few seconds, then the Governor shakes hands with the Mother Superior, starts out, and the girl follows him, but for only a few steps, the Mother Superior takes her by the arm and she does not try to get away, she only lowers her head, Don Julio, did she have a name?, because they would have to baptize her. The girl, Mother? He didn't know, in any case she probably didn't have a Christian name, they should find one for her. He bows, leaves the Residence, strides across the Mission courtyard, and goes rapidly down the path. When he reaches the square, he looks at Jum: his hands tied over his head, he is hanging like a plumb bob from the capironas, and between his feet suspended in the air and the heads of the onlookers there is about a yard of open space. Benzas, Águila, Escabino are no longer there, only Corporal Roberto Delgado, some soldiers, and old and young Aguarunas gathered together in a compact group. The Corporal is no longer shouting, Jum is silent too. Julio Reátegui looks at the dock: the boats are rocking, empty, they have already finished unloading. The sun is raw, vertical, of a yellow color that is almost white. Reátegui takes a few steps toward the Government house, but as he passes the capironas he stops and turns to look. His two hands prolong the visor of his sun helmet and even then the aggressive rays touch his eyes. Only his mouth can be made out, has he fainted?, which seems to be open, does he see him?, is he going to shout Piruvians again?, is he going to insult the Corporal again? No, he doesn't shout anything, he probably doesn't have his mouth open, either. The position he is in has made his stomach disappear and his body lengthen, he looks like a tall and thin man and not the husky and big-bellied heathen that he is. Something strange emanates from him, the way he is, motionless and airy, converted by the sun into a thin luminous form. Reátegui keeps on walking, goes into the Government house, smoke has thickened the atmosphere; he coughs, shakes some hands, embraces, and is embraced. Jokes and laughter can be heard, someone puts a glass of beer into his hands. He drinks it down and sits. There are conversations around him, sweating white men, Don Julio, they were going to miss him, they were sorry to see him leave. He too, very much, but it was time now to take care of his own affairs again, he'd neglected everything, his plantings, the sawmill, the small hotel in Iquitos. He'd lost money here, friend, and he'd got older too. He didn't like politics, work was his element. Solicitous hands fill his glass, pat his back, take his helmet, Don Julio, everybody had come to pay their respects, even the ones who lived beyond the Pongo. He was tired, Arévalo, he hadn't slept for two nights and his bones ached. He dries his forehead, his neck, his cheeks. From time to time, Manuel Águila and Pedro Escabino draw aside, and between their bodies one can see the metal screen on the window, the capironas of the square in the distance. Are the onlookers still there or has the heat driven them away now? Jum cannot be made out, his earth-colored body has dissolved into the jets of light or is blending in with the copper-colored bark of the tree trunks, friends: he should not die on them. So that it would be a good lesson, the heathen had to go back to Urakusa and tell the others what had happened to him. He wouldn't die, Don Julio, it would even do him good to have a little sunbath: Manuel Águila? He should pay for the goods, Don Pedro, it must not be said that there were any abuses, they had only set things straight. Of course, Don Julio, he would pay the difference to those dunces; Escabino the only thing he asked for was to do business with them the same as before. Was it true that that fellow Don Fabio Cuesta was a man who could be trusted, Don Julio?: Arévalo Benzas? If he weren't, he wouldn't have had him appointed. He'd been working with him for years, Arévalo. A little easygoing, but loyal and helpful like few other people, they'd get on very well with Don Fabio, he could assure them. He hoped that there wouldn't be any more trouble, it was a terrible waste of time, and Julio Reátegui felt better now, friends: when he came in he felt a little nauseous. Maybe it was hunger, Don Julio. They had better go have lunch right away, Captain Quiroga was waiting for them. And, by the way, what kind of person is the Captain, Don Julio? He had his weaknesses, like any human being, Don Pedro: but on the whole he was a good person.

1

"It's been over a year since you came," Fushía shouts.

"I can't understand you," Aquilino says, cupping a hand to his ear; his eyes wander over the intermingled tops of the hardwood palms and capanahua trees, or, furtive and fearful, they peek at the cabins that stand behind a row of ferns at the end of the path. "What did you say, Fushía?"

"It's been over a year," Fushía shouts. "It's been over a year since you came, Aquilino."

This time the old man nods, and his eyes, veiled by rheum, alight on Fushía for an instant. Then they go back to wandering over the muddy water of the shore, the trees, the winding of the path, the grove: it couldn't have been so long, man, only a few months. No sound at all is coming from the cabins and everything seems deserted, but he didn't trust them, Fushía, what if they appeared, like that other time, howling, naked, and they filled up the path and ran toward him and he had to dive into the water? Was he sure they wouldn't come, Fushía?

"A year and a week," Fushía says. "I count every day. As soon as you leave I'll start to count, the first thing I do every morning is to make a mark. In the beginning I couldn't do it, but now I can use my foot like a hand, I can pick up a stick with my toes. Do you want to see, Aquilino?"

He puts his good foot forward, scratches the sand with it, scrapes together a small pile of stones, the two intact toes separate like the claws of a scorpion, close over a stone chip, lift it, the foot moves quickly, scratches the sand, draws back, and there is a tiny, straight mark, which the wind fills up again in a few seconds.

"What do you do things like that for, Fushía?" Aquilino asks.

"Did you see, old man?" Fushía says. "Every day, just like that, little marks, smaller and smaller, so they'll fit on my part of the wall, there are a lot of them for this year, something like twenty rows of marks. And when you come I give my meal to the attendant and he whitewashes it and covers them up, and I can start marking the days all over again. Tonight I'll give him my food and he'll whitewash it tomorrow."

"All right, all right"—the old man's hand asks Fushía to calm down—"anything you say, it's been a year, all right, don't get nervous, don't shout. I couldn't come any sooner, it isn't easy any more for me to travel around, I fall asleep, my arms can't take it. Can't you see that the years are going by? I don't want to die on the water; the river is fine to live on, but not to die on, Fushía. Why do you scream like that all the time, doesn't it hurt your throat?"

Fushía takes a leap and puts himself in front of Aquilino, he puts his face under the old man's, and Aquilino draws back with a twisted expression, but Fushía grunts and jumps until Aquilino looks at him: now, now he had seen, man. The old man covers his nose and Fushía goes back to where he was. That was why he couldn't understand what he was saying, Fushía; could he eat like that, with an empty mouth? Didn't he miss his teeth, didn't he choke? Fushía shakes his head several times.

"The nun soaks everything for me," he shouts. "Bread, fruit, everything in water until it's soft and breaks apart, then I can swallow it. Just that it's so fucking hard to talk, my voice won't come out."

"Don't get mad because I cover up my nose." Aquilino presses the openings of his nose with two fingers and his voice sounds twangy. "The smell is making me sick, it makes my head spin. The last time I carried the smell away with me, Fushía, it made me vomit during the night. If I'd known how hard it was for you to eat, I wouldn't have brought you the crackers. They'll scratch your gums. The next time I'll bring you some beer and some cola. I hope

I can remember, because, you know, my head isn't what it used to be, I keep on forgetting everything, I can't keep track of things. I'm old, man."

"And the sun's not out now," Fushía says. "When it is and we go down to the beach, even the nuns and the doctor cover their noses, they say it stinks a lot. I don't smell anything, I've got used to it by now. Do you know what it smells like?"

"Don't shout so much." Aquilino looks at the clouds: thick, grayish rolls and white splotches scattered here and there hide the sky, a leaden-colored light comes slowly down over the trees. "It looks like rain, but even if it rains I have to leave. I'm not going to sleep here, Fushía."

"Do you remember those flowers that were on the island?" Fushía jumps where he is, like a hairless red little monkey. "Those yellow ones that open when the sun comes out and close up at night, the ones the Huambisas said were ghosts. Do you remember?"

"I'm leaving even if it's raining hard," Aquilino says. "I'm not going to sleep here."

"That's what it's like, just like those flowers," Fushía shouts. "They open up when the sun rises and some drivel comes out, that's what stinks, Aquilino. But it does good, it doesn't hurt any more then, you feel better. We feel good and we don't fight with each other."

"Don't shout so much, Fushía," Aquilino says. "Look how the sky has clouded over and all the wind there is. The nun said this is bad for you, you have to go back to your cabin. And I'm leaving right now, it's better that way."

"But we don't smell it either when the sun's out or when it's cloudy," Fushía shouts. "We never smell anything. We smell the same thing all the time and it doesn't seem to stink any more, it seems like the natural smell of life. Do you understand me, old man?"

Aquilino lets go of his nose and takes a deep breath. Small wrinkles appear on his face, he frowns under his straw hat. The wind ruffles his rough shirt and, at times, bares his frail chest, his protruding ribs, his bronzed skin. The old man lowers his eyes, looks aside: he stays there, in repose, like a huge crab.

"What's it like?" Fushía shouts. "Like rotten fish?"

"For the love of God, stop shouting," Aquilino says. "I have to go now. When I come back, I'll bring you some soft things so you can swallow them without chewing. I'll look around, I'll ask in the stores."

"Sit down, sit down," Fushía shouts. "Why did you stand up, Aquilino? Sit down, sit down."

In a squatting position, he leaps around Aquilino and looks for his eyes, but the old man is steadfastly looking at the clouds, the palm trees, the sleepy waters of the river, the small dirty waves. Downstream, a small island of ochre-colored earth is haughtily slicing the current. Fushía is next to Aquilino's legs now. The old man sits down.

"Just a little while longer, Aquilino," Fushía shouts. "Not yet, old man, you only just got here."

"Now I remember, there's something I have to tell you." The old man slaps his forehead, and for a second he looks: the healthy foot is scratching in the sand. "I was in Santa María de Nieva in April. Look what's happened to my head. I was going to leave without telling you. The Navy hired me, their pilot was sick, and they took me on one of those gunboats that fly along the water. We were there for two days."

"You were afraid I was going to grab you," Fushía shouts. "That I was going to hug you around the legs, and that's why you sat down, Aquilino. Otherwise you would have just slipped away."

"Don't give me any more of those shouts, let me finish telling you," Aquilino says. "Lalita's got fat as the devil, at first neither one of us recognized each other. She thought I'd died. She began to cry."

"You used to spend the whole day," Fushía shouts. "You'd sleep in your boat and the next day you'd come back and talk to me, Aquilino. You'd spend two or three days. Now you want to leave as soon as you get here."

"They put me up in their house, Fushía," Aquilino says. "They've got a bunch of kids, I don't remember how many, a lot. And Aquilino is a grown man now. He was working as a ferryman, and now he's gone off to work in Iquitos. He doesn't look the way he used to when he was a kid, he doesn't have those slant eyes any more. They're almost all boys, and if you could see her you wouldn't believe it was

Lalita, she's got so fat. Do you remember how I helped her give birth with this very pair of hands? Aquilino is a big fellow, very nice too. And Nieves' kids too, and the policeman's. You can't tell them apart; they all look like Lalita."

"Everybody used to be jealous of me," Fushía shouts. "Because you came to see me and nobody comes to see them. And then they'd tease me because you took so long in coming back. He'll be here soon, it's because he travels, he does business on the rivers, but he'll be here tomorrow, or the day after, but he'll be here in any case. Now it's as if you never came at all, Aquilino."

"Lalita told me about her life," Aquilino says. "She didn't want any more children, but the soldier did and he went on keeping her filled up, and in Santa María de Nieva they call the kids the Fats boys. Not just the guard's kids, Nieves', and your boy too."

"Lalita?" Fushía shouts. "Lalita, old man?"

A rose-colored agitation breaks out, moans, along with putrid exhalations, and the old man covers his nose, throws his head back. It has started to rain and the wind is hissing among the trees, the underbrush is dancing on the other shore, there is a rustling of leaves. The rain is still fine, invisible. Aquilino stands up:

"Now you see, it's begun to rain, I have to leave," he twangs. "I'll have to sleep in the boat, get soaked all night. I can't go upstream in the rain, if the motor quits on me I won't have enough strength and the current will carry me, it's happened to me before. Did you get sad because of what I told you about Lalita? Why've you stopped shouting, Fushía?"

He is huddled over more than before, curved, ovoid, and he does not answer. His good foot is playing with the pebbles scattered on the sand: it scatters them and piles them up, scatters them and piles them up, makes them even, and in all these slow and minute movements there is a kind of melancholy. Aquilino takes two steps, now he does not take his eyes off that glowing back, those bones being washed by the rain. He draws back a little more, and now it is impossible to distinguish between ulcers and skin, everything is one surface, purple, violet, iridescent. He releases his nose and takes a deep breath.

"Don't be sad, Fushía," he murmurs. "I'll be back next year, even if I'm worn out, my word of honor. I'll bring you some soft things. Did you get angry because of the Lalita business? Did you remember the old days? That's life, man, at least it's been better for you than for a lot of other people; think about Nieves."

He murmurs and keeps on withdrawing, now he is on the path. There are puddles in the low spots, and a very strong breath of vegetation invades the atmosphere, a smell of sap, resin, and germinating plants. The old man continues withdrawing, the small pile of living and bloody flesh is still motionless in the distance, it disappears behind the ferns. Aquilino turns around, he runs toward the cabins, Fushía, he would be back next year, whispering, he should not be sad. It is raining very hard now.

2

"Hurry, Father," Wildflower said. "I've got a taxi waiting over there."

"Just a minute." Father García coughed, rubbing his eyes. "I have to get dressed."

He disappeared into the house, and Wildflower signaled the driver to wait. Swarms of insects were buzzing around the street lights on the deserted Plazuela Merino, the sky was high and starry, and along the Avenida Sánchez Cerro, roaring, the first nocturnal trucks and buses were appearing now. Wildflower waited on the sidewalk until the door opened again and Father García came out, his face hidden behind a gray scarf, a wool hat that came down to his brows. They got into the taxi and it went off.

"Go fast, driver," Wildflower said. "As fast as you can, driver."

"Is it far?" Father García asked, and his voice turned into a long yawn.

"A little bit, Father," Wildflower said. "Near the Club Grau."

"Why did you come all the way here, then?" grumbled Father García. "What do you think the Buenos Aires parish is for? Why did you have to get me out of bed and not Father Rubio?"

The Tres Estrellas was closed, but light could be seen inside, Father: the lady wanted it to be him who came. Three men embracing each other were singing on the corner, and another, a little farther on, was urinating up against a wall. A truck overloaded with crates was boldly going down the center of the street, the taxi driver honked to get by, turning his lights off and on in vain, and suddenly the wool hat went right over to Wildflower's very mouth: what lady wanted him to come? The truck finally pulled over and the taxi was able to pass, Father, Señora Chunga, a sudden start, what?, who was dying?, the cassock began to shake and a kind of nausea was strangling Father García's voice under the scarf: whose confession was he going to hear?

"Don Anselmo's, Father," Wildflower whispered.

"Is the harp player dying?" the driver exclaimed. "What did you say? Was it him?"

The taxi braked suddenly, squealed onto the Avenida Grau, then took off forward with greater speed, and the long beams of its headlights made the speed seem even faster, and he did not slow down at intersections, limiting himself to announcing his rapid passing with a strong blowing of the horn. In the meantime, the wool hat was swinging fretfully in front of Wildflower's face, and Father García's throat seemed locked in a hoarse battle with something that was obstructing it and stifling him.

"He was playing, just as happy as he could be, and all of a sudden he fell onto the floor." Wildflower sighed. "He turned all purple, poor man, Father."

A hand flew out of the shadows, it shook Wildflower on the shoulder and she moaned, were they going to the house of prostitution?, startled, and she huddled against the car door: no, Father, no, to the Green House. That was where he was dying, why had he shaken her like that, what had she done to him, and Father García let go of her and snatched the scarf from around his neck. Breathing with difficulty, he put his mouth close to the window and remained that way for a moment, leaning forward, his eyes closed, inhaling the thin night air with anguish. Then he fell back against the seat and wrapped himself in the scarf again.

"The Green House is a house of prostitution, you wretch!" he roared. "Now I know who you are, now I know why you're half naked and all made up."

"Haven't they called a doctor?" the driver asked. "That's a sad piece of news, Miss. Excuse me for butting in, but I know the harp player very well. Who doesn't, and we all think a lot of him."

"Yes, they called one," Wildflower said. "Dr. Zevallos is already there. But he says it'll be a miracle if he doesn't die. They're all crying, Father."

Father García had folded up on the seat and he was not speaking, but, intermittently, weakly, stubbornly, the sound was still coming out from under the scarf. The taxi stopped in front of the gate of the Club Grau; the motor was still roaring and steaming.

"I'd go right into the settlement," the driver said, "but the sand is soft and I'd be sure to get stuck. I'm sorry about what's happening, I really am."

While Wildflower was unfolding a handkerchief, taking out the money, and paying the driver, Father García got out and shut the door angrily. He started walking through the sand with long strides. Every so often he would stumble, he was going up and down on the unequal surface, and in the clear night he could be seen advancing between the yellowish dunes, hunchbacked and dark, like a huge vulture. Wildflower caught up to him halfway there.

"Did you know him, Father?" she whispered. "Poor man, don't you think? If you could have seen how he played, it was so pretty. And he could barely see."

Father García did not answer. He was walking all hunched over, with his legs wide apart, at a quick rhythm, his breathing more and more anxious.

"Isn't it strange, Father," Wildflower said. "You can't hear a sound now, and every night you can hear the music of the orchestra from here. Even farther away, it's very clear; even on the highway."

"Quiet, you wretch," Father García roared, without looking at her. "Keep your mouth shut!"

"Don't get angry, Father," Wildflower said. "I don't know what I'm saying. I'm just so upset, you don't know what Don Anselmo was like."

"I know only too well, wretch," Father García muttered. "I've known him since before you were born."

He said something else, incomprehensible, and again the strange raucous and urgent sound came out. In the doors of the shacks of the settlement there were people, and as he passed whispering could be heard, good evening, some women crossed themselves. Wildflower knocked on the door, and right away a woman's voice: they were closed, they weren't open for business, Ma'am, it was she, Father was here. There was a silence, hurried footsteps, the door opened and a smoky light illuminated Father García's thin and decrepit face, the scarf dancing around his neck. He went into the place, followed by Wildflower, he did not reply to the greeting of two male voices from the bar, perhaps he did not even hear the respectful whispering that had arisen at two tables surrounded by hazy figures. He stood, severe and motionless, by the empty dance floor, and when a faceless form appeared before him, where was he?, he grunted quickly, and Chunga, who had put out her hand to him, changed its course and pointed to the stairs: where, they should take him. Wildflower took him by the arm, Father, she would show him. They went across the room, they went up to the second floor, and in the corridor Father García pulled away from Wildflower's hand. She softly touched one of the four identical doors and opened it. She stood aside, and when Father García had gone in she closed it and went back down to the main room.

"Was it cold out?" Jocko asked. "You're shivering."

"Have a glass of this," Kid Alejandro said. "It'll warm you up."

Wildflower took the glass, drank, and wiped her lips with her hand.

"The priest got furious all of a sudden," she said. "In the taxi he grabbed me by the shoulder and shook me. I thought he was going to hit me."

"He's a grouch," Jocko said. "I didn't think he'd come."

"Is Dr. Zevallos still there, Ma'am?" Wildflower asked.

"He came down a while ago to have a cup of coffee," Chunga replied. "He said there was no change."

"I'm going to have another drink, Chunguita, I need it for my nerves," Jocko said. "I haven't got any money, take it out of my pay."

Chunga nodded and filled up both their glasses. Then, with the bottle in her hand, she went over to the tables around the dance floor where the inmates were discreetly whispering: did they want a drink? They didn't want any, Ma'am, thank you, and there was no use for them to stay either, they could leave. Another round of whispering started, more prolonged, a chair creaked, Ma'am, if she didn't mind, they'd rather stay, could they?, and Chunga, sure, whatever they wanted, and she went back to the bar. The shadows went on with their muffled dialogues and the musicians were drinking in silence, looking at the stairs from time to time.

"Why don't you play something?" Chunga asked, in a low voice, with a vague gesture. "If he can hear you, he'll probably like it; he'll think that you're accompanying him."

Jocko and the Kid were doubtful, Wildflower yes, yes, she was right, he'd like it, and the shadows stopped whispering: all right, they'd play for him. They went over to the orchestra corner, slowly, Jocko sat down on the bench against the wall, and the Kid picked his guitar up from the floor. They started with a sad song, and only after some time did they dare to sing, mumbling, without conviction, but little by little they began raising their voices and they ended up recovering their usual ease and vivacity. When they played one of the Kid's songs, they were noticeably more emotional, they sang the words very slowly and sentimentally, and sometimes Jocko would get off key and fall silent. Chunga brought them some drinks. She seemed upset too, and she was not walking with her usual slightly arrogant assurance, but on tiptoe, without moving her arms or looking at anybody, as if frightened or confused, Ma'am: there comes Dr. Zevallos. Jocko and the Kid stopped playing, the inmates got up, Chunga and Wildflower ran to the stairs.

"I gave him an injection." Dr. Zevallos was mopping his brow with his handkerchief. "But we shouldn't get our hopes up. Father García's with him. That's what he needs now, prayers for his soul."

He ran his tongue over his lips, Chunga, he was terribly thirsty: it was hot up there. Chunga went to the bar and came back with a glass of beer. Dr. Zevallos sat at a table with the Kid, Jocko, and Wildflower. The inmates had gone back to their seats and were whispering again, in a monotone.

"That's the way life is." Dr. Zevallos drank, sighed, closed and reopened his eyes. "We all have to go someday. Me a lot sooner than the rest of you."

"Is he suffering very much, Doctor?" Jocko asked, with a drunken voice; but his look and his movements were sober.

"No, that's why I gave him the injection," the Doctor said. "He's unconscious. He comes to every so often, for a few seconds, but he doesn't feel any pain."

"They were playing for him," Chunga whispered, with a voice that was also altered and with irresolute eyes. "We thought he'd like it."

"You can't hear it from his room," the Doctor said. "But I don't hear very well, Anselmo could probably hear it. I'd like to know exactly how old he is. Over eighty, I'll bet. He's older than I am, and I'm pushing seventy. Could I have another beer, please, Chunga."

Then they were silent and remained that way for a long time. Chunga would get up every so often, go to the bar, and bring back beers and glasses of pisco. The whispering of the inmates was still there, sometimes harsh and nervous, sometimes muffled and almost inaudible. And suddenly they all stood up again and ran to the stairs, where Father García was coming down, hatless and without his scarf, having some difficulty, motioning to Dr. Zevallos. The Doctor went up the stairs, holding on to the banister, disappeared into the corridor, Father, what had happened, several questions burst out at the same time, and as if the noise of it had startled them, they all became quiet together: Father García was mumbling something, choked up. His teeth were chattering very hard and his wandering look did not stop on any face. The Kid and Jocko were holding each other and one of them was sobbing. A short time later the inmates began to wipe their eyes, moan, cry aloud, throw themselves into each other's arms, and Chunga and Wildflower were left to hold up Father García, who was trembling and rolling his eyes in a tense and tormented way. Between the two of them, they dragged him over to a chair, and he, inert, let himself be seated, have his forehead wiped, and he drank the glass of pisco that Chunga poured into his mouth without resistance. His body was still trembling, but his eyes had become serene and they were staring into space, encircled by large, dark rings. A little later, Dr. Zevallos appeared on the stairs. He came down slowly, head down, heavily rubbing his neck.

"He died at peace with God," he said. "That's all that matters now."

The shadows at the tables in the back had also calmed down, and the whispering began again, still timid, painful. The two musicians, in each other's arms, were weeping, Jocko very strongly, the Kid noiselessly and shaking his shoulders. Dr. Zevallos sat down, a melancholy expression crossed his chubby face, Father: had he been able to speak to him? Father García shook his head no. Wildflower was stroking his forehead and he, hunched over in the chair, was making an effort to speak, he hadn't recognized him, and a hoarse whistle was coming from his mouth, and, once more, his look renewed its wandering, an incessant exploration of the things around: all the time the Estrella del Norte, the only thing he could understand. His voice, drowned out by Jocko's weeping, could barely be heard.

"It was a hotel that used to be here when I was a young man," Dr. Zevallos said to Chunga, with a certain nostalgia, but she was not listening to him. "On the Plaza de Armas, where the Hotel de Turistas is today."

3

"You've spent all your time sleeping, you haven't enjoyed the trip at all," Lalita says. "And now you're going to miss our arrival."

She is leaning on the rail, and Huambachano, on the deck, his back against some coils of rope, opens his bulging eyes, he wished he was sleeping, his voice sounds weak and ill, he had his eyes closed so that he wouldn't vomit any more, Lalita: he'd already got rid of everything he had in him, but he still felt like it. It was her fault, he'd wanted to stay in Santa María de Nieva. With her body half over the edge, Lalita is feasting her eyes on the horizon of reddish roofs, the white fronts, the tall palm trees that rise up in the city, and the figures, quite clear now, moving about the dock. The people on deck struggle to find a place by the railing.

"Fats, don't be lazy, you're going to miss the best part," Lalita says. "Look at my town, Fats, see how big, how pretty it is. Help me look for Aquilino."

Huambachano's mournful face traces an imitation of a smile, his chunky body twists and finally rises with great effort. An active bustle takes over on deck; the passengers inspect their bundles, throw them onto their shoulders, and, affected by the excitement, the pigs grunt, the chickens cackle and flap their wings frantically, and the dogs run back and forth, barking, their ears standing up, their tails wagging. A whistle pierces the air, the black smoke from the stack thickens, and particles of carbon fall on the people. Now they have entered the harbor, they go along through an archipelago of motor launches, rafts loaded with bananas, canoes, Fats, was he looking?, he should watch closely, he had to be there, but Fats was upset again: damn the luck. He has an attack of heaving, but he does not vomit, he contents himself with spitting angrily. His greasy face is contrite and purplish, his eyes have become very red. From the bridge, a small man is shouting orders, gesticulating, and two barefoot crewmen, stripped to the waist, up on the prow, ready the lines.

"You ruin everything, Fats," Lalita says, without ceasing to look at the harbor. "I come home to Iquitos after such a long time and you get sick."

In the swaying of the oily water, tin cans, boxes, newspapers, trash are rocking. They are surrounded by launches, some newly painted and with pennants on their masts, by rowboats, rafts, buoys, and barges. On the dock, beside the gangplank made of boards, a small, amorphous crowd of porters is shouting and whistling at the passengers, they give their names, beat on their chests, they all try to get the first spot by the gangplank. Behind them there is a wire enclosure, some wooden sheds, where the people waiting for the passengers are crowded in: there he was, Fats, the one in the hat. How big, what a good-looking boy, he should wave to him, and Huambachano opens his glassy eyes, he should say hello, Fats, he raises his hand and waves it weakly. The ship has stopped moving and the two soldiers leap to the dock holding the lines, they tie them to some moorings. Now the porters are howling, jumping, and with grotesque facial expressions and gestures they try to catch the attention of the passengers. A man in a blue uniform and a white cap is strolling indifferently in front of the planks. Behind the fence, the people are waving their hands, laughing, and in the midst of the uproar, at regular intervals, the strident whistle keeps blowing: Aquilino! Aquilino! Aquilino! The color comes back to Huambachano's face and his smile is more natural now, less pathetic. He makes his way among the women loaded down with bundles, dragging a bulging suitcase and a bag.

"He's put on weight, did you notice?" Lalita says. "And look how he's all dressed up to meet us, Fats. Say something, show your thanks, maybe you've forgotten everything he's done for us."

"Yes, he's heavier and he's wearing a white shirt," Huambachano says mechanically. "It was just about time; I'm not made for sailing. My body can't get used to it. I've been suffering the whole trip."

The man in the blue uniform collects the tickets, and with a friendly push he turns the passengers over to the simian, desperate porters, who pounce on them, snatch away the animals and the packages, begging them, scolding them if they resist surrendering their luggage. There are only a dozen of them, but they seem to be a hundred from the noise they make; dirty, hairy, skeletal, all are wearing pants covered with patches, and, occasionally, tattered undershirts. Huambachano pushes them aside, boss, whatever he wanted, beat it, they go back to the luggage, sons of bitches, five cents, boss, and he beat it, let me through. He leaves them behind and reaches the fence, staggering. Aquilino comes out to meet him and they embrace.

"You've let your mustache grow," Huambachano says, "you've got your hair slicked down. You sure have changed, Aquilino."

"Here it's not the way it is back there, you have to dress up." Aquilino smiles. "How was the trip? I've been waiting for you since this morning."

"Your mother had a good trip, she was happy," Huambachano says. "But I was very seasick, I spent all my time throwing up. It's been so many years since I've been on board a ship."

"The best cure for that's a drink," Aquilino says. "What's my mother doing, why did she stay behind?"

Sturdy, her long graying hair hanging over her back, Lalita is surrounded by porters. She has leaned over one of them, her lips are moving, and she watches him very closely, with an almost aggressive curiosity: those shitheads, didn't they see that she didn't have any luggage? What did they want to do, carry her? Aquilino laughs, takes out a pack of Incas, offers Huambachano a cigarette, and lights it for him. Now Lalita has put one of her hands on the shoulder of the porter and is talking animatedly with him; he is listening with a reserved expression, he shakes his head no, and after a moment he withdraws and mixes with the others, he begins to jump, shout, run after the passengers. Lalita comes over to the wire with a springy step, her arms open. While she and Aquilino are embracing, Huambachano is smoking, and his face, hidden in the curls of smoke, looks recovered and placid now.

"You're a man now, you're getting married; pretty soon you'll be giving me some grandchildren," Lalita squeezes Aquilino, makes him step back and turn around. "And you're so elegant, so good-looking."

"Do you know where you're going to stay?" Aquilino says. "With Amelia's parents. I'd looked for a hotel, but they said no, we'll fix them up a bed in the front room. They're nice people, you'll be good friends."

"When's the wedding?" Lalita asks. "I've brought along a new dress, Aquilino, to wear that day. And Fats has to buy a necktie, the one he had was old and I wouldn't let him bring it."

"Next Sunday," Aquilino says. "Everything's all set, we've paid for the church and a small reception at Amelia's parents' house. Tomorrow I have my bachelor dinner. But you haven't told me anything about my brothers. Are they all fine?"

"Fine, but dreaming about coming to Iquitos," Huambachano says. "Even the little one wants to take off like you."

They have come out onto the Malecón, and Aquilino is carrying the suitcase on his shoulder and the bag under his arm. Huambachano is smoking and Lalita is greedily observing the park, the houses, the passers-by, the automobiles, Fats, wasn't it a pretty city? The way it had grown, none of this was here when she was a girl, and Huambachano yes, his face indifferent: it seemed pretty at first sight.

"Weren't you ever here when you were in the Civil Guard?" Aquilino asks.

"No, only in places on the coast," Huambachano says. "And later on in Santa María de Nieva."

"We can't go on foot, Amelia's parents live too far away," Aquilino says. "We'll take a taxi."

"One day I want to go where I was born," Lalita says. "Is my house still there, Aquilino? I'm going to cry when I see Belén, the house is probably there and hasn't changed a bit."

"What about your job?" Huambachano asks. "Are you making good money?"

"Not much right now," Aquilino says. "But the owner of the

tannery is going to give us a raise next year, that's what he promised. He advanced me the money for your trip."

"What's a tannery?" Lalita asks. "I thought you were working in a factory."

"Where they cure alligator skins," Aquilino says. "They make shoes, wallets. When I started, I didn't know anything, and now they've got me teaching the new people."

He and Huambachano shout at every taxi that passes, but none of them stops.

"I'm over being sick from the water," Huambachano says. "But now I'm getting sick from the city. I haven't been used to it for a long time either."

"It's because for you there's no place like Santa María de Nieva," Aquilino says. "It's the only thing you like in the world."

"That's right, I wouldn't live in the city any more," Huambachano says. "I'd rather have my little farm, a peaceful life. When I retired from the Civil Guard, I told your mother I'll spend the rest of my days in Santa María de Nieva, and I'm going to keep my word."

An old jalopy stops in front of them with a noise of tin cans, clanking as if it were about to fall apart. The driver puts the suitcase on the roof and ties it down with a rope, and Lalita and Huambachano [illegible] in the back, Aquilino next to the driver.

"I checked into what you asked me, Mother," Aquilino says. "It was a lot of work, nobody knew anything, they sent me all over the place. But I finally found out."

"What was that?" Lalita asks. She is looking with intoxication at the streets of Iquitos, a smile on her lips, emotion in her eyes.

"About Señor Nieves," Aquilino says, and Huambachano, with sudden urgency, looks out the window. "They let him out last year."

"They kept him in that long?" Lalita says.

"He's most likely gone to Brazil," Aquilino says. "People who get out of jail go to Manaus. They won't give them any work here. He probably found work there if he was as good a pilot as they say he was. Except that being away from the river for such a long time, he must have forgotten what he knew."

"I don't think he's forgotten," Lalita says, interested again in the spectacle of the narrow and crowded streets, the raised sidewalks, the house fronts, and the railings. "At least it's good that they finally let him out."

"What's your fiancée's last name?" Huambachano asks.

"Marín," Aquilino says. "She's a little brunette. She works in the tannery too. Didn't you get the picture I sent you?"

"So many years without thinking about the past," Lalita says suddenly, turning to Aquilino. "And today I see Iquitos again and you tell me about Adrián—"

"The car is making me sick too," Huambachano interrupts her. "Have we got very far to go, Aquilino?"

4

It is already dawning among the dunes behind the Grau barracks, but shadows still hide in the city when Dr. Pedro Zevallos and Father García cross the sand arm in arm and get into the taxi parked by the highway. Wrapped up in his scarf, his hat pulled down, Father García is a pair of feverish eyes, a fleshy nose that grows out beneath two bushy eyebrows.

"How do you feel?" Dr. Zevallos asks, dusting off the cuffs of his pants.

"My head's still spinning," Father García murmurs. "But I'll lie down and it'll go away."

"You can't go to bed like that," Dr. Zevallos says. "Let's have some breakfast first, something hot will be good for us."

Father García makes a gesture of annoyance, there wouldn't be anything open at that hour, but Dr. Zevallos cuts him off, leaning toward the driver: would Angélica Mercedes' be open? It should be, boss, and Father García grunts, she opened very early, not there, and his hand shakes again and goes back into its nest of folds.

"Stop saying no all the time," Dr. Zevallos says. "What does it matter where. The main thing is to warm our stomachs up a little after a bad night like that. Don't try to fool me, you know that you won't be able to close your eyes if you go to bed now. We'll have something at Angélica Mercedes' and chat a little."

A harsh snort comes through the scarf, Father García turns in his seat without answering. The taxi enters the Buenos Aires district, it goes past chalets with ample gardens, one after another on both sides of the highway, it goes around the dark monument and slips off toward the sombre bulk of the cathedral. A few shopwindows on the Avenida Grau are sparkling in the dawn, a garbage truck is in front of the Hotel de Turistas and men in overalls are going toward it carrying trash cans. The taxi driver has a cigarette in his mouth, a gray wake travels from his lips to the rear seat, and Father García begins to cough. Dr. Zevallos opens the window a little.

"Haven't you ever been back to Mangachería since Domitila Yara's wake?" Dr. Zevallos asks; there is no answer: Father García has his eyes closed and is snoring softly.

"Do you know that they almost killed him that time, at the wake?" the driver asks.

"Quiet, man," Dr. Zevallos whispers. "If he hears you, he'll fly into a rage."

"Is it true that the harp player died, boss?" the driver asks. "Is that why they called the two of you out to the Green House?"

The Avenida Sánchez Cerro stretches out like a tunnel, and in the shadows of the sidewalk, at certain intervals, the figures of small trees can be made out. Toward the end, over a vague horizon of roofs and sand dunes, a circular iridescence is beginning to glimmer.

"He died early this morning," Dr. Zevallos says. "Or did you think that Father García and I are at an age where we can spend the night at Chunga's?"

"Age doesn't matter for that, boss," the driver says, with a laugh. "A buddy of mine took one of the women over to get Father García, the girl they call Wildflower. He told me that the harp player was dying, boss, it's a shame."

Dr. Zevallos is looking distractedly at the whitewashed walls, the outside doors with their knockers, the new building the Solaris put up, the newly planted carob trees on the sidewalks, fragile and graceful in their squares of earth: the way news travels in this town. But he had to know, boss, and the driver lowers his voice, was it true what people said?, he takes a look at Father García in the rear-view mirror, is it true that Father burned the Green House down on the harp player? Had he known that brothel, boss? Was it as big as they said, a first-class place?

"Why are Piurans like that," Dr. Zevallos says. "After thirty years haven't they got tired of kicking that same story around? They've made this poor priest's life a living hell."

"Don't say anything bad about Piurans, boss," the driver says. "Piura's my home town."

"Mine too, man," Dr. Zevallos says. "Besides I'm not talking, I'm just thinking out loud."

"But there must be some truth in it, boss," the driver insists. "Otherwise why would people talk, why would there be that business of firebug, firebug."

"How should I know," Dr. Zevallos says. "Don't you dare to ask Father?"

"With his hot temper! Not in a million years." The driver laughs. "But tell me at least if that brothel really existed or if people just made it all up."

Now they are going along the new part of the avenue: the old highway will soon have an asphalt surface and the trucks that come from the south and continue on to Sullana, Talara, and Tumbes will no longer have to go through the center of the city. The sidewalks a wide and low, the gray lampposts are newly painted, that tall skeleton of reinforced concrete will be a skyscraper, perhaps taller than the Hotel Cristina.

"The most modern district is going to be rubbing elbows with the oldest and the poorest," Dr. Zevallos says. "I don't think Mangachería has very long to go."

"The same thing'll happen to it as happened to Gallinacera, boss," the driver says. "They'll bring in bulldozers and build houses like these, for rich people."

"And where the devil will the Mangaches go with their goats and their donkeys?" Dr. Zevallos asks. "And where will a person be able to get any good chicha then?"

"The Mangaches are going to be very sad, boss," the driver says. "The harp player was like a god to them, even more popular than Sánchez Cerro. Now they'll light candles for Don Anselmo too, and pray to him the way they do to Domitila, the holy woman."

The taxi leaves the avenue and, bouncing, rocking, it goes along a narrow unpaved street between shacks made out of wild cane stalks. It raises a great cloud of dust and infuriates the stray dogs, who run close to the fenders, barking at it, boss: the Mangaches were right, dawn comes up earlier here than in Piura. In the blue clarity, through clouds of dust, figures lying on mats can be made out at the doors of the houses, women with jugs on their heads crossing at the corners, donkeys with dreamy and apathetic looks. Attracted by the roar of the motor, children come out of the shacks, and, naked or in tatters, they run behind the taxi waving, what was up, yawning, what was going on: nothing, Father, they were now in forbidden territory.

"Let us out here," Dr. Zevallos says. "We'll walk a little."

They get out of the taxi and, arm in arm, slowly, supporting each other, they go along a crooked path, escorted by urchins who are jumping about, firebug!, they shriek and laugh, firebug!, firebug!, and Dr. Zevallos pretends to pick up a stone and throw it: little shits, shitty little kids, it was just as well they were almost there.

Angélica Mercedes' house is larger than the others, and the three small flags that wave over its adobe front give it a gallant and coquettish air. Dr. Zevallos and Father García go in, sneezing, choose two stools and a table made of rough planks, sit down. The floor has been recently wet down and the smell is of damp earth, coriander, and parsley. There is nobody at the other tables or at the bar. Grouped in the doorway, the children are still shouting, they stretch out their dirty, hairy heads, Doña Angélica!, their thin arms, Doña Angélica!, they laugh, showing their teeth. Dr. Zevallos rubs his hands thoughtfully, and Father García, between yawns, watches the door out of the corner of his eye. Angélica Mercedes finally comes out, fresh, plump, morning-like, the hem of her broad skirt tracing cable marks on the stools. Dr. Zevallos gets up, Doctor, she opens her arms to him, such a pleasure, what a miracle to see him there at that time of the morning, it's been so many months since he had been there, and she was getting prettier every day, Angélica, what did she do to stop from getting old?, what was her secret? And they finally stop patting each other on the back, Angélica, didn't she see whom he'd brought?, didn't she recognize him? As if fearful, Father

García puts his feet together and hides his hands, good morning, the scarf grunts gruffly and the hat shakes for a second, Holy Virgin!: it was Father García. Her hands clasped over her heart, her eyes excited, Angélica Mercedes leans over, dear Father, how happy she was to see him, he didn't know, how wonderful that you brought him, Doctor, and a bony and hesitant hand rises coldly toward Angélica Mercedes, draws back before she can kiss it.

"Could you fix something hot for us, friend?" Dr. Zevallos asks. "We're half dead, we've been up all night."

"Of course, of course, right away." Angélica Mercedes cleans the table with her skirt. "Some hot soup and some spicy hors d'oeuvres? Some light chicha too? No, it's too early for that, I'll make you some juice and coffee and milk. But how come you haven't gone to bed yet? You're spoiling Father García."

A sarcastic grunt comes up from under the scarf and the hat straightens up, Father García's deep eyes look at Angélica Mercedes, and she stops smiling, turns her wondering face toward Dr. Zevallos, who, chin in his fingers, has a melancholy expression now: where had they been, dear Doctor? Her voice is timid, her hand grasps the hem of her skirt close to the table, and she is motionless: at Chunga's. Angélica Mercedes gives a little shout, at Chunga's?, her expression changes, at Chunga's?, she covers her mouth.

"Yes, old friend, Anselmo is dead," Dr. Zevallos says. "It's a sad piece of news for you, I know. For all of us. What can we do, that's the way life is."

Don Anselmo? Angélica Mercedes stammers, her mouth half open, her head to one side, is he dead, dear Father?, and her nose quivers rapidly, dimples appear on her cheeks, the children at the door have run off, and she shakes her head, rubs her arms, is he dead, Doctor?, she weeps.

"Everybody has to die someday!" Father García roars, pounding on the table; the scarf opens and his livid, unshaven face is deformed by the trembling of his mouth. "You, I, Dr. Zevallos, it's going to come to all of us, nobody can escape."

"Take it easy, man." Dr. Zevallos embraces Angélica Mercedes, who is sobbing, clutching her skirt to her eyes. "You take it easy too. Father García's very nervous, it's best not to talk to him, don't ask him anything. Go ahead, fix us something hot, don't cry."

Angélica Mercedes nods, still weeping, and goes away, her face in her hands. In the other room she can be heard talking to herself, sighing. Father García has picked up his scarf again, he wraps it around his neck, and he has taken off his hat: erect, gray, the tufts of hair at his temples only partially hide his smooth skull and the moles on it. He leans his chin on his fist, a thoughtful wrinkle crosses his brow, and the stubble of his beard gives his cheeks the look of something worn and dirty. Dr. Zevallos lights a cigarette. It is daytime now, and the sun which is flooding the place and gilding the stalks has dried the floor; blue and buzzing flies invade the air. Outside, voices, barking, bleating, braying, and domestic sounds gradually increase, and on the other side Angélica Mercedes has begun to pray, she mumbles the name of the holy woman mixed in with invocations to God and the Virgin, Doctor: that lesbian did it on purpose.

"But for what reason," Father García murmurs. "For what reason, Doctor?"

"What difference does it make," Dr. Zevallos says, watching the smoke become dissipated. "Besides, maybe there wasn't any reason behind it. It could have been coincidence."

"Nonsense, she had you and me called for some reason," Father García says. "She wanted to give us a bad time."

Dr. Zevallos shrugs his shoulders. He receives a ray of sunlight in the center of his forehead, and half his face is golden and bright; the other half is a lead-colored mole. His eyes are sunken in a soft drowsiness.

"I'm not very observant," he says, after a moment. "It hadn't even occurred to me to think about that. But you're right, she probably wanted to give us a bad time. She's a funny woman, Chunga. I didn't think she knew."

He turns to Father García and the mole increases its territory, occupying his whole face, only an ear and his jaw receive the yellow bath now; that she didn't know what? Father García looks at Dr. Zevallos from an angle.

"That I brought her into the world." Dr. Zevallos raises his head and it lights up, his bald spot stands out, shiny and granular. "Who could have told her? Not Anselmo, I'm sure of that. He thought that Chunga had been fooled."

"In this gossipy, dirty little town everything ends up being known,"

Father García says with a grunt. "Even if it's thirty years later, everything that happens comes to be known."

"She never came to my office," Dr. Zevallos says. "She never called me for anything, and now she does. If she wanted to give me a bad time, she succeeded. She made me relive the whole thing all at once."

"Your part is obvious," Father García grunts, as if he were speaking to the table. "This fellow saw my mother die, so he should see my father die too. But why did that lesbian have to call me?"

"What's this all about?" Dr. Zevallos says. "What's going on?"

"Come with me, Doctor." The voice comes from the right, it echoes off the high ceiling of the entranceway. "Right now, just the way you are, Doctor, there isn't any time."

"Do you think I don't recognize you?" Dr. Zevallos says. "Come out of there, Anselmo. What are you hiding for? Have you gone crazy, man?"

"Come, Doctor, hurry," a broken voice in the darkness of the entranceway which the echo repeats up above. "She's dying, Dr. Zevallos, come."

Dr. Zevallos raises the lamp, he searches and finally he finds him, not far from the door: he is neither drunk nor mad, but cringing with fear. His eyes are rolling madly in their swollen sockets and his back is pressed against the wall as if he were trying to push it down.

"Your wife?" Dr. Zevallos says, with astonishment. "Your wife, Anselmo?"

"They can both be dead and I still won't accept it." Father García pounds on the table and his stool creaks. "I won't accept that infamy. Even after a hundred years, it will still be infamous as far as I'm concerned."

The door of the vestibule has opened and the man retreats as if he saw a ghost, he escapes from the cone of light coming from the lamp. The small figure wrapped in a white robe takes a few steps into the courtyard, son, she stops before she reaches the entranceway: who was there?, why didn't they come in? It was he, mama, Dr. Zevallos lowers the lamp, hides Anselmo with his body: he had to go out for a while.

"Wait for me on the Malecón," he whispers. "I'm going to get my bag."

"Start with the soup." Angélica Mercedes puts two steaming gourds on the table. "It already has salt in it, and I'll bring the snacks in just a little while."

She is no longer crying, but her voice is mournful and she has thrown a black shawl over her shoulders. She goes off to the kitchen, and now there is a slight sway to her walk. Dr. Zevallos stirs his soup thoughtfully, Father García lifts his gourd with four fingers, brings it close to his nose, and inhales the warm aroma.

"I never understood it either, and I think that back then I thought it was infamous too," Dr. Zevallos says. "Now I'm old, I've seen a lot of water go over the dam, and nothing seems infamous to me any more. If you'd been there that night, you wouldn't have hated poor Anselmo so much, I swear, Father García."

"God will reward you, Doctor," the man sobs as he runs, bumping into trees, benches, the railing of the Malecón. "I'll do whatever you ask, I'll give you all my money, Doctor, my life, Doctor."

"Are you trying to work on my emotions?" Father García grumbles, looking at Dr. Zevallos, hiding behind the gourd that he is sniffing. "Am I supposed to start crying too?"

"Actually, I don't give a damn about any of that now." Dr. Zevallos smiles. "Gone with the wind, my friend. But because of what Chunguita did last night, it came back into my mind and it's still there. I'm talking about it to get rid of it; don't pay any attention to me."

Father García tests the temperature of the soup with the tip of his tongue, he blows, sips, belches, grunts an apology, and continues sipping and blowing. A short time later, Angélica Mercedes returns with a plate of snacks and some lúcuma juice. She has covered her head with a shawl, Doctor, wasn't it good?, and his voice makes an effort to be natural, yes, Ma'am, very good. A little hot, as soon as it cooled off he'd drink it, and the snacks she'd made for them looked good. Now she was warming up the coffee for them, anything else they wanted, just call, dear Father. Dr. Zevallos rocks the gourd with a finger, he carefully examines the muddy round surface that is going back and forth, and Father García has begun to cut small pieces of meat and chew them vigorously. But suddenly he pauses, had they all known?, and he remains with his mouth open: the wretches that were there?

"They knew about the romance from the very beginning, as is logical," Dr. Zevallos murmurs, stroking the edge of the gourd, "but I don't think anybody else found out. There was a small stairway that opened onto the back yard, and we went up to the tower that way, the people in the main room didn't see us. A wild noise came from downstairs, and Anselmo must have told the girls to give the people a good time and not let them suspect what was going on."

"How well you knew the place." Father García is chewing again. "It couldn't have been the first time you'd been there, I imagine."

"I'd been there dozens of times," Dr. Zevallos says, with a fleeting gleam in his eyes. "I was thirty years old then. In the flower of my youth, my friend."

"Filth, stupidity," Father García grunts, but his hand lowers the fork he had raised to his mouth. "Thirty years old? I must have been the same age, more or less."

"Naturally, we belong to the same generation," Dr. Zevallos says. "Anselmo too, although a little older than us."

"There aren't many left from those days," Father García says, with hoarse humor. "We've buried them all."

But Dr. Zevallos is not listening to him. He is moving his lips, blinking, shaking the gourd until he spills some drops of soup on the table, man, how was he ever to imagine, not even when he saw the figure in the bed did he guess, man, who could have guessed.

"Don't start talking to yourself," Father García says, "don't forget that I'm here. What couldn't anybody have imagined?"

"That his wife was that child," Dr. Zevallos says. "When I went in, at the head of the bed I saw a fat redhead, the one they called Firefly, and she didn't look sick to me, and I was going to crack a joke, but then I saw the shape on the bed and the blood. You can't imagine, my friend, on the sheets, on the floor, the whole room was one big stain. It looked as if they'd butchered somebody."

Father García is not cutting, he is squashing the pieces of meat ferociously, he picks them up with the fork, twists them against the plate. The dripping pieces do not reach his mouth, the child was bleeding?, remain trembling in the air like his hand and the knife and fork, blood all over?, and a sudden hoarseness comes over him, the blood of that child? A thread of transparent drivel runs down her chin, idiot, he should let her go, it was no time for kisses, he was smothering her, they had to make her shout, idiot: it would be better to slap her. But Josefino raises a finger to his mouth: no shouting, couldn't she see that there were so many neighbors?, couldn't they hear them talking? As if she had not heard them, Wildflower screams even louder, and Josefino takes out his handkerchief, he leans over the cot and covers her mouth. Without changing her expression, Doña Santos keeps on poking, skillfully manipulating the two dark thighs. And then he had seen her face, Father García, and his arms and legs began to tremble, he forgot that she was dying and that he was there to try to save her life, all he could do was, yes, yes, look at her, there was no doubt: it was Antonia, my God. Don Anselmo was no longer kissing her, fallen down at the foot of the bed, he was offering his money again, Dr. Zevallos, his life, save her!, and Josefino was frightened, Doña Santos, she hadn't died, had she? She wasn't going to kill her, she wasn't going to kill her, Doña Santos, and she hush: she'd fainted, that was all. It was better, there wouldn't be any noise and she could get it over with quicker, he should moisten her forehead with the cloth. Dr. Zevallos handed him the washbasin quickly, they should boil more water, idiot, crying instead of helping. He is in his shirt sleeves, his collar open, and very calm now. Anselmo cannot hold the washbasin, it falls out of his hands, Doctor, she shouldn't die, he picks up the washbasin and tiptoes over to the door, Doctor, she was his life, and goes out.

"You son of a bitch," Dr. Zevallos mutters. "It's crazy, Anselmo, how could you have done it, man, what a terrible thing you've done, Anselmo."

"Hand me the bag," Doña Santos says. "And now I'll give her a little tea and she'll wake up. Take this and bury it well, and don't let anyone see you."

"Was there any hope?" Father García grunts, martyrizing the pieces of meat, spearing them and dragging them from one side to the other. "Was it impossible to save the girl?"

"In a hospital, perhaps," Dr. Zevallos says. "But she couldn't be moved. I had to operate on her almost in the dark, knowing that she was dying. It was more of a miracle that I was able to save Chunguita, she was born after her mother was already dead."

"A miracle, a miracle," Father García says. "Everything is a miracle around here. They also said it was a miracle when the Quirogas were killed and the girl was saved. She would have been better off if she'd died back then."

"Don't you think about the girl when you go by the bandstand?" Dr. Zevallos asks. "I do, I always seem to see her sitting there, taking the sun. But that night I came to feel sorrier for Anselmo than for Antonia."

"He didn't deserve it." Father García snorts. "No sorrow, no pity, no anything. The whole tragedy was his fault."

"If you could have seen him, kicking, kissing my feet so I'd save the girl, you would have taken pity on him too," Dr. Zevallos says. "Do you know that if it hadn't been for my friend here that Chunguita would have died on me too? She helped me take care of her."

They remain silent and Father García lifts a piece of meat to his mouth, but he puts on a look of distaste and lets go of the fork. Angélica Mercedes returns with another pitcher of juice, she shoos the flies away with one hand.

"Did you hear us, friend?" Dr. Zevallos asks. "We were recalling the night that Antonia died. It seems like a dream now, doesn't it? I was telling Father that you helped me save Chunga."

Angélica Mercedes looks at him very seriously, without surprise or alarm, as if she had not understood.

"I don't remember anything, Doctor," she says finally, in a low voice. "I was a cook, but I don't remember that either. We shouldn't talk about that now. I'm going to eight-o'clock mass to pray for Don Anselmo so he can rest in his grave. And then I'm going to his wake."

"How old were you then?" Father García asks. "I don't remember what you were like. Anselmo and those wretches yes, but not you."

"I was just a kid, dear Father." Angélica Mercedes' hand is a quick, efficient fan: no fly comes close to the food or the juice.

"Not more than fifteen," Dr. Zevallos says. "And you were very pretty. We all had our eyes on you, and Anselmo would say hold it, she's not one of the inmates, you can look but you can't touch, taking care of you as if you were his own daughter."

"I was a virgin and Father García wouldn't believe me." A roguish gleam lights up Angélica Mercedes' eyes,. but her face is still a severe mask. "I used to tremble when I went to confession, and you always told me leave that house of the devil, you're condemned already. Don't you remember either, Father?"

"What's said in the confessional is a secret," Father García says, with a kind of hoarse joviality. "Keep those stories to yourself."

"A house of the devil," Dr. Zevallos says. "Do you still think that Anselmo was the devil? Did he really smell of brimstone, or was it just to frighten churchgoers?"

Angélica Mercedes and the Doctor smile, and under the scarf, after a moment, something unexpected and harsh is heard, a hybrid sound like an attack of coughing and a suffocating laugh.

"In those days he was only there, in the Green House," Father García says, clearing his throat. "The devil is everywhere now. In the lesbian's house, in the streets, and in the movie theatres; the whole of Piura has become the house of the devil."

"But not Mangachería, dear Father," Angélica Mercedes says. "He's never set foot in here, we won't let him, Saint Domitila helps us in that."

"She's not a saint yet," Father García says. "Weren't you going to make us some coffee?"

"Yes, it's ready now," Angélica Mercedes says. "I'll go get it."

"It's been at least twenty years since I've stayed up all night," Dr. Zevallos says. "And now I don't feel sleepy at all."

The flies, as soon as Angélica Mercedes turns around, return and fall on the food, sprinkling it with dark spots. Ragged children run past the door again, and through the cane stalks people talking loudly can be seen passing, and a group of old men taking the sun and chatting in front of the shack across the way.

"Did he feel remorse at least?" Father García grunts. "Did he realize it was his fault that the girl died?"

"He ran out after me," Dr. Zevallos says. "He was rolling around in the sand, he wanted me to kill him. I took him home, I gave him an injection, and I sent him away. I don't know anything, I haven't seen anything, go away. But he didn't go away, he went down to the river and waited there for the washerwoman, what was her name?, the one who raised Antonia."

"He was always crazy," Father García grunts. "I hope for his sake that he repented and that God has forgiven him."

"And even if he didn't repent, he's had enough punishment already with what he's been through," Dr. Zevallos says. "Besides, one would have to know whether he really deserved to be punished. And what if Antonia hadn't been his victim but his accomplice? If she had fallen in love with him?"

"Don't talk nonsense," Father García says. "I'm beginning to think you've turned soft."

"It's something I've always wondered about," Dr. Zevallos says. "The girls said that he gave her everything, and that she seemed to be happy."

"Now you think it's normal?" Father García grunts. "Stealing a blind girl, taking her to a house of prostitution, getting her pregnant. Perfectly all right to do that? The most normal thing in the world? Was he supposed to be given some kind of prize for that benevolence?"

"There's nothing normal about it at all," Dr. Zevallos says, "but don't raise your voice so much, watch out for your asthma. I'm only saying that nobody knows what she was thinking. Antonia didn't know right from wrong, and after all, thanks to Anselmo, she became a whole woman. I've always thought—"

"Be quiet, man!" Father García attacks the flies with his hands and they flee in terror. "A whole woman! Are nuns not whole? Are we priests not whole because we don't do filthy things? I won't allow you to come out with such stupid heresies."

"You're fighting ghosts," Dr. Zevallos says, smiling. "I only wanted to say that I think Anselmo really loved her and that she probably loved him too."

"I don't like this conversation," Father García says. "We'll never come to any agreement, and I don't want to fight with you."

"That's all we needed," Dr. Zevallos murmurs. "Look who's coming in."

It was the champs, work wasn't for them, they lived off the others, they played their cards neat, they were the champs, and they were coming to eat, hey: look who was there.

"Let's leave," Father García grunts, exasperated. "I don't want to be around those hoodlums."

But the Leóns do not give him time to get up and they fall on him, clapping their hands, Father García, their hair disheveled, dear Father, their eyes filled with the dregs of the night. They jump around

Father García, snow would fall in Piura today instead of sand, they try to shake his hand, it was the miracle of miracles, they pat him on the back, a day for celebrating by the Mangaches for having received this visit. They are in their undershirts, no socks, their shoes untied, they smell of perspiration, and Father García, hiding behind his scarf, underneath the hat he has put on with great speed, remains motionless, staring at the food that is being attacked by the flies once more.

"I won't allow you to be disrespectful to him," Dr. Zevallos says. "Keep those tongues under control, boys. He's a man of the cloth and he has gray hair."

"But nobody's being disrespectful, Doctor," Monk says. "We're very happy to see him here, honest, we just want him to shake hands with us."

"You never saw a Mangache who didn't show hospitality, Doctor," José says. "Good morning, Doña Angélica. We have to celebrate the event, bring us something so we can drink a toast with Father García. We're going to make peace with him."

Angélica Mercedes comes over with two demitasse cups of coffee in her hands, very serious.

"Why are you looking so annoyed, Doña Angélica?" Monk asks. "Aren't you happy with your visitors?"

"You're the worst element in the city," Father García grunts. "The original sin of Piura. I wouldn't drink with you if they killed me."

"Don't blow up, Father García," Monk says. "We're not teasing you, we really are glad that you've come back to Mangachería."

"Low-lifes, tramps." Father García has started a new offensive against the flies. "What right do you have to address me, you good-for-nothings!"

"You see, Dr. Zevallos," Monk says. "Who's being disrespectful to whom?"

"Leave Father alone," Angélica Mercedes says. "Don Anselmo's dead. Father and the Doctor were attending him, they haven't slept all night."

She puts the cups on the table, goes back to the kitchen, and when her figure disappears into the back room all that can be heard is the tinkling of the spoons, Dr. Zevallos sipping his coffee, Father

García's anxious breathing. The Leóns are looking at each other as if sick to their stomachs.

"Now you see, boys," Dr. Zevallos says. "It's no time for jokes."

"Don Anselmo's dead," José says. "Our harp player's dead, Monk."

"He was the finest man there ever was, Doctor," Monk babbles. "He was a great artist, Doctor, one of the glories of Piura. You couldn't find a nicer man. It's heartbreaking, Dr. Zevallos."

"He was like a father to all of us, Doctor," José says. "Jocko and the Kid must be all broken up, Monk. His followers, Doctor; just like his own flesh and blood to the harp player. You don't know how they looked after him, Doctor."

"We didn't know, Father García," Monk says. "Please forgive us for fooling around."

"Did he die just like that, all of a sudden?" José asks. "Only yesterday he was fit as a fiddle. Last night we ate with him here, Dr. Zevallos, and he was laughing and joking."

"Where is he, Doctor?" Monk asks. "We have to go see him, José, we have to borrow some black neckties."

"He's there, where he died," Dr. Zevallos says. "At Chunga's."

"He died in the Green House?" Monk says. "They didn't even take the harp player to the hospital?"

"This is like an earthquake for Mangachería, Doctor," José says. "It'll never be the same without the harp player."

They shake their heads, confused, incredulous, and go on with their monologues and their dialogues, while Father García drinks his coffee without removing the cup from his lips, which are barely exposed through the scarf. Dr. Zevallos has already drunk his, and now he is toying with the spoon, trying to balance it on the tip of his finger. The Leóns are silent at last, and they sit down at a nearby table. Dr. Zevallos offers them cigarettes. When Angélica Mercedes comes back in a while later, they are smoking in silence, equally depressed and frowning.

"That's why Lituma hasn't come," Monk says. "He's probably staying with Chunguita."

"She may act indifferent, the cold woman," José says. "But she's probably bleeding inside too. Don't you think so, Doña Angélica? Blood's thicker than water."

"She's probably mourning," Angélica Mercedes says. "But you never can tell with that one; was she ever a good daughter?"

"Why do you say that, old friend?" Dr. Zevallos asks.

"Do you think it was right for her to have her father working for her?" Angélica Mercedes says.

"Dr. Zevallos thinks everything is all right," Father García grunts. "He's discovered with age that there's nothing bad in the world."

"You say it with sarcasm." Dr. Zevallos smiles. "But think about it, there is a grain of truth in it."

"Don Anselmo would have died if he couldn't play, Doña Angélica," Monk says. "Artists live for their art. What was wrong with his playing there? Chunguita paid him well."

"Hurry up with your coffee, my friend," Dr. Zevallos says. "I've become sleepy all of a sudden, I can't keep my eyes open."

"Here comes our cousin, Monk," José says. "Look at the mournful face on him."

Father García sinks his nose into the cup of coffee, gives off a dull grunt when Wildflower, her shoes in her hand, her eyes all made up and her mouth without any lipstick, leans over him and kisses his hand. Lituma shakes off the dust that has dirtied his gray suit, his green-spotted tie, his yellow shoes. His hair is uncombed and shining with vaseline, his face is sunken, and he greets Dr. Zevallos very gravely.

"They're going to have the wake here, Doña Angélica," he says. "Chunga told me to tell you."

"In my house?" Angélica Mercedes asks. "And why don't they leave him where he is? Why do they want to move him, poor man."

"Do you want the wake to be in a house of prostitution?" Father García roars. "Use your head."

"I'm happy to let them have my house, Father," Angélica Mercedes says. "It's just that I thought it was a sin to drag a dead person around from one place to another. Isn't it a sacrilege?"

"Do you know what the word sacrilege means?" Father García says. "Don't talk about things you don't understand."

"Jocko and the Kid have gone to buy the coffin and arrange things at the cemetery." Lituma has sat down between the Leóns. "Then they'll bring him over. Chunga will pay for everything, Doña Angélica, drinks, flowers, she says that all you have to do is lend them your house."

"I think it's right that the wake should be in Mangachería," Monk says. "He was a Mangache, his brothers should sit up with him."

"And Chunga would like for you to say the mass, Father García," Lituma says, trying to be natural, but his voice is too slow. "We stopped by your house to tell you, but nobody answered. It's lucky I found you here."

The empty gourd rolls to the floor and there is a whirlwind of black folds over the table, who gave him permission, Father García hits the plate of snacks, who had authorized him to address him, and Lituma jumps up, firebug, what way was that to talk: firebug. Father García tries to get up and gesticulates in Dr. Zevallos's arms, swine, jackal, and Wildflower tugs at Lituma's coat, he should be quiet, giving little shouts, he should show respect, he was a priest, they should make him be quiet. But he would see him in hell someday, swine, he would pay for everything there, did he know what hell was, swine? His face inflamed, his mouth twisted, Father García is trembling like a piece of cloth, and Lituma shakes Wildflower but cannot make her let go, firebug, he wasn't insulting him, he didn't call him swine, firebug, and Father García keeps losing and recovering his voice, he was worse than that wretch who supported him, and he stretches out his exasperated hands, a parasite living on filth, a jackal, and now the Leóns are holding Lituma back: he was going to bust that old man in the chops, he wasn't taking that even if he was a priest, fucking firebug. Wildflower has begun to weep and Angélica Mercedes has a stool in her hand, she waves it in front of Lituma as if ready to break it over his head if he moved an inch closer. At the door, behind the cane stalks, all around the place, there are attentive and excited heads, eyes, long hair, elbowing, and a growing shouting that seems to spread all over the district, and the names of the harp player, the champs, and Father García stand out at times over the shrill chorus of the urchins: firebug, firebug, firebug. Now Father García coughs, his arms in the air, beside himself, red as a hot coal, his tongue hanging out, and he sprays saliva all about him. Dr. Zevallos holds his hands up, Wildflower fans him, Angélica Mercedes pats him gently on the back, and Lituma seems confused now.

"Anybody will let his tongue run away with him when he's been insulted, that's all it takes," he says, with a hesitant voice. "It's not my fault, you all saw how he started it."

"But you didn't show him any respect, and he's an old man, cousin," Monk says. "He's been up all night, he hasn't had any sleep."

"You shouldn't have done it, Lituma," José says. "Tell him you're sorry, man, look at the state you've got him into."

"I'm sorry," Lituma stammers. "Take it easy, Father García. It wasn't anything."

But Father García is still shaken by coughing and heaving, and his face is wet with mucus, drivel, and tears. Wildflower wipes his forehead with her skirt, Angélica Mercedes tries to get him to drink a glass of water, and Lituma grows pale; he was telling him he was sorry, Father, and he starts to shout, what more did they want him to do, terrified, he didn't want him to die, God damn it, and he twists his hands.

"Don't get frightened," Dr. Zevallos says. "It's his asthma and the sand he's got in his throat. It'll go away soon."

But Lituma cannot dominate his nerves, he insulted him and he got upset too, and he moans, almost weeping, between the Leóns, who have their arms around him, a person got bitter with so much bad luck, he pouts, and for a moment it looks as if he is going to break out into sobs, cousin, calm down, they understood, and he, beating his chest: they'd had him undress the harp player, wash him, dress him again, a person couldn't take it, a person was only human. And they he should take it easy, cousin, buck up, but he couldn't, God damn it, God damn it, he couldn't, and he collapses onto a stool, his head in his hands. Father García has stopped coughing, and although he is still breathing with effort, his face is calmer. Wildflower is kneeling beside him, dear Father, did he feel better? and he nods, besides being a wretch, what did he care, grunting, unfortunate, but she must have been really stupid to condemn herself by supporting a loafer, a murderer, she must have been really stupid, and she yes, dear Father, but he should not get angry, he should take it easy, it was all over now.

"Let him insult you if that'll calm him down, cousin," Monk says.

"All right, I'll let him, I'll take it," Lituma whispers. "Let him insult me, murderer, loafer, let him keep on, anything he wants."

"Be quiet, you jackal," Father García grunts, without strength, with an obvious lack of desire, and at the door, behind the stalks, there is a wave of laughter. "Silence, jackal."

"I'm quiet!" Lituma roars. "But don't insult me any more, I don't like it, keep your mouth closed, Father García. You ask him to, Dr. Zevallos."

"It's all over, Father," Angélica Mercedes says. "Don't use bad words, with you it sounds like a sin, Father, don't get so mad. Do you want another cup of coffee?"

Father García takes a yellowish handkerchief out of his pocket, all right, another cup of coffee, and he blows his nose strongly. Dr. Zevallos smooths his hair, wipes the saliva from his lapels with a gesture of fastidiousness. Wildflower passes her hand over Father García's forehead, she smooths the tufts of hair at his temples, and he lets her do it, frowning and docile.

"My cousin wants to ask you to forgive him, Father García," Monk says. "He's very sorry for what happened."

"Let him ask God for forgiveness and stop exploiting women," Father García growls peacefully, completely pacified. "And the two of you should ask for God's forgiveness too, you tramps. Do you support that pair of loafers as well?"

"Yes, dear Father," Wildflower says, and there is a new wave of laughter in the street. Dr. Zevallos is listening with an amused look.

"Nobody can accuse you of not being frank," Father García says, picking his nose with his handkerchief. "What a thorough idiot you are, you poor wretch."

"That's what I tell myself lots of times, Father," Wildflower admits, massaging Father García's wrinkled brow. "And I tell them to their faces too, believe me."

Angélica Mercedes brings another cup of coffee, Wildflower goes back to the Leóns' table, and people crowding around the doorway and behind the stalks begin to disperse after a moment. The urchins go back to their dusty running, their shrill, thin voices are heard once more. The passers-by stop in front of the chicha bar, stick their heads in, point at Father García, who, hunched over, is sipping his coffee, leave. Angélica Mercedes, the champs, and Wildflower talk in low voices about food and drink, calculate how many people will come to the wake, ponder names, figures, and discuss prices.

"Have you finished your coffee?" Dr. Zevallos asks. "We've already had more than enough excitement for today, let's go to bed."

There is no answer: Father García is sleeping peacefully, his head hanging over his chest, a corner of the scarf submerged in the cup.

"He's fallen asleep," Dr. Zevallos says. "I don't feel like waking him up."

"Do you want us to fix up a bed for him?" Angélica Mercedes asks. "In the other room, Doctor. We'll cover him up good, we won't make any noise."

"No, no, let him wake up by himself and I'll take him home," Dr. Zevallos says. "He never lets anyone know how he feels, but I know him. Anselmo's death has upset him quite a lot."

"I would have thought he'd be glad," Monk whispers mournfully. "Whenever he saw Don Anselmo on the street, he'd insult him. He hated him."

"And the harp player wouldn't answer him, he'd make believe he didn't hear and cross over to the other sidewalk," José says.

"He didn't hate him so much," Dr. Zevallos says. "At least not in these last few years. It was just a habit with him, an addiction."

"When it should have been the other way around," Monk says. "Don Anselmo did have plenty of reason to hate him."

"Don't say that, it's a sin," Wildflower says. "Priests are ministers of God, they can't be hated."

"If it's true that he burned the Green House down on him, then you can see how bighearted the harp player was," Monk says. "I never heard the least word against Father García from him."

"Did they really burn that house down on Don Anselmo, Doctor?" Wildflower asks.

"Haven't I told you the story a hundred times?" Lituma says. "What do you have to ask the Doctor for?"

"Because every time you tell it to me it's different," Wildflower says. "I'm asking because I want to know what it was really like."

"Shut up, let us men talk in peace," Lituma says.

"I loved the harp player too," Wildflower says. "I was closer to him than you; didn't he come from the same part of the country as I do?"

"The same part of the country?" Dr. Zevallos asks, breaking off a yawn.

"Of course, girl," Don Anselmo says. "Just like you, but not from Santa María de Nieva, I don't even know where that village is."

"Really, Don Anselmo?" Wildflower asks. "You were born there too? Isn't it true that the jungle's beautiful, with all the trees and all the birds? Isn't it true that people are nicer back there?"

"People are the same everywhere, girl," the harpist says. "But it is true that the jungle is beautiful. I've forgotten everything about what it's like there now, except for the color, that's why I painted my harp green."

"They all look down on me here, Don Anselmo," Wildflower says. "When they call me Wildflower, it's like an insult."

"Don't take it that way, girl," Don Anselmo says. "More likely it's friendly. It wouldn't bother me if they said I was from the jungle."

"That's strange." Dr. Zevallos rubs his throat as he yawns. "But possible, after all. Did he really paint his harp green, boys?"

"Don Anselmo was a Mangache," Monk says. "He was born right here in the district and he never left here. I've heard people say a thousand times that he was the oldest Mangache there was."

"Yes, he did," Wildflower said. "And he used to have Jocko repaint it for him too."

"Anselmo from the jungle," Dr. Zevallos says. "It's possible, after all, why not, but it's strange."

"It's one of this one's lies, doctor," Lituma says. "Wildflower never told us that before, she made it up just now. Come on, why did you wait till now to tell it?"

"Nobody asked me," Wildflower says. "Don't you always say that women should keep their mouths shut?"

"And why did he tell you?" Dr. Zevallos asks. "Back then, when we'd ask him where he came from he'd change the subject."

"Because I'm from the jungle too," she says, and looks around proudly. "Because we came from the same part of the country."

"You're pulling our legs, you damned orphan," Lituma says.

"An orphan, but you sure like my money," Wildflower says. "Do you think my money is an orphan too?"

The Leóns and Angélica Mercedes smile, Lituma has wrinkled his brow, Dr. Zevallos is still rubbing his neck, his eyes are meditative.

"Don't get me worked up, sweety." Lituma smiles artificially. "This isn't any day for arguments."

"Watch out that she doesn't get worked up instead," Angélica Mercedes says. "And leaves you and you'll starve to death. Don't argue with the man of the house, champ."

The Leóns are enjoying it, their faces are no longer in mourning but are happy, and Lituma ends up laughing too, Doña Angélica, with good humor, she could leave any time she wanted to. She stuck to them like a barnacle, she was more scared of Josefino than she was of the devil. If she left him, the guy would kill her.

"Did Anselmo tell you anything else about the jungle, girl?" Dr. Zevallos asks.

"He was a Mangache, Doctor," Monk assures him. "This one has made it up that he came from the same place she does because he's dead and can't defend himself and she can make herself sound important."

"Once I asked him if he had any family there," Wildflower says. " 'Who knows,' he said, 'they must all be dead by now.' But other times he'd say no and tell me, 'I was born a Mangache and I'll die a Mangache.' "

"See, Doctor?" José says. "If he ever told her he was from the same part of the country she was, he was probably teasing her. You're telling the truth at last, cousin."

"I'm not your cousin," Wildflower says. "I'm a whore and an orphan."

"Don't let Father García hear you or he'll fly into another rage," Dr. Zevallos says, a finger to his lips. "And what about that other champ, boys? How come he's not with you any more?"

"We had a fight, Doctor," Monk said. "We've put Mangachería off limits for him."

"He was a bad lot, Doctor," José says. "Real bad. Did you know that he's sunk even lower? He was even arrested for robbery."

"But you used to be together all the time and you'd go around testing the patience of all Piura with him," Dr. Zevallos says.

"It's because he wasn't a Mangache," Monk says. "A false friend, Doctor."

"We have to go hire a priest," Angélica Mercedes says. "For the mass and so he can come and pray at the wake too."

When they hear her, the Leóns and Lituma all turn serious at the same time, frown, nod.

"One of the Salesian Fathers, Doña Angélica," Monk says. "Do you want me to go with you? There's one nice priest who plays soccer with the kids. Father Doménico."

"He knows his soccer, but he doesn't know any Spanish," the scarf grunts atonally. "Father Doménico, what nonsense."

"Whatever you say, Father," Angélica Mercedes says. "It was so the wake would be the way God wants it, you see. Who can we get, then?"

Father García has stood up and is adjusting his hat. Dr. Zevallos has also arisen.

"I'll come." Father García makes an impatient gesture. "Didn't that lesbian ask me to come? Why all the talk, then?"

"Yes, dear Father," Wildflower says. "Señora Chunga wanted you to come."

Father García heads toward the door, bent over and dark, without lifting his feet from the ground. Dr. Zevallos takes out his wallet.

"No, no, Doctor," Angélica Mercedes says. "You were my guest, for the pleasure you gave me by bringing Father along."

"Thank you, old friend," Dr. Zevallos says. "But I'll leave you this in any case, to help pay for the wake. Until tonight, then, I'm coming too."

Wildflower and Angélica Mercedes accompany Dr. Zevallos to the door, they kiss Father García's hand and go back into the chicha bar. Arm in arm, Father García and Dr. Zevallos walk through a breeze, under a lively sun, among donkeys loaded with wood and water jars, furry dogs and urchins, firebug, firebug, firebug, with biting and untiring voices. Father García is not affected: he drags his feet along doggedly and goes with his head hanging down, coughing and clearing his throat. As they turn down a straight, narrow street, a strong sound comes up to meet them, and they have to flatten themselves against a wall of cane stalks so as not to be trampled by the mass of men and women escorting an old taxi. A feeble and tuneless horn keeps cutting the air. People come out of the shacks and join the tumult, and some women are shouting now while others hold their fingers up to heaven in the shape of a cross. An urchin stops in front of them and without looking at them, his eyes lively and excited, the harp player died, he tugs at Dr. Zevallos's sleeve, they're bringing him in that taxi, they're bringing him with his harp and everything, and he runs off waving his arms. Finally, the crowd goes past. Father García and Dr. Zevallos reach the Avenida Sánchez Cerro, taking very short, exhausted steps.

"I'll stop by and pick you up," Dr. Zevallos says. "We'll go to the wake together. Try to get at least eight hours of sleep."

"I know, I know," Father García says, with a grunt. "Don't be giving me advice all the time."